Meet Me in *Paris*

ALSO BY KRISTIN HARMEL

The Stolen Life of Colette Marceau

The Paris Daughter

The Forest of Vanishing Stars

The Book of Lost Names

The Winemaker's Wife

The Room on Rue Amélie

When We Meet Again

How to Save a Life

The Life Intended

The Sweetness of Forgetting

Meet Me in *Paris*

Kristin Harmel

GALLERY BOOKS
New York Amsterdam/Antwerp London
Toronto Sydney/Melbourne New Delhi

Gallery Books
An Imprint of Simon & Schuster, LLC
1230 Avenue of the Americas
New York, NY 10020

First Gallery Books hardcover edition July 2026

Interior design by Ritika Karnik

Manufactured in the United States of America

10 9 8 7 6 5 4 3 2 1

Library of Congress Control Number: 2026935109

ISBN 978-1-6680-9253-8
ISBN 978-1-6682-4189-9 (Int/Can Exp)
ISBN 978-1-6680-9255-2 (ebook)

To Jason and Noah,
because all my love stories lead back to you.

Meet Me in *Paris*

CHAPTER ONE

The top of the Eiffel Tower came into view, glittering in the morning sunshine over a row of zinc-roofed Haussmann buildings, and Julia Glover's breath caught in her throat. She was here. She was really here, and Paris was just as magical as she remembered.

So much life had happened since she'd spent an idyllic summer in an apartment in the Latin Quarter twenty-seven years earlier. As she closed her eyes now and breathed in the familiar yeasty, grassy scent of Paris through the open window of her taxi's back seat, she pictured herself at the age of twenty-two, stretched out on a blanket in the Champ de Mars, the park beneath the Eiffel Tower, scribbling furiously in a notebook. She had dreamed then of being a newspaper columnist, or maybe a magazine writer, the whole world stretching out in front of her in a series of seemingly infinite possibilities.

What had happened to those dreams, to all those open doors she was so sure she would walk through? She bit her lip, wishing she could go back and tell that naïve, hopeful version of herself to take more chances, to not be so afraid to spread her wings, to never take no for an answer. But it was too late now, wasn't it?

"Mom?" Piper said, interrupting Julia's spiral of self-pity. "You okay? You look upset."

Julia turned to her twenty-three-year-old daughter, her only child, who was sitting beside her in the cab. Piper was the only thing she was certain she'd done right in life, the thing she was proudest of. "I'm fine," she said, smiling. "Just wishing that I'd come back sooner."

Piper reached for her hand and squeezed. "But we're here now, Mom."

"We're here now," Julia echoed as the taxi turned a corner and the Eiffel Tower disappeared behind a building. Piper sighed contentedly and turned back to look out the window at the city rolling by.

Julia had always meant to bring Piper to the place that had captured her heart all those years before. That summer had been everything to her, and somehow, Julia had forgotten.

She snuck another glance at her daughter. Piper's wavy dark hair hung to the middle of her back, and her coffee-brown eyes sparkled with excitement. A few freckles danced across the bridge of her nose, and she had two deep dimples that matched those of her father, Julia's ex-husband, Ryan. They'd split up when Piper was just ten, and though Ryan hadn't been a bad father, he had drifted away as Piper had gotten older.

"Mom?" Piper said, turning back to her. "You're doing it again."

"Doing what?"

"Staring at me like a weirdo."

Julia laughed. "But I am a weirdo."

"Yeah, you are." Piper gave her a small smile, but Julia could see the sadness in her eyes. "But you're my favorite weirdo."

"You're my favorite weirdo, too, kid," Julia said as the Seine finally came into view and they could see the Eiffel Tower again in all its glory, glimmering in the late morning sunshine across the water on the Left Bank.

"I can't believe we're here," Piper said, and Julia could hear the awe in her voice.

"It's going to be an amazing week," Julia said with a confidence she didn't feel, and when Piper turned to glance at her, Julia could see tears in her daughter's eyes. Her aching stomach twisted with guilt.

"You sure you're okay, Mom?" Piper asked, giving her a wobbly smile. Piper asked that question a lot these days, and it broke Julia's heart every time.

"Just fine, honey." Julia knew, though, that Piper could see right through her. How could she not?

The truth was, Julia was dying. She had just turned forty-nine, and she wouldn't live to see her fiftieth birthday.

For Henry McGee, it all began with a letter.

No, that wasn't quite right. In fact, the story of Henry and Celeste Didier had begun some eighty years earlier in a run-down, top-floor apartment on the rue Dante. But Henry had always believed that the story had ended in Paris, too, in 1943, when Celeste had been arrested, imprisoned, and ultimately executed for her involvement with the French Resistance.

But impossibly, Celeste had lived after all—or so said the message he'd received last week from her grandson, Jean-Luc, who'd been cleaning out his grandmother's belongings in Paris when he'd come across her diary from the fall of 1945, which she'd written after she'd returned to France from the Ravensbrück concentration camp.

Your name was repeated often in those pages, Jean-Luc had explained, adding that he'd tracked Henry down with the help of a private investigator. *My grandmother believed you had perished. It is clear she loved you deeply, and as I work to put her affairs in order, it felt right that you should know.*

Jean-Luc hadn't explicitly invited Henry to fly across the ocean for a reunion with Celeste, but how could he do anything but? The lost love of his life—the woman he'd spent an entire career writing songs about—was alive.

I am coming to see her. Henry had replied to Jean-Luc immediately, using the email address the younger man had included at the end of his note. *I will arrive on Monday.*

Jean-Luc's response had been swift. *Sir, I regret to inform you that my grandmother is in a care home, without any memory of the past. I'm afraid a visit to Paris would be a waste of your time.*

But Celeste would know him. Henry believed that with every fiber in his being. She had to, didn't she? Henry knew in the depths of his soul that a love like the one they'd once shared never disappeared, even if it became buried in the shadows of the years. As long as Celeste was still alive, Henry would go to her. *Music will bring her back*, he had replied to Jean-Luc. *Long ago, I used to sing to her, and I know that if she can hear the music, she'll remember.*

"Sir?"

Henry's eyes flew open, his thoughts interrupted by the arrival of a thin, dark-haired Air France flight attendant, with eyes the color of twilight and lips painted scarlet. She reminded him a bit of the Celeste he'd known eighty years ago, an eighteen-year-old spitfire whose fierce passion for the French Resistance had nearly ended her life.

Henry blinked up at her from his seat in first class. "Yes?"

She looked relieved. "I was just checking . . . well, to see if you were all right."

Her accent even sounded like Celeste's. He gave her a half smile. "I suspect you were checking to make sure I hadn't kicked the bucket mid-flight."

A flush crept up her neck, and her eyes widened. "No, sir! Of course not, sir. I was just making sure . . . you didn't need anything."

"It's all right," he said. "I appreciate your concern. I'm just fine, ma'am, but while you're here, might I trouble you for a cup of coffee? I'll need my wits about me as soon as we arrive."

"Yes, sir. Right away, sir." She looked relieved to be hurrying off, and Henry chuckled to himself. He had been told he looked good for his age—barely a day over eighty, his granddaughter, Melanie, had assured him when she'd last visited at Christmastime. But the fact was, he'd been born nearly a century ago, and his doctor would have sternly warned against a transatlantic journey like this one. Henry wouldn't have listened, though. He would have traveled to the ends of the earth to see Celeste again.

"Sir?" The flight attendant was back, holding a steaming cup. "Cream and sugar?"

"No, thank you," he said with a smile, taking the drink from her. As she moved away, his heart thudded. Ninety minutes until he was back in Paris. Ninety minutes until the past caught up with the present.

Ninety minutes until his future began.

As worried as Melanie Chaulet was about her grandfather traveling by himself from New York to Paris at his age, she was also secretly glad that he was coming. Grandpa Henry was the only family she had left—and right now, she needed to be around someone who loved her unconditionally. She was, however, completely confused about his reason for this trip.

She'd known, of course, that Grandpa Henry had served in France during the Second World War, but most of her questions over the years about that period of his life had gone unanswered, even when she herself had moved to France two decades before to marry Gilles.

"It's remarkable to think that your life will unfold in the city where I once thought I'd spend mine," he'd said then, tears in his eyes, but he hadn't elaborated, and Melanie had been too caught up in her own love story to give her grandfather's past more than a second thought. He'd never mentioned Paris again, and even though she'd visited him twice a year at his home in New York, he'd never come to visit her, which she had always assumed was because of a reluctance to travel at his age.

But then he'd called yesterday and told her he was arriving the next morning on a flight from JFK that landed at 8:05 a.m. "I have just learned that the woman I loved in Paris is still alive," he'd said, the emotional tremor in his voice unmistakable.

"The woman you *loved*?" Melanie had repeated in confusion. Grandpa Henry—a humble songwriter who had penned some of the most popular hits of the past five decades—had been married to Melanie's grandmother from the time he was twenty-six right up to her death thirty-five years ago. "Before you married Grandma Betsy, you mean?"

Grandpa Henry had hesitated. "Yes, before I married your grandmother," he acknowledged, a note of apology in his voice. "I thought—I thought my Celeste had died, you see. And now, there's not a moment to waste."

"I see. Well, of course you'll stay with us," Melanie said quickly, though her blood pressure was already rising at the complication of an unexpected houseguest when her life was in the midst of falling apart. Not that Grandpa Henry knew that. No one knew. "I'll pick you up at the airport."

And now, she was on her way to Charles de Gaulle, a thousand questions running through her head. She'd always thought that her grandparents had been each other's first loves.

My Celeste, he'd called her. Who was this woman? How had her grandfather met her? Had he managed to erase her from his heart before marrying Grandma Betsy, or had she always been there, a silent third party to their decades-long marriage?

As Melanie crept along in her Peugeot 208 through near-standstill traffic on the Boulevard Périphérique, her thoughts turned to the not-so-silent third party in her own marriage.

Amandine. A woman named after a nut, who had apparently seduced Melanie's husband. Or was it Gilles who had seduced her? Either way, it was clear there was an affair in progress.

The text had pinged through a few evenings ago when Gilles was in the shower, his phone sitting on the bathroom counter, just beside the sink. She had glanced down while brushing her teeth, not meaning to read it, and her throat had tightened when she'd realized what she was seeing.

I can still smell you on my skin, the text said in French. *Until we meet again, Kisses from your Amandine.*

In case there was any confusion as to Amandine's meaning, the woman had also helpfully added a multitude of heart and kiss emojis.

Melanie had stared at the text in disbelief, then she had swallowed down the bile rising in her throat, snapped a quick picture in case she needed it, and hastily walked away before she had to acknowledge what she'd seen.

She had just turned fifty, and she and Gilles were set to celebrate their twentieth wedding anniversary this summer. She knew, of course, that she wasn't as shiny and new as she had been two decades earlier, when Gilles, ten years her senior, had swept her off her feet. There was more weight around her middle than there had been then, and the pieces of her that had once been pert had begun to sag, a cruel trick of gravity and time. But she had a reliable *coiffeur*, who kept Melanie's thick hair a youthful chestnut brown, and an *esthéticienne*, whose monthly facials allowed her to maintain skin that was mostly wrinkle-free.

More importantly, though, she was a woman who read widely and was interested in politics and art and could hold a conversation with anyone, anywhere—qualities she'd thought Gilles valued. Beyond that, she was a woman who had sacrificed her own desire to have children, because Gilles hadn't wanted them. She was a woman who had uprooted her life and moved across an ocean because she loved her husband.

But now, it seemed, she was merely a woman who was a fool.

She was also a woman who couldn't decide how to proceed. Should she confront Gilles? Then again, what if his explanation was that she was past her expiration date? That he'd decided to move on to perkier pastures and wanted a divorce? That an affair wasn't such a big deal and she should live with it or leave? She wasn't ready yet to tell Grandpa Henry about Gilles, because that would mean she'd have to face the situation—and she had no idea what came next.

Traffic was moving again on the Boulevard Périphérique, and as Melanie accelerated toward the airport, toward her beloved grandfather, she practiced a breezy smile in the mirror. If Gilles hadn't noticed in the past few days that Melanie wasn't acting like herself, maybe Grandpa Henry wouldn't, either.

CHAPTER TWO

George Gallagher still couldn't believe he'd said yes to coming to Paris, a decision that was entirely out of character for him. He wasn't a man who took chances; he had spent a lifetime playing everything as safe as possible.

But when Lou Robinson had called two months earlier, asking George to join him on a trip for Vietnam veterans who wanted to see where the peace accords ending the war were signed, George had agreed before he could stop himself, even though he hadn't traveled more than a couple of hours from home since his wife, Sally, had died a decade before. She'd always been the one to plan their vacations.

"Come on, when's the last time we had an adventure?" Lou had said over the phone. "Besides, I can't imagine taking a tour for Vietnam vets without you, George."

George couldn't imagine it, either. Lou had been his closest friend since they'd served together in the 198th Light Infantry Brigade, 1st Battalion, 46th Infantry, D Company, more than fifty years earlier. That they'd both survived the horrors of that war was the first miracle; that they were still friends after all this time was the second. They lived ninety minutes from each other in Florida and made a point to get together for lunch once a month, which was pretty much the extent of George's social life since he'd retired from his career as an economics professor.

The other Vietnam vets in their tour group were strangers to them—two Army nurses who'd served together; three combat vets and their wives, and a fourth combat vet, widowed like George and Lou, who seemed to be on a mission to throw himself at every woman in a one-hundred-foot radius. The fact that the man—who had introduced himself as Cliff—was also wearing a black beret on his balding head was just the icing on the cake of his ridiculousness.

Now, as George and Lou brought up the rear of their little tour group, they were having a hard time keeping straight faces as the bereted widower tried once again to hit on the two nurses in their group.

George looked at Lou and rolled his eyes. "Imagine having that much confidence," he said in a low voice.

"Not to mention that much belief in your appeal to the opposite sex," Lou replied with a chuckle. "So are you like that around the ladies of Gainesville?"

"Oh, yes," George said with a grin. "I seduce them left and right while wearing my beret."

As Lou laughed, George fought to keep the smile on his face. The truth was, he would have loved to have the widower's brazen self-assurance.

"He's shameless," Lou said. "What a way to go through life, huh?"

"What a way," George agreed with a shake of his head.

"What're you brooding about over here?" Lou asked a moment later, elbowing him as they walked. George could still remember meeting Lou—one of only four Black men in their unit—for the first time in the spring of '69. *Lou Robinson*, Lou had said, extending his hand to the fellow beside George as he went down the line, but the jackass had refused to shake Lou's hand. *I don't need no Negro friends*, the boy had said, spitting in the dirt, and George had turned to the boy and said, *Too bad for you, you moron, since Lou here might one day have to choose whether or not to save your life*. George had shaken Lou's hand, firmly and pointedly, and the two had been friends ever since.

"Oh, just wondering if Romeo over there ever lets up," George said, jerking his head toward the man, who was now peacocking for yet another group of women passing by.

"You got to hand it to him." Lou grinned. "Isn't Paris the City of Love?"

"I imagine *every* city that man visits is the city of love," George replied with a smile.

Lou laughed but didn't say anything for a moment. "Was your marriage to Sally that way?" he asked. "Romance and all that?"

George chuckled, then sobered. "Nah." He was being honest, and the words made him feel like a failure. He had never been unfaithful, but that didn't mean he'd been the husband Sally deserved. She'd been a fine woman. "How about you? Is that the way you were with Lavonda?" Lavonda had died two years after Sally had, and like George, Lou—a retired financial advisor—had never remarried.

"Not hardly." Lou frowned for a second and seemed to be on the verge of saying something else, but then the moment passed, and he nudged George. "Anyhow, looks like the joke's on us. While Monsieur Beret over there tries his luck with everyone, you and I are here growing old together."

"Hey," George said, bumping Lou with his shoulder. "Who're you calling old?"

"My apologies. We're obviously a couple of spring chickens."

The men chuckled and then quieted down as their young French tour guide raised his flag to summon the group's attention and suggested stopping for a quick spot of lunch at an Anglo pub he knew near Notre Dame.

Julia had booked a hotel on the rue Gît-le-Coeur in the Latin Quarter, the same narrow, medieval street on which she'd lived during that perfect summer twenty-seven years earlier, a street that had also famously been home to several 1960s Beat poets, including Allen Ginsberg and William S. Burroughs. When their car pulled up, her breath caught in her throat at the familiarity of it all. The restaurants on the corner had changed, and the bikes propped alongside buildings were sturdy, neon-green rentals rather than beat-up ten-speeds, but the street looked mostly as she remembered it, and there was comfort in the idea that it had been here all along, waiting for her to return.

"How are you feeling, Mom?" Piper asked as the driver pulled their suitcases from the trunk. "Are you in any pain?"

"Nope," Julia said brightly, and it was only a small lie. Her belly hurt all the time now, and she knew it would only get worse as the months passed. But the ache was manageable—especially with the help of the steroid pills her doctor had prescribed—so much so that sometimes, for a fleeting second here or there, Julia forgot she was sick. She wasn't supposed to be, after all, was she? People weren't supposed to be diagnosed with stage three pancreatic cancer in their midforties.

For a time, chemotherapy had worked. Julia's cancer hadn't

grown, hadn't spread. And though she felt exhausted and ill all the time, she was still alive and still around to be Piper's mother. Those years of treatment had at least allowed her to see her daughter through her college graduation.

But as her oncologist had warned her might eventually happen, her cancer cells grew too clever, too evasive. The cancer was in her liver now, too, and in her bones. "I'm sorry, Julia," Dr. Drayton had said gravely when he'd met with her last month during what she thought was simply a routine appointment. "We've exhausted all the standard chemotherapy options that are available to us, and we've reached the point where your treatments are no longer a benefit. It's up to you, of course, but it's my recommendation that we discontinue them; the side effects aren't worth it if your tumors are no longer being kept in check."

"Okay," Julia had said. "So what do we do now? A clinical trial? Immunotherapy?" Maybe there was even something new on the horizon that she didn't know about yet. She was young. She was in good shape, all things considered. She was supposed to have so much more time.

But Dr. Drayton looked away. "Julia, as you know, we've applied to every potential trial, but your particular disease progression hasn't been a fit for any of them, unfortunately. I still have a few feelers out, just in case. At this point, though, while we'll do our best to support your quality of life, I'm afraid that my recommendation is simply to do your best to enjoy living in the time you have left."

Her eyes had filled, and she had asked, just in case she'd misunderstood, "You're saying that I should stop treatment altogether?"

"I'm saying it's your choice. But chemotherapy doesn't seem to be helping anymore." He held her gaze. "I truly am very sorry."

She'd immediately gotten a second opinion, but the answer had been the same. She had reached the end of the road and had been very lucky to have survived with the disease as long as she had.

She supposed she should be thankful for the extra time she'd gotten. For the opportunity to see Piper leave the nest. For the time she'd had to get her affairs in order and to ease Piper into what was coming next.

But it wasn't enough. Not by a long shot. And whenever she looked at her daughter—her bold, brilliant, beautiful daughter—she wanted to scream and curse and rage at the universe. How could it be that she wouldn't be here to see Piper fall in love for the first time? To marry? To perhaps even have children of her own one day? Even if a miracle happened and a clinical trial came through, it would only prolong her life by months, not years. The cancer had already spread like wildfire through her body.

When Julia had finally summoned the courage to tell Piper what Dr. Drayton had said, Piper had hugged her and held on so tightly that Julia was certain her ribs would crack. "At least I don't have to go through chemo anymore," Julia had said with as much brightness as she could muster, trying to convince herself as much as Piper that there was any possibility of making lemonade from the rotten lemons they'd been given. "Dr. Drayton said I'd feel better for a little while before I feel worse."

Piper had wiped a tear away and then declared, "Then we'll go to Paris. As soon as possible."

"Paris?"

"You've always wanted to go back, Mom, haven't you? Now's our chance."

Piper was right; Julia had always imagined that she and Piper would have an adventure in the City of Light one day. And if cancer had taught her anything, it was that there was no time like the present. "All right, then, Paris, here we come," she had said as cheerfully as she could.

Two weeks later, they were here. Julia had been surprised by how hastily Piper, who was taking a leave of absence from her graduate program in English, had planned it all, and how insistent she'd been about the specific dates of their trip. "I have a surprise for you, Mom," Piper had said when Julia had pressed her about it. "Let's just say that there's something happening in Paris that I think will mean a lot to you. I feel like it's meant to be." She had smiled a cat-who-ate-the-canary smile and refused to say more.

"Mom, do you need a nap?" Piper asked now, as they dragged their bags through the front door of the hotel, into the lobby. "Or do you feel like going out for lunch first?"

"Let's do lunch," Julia said, forcing a smile through her exhaustion. Julia spent hours each day napping now, which meant that Piper would be on her own for much of this week. Piper had assured her that it was fine and that she'd be happy to wander solo around Paris while her mom rested up. Still, Julia was determined to do everything with her daughter that she possibly could. How else would they make the kind of memories that would survive long after she was gone?

"Are you sure, Mom?"

"*Mais oui,*" Julia said with a smile, adopting her best French accent, which was, admittedly, quite poor. "I'm starving."

"There's a place a few blocks from here called Café Le Petit Pont," Piper said. "Want to try it? It's all over TikTok."

"How could I refute the wisdom of TikTok?" Julia asked. "Let's just freshen up, and then we'll go."

Something was eating at Melanie.

Henry had known it the moment his granddaughter had picked him up from the airport, her brow furrowed, her shoulders stiff with tension.

"Everything all right, dear?" he'd asked after he'd hugged her, thrown his small suitcase into the trunk of her shiny black Peugeot, and gotten into the car for the ride back to Paris.

She had looked startled by the question. "Oh, I'm fine. Just fine, Grandpa Henry." But the words sounded like a lie, and the way her eyebrows drew together punctuated his suspicions.

Henry's heart sank. This was obviously about Celeste. He had fretted about it the whole way here, in fact. He hadn't been as thoughtful as he could have been in the way he'd told Melanie, and now she was upset with him. "I realize I didn't explain things well," he said now, tugging at his collar. His neck felt hot with embarrassment. "You see, I knew Celeste before I married your grandmother. I was told that she'd died, and I was devastated, but I vowed to put her out of my mind. I did truly love your grandmother, very much."

Melanie gave him a look he couldn't decipher. "Oh. Okay."

Henry sighed. He was really mucking this all up, wasn't he? "My point is, Melanie, there was never another woman while I was married to your grandmother."

"Right," Melanie said.

They drove through the outskirts of Paris in silence for a few minutes, and Henry snuck a handful of glances at his granddaughter, whose knuckles were white on the wheel. She was obviously angry, which didn't seem like her, to be honest. She was his only grandchild, and with Betsy long gone and both of Melanie's parents deceased, they were each other's only family—except, of course, for Melanie's husband, Gilles.

Melanie had always had a lightness about her, but sitting now in the passenger seat beside her felt like sharing a car with a storm cloud. Henry swallowed down his guilt over the flame he'd carried for Celeste for eighty years and cleared his throat. "Melanie, are you upset with me?" He and his granddaughter had always been blunt with each other, and now was no time to dance around the truth.

"Upset with you?" Melanie blinked a few times, looking surprised. "No, of course not."

"My dear, I've known you since the day you were born. Something's eating at you, and if you're upset about Celeste, I want to make sure you understand that—"

"Gilles is having an affair," Melanie blurted out, interrupting him, and Henry was so startled that he couldn't speak for a moment.

"*Gilles*?" he finally managed to say. His granddaughter's husband was about as charismatic as a dishcloth. He had never understood what a sparkling light like Melanie had seen in a man so dull. Gilles having an affair? It felt impossible—not least of all because an affair required some degree of initiative, didn't it? "You're absolutely certain?"

Melanie nodded, and when she began to cry, she pulled onto the shoulder of the road and buried her face in her hands. Henry rubbed her back for a moment as she sobbed, and then he withdrew and balled his hands into fists.

"Why didn't you tell me?" he asked gently, and she sniffled a bit before wiping her eyes and looking over at him.

"I just found out this week." Her expression darkened. "There was a text on his phone. Amandine, her name is."

"Like the green beans?" Henry snorted. "And what did Gilles have to say for himself?"

"I haven't told him yet that I know."

"Why not?"

Melanie looked miserable. "Because . . . Well . . . It just feels like my whole world is about to be turned upside down, and I'm not ready. Besides, isn't this just what French people *do*? Maybe I have no right to be upset."

"Of course you do. You made vows to each other, Melanie." Henry sighed. Melanie's marriage had started with her giving up her own life in the States to start anew with Gilles across the Atlantic, in his home country. Gilles had gone on to have the career he'd always wanted, and Melanie had been stuck working the same job as a school headmistress that she'd taken when she'd moved here twenty years ago—and which Henry knew she had never loved.

It had not been his business to raise these issues with Melanie. After all, it was a grandfather's job to support his grandchild however he could, and besides, it was never a good idea to interfere in other people's marriages. Who knew what really went on behind closed doors? But now, Gilles had created the perfect opening for Melanie to reevaluate her choices.

"Do you love him, Melanie?" Henry asked carefully.

She looked surprised, as if the question hadn't occurred to her. "Of course I do. He's my husband, Grandpa Henry."

"But do you *love* him?"

She was silent for a moment, her eyes on the road. "It's been twenty years. Maybe it's unrealistic to have expected the spark would still be there."

"Oh, Melanie. I'm not so sure that's true." How he wished that Melanie's parents were still alive. They would know what to say, wouldn't they? But they'd both died in their seventies, several years before. Henry was all Melanie had left, and he felt wildly ill-equipped to handle anything related to love, since he'd secretly spent a lifetime writing love songs for the woman he'd lost, rather than for the dutiful wife who'd given him a beautiful son and a wonderful life. In a way, he was no better than Gilles. "You must be honest with him, Melanie." This, at least, Henry was sure of. "You must tell him that you know about the affair. And you must listen very carefully to how he responds. You've sacrificed so much to make this marriage work. It's his turn to bend."

"And if he doesn't want to?"

"Then he's a fool who doesn't deserve you."

She sniffled a few times and then smiled slightly, a real smile this time. "I'm glad you're here, Grandpa Henry."

"I'm glad I'm here, too."

As she put the car in gear and pulled back into traffic, he snuck a look at her. She still seemed sad, but it was as if the light inside her had been turned back on, even if it was shining only dimly.

"So," Melanie said after several minutes of silence as she and Henry crossed into Paris on the road from the airport. "Did Grandma Betsy know about Celeste?"

"Yes," Henry said, for he hadn't believed in keeping secrets from one's spouse. But he hadn't told Betsy the whole truth. He hadn't said that Celeste was forever in his heart, only that there had once been a girl he'd loved in Paris, but that she had died. Betsy had accepted this as part of Henry's past.

"How did you know her, anyhow? I know you were stationed in France during World War II, but you never talk about it."

They were nearly to Melanie's home near the Jardin du Luxembourg, and Henry paused for a moment to collect his thoughts before he spoke.

"I was a gunner on a B-17 shot down in northern France in 1943," Henry said, watching Melanie closely. "The pilot, copilot, navigator, flight engineer, and two other gunners were killed in the crash, may they rest in peace." He could still see the still and lifeless face of the pilot, a farmer's son from Kansas named Roy Little, all these years later. "Somehow, I survived, along with another gunner, the bombardier, and the radio operator. We deployed our parachutes in time and were able to hide in a nearby barn. We split up, thinking that it would be easier to avoid detection that way."

"I never knew any of this, Grandpa Henry," Melanie said, her voice hushed. "I had no idea you'd been shot down."

He nodded, surprised at how hard it was to tell this story all these years later. "The others were all found by the Germans, but I was lucky enough to be picked up by the French Resistance and sent along an escape line to Paris. I was supposed to be moved quickly on to the next stop. Instead, because there had been a betrayal on the line, I was held in place for nearly a month, which was unusual. It was Celeste who sheltered me during that time. She was eighteen years old; her mother had died when she was young, and her father was a military officer who'd been killed in May 1940 when the Germans breached the French border. Her uncle, her only living relative, was a prisoner of war. She was all by herself."

"She worked for this escape line?"

"She was part of the underground. She sheltered pilots from time to time, until 1943, when she was betrayed by someone on the line and arrested."

"This was after you left?"

"Yes." It had been the greatest regret of Henry's life. He had, for years, blamed himself for her death. If he had insisted upon staying in Paris rather than being sent over the Pyrenees, could he have saved her? He had to recalibrate his whole life, his whole sense of self, now that he knew she had lived, after all. "I received word that she had been sent to the Ravensbrück concentration camp. I went back to Paris after the war, hoping against hope that she had survived, and I met her uncle, who told me she was dead and that I should forget about her if I knew what was good for me."

Melanie put a hand over her mouth. "But why would he do that?"

"Maybe he feared I would take her away to America and he'd never see her again. Or maybe he thought I'd be a reminder of all she'd lost. I may never know his motives. But I believed him, of course, and I could not forgive myself for leaving, you see. It took me a very long time to put all of it behind me. In fact, I'm not sure I ever entirely did."

"That's why it took you so long to marry Grandma Betsy after the war."

"Yes."

"And you loved her? This Celeste?"

Henry swallowed the lump in his throat. "Very much so."

Melanie pulled the car into the underground car park on the rue Soufflot, near the apartment she shared with Gilles. She didn't say anything until after she had steered the car into a spot and cut the ignition. "Then you should go to her."

"I will," Henry said. "But first, I'll be right here with you as you talk to Gilles."

CHAPTER THREE

Jackson Quick's private jet touched down at Charles de Gaulle Airport northeast of Paris just past 10 a.m.

Well, it wasn't *his* private jet, exactly. It belonged to the concert promoter who'd booked the show Jackson would be playing in Paris in just four days, the first of six stadium shows across Europe. Jackson was secretly worried that they'd all be massive flops.

It had been a decade since his last tour, and the experience was already much different from how it used to be, which startled him. Take today's hired driver, for instance. She was a young French woman who introduced herself as Manon and who barely gave him a second glance after he'd slid into the back seat of her sleek Audi. Thirty years ago, a young woman like that would have been going gaga over him. But Manon hadn't even been born when Jackson was at the height of his fame, and if she had any clue who her passenger was, she wasn't letting on.

Or maybe she just didn't care.

Jackson had been twenty-six when he'd had his big breakout hit in the mid '90s. Now he was fifty-five, a number he could hardly believe when he looked in the mirror. Old enough to be someone's grandfather, though he wasn't. He had never settled down, had never gotten married. It wasn't that he hadn't wanted to; at first, there'd been no time—he was on the road constantly, playing to screaming, sold-out crowds. And then, just as instantaneously, his career was circling the drain, and he'd been busy ever since trying to revive it.

By that point, he'd had too many experiences with women who wanted him for the wrong reasons, and it had made him wary, not just of the women who approached him, but also of his own poor judgment. He had a long history of making bad choices when it came to dating—so much so that he had begun to wonder if he had ever had any ability to see people for who they were.

But now he was lonely sometimes, which was a strange thing to admit to himself. Loneliness wasn't very rock 'n' roll, was it?

"Excuse me," Jackson said a few minutes after Manon had pulled out of the airport, headed for Paris. "Would you mind taking a bit of a detour on the way to the hotel?"

"A detour?" she asked, glancing at him in the rearview mirror. "You want to see some of the tourist sites, monsieur? The Eiffel Tower, maybe? Or the Champs-Élysées?"

Jackson smiled. "Not exactly." He gave her an address in the fifth arrondissement, and she scrunched up her nose.

"The *Quartier Latin*? Is it Notre Dame you want to see, then, sir? Many of the tourists want to go there, especially after the fire."

"No," Jackson said. "I mean, yes, I would love to see Notre Dame. But it's my old street I'd like to visit. We don't need to stop. I just want to remind myself what it felt like to be here."

"Monsieur?" Manon's eyes met his in the rearview again. "Your old street?"

"I lived here for a summer when I was twenty-five. Feels like a different lifetime now." It had been just before he'd been discovered, just before he'd signed his first record contract, just before he'd stepped aboard a bullet train that went only one way. He'd spent three sunshine-soaked months here, busking on street corners, and when people stopped to watch him sing, or tossed a few coins in his upturned baseball cap, it had been because of *his* words, *his* songs.

And then he'd gone home to the States and been plucked from obscurity by a record executive, who'd heard him singing in New York and had suggested he record a love song called "City of Light," written by a Grammy-winning songwriter named Henry McGee, and it had felt like fate, since Jackson had just come back from Paris. "This one is special, man," the exec had said. "The story goes that McGee wrote it for a girl he loved in the Second World War, and that every decade, he updates it to make it sound more modern. He's finally ready to let the world hear it, and, well, I can't think of a voice more well-suited to the song than yours." As Jackson had listened to the backing track and read over the lyrics, he had agreed. The song felt like opening a vein and bleeding one's heart onto the stage. Jackson had considered himself a decent songwriter, but he wasn't capable of anything remotely like this.

The next summer, the single rocketed to number one and introduced the world to Jackson Quick's rich baritone, which critics had immediately likened to that of a modern-day Elvis with a little Eddie Vedder thrown in for good measure.

"My mother said you were famous," Manon admitted, her eyes meeting his again. "She said she liked you when you were young."

He smiled slightly. "When I was young, huh? Feels like a long time ago, now."

They lapsed into silence after that; Manon didn't say another word until after she'd driven him past his old apartment on the rue

Xavier Privas. "Would you like to see Notre Dame now, sir?" she asked, breaking the silence between them. "It's quite close."

Jackson knew that it was; he had walked there from his apartment nearly every day with his guitar to play for tourists. "No, thanks," he said. "Actually, would you mind dropping me off here and bringing my bags to my hotel? I'd like to walk around for a little while."

Manon glanced at him. "Won't you be recognized?" she asked.

Jackson chuckled. "You'd be surprised." Middle age—okay, let's be honest, *late* middle age—was like a disguise. People didn't look twice at a fiftysomething man. And even if he did look familiar, they couldn't quite place him.

It would be different when he took the stage four days from now at Paris's La Défense Arena. The fans there would know him the moment he stepped into the spotlight.

But until then, maybe he could just be a guy strolling through the familiar streets of the most beautiful city in the world.

Twenty minutes after checking into their hotel, Julia and Piper walked several blocks to the Café Le Petit Pont. Julia was exhausted; she knew she would need a nap after this, but she was determined not to miss Piper's first interaction with the city that had so captured Julia's heart. She had slept fitfully on the plane, but it was enough to keep her going for another hour or so.

The café was just across a sliver of the Seine River from Notre Dame, and the view of the soaring cathedral was spectacular from outside the restaurant, the front of which was shaded by broad, rose-colored awnings, the name of the café in luminous script overhead. Inside, the place was exuberantly French, with maroon-backed woven café chairs and vintage alcohol advertisements. A hostess showed them to a table on the front patio, which had a view of Notre Dame's towers over the trees, and handed them menus in English. "Want a glass of white, Mom?" Piper asked as she scanned the wine list.

"You know what? Sure. Why not?" Julia had abstained from alcohol entirely during her two years of chemotherapy, but now there was no longer a reason to swear off a glass of wine here or there; an occasional drink would not change the outcome, and she might as well enjoy it while she could, in the brief window of time where she felt almost like herself.

A waiter a few years older than Piper appeared at their table a moment later. "*Bonjour.* My name is Nicolas, and I will be your waiter today." His English, flecked with a French accent, was surprisingly perfect. "May I interest you in a drink to begin? An aperitif, perhaps, or a glass of wine?"

Julia waited for Piper to order since she was still clutching the wine list, but instead of her daughter's self-assured voice, she heard only silence. She looked up to see Piper staring at the waiter—and the waiter staring back at her, both of them oddly frozen. "Honey?" Julia prompted.

Piper seemed to snap out of it, coughing and awkwardly shuffling the wine list and the menu until she dropped them both. She and the waiter bent to pick them up at the same time and nearly knocked heads. "Oh my gosh, I'm so sorry!" Piper yelped.

"*Ah, excusez-moi, mademoiselle!*" The waiter sounded equally mortified as he handed the wine list and the menu back. "The fault is mine. Now, ah, may I bring you something to drink?"

But instead of ordering, Piper just continued to stare. "Uhhhh," she said, as if she'd forgotten how to speak.

"We'll have two glasses of Sancerre, please," Julia interjected helpfully.

The waiter tore his eyes away from her daughter long enough to ask, "The smaller size, or the large, madame?"

"How about the large," Julia said, and the waiter stood there for another second before blinking a few times.

"Yes, of course, right away." He finally turned and hurried away.

When Julia looked back at Piper, she was unsurprised to see her daughter staring after him. In fact, the three thirtysomething women at the next table over all seemed to be gawking at him, too. Julia stifled a smile. "Well, he seems nice," she said in the most benign tone she could manage. "I think he thought you were cute."

"What?" Piper's cheeks were pink as she avoided Julia's gaze. "No way. Anyways, he's probably like that with all the girls he waits on."

"Yeah, I don't think so." Julia nodded at the waiter, who had stopped at the table of thirtysomethings. One of the women, a redhead, was unabashedly batting her eyelashes at him, but he seemed not to even notice.

As he walked away from the women, he glanced over, smiling at Piper, who looked quickly away. "Anyways, it doesn't matter," Piper said. "This is our trip. I'm not here to meet some guy."

Julia felt a surge of guilt. Over the past two years, even as she'd finished her senior year of college, Piper hadn't dated at all—and Julia knew it was her own fault. Piper had come home almost every weekend to be with her, which hadn't left time for much of a social life.

"Honey." Julia reached across the table for her daughter's hands. "You've been there for me in every way I could have imagined, and I hope you know how much I appreciate that. I know it's been hard. But I never intended for you to put your own life on hold so that you could deal with mine."

Piper's eyes widened. "Mom, I—"

"You and I are going to have plenty of time together on this trip. But I worry about what will happen to you after I'm not here anymore."

"Mom," Piper began, but whatever she was about to say was erased by the reappearance of their cute waiter, who had two large glasses of white wine balanced on a tray. He didn't take his eyes off Piper as he set them down on the table.

"Mesdames, are you ready to order?" he asked, but Julia might as well have not been there at all as he and Piper drank each other in. "Our salads are very popular, and our foie gras de canard is lovely."

Piper again seemed to be at a loss for words, so Julia spoke for her. "Let's have the foie gras and two small salads, then, with some french fries." She handed the menus back and smiled at the young man with thick, dark hair, strong features, and long eyelashes. "And, Nicolas, was it?"

"*Oui*, madame." He looked flustered when he finally turned to her.

"This is my daughter, Piper. It's her first time in Paris."

Piper had now turned scarlet. "Mom!" she choked out.

"Well. Welcome to Paris, Piper." Nicolas smiled at her. "It's very nice to meet you."

"You, too," Piper mumbled.

He hesitated for a second. "Is there anything else I can get you ladies?"

"We're okay for now," Piper said quickly, obviously heading Julia off before she could do something like offer the waiter her daughter's phone number.

"I'll be back shortly, then," he said, smiling at Piper once more before walking away.

"Mom, what are you doing?" Piper groaned once he was out of earshot.

"You should ask him what time his shift ends," Julia said.

"Why would I do that?" Piper's eyes practically popped out of her head. "I mean, it's not like I even live here or anything."

"So what?" Julia asked. "Take some chances! Life isn't just about making all the smart, safe moves." Julia had learned that far too late. "Anyhow, you're going to be all by yourself later on today while I catch up on sleep. Wouldn't it be more fun to see Paris with a cute guy?"

Piper buried her head in her hands. "This is so embarrassing."

"Just trying to help," Julia said with a sly grin. What she didn't say was that it would make her rest more easily to have a glimpse, even if it was just a small one, of the shape Piper's life might take after Julia was gone.

Shelby Anderson had a hangover.

It had been a long time since she'd felt like this. No, that wasn't exactly true, was it? She'd had a hangover last week, too. But that one had been from polishing off an entire bottle of chardonnay by herself at home. At least this morning's hangover felt well-earned; she was on a girls' trip, and she'd stayed up most of last night on the flight to Paris with Corinne and Vanessa—her two closest friends—swapping stories and laughing, though for Shelby, it was all she could do to fight back tears.

She wasn't supposed to be here. She was supposed to be with

Brandon. At home in Alabama. Ideally with a toddler or two following her around.

Instead, she was on another continent, on a trip that Corinne and Vanessa were cheerfully referring to as her "divorce party."

The problem was that Shelby didn't want a party. She didn't want a divorce. But she had allowed herself to be swept along by her friends' enthusiasm, and by the time she admitted to herself that she didn't want this trip at all, she was already on a flight.

They'd arrived this morning, and after quick power naps, they'd grabbed lunch near their hotel at a little place called Café Le Petit Pont, where Corinne and Vanessa—both currently single—flirted shamelessly with the cute waiter, who couldn't have been more than twenty-four or twenty-five, a full decade and a half younger than them.

But the waiter had no interest in any of them, though he was friendly and polite. It was obvious he was smitten with the twenty-something American girl with long dark hair at the next table over, who seemed to be on a trip with her mother.

"Oh my God," Corinne whispered loudly at one point, her eyes wide as the others leaned in. "I think that girl's mom is flirting with the waiter!"

"Really? Is he flirting back?" asked Vanessa, who looked forlorn, as if she'd missed an opportunity to win the waiter's affection.

"No, wait," Corinne said. "Actually, I think the mom's trying to *pick up* the waiter for her daughter. Bold move, mom, bold move. The daughter looks completely mortified."

"Wouldn't you be?" Vanessa asked with a laugh.

"Now the mom's telling the daughter she should go see Paris with the waiter," Corinne reported, still eavesdropping. Corinne had hearing like a bat. When they'd all been in college together at the University of Alabama nearly twenty years ago, she'd discovered that Vanessa's boyfriend at the time was cheating because she'd overheard a conversation in a crowded restaurant from four tables away.

"I wish I had a mom who tried to set me up with hot guys," Vanessa said, rolling her eyes.

Corinne laughed, and although Shelby forced a smile, too, she realized she was suddenly fighting back tears. What she wouldn't give for her own mother to be here with her right now, but her mom was too disappointed in her. *How can you just give up on your marriage like that?* her mom had demanded two months ago when Shelby had finally mustered the courage to call and tell her about the impending divorce, which Brandon had set in motion a few months earlier. Shelby had protested that *she* hadn't been the one to give up, that Brandon had been the one to leave, but her mother had brushed the words aside and given her an earful about how Shelby needed to honor her commitments.

The thing was, Shelby *had* honored her commitments. It would be almost better if he'd left her for someone else, because then she could have at least explained that to her mother. Instead, he simply hadn't wanted *her* anymore.

What her mother was really asking, Shelby knew, was how she could give up on the perks of being married to a man like Brandon Anderson, who everyone agreed was the perfect catch—a former college football player, a successful engineer, the son of a respected circuit court judge. But Brandon had been the one to unilaterally decide that their marriage was over, just after Shelby's third fruitless cycle of IVF, when she'd felt like such a failure that she could barely get out of bed.

"All you ever talk about is babies, babies, babies," Brandon had said, shaking his head in disappointment as she'd sobbed in the kitchen, pathetically begging him not to leave, to give them another chance. "I can't do this anymore. For God's sake, Shelby, there's more to life than this."

And maybe he was right. But she'd thought that he wanted a child as much as she did, and that all of this agony and despair would one day be nothing but a distant memory as they welcomed the baby that would finally make their family complete.

And now, not only had Brandon left, but Shelby had learned just last week through her divorce attorney that Brandon's new girlfriend—a yoga instructor in her late twenties named Alexis whom he'd started dating a few months after separating from Shelby—was pregnant. So Brandon would be a father after all. It just wouldn't have anything to do with her.

"Earth to Shelby!" Corinne's worried voice cut into Shelby's thoughts, and she realized she'd been zoned out for at least the last minute while the conversation had continued around her.

"Sorry," she murmured, embarrassed, and Vanessa reached for Shelby's hand under the table and squeezed.

"You okay?" Vanessa asked. "You're better off without him, you know."

"I know," Shelby said, but as Vanessa continued to look at her with concern, Shelby knew that her friend could see right through her. What if she *wasn't* better off, though? What if the problem was her? What if she'd lost the perfect guy solely because she couldn't pull herself together? What if her mom was right about everything?

"You know what?" Vanessa said abruptly. "I think we need a bottle of champagne."

Corinne grinned. "I'll call the hot waiter over."

"Actually," Vanessa said, "what do you say we pay our bill here and go find a bar? We'll have some bubbly, and then we'll grab an Uber and go see the Eiffel Tower."

Corinne shrugged. "I mean, I was thinking that maybe we

could stick around here for a little while more and see if the waiter notices us."

Shelby looked at her in disbelief. "Corinne, he's currently drooling over that cute girl."

"Plus, you're almost old enough to be his mom," Vanessa chimed in helpfully.

"Well, his loss. With age comes experience. I could teach him a thing or two." Corinne waggled her eyebrows suggestively.

Laughing, the women signaled the cute waiter for the check, paid their bill, and got up to leave, though as they walked out into the Paris sunshine, Shelby couldn't help but pause for a moment, looking up at the gorgeous, soaring architecture of Notre Dame. It had suffered a great loss, too, hadn't it? It had risen from the ashes. It had been rebuilt. Maybe, just maybe, there was hope of a better future for Shelby, too.

CHAPTER FOUR

Le Maison Grog was dead empty, and Russ Rodgers was worried.

Sure, they still did a brisk business each evening, but gone were the days when the bar was bustling at lunchtime, and he couldn't help but wonder if it was a signal that the golden age of the Anglo pub was fading here in Paris.

When he and his best friend, Benji, had moved here from Sydney a decade and a half ago and had decided to buy a bar geared toward English-speaking expats, establishments like theirs were all the rage. There was The Long Hop, the British pub a block over, and then there were all the Frog bars sprinkled throughout the city: The Frog & Princess over in Saint Germain-des-prés; The Frog & Rosbif over in the second arrondissement, and several other locations around Paris. And while those anglophone pubs had continued to thrive, somehow the daytime business at Le Maison Grog had slowed down.

They'd both been thirty when they'd bought the pub, which had been previously owned by a pair of Brits and was called The Red Telephone Box, a stupid name for a pub if Russ had ever heard one. They'd promptly renamed it, hanging flags from not only Australia and New Zealand, but also from the States, Canada, the UK, Ireland, and South Africa to broaden the anglophone appeal.

And at first, it had been gangbusters. They were the hot new thing in town, and they were making so much money that it made Russ's head spin. Russ had thought they might open a second branch across the Seine, but it became clear fairly quickly that Benji was more interested in bedding the hot expats who wandered through their door each night than he was in expanding their business. And that was fine when they were young. They were having fun and making a quid, and Russ had always figured that, eventually, they'd sell the bar and return to their real lives.

But somehow, fifteen years had gone by in a blink, and they were both forty-five now, both still single, both still working twelve-hour days at the bar. And that seemed well and good for Benji, who hadn't grown out of hooking up with a different twentysomething each night. But Russ was restless. He wanted more out of life.

The front door of Le Maison Grog banged open and Russ looked up. The man who entered first—twenty-five or so, dark-haired, probably French—was a common enough sight, perhaps a local office worker wandering in on his lunch break. But the group behind him—six men and five women who all looked to be in their seventies—weren't the usual clientele of the bar.

"G'day, mates!" he called out, because that's what people wanted when they walked into an Aussie pub.

"*Bonjour*," the young man greeted him, adding in French, "I'm giving a tour to a group of American Vietnam veterans here. Thought they might like a little taste of home." He looked around skeptically. "You *do* serve American food? And you *are* currently open?"

"*Oui*," Russ said, trying not to be embarrassed by the emptiness of the place. "We have a full kitchen in the back, and a nice menu of British, Aussie, and American favorites. Here, let me drag some chairs over so you can all sit together." Hastily, he combined two six-tops into a table for twelve.

The young French man, who hadn't lifted a finger to help, gestured grandly for all of them to sit, as if he'd been the one to single-handedly arrange their seating.

"G'day," Russ repeated, amping up his Australian accent, as he always did. "Can I start you lads and ladies off with something to drink?"

"British, are you, young man?" asked one of the men, who looked ridiculous in a oversized black beret. "I'd know the accent anywhere." The two men next to him exchanged looks of exasperation.

"No, sir. I'm from Australia, actually," Russ replied pleasantly. If he had a euro for every American who assumed he was British, he'd be able to afford a three-bedroom apartment overlooking the Seine rather than the run-down, one-bedroom walk-up he rented in the Latin Quarter. "Vietnam vets, are you? My granddad was a veteran, too—World War II, in fact. I have a deep respect for anyone who served in the military."

The bereted man nodded, already distracted by scooting his chair closer to two of the ladies, who immediately slid away. The fellow next to the bereted guy—African American with a thick shock of white hair and deep brown eyes—held Russ's gaze. "That's wonderful, son," he said kindly. "We appreciate your grandfather's service."

"And I appreciate yours, sir," Russ said, meaning it. The older Russ had gotten, the more he'd understood just how honorable it was to risk one's life for one's country.

"Yes, well, it does take a great deal of bravery to do what we did," said the man with the beret. "Though I didn't realize you Kiwis played much of a role in World War II."

"Actually, sir, Kiwis are New Zealanders." Russ resisted the urge to laugh as the Black man, and the white man next to him—gray-haired with a strong jaw and wire-rimmed glasses, kind of like an older Clark Kent—exchanged looks again. "Nearly a million Australians fought on the side of the Allies, and I think another 150,000 or so men and women from New Zealand served, too."

"Oh, well, as I said," said the bereted man, waving away his mistake, "very brave."

The table ordered drinks—beers for the pompous man, the tour guide, two of the women, and three more of the men, wine for the other three women, and scotch on the rocks for the two men who seemed to be close friends.

Out back, Russ told Benji that a group had come in and he needed some help. Fortunately, the cook—a burly Scottish fellow named Jagger—was out having a smoke, too, and both men stubbed their cigarettes out and hurried inside.

On the way back in, Russ nearly collided with the man with the Clark Kent glasses, the one who'd been exchanging glances with his friend each time the beret-wearing guy opened his mouth.

"Sorry!" the man exclaimed as they narrowly dodged crashing into each other. "I was just looking for the restroom."

Russ smiled. "It's just back there, down the spiral staircase, second door on the right at the bottom of the steps."

The man nodded, but he didn't move. "Listen, I want to apologize for the member of our group over there." He jerked a thumb at the man in the beret, who was currently chattering excitedly at two of the women at their table, though they had turned their backs to him. "I can't say I know him well, but I hope he didn't offend you."

Russ smiled. "Ah, no worries, mate," he said. "He isn't the first to come in here with a bit of bluster."

The older man chuckled. "To be honest, I wish I had half his confidence. Though I'd like to think I'd use it more responsibly."

Russ glanced once more at the man. "Maybe the confidence comes with that ridiculous hat. He seems to think it makes him irresistible, doesn't he?" He quickly shut his mouth. "I'm sorry. I shouldn't be talking about customers that way."

But the man didn't look judgmental. "Still, you've got to hand it to him. He's playing an odds game, isn't he? I suppose he's banking on the idea that if he throws himself at enough women, sooner or later, one of them has to say yes."

Russ chuckled. "Yeah, well, my two cents? That's not how love works. It's not about the number of people you take a shot with. It's about taking a shot with the right one." Russ immediately felt ridiculous; he sounded like some sort of romantic sage instead of a bar owner who had never actually been in a long-term relationship. "But what do I know?" he added hastily.

But the man was nodding slowly, as if Russ had said something profound. "Sounds to me like you know more than you're giving yourself credit for." With that, he patted Russ on the shoulder and shuffled off toward the bathroom, leaving Russ feeling oddly bereft.

Russ turned to retrieve the drinks Benji had poured for the group, but at that moment, the front door opened, revealing a second group backlit by the early afternoon sunshine.

"G'day!" Russ called out his standard greeting, and when the door closed, he saw three women around his age, maybe a few years younger, giggling and looking around. Already halfway to drunk, if he had to guess, which boded well for sales. "Have a seat wherever you'd like," he called. "I'll be with you in just a moment."

Two of them shuffled off obediently toward the bar, already appraising Benji, who had just perked up. But one of them stayed rooted to the spot for an extra moment, her gaze roaming the room.

She was the prettiest of the three, though not in an obvious way. The other two were heavily made up, their hair fluffed and spritzed in that mysterious way that women had, which looked like it took some effort. The one by the door, though, wore her wavy blond hair loose around her shoulders in a style that didn't look deliberate, and she appeared to be wearing little makeup. What struck Russ the most, though, was how sad she looked—and how he had a sudden, visceral urge to comfort her, even though he had no idea what was wrong.

He was jolted out of his staring by the reemergence of the man from the restroom. "Ah," the man said, coming up beside him and taking in the scene. The girl with the wavy blond hair was moving toward Russ. "Maybe it's time to take that shot."

The man smiled as he headed back toward his table, and then, the girl was beside Russ. "Hi," he said, because he couldn't even muster a second obligatory *G'day*.

"Hi," she said, and then, even though her eyes still looked sad, her lips parted in a small smile that lit up her whole face, and Russ felt the world shifting beneath his feet.

Piper's mom was *dying*.

It still didn't feel real. And here they were in Paris, and her mother was yawning and trying hard to keep her eyes open, and

Piper couldn't help but feel she was already losing her, bit by bit, even though she was still here.

"Mom," she said now as they walked back to their hotel after their meal at Café Le Petit Pont. "I know you need to sleep, but I don't want to do anything without you. I'm just going to stay in and read a book or something while you nap, okay?"

"That is most certainly *not* okay," her mom replied. "This is your very first time in Paris, and you're not wasting it holed up in a hotel room with me. Look, I just need to recharge my battery tonight, and then I'll be ready to hit the ground running tomorrow."

"Are you sure?" Piper asked, a familiar wave of guilt washing over her.

"Honey, I'll be mad at you if you don't go out and see a bit of the city."

"Yeah, all right. I'll just stick around this neighborhood, though, okay? I'll save the Eiffel Tower and everything for when you can go with me."

"If I were you, I'd go back to the café and strike up a conversation with that cute waiter," her mom said, grinning at her.

"It wouldn't be nearly as fun without you there to humiliate me."

Her mom laughed. "Look, honey, I know I push sometimes. But when you're young, you have to seize the opportunities that come along, or you'll have regrets. Believe me, I know."

Piper didn't say anything for a moment as they crossed the bustling Place Saint-Michel and turned down a much quieter side street. "Do you have regrets, Mom?" she asked quietly as they reached their hotel, a few doors down on the left.

Her mom paused at the hotel's door. "A million of them, sweetie." She looked Piper right in the eye and added firmly, "But not a single one of them has to do with you. I am the luckiest woman in the world to have a daughter like you."

"And I'm the luckiest daughter," Piper said.

"No, you're not," her mom said as she pulled the hotel's door open. Her voice trembled as she added, "The luckiest daughter would get to have her mother until she was an old woman herself."

Piper nodded, too choked up to reply right away. She waited until they were in the small elevator, heading up to their room on the third floor, before saying, "I'm still the luckiest. To have had you for the time I've had."

Her mom reached out to gently touch Piper's cheek. "I feel the same way, my love. I wouldn't trade a second of it." She yawned, looking exhausted.

"Mom?" Piper ventured. "You sure you don't want me to stay with you?"

"Go, honey," her mother said firmly. "Explore Paris. Check out Notre Dame or Sainte-Chapelle or something." They had reached their hotel room door, and her mother used the tasseled hotel key to open it, turning the lock twice counterclockwise and turning the knob. "I mean it. Stop worrying about me. Go have fun, get a nice dinner somewhere, and we'll have a great day tomorrow, okay?" She didn't wait for a response. She gave Piper a small smile, then handed her the key, which was to be left at the front desk whenever they went out, and slipped inside, pulling the door pointedly closed behind her.

Piper hesitated, frozen in place. She could follow her in, but she knew her mother needed her rest. After a moment, she sighed in resignation and pulled out her phone.

She'd been dying to visit Shakespeare and Company, the English-language bookstore near the hotel, because she loved the story of its welcoming approach to visitors: penniless aspiring writers had long been allowed to sleep in the store overnight in exchange for promising that they'd read a book a day, help in the shop, and write a one-page autobiography before they left. Tumbleweeds, they were called—and Piper liked the idea of being blown in by the wind and finding a sort-of home before one had figured life out. It was comforting to think that there was a place for people like her, who were still in the process of becoming who they were.

Taking a deep breath, she pulled up walking directions to the bookstore. It was only six minutes away, back in the direction from which she and her mother had just come.

As she exited the hotel and crossed through the bustling Place Saint-Michel, she wiped at her eyes. At least her mom wasn't around now to see her come undone.

She knew that her mom was sicker than she was letting on. She could see it in the way she moved, the way that she winced with the effort of standing up or sitting down, the way that she lost her breath so easily these days, sometimes trailing off in the middle of a sentence because her lungs couldn't keep up anymore. Piper also knew that her mother wanted badly to convince her that everything was normal. But things hadn't been normal since the day her mother had called, just over two years ago, and said the dreaded words, "Honey, I have cancer."

The Café Le Petit Pont loomed just ahead to the right, and Piper hurried past it, glancing inside to look for the cute waiter and then looking quickly away just in case he spotted her. She was still mortified by the way her mother had acted in front of him.

When she had safely cleared the café, she looked up and was surprised to see that she was already standing in front of Shakespeare and Company. She hadn't realized that they'd been so close to it earlier. The front of the store was green, with yellow signage and lettering, quotes written on chalkboards, and a square, black-and-white image of Walt Whitman on the wall to the right, surrounded by a quote in French. She'd expected a line outside the famous store, but there wasn't one, so she approached the front door and went in.

She drew in a deep breath the moment she walked through the first narrow doorway inside, over a small step that was painted with the words LIVE FOR HUMANITY. There were books as far as the eye could see, stuffed onto shelves, lining every wall, all the way up to the ceiling. The managed chaos was utterly beautiful, and Piper stopped for a moment and just inhaled, the scent of spines and pages and ink all blurring together into one perfect perfume of print. She headed toward the back of the store, and then made her way up the narrow staircase, reading the words painted on the stairs as she climbed: I WISH I COULD SHOW YOU, WHEN YOU ARE LONELY OR IN DARKNESS, THE ASTONISHING LIGHT OF YOUR OWN BEING. It was a quote from Hafiz, and it touched her to the core.

As she wandered through tiny, book-lined rooms upstairs, her gaze landed on a sign—BE NOT INHOSPITABLE TO STRANGERS LEST THEY BE ANGELS IN DISGUISE. Her heart did a little flip of recognition as she stared up at it. She'd read the phrase before; it had been the mantra of the store's founder, George Whitman, who'd attributed it to Yeats. But today, standing inside this store an ocean away from home, knowing that soon her mother would be gone and she'd be adrift in the world, looking for a place to call her own, the words felt like they'd been written just for her, a stranger in an unfamiliar land, facing an unknowable future.

"Piper?" A deep voice cut into her thoughts, and she looked down from the sign only to realize, with a start, that the cute waiter from Café Le Petit Pont was standing in front of her, clutching a narrow book in his hand.

"Nicolas?" she managed to choke out. She could feel her cheeks heating up, her pulse beginning to race. "Uh, what are you doing here?"

"I'm on my lunch break."

"I mean . . . in an English language bookstore." She had figured a place like this was mostly for tourists.

"Oh." He smiled at her. "Don't let my French accent fool you; my dad was an American. I grew up speaking English, but I've let myself get rusty." He held up the book in his hand and shrugged, a bit of color rising to his own cheeks. "Perhaps it's silly, but I've been trying to improve by reading poetry."

"Poetry?"

He looked her in the eye. "It's just, I think you can't really speak a language with fluency until you fall in love with it, can you? And how better to fall in love than to know the most lyrical way the language's words can be used?"

"That's . . . beautiful," she said, feeling a bit like the wind had been knocked out of her.

"I just wish I spoke better." He shrugged, looking embarrassed.

"You speak wonderfully. Really, you do." She glanced at the title of the book he was holding and looked back up at him. "*Leaves of Grass*?"

"You know it?"

"Well . . . Yeah. Walt Whitman is my favorite poet."

Nicolas's eyebrows arched in surprise. "You like poetry, too?"

"I wrote my college thesis on American poets of the nineteenth century." She glanced down at the book in his hands. "Have you read Whitman before?"

"Have I read Whitman?" He grinned. "'When lilacs last in the dooryard bloom'd, and the great star early droop'd in the western sky in the night, I mourn'd, and yet shall mourn with ever-returning spring.'" He hesitated. "Did I get it right? It was one of my father's favorites."

Piper nodded, at a loss for words, because Whitman's famous poem—an elegy for Abraham Lincoln, after his death—always made her think of people being gone too soon, in the wrong seasons of their lives, and of course that made her think of her mother, and suddenly, surrounded by books and wisdom and looking into the eyes of the most attractive guy she'd ever met, she felt tears forming, and oh, my gosh, was she actually about to cry?

"Piper?" Nicolas asked with concern. "Are you all right?"

But she wasn't all right at all—she hadn't been in two years—and even with the solace of being surrounded by books, she could feel the familiar swell of grief rolling in, and she had to get out. "Uh, excuse me," she managed to say, turning and dashing down the stairs and out of the store before he could see her burst into tears.

On the sidewalk outside, she faced Notre Dame and took big, deep breaths, gulping in the air until her racing heart slowed and the tide receded and the fear and hurt were back where they belonged, deep beneath the surface. But once the pain had tucked itself back in, she felt an overwhelming sweep of embarrassment. Had she just run out of a bookstore, mid-conversation, like a total crazy person? If her mom hadn't scared Nicolas off earlier, surely she'd just done the job herself.

A moment later, she felt him appear behind her, the air around her growing charged. "Piper?" he said. "What happened there?"

His tone was gentle, concerned, but she still felt like an idiot. "Nothing," she said quickly, rearranging her face into something she hoped looked normal. She'd become an expert at that since her mother's diagnosis, carefully wiping away the signs of her own emotion so that they weren't an extra burden. "I'm sorry. It's nothing."

She turned to face him, and she could read two things in his expression: that he didn't believe her, and that he genuinely cared. She averted her eyes, because she didn't want his pity. But she could still feel him looking at her with concern.

"Whatever it is, it isn't nothing," he said a moment later. "If you don't want to talk about it, that's fine. But if you do . . ."

She allowed herself to look back at him, and to imagine a world in which she could just be a carefree girl flirting with a cute guy in Paris. Instead, she was a girl who'd spent two years under the shadow of her mom's impending death, and she'd all but disappeared into the darkness. She thought of the Hafiz quote on the stairs inside about finding the light of her own being, but she had no idea how to do that. "I'm okay," she said, pasting on a smile. "Really. Mostly, I'm just embarrassed."

He didn't break eye contact, and she couldn't shake the feeling that he was looking right into her soul. "'When it is dark enough, you can see the stars,'" he said after a moment, and her heart lurched, because how had he known she'd been thinking about the darkness that had eclipsed everything good in her life?

"What?" she asked.

He smiled slightly. "Another quote. Ralph Waldo Emerson. But I always liked it because it reminds us that when things are at their worst, there's always light. You just have to remind yourself to look up and see it."

"Yeah, but . . ." She swallowed hard. "What if the light's all gone?"

"It's never gone, though."

"Yeah, well, my mom is dying, so things are pretty dark for me," she said. What did it matter, anyhow? She'd never see him again. Once the words started pouring out of her mouth, she realized it felt good to say them, to share them with someone else rather than keeping them all inside. "She's dying from cancer, and this is our last trip together, and I don't know what I'm going to do when she's gone because I don't know who I am without her, and I don't know how I'm supposed to be okay with any of this."

"Oh, Piper."

She couldn't see his face because she was too embarrassed to look up. She studied her feet like they were the most interesting things in the world.

"Piper?" he said a moment later when she still hadn't met his eye. "I'm truly very sorry."

"Thanks," she muttered to her feet. "I'm sorry, too. It's not your problem, and I shouldn't have said anything. It's just—I mean, I feel like a crazy person sometimes. I wish I knew how to handle all of this better."

"Piper?" he said again, and this time, he waited until she looked up and met his gaze, which didn't hold the judgment she expected. "You're not a crazy person. You're very strong, I think."

"Nicolas, let's be honest, I'm standing here on a sidewalk, word-vomiting out my feelings to someone I don't even know."

He shrugged. "I don't mind. Besides, we know each other now, don't we?"

She looked into his green eyes. "Yeah, well, it's not like there's anything you can do," she said softly.

"I can listen," he replied, still holding her gaze, and finally, Piper felt a bit of the weight lift from her shoulders. Finally, he broke eye contact and looked down at his watch with a groan. "Piper, I'm very sorry, but I have to get back to work. If you have some time tomorrow, though, would you like to go for a walk with me between shifts?"

"A walk?"

"It's the best way to see Paris."

"No, I mean, you want to take a walk with *me*? After all of . . . that?"

"Ah, well. My father died when I was ten, you see. So while I can't say I know exactly what you're feeling right now, I understand it. I do."

"I'm so sorry about your father," Piper said.

Nicolas shrugged and gave her a sad smile. "When he was still alive, he used to take me on long strolls around the city, nearly every day. Since he's been gone, I've found comfort in walking, and I thought you might, too. If you'd like to join me."

"Okay," she said tentatively. "I—I'm supposed to be hanging out with my mom, but she usually takes a nap in the afternoon these days."

"If you can spare the time, I'll be in front of Notre Dame at two o'clock. And if you can't come, that's all right, too."

"Okay. And . . . thanks," Piper said. And as Nicolas smiled and turned to head back to the café, Piper had a sudden sense of the world rearranging itself into something she didn't recognize. For the first time in two years, she felt a little less alone, and with his words about light in the darkest times ringing in her ears, and with the rest of the afternoon to kill, she set off toward the Seine to see where her feet would take her.

CHAPTER FIVE

Jackson had been wandering around Paris for two hours, and though he knew he should probably check in and catch a nap before meeting with the concert promoter tonight, he wasn't ready to leave his old neighborhood and reenter a world in which people would fawn over him the moment he set foot in his hotel.

It wasn't that he didn't think he'd like the Four Seasons Hotel George V. It was that for at least the next few minutes, he didn't want to be Jackson Quick. He wanted to be an anonymous guy on the streets of Paris.

In two hours, not a single person had said a word to him, aside from the vendor he'd bought a snack from fifteen minutes after the driver had dropped him off. And the guy had hardly even looked at his face; he had just grunted, "*Treize euros*," before accepting Jackson's twenty-euro note, flipping a few coins back to him, and handing over a warm sugared crepe and a cold Orangina.

Since then, Jackson had wandered around the Place Saint-Michel, had crossed the Seine to Notre Dame, and strolled west to the tip of the Île de la Cité, where he'd settled on the wall along the river and watched the world go by for a bit. He'd crossed back over the Seine on the Pont Neuf and had woven his way to the rue de la Huchette, where he'd often gone for cheap meals and even cheaper wine after long days of busking nearby. Even there, on a road packed shoulder to shoulder with tourists studying menus and spilling in and out of souvenir shops, he got only a few second glances. He could practically see the thought process of those who looked twice at him. *He looks familiar, but I can't place him.* Checking nonexistent text messages on his phone reliably spared him any further interaction as he passed.

But now he was hungry. His Apple Watch told him he had walked nearly four miles in the past couple of hours, and he'd long since burned off the crepe and soda. Up ahead, he spotted a pub with British, American, Canadian, and Aussie flags flying, and he was struck with a sudden sense of familiarity. *The Red Telephone Box.* He was almost certain that had been the name of the anglophone pub when he'd lived here, and if he remembered correctly, it served a decent lunch. It would be an ideal place to be anonymous just a little while longer.

The sign over the door had changed—it was called LE MAISON GROG now, which made Jackson's heart hurt a little. It was probably a perfectly nice place—actually, it was probably indistinguishable from The Red Telephone Box—but there was something depressing about returning to a neighborhood you'd once called home and finding that everything was different.

He pulled open the door to the pub and went inside, encouraged to see that it looked largely as he'd remembered it—a long wooden bar against the back wall and worn wooden tables throughout—though the decorations had changed from kitschy telephone receivers and phone books to boomerangs and pictures of kangaroos, along with a few neon signs advertising Foster's. Fortunately, it was nearly empty, though there were two other parties here: a big table of older folks on one side of the room, and three young women perched at the far end of the bar.

Jackson hesitated for a moment, squinting at the women. Not one of them had looked his way yet, but he could see that they were all in their thirties. A little too young to have been his fans back at the height of his career, though their mothers might have been.

He made his way toward the opposite end of the bar and sat on one of the wooden stools, which looked old enough that he suspected they'd been here thirty-five years ago, when the bar had borne a different name.

"G'day, mate!" said the bartender, obviously an Aussie, a decade or so younger than Jackson. For a split second, Jackson found himself thinking about roads not taken. What if he'd worked in a bar in Paris instead of pursuing his musical dreams? Would he be more fulfilled than he was now? Less lonely?

"Hey," Jackson said, picking up the menu the Aussie bartender placed in front of him and using it to partially block the view of his face. Jackson had been big in Australia and New Zealand back in the day, and the bartender was in the right range to have been at least tangentially aware of Jackson's existence.

"What can I get you, mate?" the bartender asked, giving Jackson a puzzled look. Probably wondering what kind of weirdo comes to a bar and hides his face. Jackson reluctantly lowered the menu and watched as the bartender frowned in concentration, trying to place him.

"Have any IPAs?" Jackson asked.

"We have Balter in a can." The bartender was still squinting at him. "It's from the Gold Coast."

"That sounds great." Jackson could see the moment the bartender realized who he was—the man's eyebrows went up as his eyes widened in surprise—and he waited to have his cover blown.

But instead, the bartender glanced down the bar at the women and seemed to make a decision. "Coming right up," he said neutrally. "Why don't you have a look at the menu, and I'll be back in a moment to see what you want."

Jackson felt a wave of relief sweep through him. "Great." He leaned in and added, "And thank you."

Thirty minutes later, Jackson had polished off a sausage roll and chips—exactly the same as he remembered them tasting three decades ago—and had chased the beer with a strong cup of coffee, since he was currently fighting the wave of exhaustion that had been threatening since that morning.

Meanwhile, he surreptitiously watched the other two groups in the restaurant—he loved trying to figure out what made strangers tick—and had already ascertained that the Aussie bartender was interested in one of the three women, and that the older folks at the table were on some sort of tour.

"I remember this place back when it was The Red Telephone Box," Jackson said when the bartender, who had introduced himself as Russ, came to deliver his check.

"Do you?" The bartender looked surprised. "Terrible name, really. When my business partner and I bought this place, the name was the first thing to go."

Jackson laughed and looked down at the bill. The bartender had only charged him for the fish and chips and coffee. "You forgot to charge me for my beer, man," he said.

"Nah, it's on the house," the bartender said, his voice low. "Not every day the voice of a generation walks into my bar."

"The voice of a generation?" Jackson had to laugh. "I don't think anyone calls me that."

The bartender shrugged. "I don't know, mate. I grew up on your songs. Come back anytime, all right? We may not be The Red Telephone Box anymore, but we're happy to be a home away from home in Paris if you need one."

"Thank you," Jackson said. He glanced once more down the bar at the girls and then smiled at the bartender. "And, hey, do you mind a bit of advice from the voice of a generation?"

The bartender laughed. "I'd be honored, mate."

"That girl down there that you've been eyeing for the past hour? You've got nothing to lose by taking a chance."

And with that, Jackson left a twenty-euro note and departed the relative anonymity of the bar for the hour-long walk to his hotel on the other side of the city. It would be easier to call a car, but he wanted to revel in being alone and unrecognized for just a little while longer.

When she and her grandfather walked into the apartment overlooking the Jardin du Luxembourg, Melanie was braced for a confrontation. Grandpa Henry was right. She had to tell Gilles that she knew and let the chips fall where they may.

But the apartment was silent. "He's not here," she said, turning in disbelief to her grandfather, who had insisted on dragging his own bag into the elevator and down the hall, muttering something about how he wasn't dead yet. "He said he'd be working from home today."

"Well, then," her grandfather said, "we'll have a moment to figure out what you want to say."

A wave of relief washed over Melanie. The longer Gilles was gone, the longer she could put off the inevitable. But just then, the apartment door opened behind her, and she turned to see Gilles, who looked as put together as ever in a sharp charcoal suit, his thinning hair gelled to perfection. "*Ma chère*," he said, kissing her quickly as he stepped into the foyer. "And, Henry, how nice to see you again. You're looking well."

Gilles turned to beam at her grandfather. Grandpa Henry didn't say a word; he just stared murderously at Gilles.

"Are you all right, Henry?" Gilles asked a bit more loudly. "Is your hearing going? I said you look very well."

"Oh, I heard you all right," her grandfather growled, and for the first time, Gilles seemed to understand that something was wrong. His forehead creased in confusion, and he looked at Melanie for an explanation.

But she couldn't do it. Her tongue felt thick in her mouth.

"Melanie?" her grandfather prompted, gently placing a hand on her elbow. "I'm right here."

"*Ma chère*," Gilles said, glancing uncertainly at her grandfather before looking back at Melanie. "What is this all about?"

Her grandfather squeezed her elbow, and Melanie took a deep breath and dove headfirst into the future, blurting out, "Amandine. I know about Amandine, Gilles."

You could have heard a pin drop in the long beat of silence that followed. Gilles looked nervously at her grandfather before turning back to Melanie. "I—I don't know what you're talking about." But his stammer belied his words.

Saying nothing, Melanie pulled her phone from her pocket and turned it around to show Gilles the photo she'd taken of his text exchange.

"'I can still smell you on my skin . . .'" Melanie recited.

"*Attends, je peux t'expliquer*," Gilles said, holding up his hands in surrender. All the color had drained from his face.

Melanie held his gaze, then continued. "*Until we meet again, Kisses from your Amandine.* How would you like to explain *that,* Gilles?"

He coughed and shot another glance at Melanie's grandfather, who was still glowering at him. "I think perhaps this is a conversation between husband and wife," Gilles said nervously.

"Yes, well, I thought our marriage was between husband and wife, too, but clearly I was wrong about that." Melanie felt a surge of confidence as her grandfather nodded his approval. Still, as much as it comforted her to have him here, this was her battle, not his. "But, Grandpa Henry, I think maybe Gilles is right. He and I need to have a chance to talk alone."

Grandpa Henry was glaring at Gilles now like he wanted to rip him limb from limb. Gilles, clearly shaken, took a small step away from him. "Are you sure, my dear?" Grandpa Henry asked.

"I am." She could see in her grandfather's eyes that he understood that as much as she wanted his support, this was something she had to face up to on her own. "I'm fine. Why don't you go see Celeste? Gilles and I have some things to talk about."

"I'm happy to stick around in case you need me," her grandfather said, shooting another threatening look at Gilles.

"Grandpa Henry," she said, turning to him. "You flew across an ocean to see the woman you thought you'd lost forever. Go to her. I know how much it means to you. I'm okay. And I'll be right here when you get back."

Grandpa Henry searched her face for a moment. "Yes, all right." He narrowed his eyes at Gilles. "You're a very stupid man," he said, and Gilles's mouth fell open. Her grandfather turned back to her, planted a kiss on her cheek, and whispered, "Good luck, my dear."

"You, too, Grandpa Henry," she murmured, kissing him on the cheek, too.

And then, he was gone, leaving her alone with Gilles, who was staring at her as if he'd never really known her at all.

Henry's heart was heavy with concern as he made his way toward Celeste's retirement home, just a ten-minute walk from Melanie's apartment near the Jardin du Luxembourg. He could have made it in five if he was younger and didn't need a cane for support. The proximity of his lost love to his granddaughter should have astonished him, but the truth was that in Paris, each arrondissement was like its own little village, and this was the same neighborhood Celeste had lived in all these years before, when he'd first met her. The coincidence was that Melanie and Gilles had chosen to settle in the same area; it was one of the reasons why Henry had avoided visiting his granddaughter during the two decades that she had lived here. It wasn't that he hadn't wanted to come; it was that he was certain he couldn't bear being within blocks of the apartment where he had loved and lost Celeste.

But now he knew that he hadn't lost her at all. She'd been out there living, breathing, having an entire existence without him. The thought made his heart happy and broke it into a million pieces at the same time.

How differently might his life have turned out? He knew without a shadow of a doubt that he would have come back for her, and he would have done whatever it took to be with her. But if he had found her, he wouldn't have married his wife or had his son. Melanie would never have existed. And how could he wish away a wife who'd been good to him, a son he'd loved from the very depths of his soul, and a granddaughter who was his favorite person in the world?

Beyond that, what would have become of his career? All the songs he'd written over the years were about the deep love and the sense of bottomless loss he felt when he thought of Celeste. Without the grief of losing her, without the overwhelming need to revisit their love again and again in his lyrics and melodies, what would he have written about?

He was so deep in thought that he almost walked right by the home. He had expected a sign out front identifying it as an elder-care facility, but instead, it looked like any other building on the street. He checked the address on his phone once more. Number 18 on the rue Royer-Collard, just off the bustling rue Gay-Lussac. He steeled himself and went in.

"*Bonjour*," said the young blond woman behind the check-in desk. "*Puis-je vous aider, monsieur?*"

"*Bonjour*," Henry replied, adding haltingly, "*Je suis ici pour rendre visite à Celeste Didier.*" His French was rusty. He had taken classes just after the Second World War as a surprise for Celeste, when he'd still believed they'd be reunited. He had been fluent by the time he'd received word that she was dead—but he had barely spoken the language since then.

"And your name, monsieur?" the woman asked, switching smoothly to English. Clearly his accent had been a dead giveaway.

"Henry McGee," he said, and she jotted something down on a ledger.

"Yes, Monsieur McGee, Madame Didier's grandson has left your name on the list of approved visitors. You are here from the United States?"

"Yes." It was all he could manage. His voice was hoarse, and he knew he sounded as desperate as he felt.

"Welcome. Right this way, monsieur."

He was trembling as he followed her down a long hall to a

locked door. She entered a code on a small pad to the right, and after the door buzzed, she pushed it open and gestured for him to follow.

Inside, the facility looked much like an old French apartment building. In fact, it reminded Henry a bit of the place where Celeste had hidden him eight decades before. "Is there no common area?" he asked, thinking of the retirement homes he knew from the States, spacious buildings with bustling activity rooms and restaurant-style dining.

"There is a room where the residents eat on the first floor. They're able to take the lift, just there." She gestured to a modern-looking elevator that looked out of place in the old building. "Aside from that, though, the residents spend most of their time in their own units. The building has been modified to accommodate the needs of memory-care patients, but it is designed to look and feel just like the apartments many of them spent their lives in."

"Memory care," Henry repeated. "How lucid is she?"

The receptionist frowned. "She has good days and bad ones, sir." She didn't elaborate further as she led him down a hall. "Here we are. Madame Didier's apartment."

She stopped outside of a door marked 0-B, and knocked loudly.

Henry held his breath, exhaling only when the door opened a moment later, revealing a small woman with long white hair that fell around her shoulders. He knew her instantly and took a step forward without meaning to. "Celeste," he whispered.

But she looked at him without a spark of recognition. "*Je vous connais?*" she asked, and Henry had to blink rapidly to stop himself from crying.

"Yes, Celeste," he answered in English, for when he'd known her, she'd been nearly fluent and eager to practice. "It's me, Henry."

When she continued to stare at him, puzzled, he added, "Henry McGee," his voice cracking.

"Madame Didier, Monsieur McGee is an old friend of yours," the receptionist explained in French as Celeste squinted at her. "Your grandson, Jean-Luc, called ahead and said he would be visiting."

"Grandson?" Celeste frowned and said in French, "How perfectly ridiculous. I'm not old enough to have a grandson."

The receptionist shot Henry a look of apology. "I will leave you to it," she said, switching back to English. Then she turned on her heel and walked away, leaving Henry alone in the hall with the love of his life, who was staring at him like he was a stranger.

"Celeste," he said in English. "It's me, Henry. I knew you eighty years ago, when we were both very young."

She was watching his lips closely. "Eighty years!" she repeated with a little bubble of a laugh. It was the same laugh he remembered from 1943, and hearing it brought tears to his eyes. So much had changed, but so much had stayed the same, too. Her eyes were a brilliant blue, though they were foggier now, and though her hair had gone from raven black to snow white, it was still long and loose, and he yearned to run his fingers through it. On her skin, the smoothness of youth had been erased by the creases of age, but her cheeks were still pink, her mouth still a perfect rosebud that he longed to kiss. "If that's a joke, I don't understand it, I'm afraid," she said.

She had switched seamlessly to English, which gave him a little surge of hope. If she could remember another language that she'd learned so long ago, surely she could remember him.

"Celeste," he said again, staring at her, willing her to remember him. "I know I must look very different to you now. We knew each other when I was nineteen, and you were eighteen. You were the most beautiful girl I'd ever seen. It was during the Second World War, and you saved my life. You sheltered me in your apartment and . . ." He swallowed hard. "Celeste, we fell in love."

"I remember the war . . ." She continued to gaze at his lips as he spoke, as if she was having trouble following him. "But love? How did you say we knew each other?"

The knots in Henry's stomach were twisting tighter, and he fought back tears. "I was a gunner shot down over northern France and—"

"How terrible," she breathed, clapping a hand over her mouth.

"But it led me to you. You were working with the French Resistance, and—"

"Me?" Her eyes widened.

"You were a hero." His voice cracked. "Later, after I left you—"

She cut him off again, her voice slicing into him. "But *why* did you leave me?"

"I was an American soldier. I was trying to get home." It sounded like a feeble excuse, the biggest mistake of his life. "I had no choice, I—"

Just then, a young care worker in faded black scrubs came up behind him. Henry was still standing in Celeste's doorway; she hadn't invited him in, and he hadn't wanted to ask, for fear she'd say no.

"Madame Didier, you have a visitor, I see," the care worker said loudly in French, giving Henry a small smile.

"It's all right, you can speak English," Celeste said, and the nurse's eyes widened.

"*You* speak English, Madame Didier?" the care worker asked, switching to English, her accent clearly American. "But I've known you for two months and you've never—"

"Of course I speak English. So does my visitor, who insists I know him."

Henry's spirits were sinking by the second. He turned to the care worker, whose name tag read KAYLA. She was perhaps twenty-four or twenty-five, with brown curls that fell to her shoulders and the kind of gleaming, rosy cheeks that only came with youth. "Celeste was the love of my life," he said, his throat constricting, "and it seems she has forgotten me."

The worker gave him a look of sympathy. "I'm very sorry, sir. Some of our residents struggle to remember things."

"But we were everything to each other." Henry knew he sounded desperate. He looked back at Celeste. "I've spent a lifetime writing songs for you, Celeste."

"For *me*?"

"I wrote the first of them when we were together in your apartment. I was watching you sleep, and I—"

"Well, sing it, then," Celeste said.

The care worker gave Henry an encouraging smile. "Studies have found that music does sometimes break through the fog, sir."

"But you see, I—I can't sing anymore, Celeste," Henry said. "My vocal cords are damaged."

She blinked at him a few times and harrumphed. "That sounds like a convenient excuse."

And before Henry knew what was happening, she had shut the door in his face, leaving him alone in the hallway with the care worker. He stared at the floor for a moment, blinking back tears, then he looked up at her in astonishment.

"How can she not know me?" he whispered. "She's the love of my life."

The young woman put a hand on his arm. "It's the disease, sir. The memories are there. She just can't always access them."

"But . . . I thought that . . . with the way we loved each other . . ." He stopped abruptly, worried that he'd gotten it all wrong. Had she forgotten him the moment he'd left her apartment? Had he carried a flame for eighty years for a woman who'd never given him a second thought?

An uncomfortable silence settled over them as the care worker shifted from foot to foot. "I wouldn't know about that, sir," she said. "But I do know that music has been known to jog the memories of dementia patients. Maybe you could come back tomorrow and try the best you can to sing it to her, even if it's not perfect? Or is there anyone else who knows the song?"

Henry laughed through his tears. It was one of the biggest hit songs of the past thirty years, though the young woman couldn't know that. "There is a recording of the song, actually."

"Wonderful! Maybe if you play it for her, she'll remember."

Henry felt a small flicker of hope. "I'll try tomorrow, then. Thank you very much."

The care worker smiled. "Can I show you the way to the exit, sir?"

Henry glanced once more at Celeste's door. "I—I suppose so." He coughed to cover the sob that threatened to escape. "Maybe tomorrow will be better."

CHAPTER SIX

Kayla Brock looked up at the Eiffel Tower as she exited the Pont de l'Alma RER train station. She still had to pinch herself at the realization that she lived here.

It had been another long day at work at the assisted-living home on the rue Royer-Collard, but at least she'd been able to spend some of the day with Celeste Didier, who had quickly become her favorite patient; the woman might not have much of her memory intact, but man, was she smart and feisty. It boggled Kayla's mind how someone who sometimes forgot the way to her room could speak flawlessly in a second language and could always guess the answers to the puzzles on the old reruns of French game shows that seemed to be playing at all hours of the day in the dining room. How was it that some pieces of the brain seemed to vanish like mirages while others were always there?

And now Celeste was at the center of a love story that had captured Kayla's imagination. The man who'd come to see her had called her the love of his life and had said he'd spent a lifetime writing songs for her. Kayla couldn't imagine being loved that deeply;

in fact, if you had asked her this morning, Kayla would have said she wasn't sure she even believed in love like that at all.

Certainly her own parents hadn't had it—her mom and dad had met here in Paris back in the late nineties and dated for just a few months before her mom had gotten pregnant. Kayla's dad—Simon—had wanted nothing to do with being a father, so Kayla's mom had returned to the States and raised Kayla alone. Kayla's only connections with her father during her childhood had been a card every Christmas and the child support payments he sent to her mother monthly until she was eighteen. The biggest perk to being his child was that his nationality had given her dual citizenship.

Her mom had always dissuaded Kayla from pursuing a relationship with him, but Kayla was twenty-six and trying to figure out who she was and who she was supposed to grow into, so when the opportunity had arisen to put her nursing degree to some use in France as a care worker at an elder-care facility in Paris, she had jumped at it. She had emailed her father—a successful real estate agent—to tell him that she was thinking of spending a year in Paris and that she would love to get to know him. He had written back to say that he would be happy to meet her. Filled with hope, and ignoring her mother's warnings, she had exchanged several emails with him, asking him advice about where to find a good apartment. She'd ultimately chosen a *chambre de bonne*, a small converted maid's chamber, on the top floor of a building on the rue du Général Camou, a few blocks away from the father she'd never known.

She had imagined long meals together, where she'd learn about his life and tell him all about hers, filling him in on all the years he'd missed. But as it turned out, he was a workaholic, leaving early to meet with clients and coming home most nights after dinner, so she was lucky if they had a conversation with each other once a week. She had always assumed that the lack of communication between them over the years was because her mother hadn't wanted them to know each other. But now that she was here and he seemed to be in no hurry to get to know her, she couldn't help but feel the sharp sting of rejection.

Kayla's mother was so annoyed at her for the decision to decamp to France that they'd hardly talked since she'd arrived in Paris. Maybe Kayla should call her now and tell her the story of Celeste Didier and her long-lost American love; it was the kind of romantic story her mother would eat right up. That's what she was thinking as she hurried along the broad dirt path of the Esplanade David Ben Gourion, the Seine sliding by to her right, the Eiffel Tower slicing into the bright blue sky over the treetops to the left. It was six o'clock in Paris, which meant that it was only noon back home in New York.

She pulled out her phone and was just about to tap *Mom*, the first contact in her Favorites list, when a deep voice just ahead of her to the left interrupted.

"*Excusez-moi, mademoiselle.*"

She looked up, startled, and saw a guy around her age, maybe a few years older, sitting on a bench facing the water. He had dark, curly hair, soulful brown eyes, and olive skin, and he was smiling right at her.

"*Moi?*" she asked, looking around to make sure he wasn't talking to someone else, which seemed to make his smile widen.

"I don't mean to impose," he said in French. "I just have a question. Or perhaps you could call it a request for a favor."

The small park bustled with tourists, so she felt comfortable stopping to talk to a stranger for a moment, especially because he looked pleasant. On closer inspection, there was a cleft in his chin and a dimple in his right cheek. Okay, so not just pleasant but cute. "Yes?"

"I was wondering," the young man said, and it was then that Kayla realized that he was nervous, "if you'd mind stopping for a few moments. That is, unless you're in a hurry to get somewhere."

"Stopping?"

"Er, yes." The man cleared his throat. "I've been . . . I've been wanting to paint you. But you hurry by so quickly that I've never had the chance."

Kayla blinked at him in confusion. "*Paint* me? I don't understand."

He gestured to the easel in front of him and the wide array of pastels laid out in a row beside it, which Kayla had only just noticed. "I come here nearly every evening to paint—and for the past two months, I've seen you most days, too."

Kayla's mouth fell open. She had never noticed the guy before, but he'd been watching her for two months? She didn't know whether to be flattered or creeped out.

"You always look lost in thought," he added after a pause. "And then, you look up and see the Eiffel Tower, and your face changes. I wanted to capture that moment. I've been trying to paint it, in fact, for the past few weeks. But you disappear so quickly."

Kayla arched an eyebrow. "This feels like a really bad pickup line."

The man laughed and turned his easel around to show her what he'd been working on. "See for yourself."

Kayla stared at the half-finished painting, which was as beautiful as anything she'd seen in the Louvre. It showed the Seine under a bright blue sky, the buildings of the Right Bank just visible across the water, and in the foreground of the picture, a dark-haired woman was walking along, her head tilted up. But she could see what the man was saying; she recognized the body language as her own, but the face didn't look like hers. Still, it was stunning. "*You* painted this?" she asked.

He ducked his head modestly. "The look on your face, it's hope and joy and optimism all wrapped into one perfect moment. I just can't seem to get it right on the canvas." He smiled and stood. He was taller than she'd realized, his shoulders broad. "I'm sorry. I should introduce myself. I'm Nadim."

"Nadim," she repeated, shaking his outstretched hand. His fingers were strong and callused, his palm soft. "I'm Kayla."

"And you are not French?" he asked. When she looked at him in confusion, he clarified. "Your accent."

"Oh. Right. I'm American, but my father is French. I'm living here for a while, trying to get to know him."

"You do not know him well?" Nadim looked confused. "Your own father?"

"It's kind of a long story."

"I have time," Nadim said. "What I mean is, perhaps you could tell me. I would love to sketch you, and we can talk as I draw." He stopped abruptly and searched her eyes. "That is, if you want to."

"Oh," Kayla said. The fact that he'd noticed her—when her own father barely seemed aware that she was alive—meant more to her than she could say. "I mean, yeah. I can sit for a few minutes if you want."

A look of relief swept over his handsome face. "Oh, thank you. I was worried that I'd scared you away."

She laughed. "If you didn't have the painting to back you up, you might have." She glanced at his easel again. "You're really talented, Nadim."

He ducked his head again. "I am not as good as I would like to be."

"Neither am I," Kayla said quietly. When he looked up at her, confusion written across his face, she laughed. "Not at painting, I mean. I'm terrible at painting. But I mean at life, you know? None of us are ever as good as we would like to be, are we?"

"Indeed." Nadim was staring at her as if seeing her for the first time, and they stood that way, for a long moment, looking into each other's eyes.

It was Kayla who broke the silence by sliding her gaze away. "So where should I sit?"

"Oh. Um, just beside me here, if that's all right with you."

She nodded and sat beside him on the bench.

He sat back down, pushing his easel aside, and pulled a large sketchpad and several pencils from the backpack that lay at his feet. "So, tell me about your father, Kayla."

She raised her eyebrows at him. "You really want to hear about this?"

He nodded. He hadn't started sketching yet, but he was studying her face in a way that made her blush.

"Okay." Kayla drew a deep breath. "I didn't have a relationship with him when I was a kid, and I've always felt like that's a piece of my life that's sort of incomplete. Does that sound crazy?"

"Not at all," Nadim murmured, still staring intently at her. "It sounds very human. Our parents are part of who we are."

"I just—I thought he would feel like that, too, you know? But I've been here for two months now, and I've barely seen him. He's always too busy. I just wish he'd make time for me."

"Of course. Does he have other children?" Nadim asked.

Kayla shook her head. "He never married. I'm pretty sure he didn't want kids at all. Maybe I'm crazy to think he'd want to get to know me now."

"That's not crazy at all to imagine that a parent would want to know his child," Nadim said gently. "Perhaps he feels he doesn't know how to be a father. Maybe he's even feeling guilt over his absence from your life, and he doesn't know how to face that."

Kayla thought about that for a moment. "Maybe. I guess I never considered that."

"Maybe he truly doesn't understand that you're here to know him better," Nadim said. "Could you invite him to meet you, perhaps at a café? Be honest with him about what's on your mind?"

"Yeah," Kayla said, nodding slowly. "Thanks, Nadim. That's really good advice."

"I think," he said, picking up a pencil, "that anyone would be lucky to know you, Kayla. I hope your father sees that as clearly as I do." Then, with an intensity she'd never seen before when a man looked at her, he studied her eyes and then her lips. Finally, he began to draw.

After they'd finished their bottle of champagne at Le Maison Grog, Shelby suggested heading back to their hotel to settle in and take a quick nap before dinner, but Corinne had already ordered a second bottle, and she and Vanessa seemed determined to stay. Shelby guessed that this might have had something to do with the fact that the clock had just struck five, and the local businesses had apparently offloaded their young French male employees directly into the bar.

In the space of forty-five minutes, they had gone from being nearly the only ones in the place—aside from a group of older tourists, and one sad-looking middle-aged guy at the far end of the bar—to swimming in a sea of French men who seemed thrilled that there were already three on-the-way-to-drunk Americans ready and waiting for them. Never mind that Shelby and her friends were at least a decade older than most of the men; no one seemed to care.

A few of the French men had tried to chat Shelby up, and she knew she should be flirting and giggling and throwing back glasses of champagne until her inhibitions vanished and all the warning bells in her head stopped ringing. Shelby wondered, not for the first time, if there was something terribly wrong with her. She knew she was supposed to be getting back on the horse, so to speak, with a hot French guy this week, so why was she standing here thinking about Brandon? Not that it mattered; the other two women seemed happy to saddle up in Shelby's place, and after a while, the guys who had tried to talk with her had realized they'd been focusing their attentions on the wrong American and had drifted away to where her two friends were currently holding court.

"Someone's birthday, eh?" the bartender asked as he topped off her flute.

She looked at him, startled to have been spoken to. She'd said hello to him when she'd first come in, but after that, he'd been busy serving the table of older folks, who were also American from the sound of it, and then the middle-aged guy had come in, and they'd gotten into a conversation that appeared to be about beer.

She looked over her shoulder, in case Vanessa or Corinne had snuck up behind her and were actually the ones the bartender was addressing in a tone that sounded flirtatious. But they weren't there, and when she turned back around, he was still looking right at her. "Um, something like that," she said.

He smiled. "Bachelorette party, then? We get a lot of those here." His Australian accent was thick, and Shelby resisted the urge to be charmed by it; she assumed he amped it up for the tourists, because who didn't like a hot Aussie bartender?

Shelby hesitated. "Divorce party, actually."

"A divorce party? Is that a thing?"

"Right? That's what I said!" Shelby couldn't help but smile back.

"So which one is the divorcée, then?" the bartender asked, craning his neck to get a look at her friends. "The redhead? She looks like she's going a bit wild."

"Corinne? No, that's how she looks all the time."

The bartender laughed. "The brunette beside her, then, I guess?"

Shelby hesitated. "Actually, it's me."

The bartender's attention snapped back to her. "You? But you're sitting over here, and they're—" He cut himself off, glancing at the other two women, both giggling away at something one of the French guys had said, and then looking back at Shelby. "Ah. But you're not celebrating. You still love him, then, do you?"

"No, not exactly." She wasn't even sure anymore that it was Brandon she missed, or whether she just missed the future she'd assumed she'd have when they'd still been together. "It's just that . . . endings are sad, you know? And I feel like . . . I've lost something." She abruptly stopped talking. What was wrong with her? "I'm sorry," she said quickly. "I don't usually blurt out everything in my head to strangers."

The bartender looked amused. "In that case, I'm Russ." He stuck out his hand, and she looked at it uncertainly. "Go on, then, tell me your name. Then we won't be strangers anymore."

She laughed and shook his hand. "I'm Shelby."

"Well, Shelby, don't look now, but there's a toddler eyeing you up."

Shelby turned to see one of the young French men, who couldn't have been a day over twenty-one, ogling her. She turned back to Russ with a laugh. "Not my type, I'm afraid."

"Luckily for him, he seems to be your redheaded friend's type."

They both watched as Corinne slung an arm drunkenly around the young man's shoulders and planted a big kiss on his cheek.

"*Everyone* is Corinne's type," Shelby said.

"Well, aren't those French boys lucky, then?"

Shelby laughed, but as the smile faded from her face, she just felt sad. "I'm supposed to be acting like that, you know. Flirting with all the boys. Putting my marriage behind me."

"Ah, so that's what a divorce party is? I was wondering." Russ studied her for a moment. "Look, Shelby, I think that maybe the end of a relationship is like closing a chapter, but that can be hard to do when you're not ready. I hope that isn't too bold of me to say."

"Bold? I basically just told you my life story. I think you're entitled to weigh in." She thought about his words for a moment. "But yeah. Maybe you're right; I just wasn't expecting the chapter to be over."

"That's the thing about chapters, though, you know? They're only a part of your story."

She looked up and met his gaze. His eyes were a deep, complex brown. "Yeah?"

"Yeah." His eyes hadn't moved from hers even though she was dimly aware now of Vanessa down the bar announcing that she was out of champagne.

The moment was interrupted by Corinne bouncing up beside her, her red hair wild and loose, her cheeks flushed. "Come on!" Corinne said, not even giving Russ a glance. "We're going to get crepes!"

"Crepes?" Shelby echoed.

"With those cute guys." Corinne pointed at the French guys who were currently laughing at something Vanessa had said. "They said there's a place right down the street."

"I—I don't really feel like a crepe."

"Oh, come on, Shelb!" Corinne giggled and hiccuped. "It's *Paris*! They're *French*! You're about to be *divorced*!" Her exclamation was punctuated by a second hiccup, but that didn't remove the sting from the final word. "You're supposed to be hooking up to put Brandon behind you, remember?"

"Yeah, I know," Shelby said quietly. She turned back to the bartender, but he had already moved away to take another customer's order. Had she imagined the spark between them?

She shook her head at herself. She was projecting all her loneliness on a man whose job it was to charm his customers. Besides, she was here for a French fling—Vanessa and Corinne were insisting—and flings didn't start with heart-to-heart conversations, did they?

"Okay," she said, sliding off her barstool and forcing a smile. "Let's go get some crepes."

A moment later, as she was swept out of Le Maison Grog on a tide of eager, young French men, she resisted the urge to look back.

CHAPTER SEVEN

After a group dinner at a brasserie near their hotel, George and Lou—who were sharing a room—were just getting ready to turn in when there was a knock at their door.

They exchanged looks, and then George checked the clock on his bedside table. It was nearly 10 p.m. "Who could it be at this hour?" he asked.

Lou shrugged and headed for the door. When he opened it, Cliff, the widower in the black beret, was standing there, dressed in slacks and a silky black shirt unbuttoned nearly to his navel, showing off more gray chest hair than George would have thought possible for anyone to possess.

"Hello, fellows," Cliff said. "Want to join me for a night out on the town?"

"A night out on the town?" Lou repeated, like he couldn't understand the words.

"Well, sure. Three eligible bachelors like us? Got to make the most of it, right?" He grinned and thrust his chest out, the gray hairs catching the light.

"I think you missed a button, Cliff," Lou said.

"Me?" Cliff looked down, confused. "No, no, this is deliberate, Lou. Got to give the ladies a glimpse of the goods."

Lou and George exchanged looks again. Impossibly, it appeared that Cliff was being entirely unironic.

"Right," George said. "And the beret? Is that part of the seduction, too?"

Cliff touched his headwear. "This? No, this is just to fit in here in Paris. You two should get berets, too. You'll look less like tourists."

"Thanks, but I'm not much of a hat guy," Lou said, and when George looked over at him, he could see his friend trying to keep a straight face.

"Me neither," George said. "I just don't have the head for it."

"Hmm." Cliff seemed to be examining the shape of George's skull. "I do see your point. Bit of a square noggin there, huh? Anyhow, I'm headed back to that Australian bar where we had lunch. Pierre told me it's quite the scene at night. I think those two smokin' Army nurses overheard, and so I'm going on the chance they might be there."

"Um, thanks for the invitation," George said. "But actually, Lou and I were just about to go to sleep."

Cliff looked him up and down, seeming to notice for the first time that George was in a pressed pair of button-down pajamas, Lou in an undershirt with sweatpants. "But it's only ten."

"Past my bedtime," Lou said with a smile.

"Mine, too," George added.

Cliff looked shocked. "But . . . you're both single. How do you meet women if you're in bed so early?"

"Believe it or not, Cliff, that hasn't been much of a priority for me," Lou said.

"Me neither," George chimed in, and Lou smiled at him, holding his gaze.

George nodded as Cliff's shoulders slumped. "Fine. But you'll be missing out on a wild night in Paris."

"I'm afraid it's a chance we'll have to take, Cliff," Lou said. "Enjoy your evening, all right?"

"It's your loss. You fellows sure? I don't want to—" But the rest of Cliff's sentence was cut off as Lou politely but firmly shut the door in his face.

George looked at Lou, who finally cracked a smile. "Too bad about that 'square noggin' of yours," Lou said.

George began to laugh, and then Lou did, too, and before they knew it, they both had tears rolling down their faces, and they were holding their sides and trying to catch their breath. George couldn't remember the last time he'd laughed so hard.

But when the laughter finally slowed and Lou went to brush his teeth, George felt a familiar sense of failure creep in as the silence settled around him. He'd had a million chances to change his circumstances, hadn't he? And he'd chickened out of every one.

What was it about the American girl? *Shelby.* Russ couldn't stop thinking of her and the way she'd looked so sad and vulnerable when she'd told him about her divorce.

Her friend had said they were going to get crepes, and he could think of at least two dozen places within a four-block radius that they might have decamped to. He kept hoping they'd return, hopped up on Nutella and bananas and ready for another bottle of champagne, and each time the door to Le Maison Grog opened, he found himself looking up hopefully, expecting it to be her. But as the hours ticked by and the bar filled up, she didn't materialize, and he admitted to himself around midnight that she probably never would. Even if he hadn't imagined the spark between them, it wasn't like she was in Paris looking for something serious.

What a strange day it had been. Between the Vietnam veterans and the divorce party, it had been an odd afternoon crowd, and on top of that, Jackson Quick had walked in and nursed a beer at the bar. *The* Jackson Quick! Russ realized that he'd been so caught up in watching the door for Shelby that he'd forgotten to tell Benji.

"You'll never guess who I poured a beer for this afternoon," he said, as Benji grabbed a cocktail shaker for a round of lemon-drop shots. A group of twentysomething American girls at the far end of the bar was ordering them as if they were going out of style.

"Hey, mate, can you grab me some lemon wedges?" Benji replied without looking at Russ. How could he when his eyes were glued to the tallest of the lemon-shot girls? A statuesque, willowy blonde, she was just Benji's type, and from the way she was batting her eyelashes at him, it seemed the feeling was mutual.

"A bit young, don't you think?" Russ couldn't resist saying as he slid a dozen lemon wedges into a rocks glass.

"Who, the American?" Benji asked innocently, shooting the blonde a dazzling smile before finally turning his attention back to Russ. "She's legal; I asked."

"Of course she's American." Benji rarely hooked up with anyone who wasn't; the Australian accent was like catnip to the twentysomethings from the States who visited their bar. Russ himself turned down at least one overt and drunken proposition each night. "But what is she, twenty-five?"

Benji shrugged, giving the blonde a wink, which made her giggle and duck her head, a cascade of hair falling over her shoulder.

She was undeniably beautiful, but also young enough to be Benji's daughter. "Something like that."

Russ groaned. That meant the girl was even younger. "Really, mate, do you ever think about dating someone your own age?"

Benji looked genuinely puzzled. "Who said anything about dating?"

And then he was off, turning his back to Russ and gallantly delivering the lemon-drop shots. The girls clinked glasses and threw the liquor back at the same time, and the blonde somehow maintained eye contact with Benji throughout.

Russ felt a sudden stab of sadness as he watched the flirtation play out. Benji did this nearly every night. He'd have a nice roll in the hay in the American's hotel room, and then he'd never call her, never talk to her again.

Was Russ jealous? He didn't think that was quite it. Not that he would have minded a hookup now and then—certainly he'd had his share in his thirties—it was just that the older he got, the more he understood that it was rarely as simple as just a night together. But Russ's feelings had no place in a bar where, let's face it, everyone was getting wasted and pairing up. Russ had spent a decade and a half providing the drinks that were a precursor to meaningless sex. Now, more and more, he found himself thinking about what the hell he was doing.

"I got her number," Benji said, returning to stand beside Russ a moment later. "Damn, do you see those legs?" He turned to Russ. "You want to come out with her group of friends after we close?"

"No, thanks."

Benji raised an eyebrow. "Must be boring to be a saint."

"I suppose it is." But at least Russ could live with himself.

"What were you going to tell me before?" Benji asked, finally tearing his eyes away from the blonde and focusing on Russ. "Someone you poured a coldie for today?"

Russ opened his mouth to tell Benji that Jackson Quick had been sitting at this very bar, but before the words were out of his mouth, the blonde called out to Benji, and Benji drifted away, seemingly without remembering that he'd been in the middle of a conversation. Russ shook his head. The American rocker had seemed relieved when Russ had treated him normally. What if he came back and Benji was the one to wait on him? Benji would no doubt act like a starstruck moron while simultaneously pretending that he was too cool to care. No, it was better left unsaid.

"No one," Russ said to the space where Benji had been a moment before. He looked at his watch. It was 1:45 in the morning. Nearly closing time. "Last call!" he said to those who were clustered around the bar. "Last call, everyone!"

Just then, the door to Le Maison Grog opened, and, backlit by the streetlamp just outside, there stood Shelby, dressed much more casually than she had been before, in jeans, a light sweater, and trainers, her hair pulled back in a ponytail. His stomach did a weird little flip as she searched the room, her eyes finally meeting his. With a small smile, she hurried over to the bar.

"You're back," he said, ignoring all the other customers who were waving cash in his face and asking for one more beer or whiskey sour or shot before they closed.

"I'm back," she said. She still looked vulnerable and sad, but there was something else there, too. As her gaze roamed to his jaw, to his mouth, and then back to his eyes, he realized with a start that what he was seeing was desire. For him? His heart beat a little more quickly.

"What happened to the divorce party?" he asked, the world narrowing to just the two of them. He had completely tuned out all the other customers, which probably meant his tips would be shit tonight, but he didn't care.

"Somehow," she said with a small roll of her eyes, "it turned into a mission for my two friends to hook up with French guys."

"And you didn't want to?" he asked, as her eyes roved his face again.

"No." She lowered her gaze and then looked right at him. "The thing is, I'm interested in someone else."

"Is that so?"

"I was, um, talking about you, in case that wasn't clear." Her cheeks went a bit pink as he laughed.

"Oh, yeah? Am I a rebound, then?" he asked, keeping his tone light.

Shelby hesitated before she answered. "Honestly? I don't think I'm capable of anything beyond that right now."

"I get it," Russ said. What else was he supposed to say? She had gorgeous eyes, blue and bottomless. He knew in that moment that he'd take whatever she was willing to give.

"I *do* know that I haven't been able to stop thinking about you all night," she added, her tone softening.

"Yeah?" he asked.

She took a deep breath, then, before he saw it coming, she hopped up on her toes, leaned across the bar, and planted a quick kiss right on his lips. "Yeah," she said, pulling away with a smile as the bar patrons around them catcalled. Her cheeks were flaming, which made her look even more adorable. "God, I'm sorry, was that too much?" she asked. "I'm—I'm really bad at this."

"Actually, it was perfect." He glanced over at Benji, who was watching with amusement. "Close up without me?" Russ said. It wasn't really a question.

Benji raised his eyebrows and nodded. Without another word,

Russ crossed from behind the bar and stood beside Shelby, who was smiling up at him.

"What do you say we get out of here?" Russ whispered in her ear.

"Really?"

"If you want to."

"I do." And with that, Shelby grabbed his hand, lacing her warm fingers through his, and led the way out of the bar.

CHAPTER EIGHT

Julia had feigned sleep when she'd heard Piper come in the evening before, waiting as her daughter brushed her teeth, showered, and climbed into the bed beside hers.

They were sharing a room with two double beds and no privacy, and Julia knew that if she'd revealed she was awake, Piper would have felt compelled to take care of her, to bustle around the hotel room making sure she had everything she needed. It was better sometimes just to let her daughter off the hook. Besides, Julia hated feeling like a patient all the time.

They were both awake the next morning by sunrise, despite the jet lag. After a mumbled good morning, Piper quickly pulled on jeans and a sweater and hurried down to the lobby. She returned a few minutes later, still bleary-eyed, with a steaming cup in each hand.

"Latte?" she asked with a smile, and Julia accepted one of the drinks gratefully and took a long, bracing sip.

"So?" Julia prompted once Piper had settled back into her own bed. "What did you do yesterday while I napped?"

Piper smiled and looked at her feet. "I . . . I kind of ran into that cute waiter."

"I *knew* it. So you went back to the café after all?"

"Actually, I saw him at Shakespeare and Company. The bookstore."

Julia raised her eyebrows. "Must be fate, then."

"I don't know about that." Piper looked embarrassed. "We just talked for a little bit. But, I mean, where could it possibly go?"

"You're always worrying about the next step, honey. Maybe just enjoy it for what it is."

"But what *is* it?"

"Maybe someone fun to keep you company this week when I need to rest. Maybe the beginning of something more. Who knows?"

Piper took a sip of her latte. "I'm here with you, though. I shouldn't be worrying about some guy."

"Can't you do both?"

"I know, I just . . ." Piper trailed off, and in the silence, Julia heard the words she wasn't saying.

"Honey, you are the best daughter I could possibly ask for. But you have the right to have a life of your own, too, you know. You deserve to be happy."

Piper shrugged, but she didn't say anything.

"So how did you leave it yesterday?" Julia asked a moment later.

"He had to go back to work, but he asked if I could meet him during his break this afternoon for a walk."

"Then you'll meet him," Julia said with a smile.

"What about hanging with you?" Piper looked uncertain.

"You know I'll need a couple of hours of downtime, anyhow. It's perfect."

"Are you sure?"

"Positive."

Piper took a long sip of her coffee. "So," she said after a minute, "remember I told you I have a surprise for you? About why we had to come to Paris this week specifically?" It had been Piper who'd insisted on the dates and taken over the planning of their trip as soon as they'd agreed to go. When Julia looked up, Piper was beaming, the uncertainty on her face erased by a ray of sunshine.

Julia smiled at her daughter. "Yeah. I'm dying to hear." She realized the moment the words were out of her mouth that the expression was the wrong one to use, given the circumstances, and she felt terrible as a shadow flitted across Piper's face.

"Right," Piper said, looking down for a second before looking back up and meeting Julia's eye. "Well, we're going to a concert."

"A concert?"

Piper nodded eagerly. "The first time he's played live in years. I couldn't believe it when I heard, Mom. His comeback tour starts on Friday, right here in Paris. I bought us tickets to see him!"

"Who, Piper?"

Piper laughed. "Sorry, I'm so excited, I'm getting ahead of myself." She paused and beamed at Julia. "Only your very favorite singer from when you were in high school."

"No *way*." Julia had been a huge Jon Bon Jovi fan back in the early '90s, but she hadn't heard he was touring again, and certainly not that he was playing in Paris.

"Yes way!" Piper chirped. "We're going to see Jackson Quick this Friday!"

"Jackson—" Julia cut herself off and forced a smile. Jackson Quick? How had Piper gotten it into her head that Julia had been a Jackson Quick fan? Sure, she liked "City of Light"—who didn't?—and she could probably sing the chorus to a few of his other hit songs, but that was where her enthusiasm ended. But Piper was sitting there grinning at her, waiting for a response, so she mustered as much excitement as she could and leaned forward to grab her daughter's hands. "Wow, I mean . . . Jackson Quick! What are the odds?"

"I've been *so* excited to tell you, Mom!" Piper hopped up without another word and grabbed her phone. "I made us a playlist to listen to this week!" She tapped her phone a few times. "But you probably know all these songs by heart anyways!"

"Uh, sure, probably," Julia agreed weakly. From what she remembered, he'd been huge in the mid-'90s and then had kind of faded into obscurity. She honestly hadn't given him a thought in thirty years.

"Here goes!" Piper chirped, and the distinctive opening chords of "City of Light" rang out over her phone's speakers.

"*A moment in time, a brush of your hand.*" Jackson Quick's deep, rich voice crooned the first lines of the song. "*The sound of your voice, now I understand, / That from the moment I saw you, my life would be new. / It was always meant to be me and you.*"

"Ooh, so romantic," Piper said with a grin as an instrumental portion took over.

But Julia was lost in the words for a moment. It had been so long since she'd heard the song, and she wasn't sure she'd ever really listened to what it was saying. But the version of love it talked about, well, it was what she'd always hoped for when she was young, wasn't it? She'd believed in it, had been so certain that this was what love was supposed to feel like, that when you found your soulmate, you'd know it in the very depths of your being.

But life hadn't turned out that way. No one had loved her the way Jackson Quick described, and she'd never loved anyone that way, either. What a waste. She swiped at the tears forming in her eyes, hoping that Piper hadn't noticed.

"Aw, you're so excited, you're crying?" Piper said with a laugh, leaning forward to give Julia a big hug. "Just don't do anything embarrassing like throw your bra at the stage, okay, Mom?"

"I promise," Julia said, forcing a smile as Jackson Quick's voice from decades before began a second verse about a kind of love Julia would never know.

Gilles Chaulet had made a mistake.

Like an imbecile, he had imagined that he could juggle a mistress on the side while still appearing to be an attentive husband to Melanie. In any case, an expectation of fidelity was a very American construct, wasn't it? Half the men he knew had discreet relationships on the side, so why not him? The error, obviously, was believing that Amandine could be trusted, that she wouldn't do something so foolish as to text him when she knew Melanie might be around.

It was as if she had done it on purpose. But that was ridiculous, too. Why would she? He didn't believe that she had any aspirations to break up his marriage; she seemed very content being treated to fine meals and extravagant gifts on the side. And though Gilles had the dim sense that *perhaps* Amandine was taking advantage of him, he also understood that in the context of an affair, particularly at his age, that was the cost of doing business.

Gilles had turned sixty earlier in the year, and it hadn't gone quite the way he'd expected. Paris was full of men his age who still cut a sharp figure in their designer suits, but Gilles was aware that no matter how many sit-ups he did in the morning, he had become wobbly around the edges. His brother Jean-Marc, two years his junior, still had a full mane of silvery hair, whereas Gilles's had begun to recede and thin a decade ago. And his brother François, older by five years, implausibly still had a square jaw, his face a study of chiseled lines, whereas Gilles's jowls sagged and the bags under his eyes seemed to grow by the day.

In short, he was no longer the man he had been. He knew it. Melanie knew it. But Amandine hadn't known him when he'd been a younger man. In fairness, that was because she'd only been in grade school. But still, she only knew how he looked *now*, and she found him attractive enough to take to bed. It wasn't as if he could turn his nose up at that.

Plus, she was a dancer. A damned ballerina with legs up to her neck, who was so flexible he sometimes wondered if her bones were made of rubber. What man in his right mind would say no to that?

It wasn't his fault, not really. He and Melanie had been married for almost twenty years now, and as he supposed was the case with all marriages, the fire was out. He had tried to reignite it, though. For example, last year, he'd woken her several times in the middle of the night because he'd been aroused. "You turn me on," he'd murmured to her, or, "You're so beautiful." But she had turned her back on him each time and mumbled something about how if he couldn't be bothered to make her feel wanted during the daylight hours, he should think twice about waking her at three in the morning.

Then, six months ago, he'd met Amandine at a bar, where he was having a post-work cocktail with an American cosmetics buyer who was in town from New York. Gilles had invited Melanie along, but she'd made an excuse—some after-school event or another she'd had to attend—and when the American had left to head back to his hotel, Gilles had decided to have just one more whiskey before heading home.

The bartender had just delivered the drink when a long-haired, slender brunette with an enormous spill of cleavage had glided up to the bar. "Handsome men should never drink alone," she had purred, sliding into the seat beside him. He hadn't known what to say—he hadn't even been certain she was talking to him, though there was no one else around—and after a moment, she had laughed. "This is the part where you buy me a drink," she'd whispered, her warm breath tickling his ear.

He had quickly summoned the bartender, aware that she was probably just using him for free alcohol, but he was willing to play the game for a few minutes of attention. She ordered a vodka soda with a twist of lemon, and when it arrived, she clinked her glass against his and leaned forward to murmur in his ear again. "And this is the part where you tell me you want to sleep with me."

Gilles spilled his whiskey on himself. As he hastily mopped up the mess, his brain spinning as he tried to formulate a reply—in retrospect, wouldn't it have been easier simply to repeat her words back to her?—she laughed again, apparently delighted to have turned him inside out.

"I'm Amandine," she said.

"Gilles," he finally managed to say.

"Oh, I know who you are," she said, and perhaps that should have been his first warning sign that she might actually have an agenda.

"Do you?"

She took a long sip of her drink and then leaned in to whisper in his ear. "You're the vice president of the Renouard-Arsenault Cosmetics Group, aren't you?"

"Well . . . I mean . . . yes," he'd sputtered. Actually, he was the vice president of North American sales for Renouard-Arsenault, which was quite a bit different, but who was he to split hairs? "How did you know?"

"I interned there a few years ago. I always thought you were very handsome."

"You . . . don't work there anymore?" One couldn't be too careful. Even *he* knew you couldn't go screwing interns.

"No," she'd said.

"I have a wife," he'd said next.

"And?" she'd asked, leaning in. "She's not here, is she?"

"No."

"But I am." This time, when she leaned in to whisper to him, she nibbled his earlobe, and suddenly, his whole body was on fire. "Do you want to get out of here?"

"Why?" he couldn't help himself from asking, and then, embarrassed, he'd clarified, "I mean, why me?"

"Because I like powerful men." The words were an aphrodisiac; Gilles didn't feel particularly powerful, but he supposed that's how he appeared to a twentysomething former intern. Frankly, he was happy to glimpse himself through the woman's eyes for a moment and not feel that he was coming up short, the way he always felt with Melanie these days.

"Oh." It was all he'd been able to manage.

"Pay for the drinks," she said. "And then meet me out front." She was gone before he could say no, but then again, he was never going to turn down an offer like that, was he?

Their affair had begun that evening—a quick romp in a hotel he'd hastily paid for in cash. He'd been covering Amandine's rent and buying her jewelry ever since, which was a headache in and of itself, because it meant he'd had to get a secret credit card.

But now the jig was up, and though Gilles would miss the sex, he had to admit he was also a bit relieved. Sneaking around was hard work, and to be honest, he'd felt guilty about betraying his marriage this way. He'd read a poll once that said more than half of married French people felt that affairs were morally acceptable; in contrast, less than 20 percent of Americans felt the same. Was it his fault that his wife was from a culture that was so uptight about such things? If he'd married a French woman, she'd be pretending not to notice, and Gilles would be having sex with a nubile twentysomething for as long as his credit card could support it.

But it was all a moot point now. Melanie had found out—and she'd had a predictably American response. Gilles had never meant to hurt her, and last night, while her grandfather had snored in the guest bedroom, he had promised, through tears, that he would break it off. He was sorry, he really was, and it was time to set it right.

He left soon after waking up on the couch the next morning, stopping along the way for a quick coffee at the café on the corner. He buzzed Amandine's apartment just past eight in the morning.

"Hello?" her voice came through the tinny speaker box of her building, sounding groggy.

"It's me," he said, and when she didn't respond right away, he had the sudden thought that perhaps she had another man in there with her. "Gilles," he clarified, feeling ridiculous. He had never shown up unannounced before.

"Come on up," she said after a pause, and then the door buzzed and he was in.

She answered her apartment door a moment later wearing a gauzy, feather-trimmed pink robe that left little to the imagination. "I didn't know you were coming."

As he'd sipped his coffee that morning, he had planned a whole speech letting her down easy, but what came out of his mouth as she gazed at him now, her nipples pert, was, "Amandine, I love my wife."

She laughed. "So you've said."

"I mean, I can't do this anymore. She's made very clear that she won't tolerate—"

"Oh, shut up and come inside," she'd said, and because the sash on the robe had come untied at some point, and she was basically standing there naked, he felt he didn't have much of a choice as she led him to the bedroom.

Afterward, she smoked a cigarette, and he tried to restore the sense of resolve he'd felt upon waking that morning. "This was the last time, Amandine," he said now, more confidently than he felt.

"Don't be ridiculous," she said lightly, turning to smile at him.

"No, I'm not—this isn't ridiculous." He was really fumbling now. "It's just, I truly do love Melanie."

"Yes, well."

"And she knows about you."

"I assumed."

"So this has to end."

She looked puzzled. "Why?"

He stared at her. Maybe it felt like they were speaking different languages because they were from two different generations. He was an old man, and she was in her twenties, young, beautiful, casual, all the things he thought he wanted, but what was he to her?

"Do you love me?" he asked, hating how pathetic the question sounded, and realizing a beat later that it was an echo of the question Melanie had asked him last night. *Of course I love you*, he'd said instantly, meaning it. But here he was, lying naked beside his mistress the very next morning. He really was an asshole, wasn't he?

"How can you ask me that?" Amandine asked, sounding wounded. "Of course I do."

"You love *me*?" he persisted. "Or you love my money?"

She put a slender finger beneath his chin and waited until he looked at her. "You, Gilles," she said firmly. "And I thought you felt the same."

Well, now he felt like an even bigger ass. "Of course I do. It's just that I made promises to Melanie. She's my wife, and—"

"Well, then, there's nothing more for me to say." Before he could protest, she was up and out of bed, covering her smooth, beautiful body in a gray cotton robe that was much less sexy than the one she'd answered the door in. She stared down at him, and he was instantly conscious of how his naked, deflated body must look. "You should go, Gilles," she said, flipping her hair and striding out of the room.

"I know," he said, puzzled, as he hastily pulled his pants and sweater back on and ran a hand through his hair. Why did it feel as if the tables had been turned? Wasn't *he* the one breaking things off with *her*? "I'm sorry," he said feebly as he walked into the parlor a moment later. Amandine already had the door open, waiting for him to leave. "Say something," he pleaded when she remained silent.

Still, she said nothing until he walked past her out of the apartment. Then, and only then, did she lean in and whisper, "You'll be back. I know you will." And then, before he could respond, the door slammed behind him, and he was left in the hall. But no matter. He would go home now and tell Melanie what he'd done. Well, not the sex part. But the breakup part, anyhow. And he would promise her that he'd win her back, whatever it took.

Amandine was wrong. He wouldn't be back. Sure, he'd have to

contact her eventually to let her know he could no longer pay the rent on her apartment. And perhaps a blow like that would land more softly if delivered in person. But he was a new man, rededicated to his wife, and he was determined to be a better husband going forward.

"You're sold out, you know."

It was just past 9 a.m., and Jackson Quick had been standing on stage at the empty Paris La Défense Arena, staring out at the sea of seats, tens of thousands of them, his pulse racing as he imagined many of them filled for his concert on Friday. His manager Cash's voice had startled him out of his reverie.

"I'm sorry, sold out?" he asked, turning, certain he'd heard Cash incorrectly.

"You're back, baby," Cash said, cracking a rare smile.

Jackson swallowed hard. He hadn't played a show in nearly a decade. Cash had sworn that if they staged a reunion show, the world would eat up the music in a nostalgic fervor, with fans in their forties and fifties reliving the glory days of their youth. This was intended to be the first salvo in a comeback tour, but investors had been reluctant to pony up until they knew Jackson could still fill an arena, so they were starting with a handful of shows across Europe before they committed to anything bigger. Cash had put all of their eggs in this Parisian basket, and Jackson had known—though neither of them had said it aloud—that if this show was a flop, the rest of his career was toast. But if he could fill up La Défense . . .

"Booking your North American tour will be a piece of cake," Cash said, reading his mind.

Jackson stared at Cash in astonishment. "But . . . how? I thought I was . . . washed up."

Cash gave him a look like he was speaking a foreign language. "You think I could book a washed-up singer into an arena like this?"

"I think you've always believed in me more than I deserved," Jackson said.

"And I think you've never believed in yourself enough," Cash said, nudging Jackson's shoulder with his own. "Look. This is the beginning of something, Jacks. Don't screw it up by becoming too self-aware." He grinned, softening the words. "You're a rock star, man. Act like it."

"Right," Jackson murmured as Cash gave him a thumbs-up and strode away to supervise the first phase of the equipment load-in.

"Band'll be here tomorrow!" Cash called over his shoulder.

"Got it," Jackson said, though Cash had already disappeared down a tunnel leading out of the arena. He'd already had four weeks of rehearsals in a rented studio in Los Angeles with a band Cash had assembled. Having musicians behind him again had felt like slipping into a comfortable pair of shoes he'd misplaced long ago, but it would still be Jackson out in front. Jackson in the spotlight. Jackson whose voice would make or break the comeback. Jackson who the fans would expect to light up the room.

It was a hell of a lot of pressure. As he stood onstage, looking out at all the empty seats, he felt a ripple of something. Possibility. Electricity. But also disbelief. The Stones had played here, as had McCartney and Elton John. How could he even be listed in the same breath as those greats? It was as exhilarating as it was paralyzing. Sometimes, he could buy into Cash's words and believe he'd earned his place here, but other times? He wondered if he deserved any of this. After all, his greatest hits weren't even written by him.

Genesis. Springsteen. Taylor Swift, maybe the greatest songwriter of her generation. They'd all played here, too. They'd all played songs *they'd* written. How could Jackson, in good conscience, breathe the same rarefied air?

"Sir?" His runaway train of thought was interrupted by a teenage French boy approaching from the wings of the stage. Jackson looked up and forced a smile, the smile of a self-assured rock star, not an insecure fifty-five-year-old baby.

"Yes?" he said as the boy walked toward him.

"May you make me an autograph?" the boy asked, timidly holding out a piece of paper and a Sharpie. "For my mother?"

"Sure," Jackson said, taking the pen and scribbling his name on the proffered paper. The boy mumbled his gratitude and hurried away.

Jackson returned his attention to the cavernous arena. He'd been told his whole career that he should do what the record label wanted, that he should sing the songs they handed to him, that he should dress the way they wanted and be the rocker they expected him to be.

And he would still do that. He knew well enough not to bite the hand that fed him, and undeniably, following along in lockstep had given him an incredible career.

But there was room for the real Jackson Quick in there, too; he was sure of it.

"*There's a wall between us, built by my hand,*" he sang quietly now, a cappella, his voice floating out from the stage. "*I've kept myself hidden, and you don't understand.*" It was a song he'd been working on for the past two years, a song he'd been trying so hard to get right. But he didn't have faith in it, did he? He hadn't even told the band, or Cash, about it. What if they laughed at him and told him to stick to the vocals and leave the songwriting to the professionals? He took a deep breath. "*I'm standing alone, babe, in no-man's-land,*" he sang a bit more loudly now, belting it out to the arena, imagining thousands of fans listening raptly. "*But it's time, yeah, it's time, to become who I am.*"

The only reply was silence.

CHAPTER NINE

Henry was surprised to realize that it was already ten in the morning when he awoke in his granddaughter's guest room.

"Melanie, I didn't mean to sleep so late," he said a moment later, shuffling into the kitchen and finding Melanie there, her back to him, as she tinkered with her Nespresso machine.

"It's the time difference," she said without turning around. "You'll adjust in a couple of days, Grandpa Henry."

Henry squinted at her. She still hadn't turned, and her voice sounded thick and strange. "Melanie, my dear? Are you all right?"

She finally looked over her shoulder at him, and he could see instantly that her eyes were bloodshot and her smile was fake. "Oh, sure, I'm fine."

He gritted his teeth, hurting for her. "You haven't told me what happened with Gilles."

She turned back to the Nespresso. "Would you like a latte, Grandpa?"

"Just black coffee for me, dear. Now, what happened?"

Melanie pushed a few buttons on the Nespresso maker, and

like some kind of miracle, it spewed out a rich-smelling dark brew into a white mug, which Melanie passed across the counter without answering his question. "Why don't you tell me about your visit to Celeste?"

He took a small sip of the hot coffee and raised an eyebrow at Melanie. "Not until you tell me about Gilles."

"He said he'd made a mistake," Melanie said quietly. "That he'd never meant to hurt me."

"Did you believe him?"

"I think," she said slowly, "that what he actually meant was that he never intended for me to find out."

Henry nodded as Melanie turned back to the Nespresso machine and made herself a drink. Melanie was a smart girl, and for this he was glad, for it meant she would land on her feet, no matter what. But sometimes, the smartest among us were the most foolish at love. A mind and a heart weren't always on the same page. He made a mental note to think about that sentiment later for a song lyric. "Do you believe he was genuinely sorry?"

Melanie turned back around, a steaming espresso in hand. "I really do."

"And do you think you can ever trust him again?" Henry asked carefully.

Her eyes flitted to his and then dropped. "I don't know."

Henry gritted his teeth, his dislike of his grandson-in-law multiplying by the second. How he wished Melanie would wake up and see her own value. "You know you're under no obligation to accept his apology."

"Aren't I?" she asked, raising her eyes to meet his. "I can't just throw away two decades of marriage, though, can I, Grandpa Henry?"

"It strikes me," Henry replied, "that you would not be the one throwing those decades away."

"Affairs are the norm here in France, though," Melanie said. "Maybe it's not fair of me to—"

"To what?" Henry interrupted. "To expect a husband who is faithful to you? It seems to me that regardless of what other people are doing, that's the very least you should expect in a marriage."

Melanie wiped at her eyes. "Maybe you're right. But enough about me. What about Celeste?"

Henry looked into his coffee like it might hold the secrets to the universe. "She did not know me."

Melanie frowned. "Oh, Grandpa Henry . . ."

"But there was something there, Melanie. She switched to speaking English when she saw me, as if it was second nature for her. Her laugh was the same; her smile was the same. She was still in there. I just couldn't reach her."

"I'm so sorry. What are you going to do?"

He gave her a shaky smile. "I'm going to return every day until she remembers. I always promised I'd come back for her, you see. I've failed her. My whole life, I've failed her."

"But you didn't know she'd lived."

"And now I do. Now I have to keep that promise every single day."

Melanie looked down. "Everybody deserves to be loved like that, I think."

He waited until she looked up and met his eyes. "Yes, my dear," he said, holding her gaze. "Everybody does."

Melanie's grandfather left thirty minutes after their conversation in the kitchen, saying he was heading back to Celeste's assisted-living facility in hopes that she might be more lucid earlier in the day. Melanie's heart ached for him; it was clear that he loved the woman deeply.

Melanie had felt like that about Gilles at the beginning, too. She'd been swept away in the romance of it all, and she'd felt loved and cherished.

But had she deceived herself? After all, they'd married quickly, after less than a year of dating. *We're not getting any younger*, Gilles had said when he'd proposed—admittedly not the most romantic line. But Melanie had agreed, because at the time, she'd thought that turning thirty had meant she was already inching toward old age. In retrospect, though, she'd still been so young and so impressionable, and she'd wanted so badly to believe in a magical love story with a handsome French man that she'd forgotten to ask herself what *she* wanted.

And even though she knew the spark was mostly gone from their marriage, the love wasn't—at least on her end. Gilles was her family, and up until she'd found the text from Amandine, she'd assumed he always would be. Now she didn't know *what* she believed.

She was putting away dishes in the kitchen, humming sadly to herself, when she heard Gilles's key in the lock. She turned just as he walked through the front door.

"*Mon amour*," he said, crossing to her immediately and trying to kiss her. She turned her head so that his lips landed on her cheek. He pulled back. "Ah, you are still angry."

Melanie stared at him in disbelief, his words reigniting her fury. "Of course I'm still angry. What, you thought you'd go out for a few hours, and I'd magically be over the fact that *you had an affair*?"

"*N'en fais pas tout un fromage*," he said, the French equivalent of accusing someone of making a mountain out of a molehill. His eyes were pleading. "It was a mistake. I told you."

"No, a mistake is tripping on the sidewalk or misspelling a word in a corporate report. This was deliberate, Gilles. You *chose* to betray me."

As he stared at her, she felt a surge of strength. She had never talked to him like this before.

"Well, I broke things off with Amandine," he said after a long pause, his eyes downcast as he said his mistress's name. "That's where I went this morning. I wanted to finish things as soon as possible."

"Excuse me, *what*? You went to see your *mistress*?"

"To end things!"

"And you couldn't do that on the phone?"

"I needed her to understand. You can't be upset about that, can you? I felt that I owed it to her to have that conversation in person."

"Oh, you *owed* it to her? How gentlemanly of you." Melanie choked out a laugh. "Why break it off, anyhow?"

"Why?" He looked up, his expression incredulous. "Because you are my wife! Because I don't want to lose you! Because you are the one I love!"

Melanie held his gaze and dared herself to be honest for once. "But what if that isn't enough?"

"Pardon?" He looked confused.

"What if that isn't enough for me? What if I want more, Gilles? What if I want someone who's really *in* this marriage, not someone who would cheat on me the moment things feel a little dull?"

Gilles raked a hand through his thinning hair. "Melanie, the affair was an error in judgment. A failing. I love you. You must know that."

Melanie looked at him for a long time. "I love you, too, Gilles. But I'm not sure how much that really matters anymore."

She felt defeated, deflated. She didn't know what she wanted.

She did know, however, that she couldn't stand the sight of him right now.

"Melanie—" he began.

"I need some time to think. You should go stay in a hotel for a few days."

His mouth fell open. "A *hotel*?"

She wanted to laugh—how could he be so surprised at being asked to leave?—but there was nothing funny about this. "I'll call you when I'm ready to talk." And with that, she put down the dish towel, grabbed her purse from the counter, and headed out the door of the apartment without looking back.

Sunshine was streaming in through Russ's bedroom windows when he awoke, tangled up in sheets, just past 10 a.m. As he squinted into the too-bright daylight, he had two sudden realizations: One, he'd had far too much whiskey last night, and two, he wasn't alone.

Shelby. The American girl slept beside him, her face turned toward him, one of her arms draped over his torso. God, she was beautiful.

He sat up in bed and surveyed the damage around the room. A bottle of Jack Daniel's sat nearly empty on the nightstand, two rocks glasses beside it, one of them lying on its side. He put a hand to his aching head, the events of the evening filtering back in.

Leaving the bar with Shelby. His arm around her shoulder as he'd led her back to his apartment. The way she'd deflated when he'd told her she was beautiful. The bottle of Jack, which had been full when he'd grabbed it from his cupboard. The first shot they'd taken, toasting to the future. A second shot, toasting good riddance to those who'd hurt them. A third shot, toasting to chance meetings. And a fourth, toasting to . . . well, now he couldn't remember.

He remembered laughing with her, and he remembered her curled up in a ball, sobbing. He remembered kissing her deeply and also realizing, as their kisses grew more frantic, that he couldn't do this, not while she was drunk and still possibly in love with her ex-husband. That's when he'd stopped, carrying her to bed and holding her until she fell asleep.

This was not what Benji would have done. Benji would have screwed her and sent her on her way. Maybe life would be easier if he could be a bit more like Benji, but that wasn't who he was. Never had been, never would be. And as Shelby opened her blue eyes and blinked at him first in confusion and then in realization, he was glad he hadn't taken advantage of the situation. It was very clear that this girl was broken.

"Good morning," he said, smiling down at her.

"Good . . . morning." She blinked a few times. "Did we . . . ?" she mumbled, putting a hand to her head, which he imagined hurt as much as his did.

"No, no, we didn't," he said quickly.

"Oh." Her face fell. "You didn't want to . . . ?"

"No, I did want to," he said hurriedly. "Very much. But you seemed so sad."

She stared at him, and he could see the moment the memories of the night before filled in, because her eyes widened, and then she closed them and groaned. "Oh my God, I cried, didn't I?"

"Only a little bit." He gave her a small smile.

"I am so, so sorry." She covered her face with her hands. "I'm absolutely mortified."

"Shelby?" He waited until she looked at him, peeking out from between a few of her fingers. "You don't need to apologize. It just seems like, well, maybe you're not ready to move on."

"But I am," she said in a small voice. "I'm supposed to be getting over him."

"Right." It wasn't as if she'd misled him, but he had hoped, after the hours of baring their souls to each other last night, that she might have seen this as something more.

Shelby groaned. "It sounds terrible, doesn't it? I didn't mean it like that, Russ. Just that, obviously, this can't go anywhere. And you seem like a nice guy, and—"

"No, I get it," he interrupted.

"I haven't been single in more than a decade and I, just . . ." She wiped her tears away. "It's just . . . I don't really know who I am right now, you know? I was so sure I'd grow old with my husband, and instead, I'm out in Paris, acting like a complete loser." She gave him a small smile.

"You didn't act like a loser," he assured her. "So this husband of yours . . ."

"Soon to be *ex*-husband," she said quickly. "The divorce will be final next week."

"Right. But this guy . . ."

"Brandon," she filled in.

"Brandon." He realized he hated knowing the man's name. It made it too easy to think of her with someone else. "So this Brandon guy, he's got to be a real idiot."

She smiled slightly. "Now you sound like my friends. But I think it's more complicated than that, you know? I mean, we both wanted to start a family, and I couldn't get pregnant, and it just drove this big wedge between us. After a while, I think Brandon just didn't want to be around me at all anymore. It caught me off guard when he told me he wanted a divorce, but I should have seen it coming."

"Okay, now I *know* the guy's an idiot," Russ said. "You were going through a rough patch, and he jumped ship? That's not what you're supposed to do in a marriage."

Shelby squinted at him like she was trying to read him. "Have you ever been married?"

"Well, I'm basically married to Benji." From her confused look, he realized she had no idea what he was talking about. "My business partner. We own the bar together. What I mean is that the two of us are like an old married couple, you know? Bickering about finances and responsibilities and who owes who what."

She cracked a small smile. "Sounds very romantic."

He laughed. "Yeah, it's a regular Jackson Quick song. Truth is, I was so focused on the bar in my thirties that a whole decade passed by without me looking up. And the older I get, the harder it is for me to imagine any life for myself other than this one."

"Is this not what you want? To be running a bar in Paris and going home with drunk American girls?"

When she put it that way, he sounded pathetic, didn't he? "For the record, I can't remember the last girl I took home."

"That tends to happen when you drink a whole bottle of Jack," she said, raising an eyebrow.

He laughed. "I mean it. This isn't something I do. Ever. Not anymore, anyhow."

She squirmed uncomfortably. "Do you wish you hadn't taken me home?"

"No," he said instantly. "I just need you to know that this isn't something I make a habit of."

"Yeah, well, me neither. I haven't been with anyone but my husband since . . ." She trailed off and looked away.

"I know," Russ said, and he did. He knew that Shelby was new at being single, new at being made to feel attractive after so long. And he also knew, in that moment, despite the many ways in which they were both broken, that he wanted to be the one making her feel that way for as long as possible, even if their time would be up in a few short days. "What do you say to breakfast? There's a little café around the corner . . ."

She looked at him for a long time, and he could see her trying to figure him out. The thing was, he wasn't very complicated. *This* wasn't complicated. So before she could further confuse herself, he leaned forward and kissed her, long and deep. When he finally pulled back, she looked dazed.

"I hope that was okay," he said. "I know I was just supposed to be a fling, so maybe you want to get out of here before—"

"Actually . . ." She cut him off. "Could you maybe kiss me like that again?"

"That could be arranged," he said, and this time, when his lips met hers and she tangled her fingers in his hair, pulling him toward her, he could feel the moment things shifted and she finally took a real step out of her past and moved a little closer to the future.

After breakfast in the hotel's dining room, Julia and Piper strolled down to the Seine and then turned left to walk along the river.

"You're sure you're all right?" Piper asked with concern after they'd strolled for five minutes, Notre Dame behind them and the enormous Louvre rising far ahead on the Right Bank.

"I'm fine, sweetheart. It feels good to get out and walk." And she meant it. The problem with chemotherapy treatments is that they knocked all the wind out of you, made it hard to draw a breath, and depleted your body such that merely getting off the sofa took a Herculean effort. Without the treatment drugs coursing through her system, she felt lighter and full of energy. She felt almost like herself again.

The problem was that now that the chemo was no longer attacking the cancer cells, they were growing unchecked. Soon, the balance would tip again, and the exhaustion would return, and this time it would be because her body was beginning to give up the fight.

But that day wasn't here yet. Today, Julia was in Paris, and the sun was shining, and the breeze was blowing, and her daughter was beaming, and she could almost believe that she had all the time in the world.

Piper slipped her arm through her mother's and leaned her head on Julia's shoulder. "I'm so glad we're doing this, Mom. I wish we'd traveled more."

"I do, too," Julia said. The truth was, there were so many things she wished she'd done differently. She'd been basically a single mom since getting divorced thirteen years ago, when Piper was in fourth grade, and money had been tight for a while. She had been so busy putting away funds for a rainy day that she'd forgotten to live in the present.

So much wasted time. So little sand left in the hourglass. But they were here now.

"So," Julia said as they walked, a large boat full of tourists slicing through the water on their right. "What time are you meeting that cute waiter?"

She glanced at her daughter in time to see Piper's cheeks turning pink. "Uh, he'll be on break around two, he said."

"And you're dragging around with your old mom instead of getting ready?"

Piper gave her a small smile. "I wouldn't trade this for anything in the world, Mom. I swear."

"I know." Julia nudged Piper as they walked. "But you're in trouble if you don't go see him. I'll need a nap before dinner, anyhow."

Piper didn't say anything for a moment, and Julia took the opportunity to take a deep breath, pulling the Parisian air into her lungs, feeling the sunshine on her face and thinking how lucky she was to be alive in this moment. "You know, sweetheart, when I'm gone—"

"Please, don't." Piper cut Julia off, and when Julia looked at her, she could see her daughter's face painted with sadness.

"Honey, we have to talk about—"

"I know," Piper said, interrupting her again. "But not in Paris, okay? Here we can pretend that we're just a mother and a daughter visiting the most beautiful city in the world together, can't we?"

Julia swallowed the lump in her throat. "Yeah."

They didn't speak again for the next fifteen minutes, as they walked slowly toward the Musée d'Orsay, the impressionist museum housed in an old railroad terminal on the Left Bank. The building had stood here, looking out over the Seine, for 125 years. It had survived two world wars and had evolved from a train station to a wartime post office to a museum. But it had weathered all the changes and still, here it was, as beautiful as ever.

As she and Piper crossed the street from the promenade along the river, Julia snuck a look at her daughter. Piper would weather the changes, too. It wasn't fair to lose one's mother at such a young age, especially with a father she'd only seen every other weekend, no grandparents still alive.

But just like the soaring building before them, Piper would survive. She would remake herself; she would rebuild; she would become something amazing that Julia couldn't even envision yet. That's what life was, a constant opportunity for reinvention, for change, for transformation.

Maybe it wasn't entirely too late for Julia to change a bit, too. After all, she was here, wasn't she? She had flown across an ocean with her daughter to a place she'd always longed to come back to. Maybe she would even become a Jackson Quick fan this week, while she was at it. The thought made her choke out a small laugh.

"Mom?" Piper looked at her with concern. "You okay?"

"Yeah." Julia smiled. It made her ache to know that Piper would continue to change into someone Julia didn't yet know. But it was also a balm to her soul to be reminded that, eventually, her girl would molt, shedding the layers of her pain. There would come a day that Piper would no longer be defined by the loss; it would merely be a piece of her. And that was a good thing. "I'm okay, kiddo."

Piper took her hand, and together, they strode into the museum to lose themselves for a few hours in paintings from another age, which would live on long after Julia was gone.

CHAPTER TEN

Henry walked into the assisted-living home just after it opened for the day, his spirits buoyed as he imagined encountering a more lucid Celeste. He knew all too well about dementia—it had claimed several of his friends over the years in addition to his wife—and he understood that those suffering from it tended to be foggier as the day went on. Maybe she would know him this morning, before her reality began to cloud over.

The same young woman he'd seen yesterday was seated behind the check-in desk, and she looked up with a smile as he entered.

"Hello, sir," she said in English, clearly remembering him. "You are here again to see Celeste Didier?"

"*Oui*," Henry said, returning her smile.

"I'll buzz you in."

Henry nodded his thanks and then walked through the door into the hall, as he'd done the day before, and let his feet carry him to apartment 0-B. He took a deep breath and knocked.

Celeste answered the door a moment later, her white hair long and loose, her blue eyes bright, and it took all of Henry's self-restraint not to pull her immediately into his arms.

"Celeste," he whispered, when she didn't say anything. She was peering at him, her gaze penetrating and unsettling. "It's me. Henry." He held his breath, hoping.

Something that looked like recognition flitted across her face for a split second, and then it was gone, replaced by a blank stare. "Do I know you?" she asked, and he had to force a smile to hide the hurt.

"You do. Or rather, you did. A very long time ago. You saved my life, here in Paris, during the war."

"Did I?" She sounded interested now. "And how did I do that?"

"I stayed with you in your apartment for nearly a month while I was waiting to get out of Paris along an Allied escape line."

She raised an eyebrow. "Well, that sounds quite improper."

"It wasn't." He cleared his throat. "Well, not at first, anyhow."

She cracked a small smile. "I see. But once you'd been there for a while?"

He didn't know what he could say except for the truth. "I fell in love with you. And . . ." He hesitated. "You loved me, too, Celeste."

She blinked a few times. "Well, in that case, I suppose you'd better come in." She didn't wait for an answer before turning and walking back into her apartment. Henry followed, closing the door behind him, before she could change her mind.

She led the way into a sitting room with a set of French doors that opened onto the building's interior garden. Red roses and something soft and white that Henry didn't recognize bloomed just outside. There was a television in the room, but Celeste's chair, which she settled into now, didn't face it; it was turned to look at the world outside.

"Tell me," she said, gesturing for Henry to sit on the couch across from her, "is it warm out today?"

It wasn't the question he'd expected, but he was determined to meet her where she was. "There's a chill in the air. Just like there was the first time I was here in Paris. This is my first time back in many years, and it's astounding to me that the air itself smells the same as it did then."

She gazed out through the French doors. "Those don't open more than a crack, you know. I suppose they're worried I'll wander away."

He didn't know what to say to that, so he didn't reply.

"I just might," she said under her breath. "What did you say your name is?"

"Henry." He was already thinking of how he might sneak her out to bask in the spring sunshine.

"Henry," she repeated slowly, as if turning the word over in her mouth, seeing if it fit. "I'm very sorry, but I don't know any Henry. You're certain you haven't confused me with someone else?"

"No," he said, blinking back tears. "I have thought of you every day for the past eighty years, Celeste. I would know you anywhere."

She raised her eyebrows. "I see."

They were at an impasse. "I wrote you a song," he blurted out, and her eyebrows went up farther.

"You wrote a song for me?"

"I did."

"Well, sing it, then." She leaned back in her chair as if she was one of the judges on that singing reality show that young people liked to watch.

"I—I can't sing anymore."

She stared at him. "It isn't as if I'm expecting Serge Gainsbourg. Go on, then."

"How about if I play you a recording instead?"

"A recording?" Her eyebrows arched. "But that wouldn't be the same, would it?"

He swallowed hard. He knew his vocal cords would betray him, but she was right; he had to try. "*A moment in time, a brush of your hand*," he choked out, but he couldn't quite hit the notes. The years stripped so much of a person. "*The sound of your voice, now I understand*," he continued feebly, but he trailed off as she scrunched her nose up.

"That's terrible," she said.

"I know," he reported miserably. "I told you. I can't sing anymore."

"I was never a very good singer myself."

"You once told me that your mother described your singing voice as cats fighting in the alley."

She stared at him. "I told you that?"

"You told me about many things, Celeste. The way you could roll a cigarette for your father in three seconds flat. The way your mother taught you to make tartes from whatever was in season. The birthmark shaped like a star on the inside of your right elbow." He blinked back tears.

She gaped for a moment and then slowly rolled up her right sleeve, showing him the star-shaped mark nestled into the tender white skin of the inner bend. How many times had he kissed that very spot as his lips had begun their journey over her body? Not nearly enough.

"How did you know?" she whispered.

"I told you," he said. "We were in love, Celeste."

They were interrupted by a knock on her door. Giving him a teary look of uncertainty, Celeste rose to answer it. It was the care worker from yesterday, the American named Kayla.

"Bonjour, Madame Didier," Kayla said, and then she glanced past Celeste and saw Henry. Her eyes lit up. "Oh, hello again, sir. Have you returned to play the song for Madame Didier?"

"I have." He pulled out his phone and fumbled with it for a moment. "I'm sorry. I don't use my phone for music very often." It was an embarrassing admission, he supposed, but he couldn't understand the world of streaming music; he'd take a vinyl or even a CD over electronic nonsense any day of the week. "I'm not certain how to find it. Do you have Apple Music on your phone?"

Kayla looked surprised. "Your song is on Apple Music? I thought you meant you had a recording of yourself singing it."

Henry chuckled. "Believe me, no one would want to hear that."

Kayla looked unconvinced, but she pulled out her phone and swiped to the music app. "What's the name of the song, sir? Maybe I can find it."

"'City of Light,'" he said, shooting a look at Celeste, who was following the exchange.

When he glanced back at Kayla, he found her staring at him. "'City of Light'?" she repeated. "Like . . . the Jackson Quick song?"

"Yes, that's the one. Have you found it?"

She nodded slowly, but still she didn't press play. "You're telling me that *you* wrote Jackson Quick's biggest hit song?"

"You know it?"

She looked at her phone and to Henry, and then back at her phone. "I think *everyone* knows this song, sir." She tapped something on her screen, and her eyes widened. "This is you?" she asked, turning the phone around to show him the credits page. There, beneath Jackson Quick's name as the *Performing Artist*, was the name Henry McGee under *Composition & Lyrics*.

"One and the same," Henry said. Celeste's head had tilted to the side in confusion, and he worried that he was losing her attention. "Please, would you play the song?"

"Of course," Kayla said, looking flustered, and after a few swipes, he heard the familiar opening chords. Kayla turned up the volume.

"*A moment in time, a brush of your hand*," crooned Jackson's deep voice from her phone's tinny speakers. "*The sound of your voice, now I understand*."

Henry and Kayla both turned to look at Celeste, but her face was blank. Henry's heart began to sink.

"*That from the moment I saw you, my life would be new*," the song continued. "*It was always meant to be me and you*."

"Do you recognize it, Madame Didier?" Kayla asked hopefully.

"I can barely hear it, dear. Can't you turn it up?"

"It's up as high as it'll go," Kayla reported.

"Can you give her the phone?" Henry said. "Maybe if she holds it up to her ear?"

Kayla handed her phone to Celeste, who obediently placed it next to her ear. Henry held his breath as Jackson Quick's deep voice continued to croon the lyrics he'd written for Celeste so long ago. But Celeste's expression remained blank, and when the song ended, she handed the phone back to Kayla with a shake of her head. "I'm afraid I've never heard this before."

Henry hung his head. How could he reach her if not through music? It was the language they had both spoken so long ago, the way he'd told her for the first time that he loved her. How could she have forgotten?

"That's okay, Madame Didier," Kayla said gently. "Monsieur McGee, can I speak with you for a moment?" At his nod, she led him into the hall, leaving Celeste's door open, and Celeste stood there, gazing at them with curiosity.

"She didn't know it," Henry said unnecessarily.

"Actually, I think her hearing is much worse than she lets on," Kayla said once they had stepped away from the door. "She's clever and she's gotten good at reading lips, so she covers for it."

That's why it had seemed like she was watching his lips closely every time he spoke. He should have recognized it, having lost some of his own hearing over the years.

"Why does she not wear hearing aids?" Henry asked.

"She refuses to," Kayla replied.

"I see. So what do you suggest? Maybe I could ask my granddaughter to borrow some speakers . . ."

"Or you could take her to the Jackson Quick concert," Kayla said slowly.

"The . . . what?"

"He's playing here in Paris at the end of this week."

Henry's mouth fell open. Jackson Quick? Here? In Paris? It sounded too perfect to be true—and a moment later, Henry realized that actually, maybe it was. It wasn't as if he and Jackson Quick knew each other; he was just the old man who'd written a hit song for a pop star decades ago.

"You know what?" Kayla said after a few seconds. "Never mind. Forget I said anything. I mean, even if she can hear the song better, bringing someone with dementia to a big rock concert could be a terrible idea. It might be really scary for her."

But Henry's mind was already spinning. "But if I could find seats close to the stage so she wouldn't feel lost in the crowd . . ." He trailed off. Yes, that was it. He would buy tickets as soon as he left here today. He would invite her grandson along, too, so she'd have someone familiar there with her.

But what if the concert made things worse? He knew it was a possibility, but he also had the feeling this could be his only chance.

What if hearing the song live—surrounded by people who knew the words, as the rhythm pulsed through their bodies—was the key to unlocking Celeste's memory? Henry knew it was a long shot, but so, too, was all of this. He wasn't meant to be here, with Celeste, eighty years after he'd last seen her. He wasn't meant to be in possession of his full mental faculties at this age. He wasn't supposed to be fit enough to fly across an ocean to reunite with the woman he loved. This was all impossible. So why not hang his hopes on the most impossible piece of all?

"Sir?" Kayla said gently, interrupting his train of thought. "Are you all right?"

"Right as rain," he murmured, giving her a quick smile. "Thanks for telling me about the concert. I'll see about getting some tickets right away."

As Piper and her mom walked out of the Musée d'Orsay into the early afternoon sunshine, Piper put an arm around her mother, whose shoulders, which had once been broad enough to carry all the weight of their little family, felt tiny and sparrow-like now. It always surprised her how much of her mother had already disappeared. "You look like you're ready for that nap," Piper said softly.

"I could definitely use some rest," Piper's mom said, her eyes bloodshot. "Besides, aren't you going to see the cute waiter?"

"Only if you don't want me to stay with you."

"You're in Paris! Go. Have fun. We'll meet up later and go to dinner at that restaurant near the Eiffel Tower tonight, okay?"

They got in line for the cab stand outside the museum, both of them knowing without discussing it that the mile-long walk back to the hotel was out of the question by this point in the day.

"Which was your favorite painting, Mom?" Piper asked as they waited.

"I think I liked *Starry Night Over the Rhône*," her mom said after a moment. "I would have liked to see Arles, the place where Van Gogh painted."

Piper glanced at her mom and looked quickly away before her mom could see the wave of emotion that had just rolled over her. There were so many things her mother wouldn't get to see and do. "At least we're here, seeing the painting," she said, forcing a smile. "We get to see Arles through Van Gogh's eyes."

"True, honey," her mom said. "Which painting did you like best?"

Piper had been astounded at how connected she felt to the vast collection of impressionist works, from Monet's jubilant and patriotic *La Rue Montorgueil* to Renoir's famed *Dance at Le Moulin de la Galette* and Manet's *Luncheon on the Grass*. They were all paintings she'd seen in textbooks, but to experience them up close was more emotional than she could have imagined; leaning in to see the brushstrokes made her imagine the artists themselves, moved by the world around them as they did their best to commit what they saw to canvas. In a way, they would all live forever, wouldn't they? These pieces of art they'd created were still here, even hundreds of years after the artists themselves were gone. "*The Church at Auvers*, I think," she said. "The violet sky was so beautiful, and the way the windows of the church seemed to be bathed in the same light . . ." She trailed off.

"I liked that one, too," her mom said, reaching for her hand and giving it a reassuring squeeze.

Back at their hotel twenty minutes later, Piper's mom changed into her pajamas and crawled into bed. "I'm really sorry, honey," she said, yawning. "I realize this isn't how you envisioned spending our time in Paris."

"Mom, I'm just glad to be here with you."

"I just—I want to see you happy, honey. Before I go."

"I *am* happy." But the tears in her eyes betrayed her. Damn it, this was supposed to be a trip where she and her mom forgot about the fact that death was stalking them; instead, it was all she could think about.

Her mom held out her arms, and Piper allowed herself to be folded into them. "Go see the boy, sweetie," her mom said. "I'll see you tonight."

CHAPTER ELEVEN

As Piper hurried across the bridge toward Notre Dame, she spotted Nicolas sitting in front of the soaring church, and her heart did a little flip. He was there waiting for her, just like he said he would be. He stood as soon as she approached, a grin spreading across his face.

"I thought perhaps you would not come," he said, giving her a kiss on each cheek. "I am glad you did."

"Listen, I have to ask. This isn't, like, a pity meetup, is it?"

"A pity meetup?" He looked confused. "What is that?"

"I mean, you're a nice guy, but just because my life is falling apart doesn't mean that you have to entertain me."

"Is that what you think?"

"I don't want to be anyone's charity project."

"Piper." When she didn't reply, he touched her chin gently and waited until she looked reluctantly back at him. "Piper, you are not a charity project."

She looked into his green eyes, losing herself there for a second. "Are you sure?"

"Completely. Besides, I can practice my English with you, yes? It's nice for me."

"Oh, so I'm just a convenient conversation practice partner, then?" She tried not to feel a little disappointed.

"Piper, you are a conversation practice partner with the prettiest smile I've ever seen. You are kind and interesting and you appreciate poetry and you like bookstores, and, well, I would like to know you better." He raised an eyebrow at her. "Now, shall we walk? Or is there more to this interrogation?"

She laughed. "Yeah, okay. We can walk."

"Maybe you can tell me about your mom."

"Really?"

Nicolas nodded. "If you'd like."

"Yeah, okay," Piper said, her pulse racing as she took a deep breath and began. As they strolled around Notre Dame, looking up at the intricate statues that flanked the massive church, Nicolas listened as Piper haltingly poured out the story of her mother's diagnosis and her fears for the future, and when she had finally finished speaking, he was still there, still beside her.

"Piper," he said when she had finally gone quiet. "I am so very sorry that you will lose her."

It was somehow exactly the right thing to say. Her friends—who had dwindled in number when Piper stopped going out on weekends in college so that she could go home to her mother—said pat things such as *It's the circle of life* and *She'll always be looking down on you*, which was perhaps true, but which didn't help. She needed someone to look her in the eye and to see how much she was hurting and to acknowledge that it was terrible and unfair and that there was nothing any of them could do about it. "I'm sorry you lost your dad, too," Piper said. "I know I should be looking at the bright side and all that and saying how lucky I am to have had her for the time I've had her."

He tilted his head to the side and searched her eyes. "No, I don't think you should be saying that right now, Piper," he said. "I think you are saying just the right things."

"Really?"

"Really."

"Will you tell me about your dad?" Piper asked.

Nicolas was silent for a few seconds, and then he took her hand, leading her back toward the square in front of Notre Dame, which they had circled entirely as they'd talked, weaving in and out of lines of tourists waiting to enter the cathedral. "He was from New York, and he met my mother when he was on a business trip here in the late 1990s. He moved here for her and never looked back; he fell in love with the city, meter by meter, and he taught me to love it, too, from the time I was old enough to walk."

"That's beautiful."

"When I was a boy, my papa used to take me here, to the Île de la Cité every weekend. We would start at *Point Zéro*. Do you know what this is?"

Piper shook her head, and Nicolas smiled at her, stopped walking, and pointed down. She was startled to realize that they were standing on a cobblestone formation that was different from the others. She blinked and looked more carefully, taking in the eight-pointed bronze star at the center, surrounded by four stones that together read POINT ZÉRO DES ROUTES DE FRANCE.

"This is the starting point of every major road leaving Paris," Nicolas explained with a smile. "The center of the city. Every week, my father would have me stand on this star, and he'd tell me that we could go anywhere from there, and that each direction was a new adventure."

"I love that," Piper said, looking up at him.

"I loved it, too. And he was right. We would set off at random, and we never took the same walk twice. There's so much to discover in this city, Piper, so much to discover in this world. My father always told me that there may be sadness in life, but there's always joy, too, right around the corner. You just have to keep walking until you find it."

Piper blinked, the words hitting home as they began to walk away from the bronze star. "How did you lose him?"

"A heart attack," Nicolas said bluntly. "In some ways, I think, the opposite of what you are going through. He was here one day—taking me for strolls around Paris—and then gone the next, in the middle of playing tennis, with no chance to say goodbye."

"I'm so sorry." It made her ache to think of her mother disappearing with no warning. Maybe in a way, as difficult as this time was for both of them, it was a blessing to have these moments together, knowing what was to come.

"Thanks." He glanced down at her. "He and my mother raised me with French as my primary language—my dad spoke fluently—but after he was gone, I always felt like the fact that I didn't really know his language, his culture, meant that I'd missed out on knowing him as well as I could have."

"And that's why you're reading American poets now?"

"My dad liked poetry, too, but I was too young when he died; that was never something he really shared with me."

"I bet he'd be proud to hear you quoting Whitman."

"I hope so." They were approaching the Pont Neuf, and Piper assumed when they got there that they'd turn left and head back over to the Latin Quarter. But instead, Nicolas led her across the street, past a statue of a king on horseback, and down a set of steep stairs into a wedge of land that narrowed to a point at the island's end, jutting into the Seine.

"The Saule Pleureur de la Pointe," Nicolas said, gesturing

ahead, to where a tree the size of a house drooped its leaves toward the water at the end of the island. "The weeping willow of the point. I sometimes take my lunch here before I go in for an afternoon shift. There's something wonderful about simply being still and letting the world go by. Shall we?"

Nicolas led Piper to the stone wall just in front of the willow, and they sat at the water's edge, their feet dangling as the Seine streamed by them. Nicolas closed his eyes and breathed in. "My favorite spot in Paris."

Piper could see why; she felt like part of the city itself as the world bustled around her, with boats sliding up and down the river and people on the Left Bank hurrying back and forth, lost in their own conversations.

Nicolas opened his eyes and stared out at the Seine and then glanced up at the sky, where white, puffy clouds hung overhead. "Every time I walk through this city, every time I discover something new, every time I remember to leave space for things that surprise me, my father's right here with me, even after all these years. I walk with his memory. I guess that's what I wanted to tell you, Piper. We never have enough time, in the end, with the people we love, do we? But your mother will be with you always, the way my father is with me."

"That's not enough, though, is it?" Piper said. "I know it sounds greedy, but I don't want to walk with her memory. I want to walk with *her*. I want her to be there at my wedding and when I have children of my own and when I need a shoulder to cry on. I want to watch her grow old. Why don't I get to have that?" These felt like selfish thoughts—Piper was making her mom's death about her—but she couldn't shake them. Losing her mom would reshape her entire world.

"Nothing can change the sense of loss you'll feel when she goes," Nicolas said after a while. "But you still have her for now, Piper. What will you do with that time?"

Piper understood that this was a question that most people asked of themselves too late. We take the moments for granted until we realize that time is running out. "Well, we're here in Paris together now. That's something we always dreamed of doing. And I'm taking her to see Jackson Quick in concert on Friday. He's her favorite singer from when she was young. I'm just afraid that when this week is over, it will be the beginning of the end, you know?"

"So we will do our best to make it memorable for both of you, yes?"

"'We'?" Piper echoed.

"It would be my honor to help. Now, what do you say we grab a coffee before I have to be back at work?" He stood and offered her his hand. She took it, and after he helped her up, he didn't let go, and she realized she didn't want him to.

They began to talk again as they strolled back toward the Pont Neuf, leaving behind the shade of the great willow and the quiet peace of the magical park as they made their way back to the real world.

The Jackson Quick concert was sold out, which complicated things for Henry.

Not that Henry wasn't happy for the kid. Or, well, Jackson Quick wasn't exactly a kid anymore, was he? When he had recorded "City of Light" all those years ago, he'd been a fresh-faced twentysomething, but he'd be in his fifties by now, wouldn't he?

My, the years went by fast. Faster still when you got to Henry's age.

But sold out? Henry couldn't wrap his head around it. As far as he knew, Jackson hadn't toured in a decade, maybe more. Who were all these people who had bought tickets to see the former pop idol in Paris, of all places?

Melanie had suggested, when he'd called her in a panic, that he try a website called StubHub, but the only resale tickets available there were in the nosebleed section. He wasn't going to bring the love of his life to a concert and stick her up in the rafters, now, was he? He needed her close to the stage, close to the speakers, in a situation that felt as nonthreatening as possible, if this had any chance at all of working.

And for that, he realized, he would need Jackson Quick's help.

It was a ridiculous thought, of course. But the fact was, Jackson had become famous using the song Henry had written for Celeste—and over the course of the next few years, the rock star had recorded another dozen of Henry's newer songs. So maybe, just maybe, if Henry could explain things, Jackson might find it in his heart to help Henry out.

Before Henry could second-guess himself, he had hailed a cab and asked the driver to take him to La Défense. Thirty-five minutes later, he found himself standing in an empty parking lot outside of a huge, silent stadium. The driver zoomed away before Henry could ask him to wait.

Henry stared up at the arena, already realizing he had made a mistake. The concert wasn't for another three days. What would make him think that Jackson Quick was hanging out inside the venue right now? Henry could kick himself for not thinking this through. Still, he was here now. Maybe there was someone inside who could reach Jackson.

He trudged up to the front of the arena, but the ticket windows were all closed. There appeared to be no one around, but Henry wasn't going to give up that easily. He walked to the first door on his right and tried it. Locked. That figured. On to the next. That one was locked, too. Henry continued around the building, patiently trying every door, until finally, under a sign for GATE 33, he pulled a handle and was stunned when the door swung open.

He slipped inside and through the dimly lit corridors until he emerged into the cavernous arena, filled with thousands of empty seats and a stage at the far end. To his relief, the place wasn't entirely deserted; there were workers loading in equipment, and already, there was a big sign above the stage that read JACKSON QUICK: THE WORLD OF LIGHT TOUR.

He made his way toward the stage, earning some strange looks from workers, but no one stopped him. He walked backstage like he belonged there, and peeked his head into every room that looked like it might house a rock star, but he came up empty. He was just about to give up and head home when a man tapped him on the shoulder.

"Hey, buddy, can I help you?" a deep voice asked in English, in a tone that sounded more confrontational than helpful.

Henry turned and found himself face-to-face with a man in his sixties with silver hair and expensive-looking clothes. So not a part of the load-in crew, then. "Yes, I'm looking for Jackson Quick," he said, trying to sound confident.

The man stared at him. "Little old to be a groupie, aren't you?"

Henry glared at the man. "I'm not a groupie."

"Which is exactly what a groupie would say," the man pointed out. "What is it you want with Jackson?"

"I need to talk to him about a song."

The man raised an eyebrow, waiting for Henry to go on.

"I'm a songwriter," Henry clarified after a pause.

The man guffawed. "Hate to break it to you, boss, but he's not looking for any new material right now."

This bothered Henry more than anything else. "Well, he should be. Talented kid like him? But I digress. No, I'm actually the writer of 'City of Light.'"

The man's eyes widened in disbelief. "*You* wrote 'City of Light'?"

"I did," Henry confirmed. "And you are?"

The man's eyes narrowed as if he was trying to puzzle Henry out. "I'm Jackson's manager, Cash James."

Henry exhaled in relief. "Mr. James. Nice to meet you. I'm Henry McGee."

"You have some ID, Mr. McGee?"

Henry pulled out his wallet and showed Cash his driver's license, which Cash studied for a moment before handing it back.

"Ninety-nine years young, huh?" Cash said, sounding impressed. "Okay, say I believe you're the same Henry McGee who wrote the song. What do you want with Jackson?"

"Well, the woman I wrote that song for is here in Paris. She has dementia. And I'm hoping . . . I'm hoping if I can bring her to the concert on Friday, maybe, maybe, the music will bring back the memories. Maybe . . . maybe Jackson Quick can even say something from the stage." It was more than he'd intended to ask, but he had to take his shot.

Cash whistled, low and slow. "That's very romantic, Henry. But I'm afraid Jackson Quick isn't in the business of taking requests."

"Please," Henry said. "I've been separated from Celeste for eighty years. I just found out she survived the war." When the manager didn't say anything, Henry added, "Without Celeste, I never would have written that song. And if I recall correctly, that's the song that kicked off Jackson Quick's career."

Cash stared at him for a long time, and Henry could tell that the manager was evaluating him. "That's some story," he said at last. "Fine. I'll call Jackson. But the final decision is up to him."

"Thank you," Henry said as Cash pulled out his phone. "Thank you very much."

"Let's see what Jackson says," Cash said as he jabbed at the phone with a meaty finger. "Don't thank me yet."

After the Musée d'Orsay, Julia fell right asleep, exhausted from all the walking she and Piper had done that morning. But she slept fitfully, dreaming that she was inside the Van Gogh painting of the church, the one with the stars over the Rhône River, and that darkness was falling, erasing all the infinite pinpricks of light. She woke with a start and grabbed her phone to check the time, assuming she'd slept until late afternoon and that Piper would be back soon, if she wasn't already. But instead, she was startled to realize that she had dozed for less than forty minutes. She closed her eyes, hoping she'd be able to drift back to sleep, but the blackness of her dream returned and jarred her awake once more, her pulse racing.

She sat up and took a drink of the water beside her bed. Piper had left a glass there for her before departing. How thoughtful her daughter was. Goodness, she was tired of being a burden on Piper, sick of being sick.

She thought for a moment about texting Piper to let her know that she was awake, but Piper was off somewhere with that cute waiter, and she didn't want to interrupt her.

Besides, there was someplace Julia wanted to go that she wouldn't drag Piper to, because it wasn't worth Piper's time. When Julia had lived here for a summer when she was twenty-two, she and her roommate, a New Yorker named Ellen, had frequented a pub not far from the hotel where Julia and Piper were staying now. It had been a trendy hangout for young American and British students from the nearby Sorbonne, and also a popular pickup spot where young French men could be assured of finding wide-eyed English-speaking girls who were charmed by their French accents and chivalry.

Julia herself had been charmed more than once—she remembered making out in the corner with a young French advertising executive named Guillaume and going on a picnic with a French computer programmer named Anton—but she suspected she was generally a disappointment to the guys who'd come here in those days, because she'd had a firm no-sleeping-with-randoms rule. She'd just graduated college, and she was the only one among her friends who was still a virgin. Ellen had urged her to sleep with a French guy as soon as possible, just to see what the fuss was all about, but Julia had been determined to save herself for someone special.

And then, she'd gone home at the end of the summer and met an attorney named Ryan, and he'd been her first, and she'd been in love with him, and she had married him on a beautiful spring day when she was twenty-five, and Piper had come along just over a year later. By the time she realized that she and Ryan weren't all that compatible after all—that he hated to read and that he disliked being outdoors and that he loved his daughter but didn't think he was necessarily obligated to play a role in parenting her and preferred to work late and go to ball games with his coworkers—she had already made her bed, as her mother reminded her, and now she had to lie in it.

And lie in it she had, until Piper was ten, and Julia had finally made the difficult choice to leave a man she still cared about but had little in common with, a man who would never put his family first, or even second or third. He wasn't a bad person. But he wasn't the right person for her, and she didn't want Piper growing up thinking that a marriage was supposed to be about settling.

That, she realized, was why she wanted to go back to the pub that had once meant so much to her. It represented the last time in her life that she was simply herself, before she'd met Ryan and her world had begun to narrow.

Before she could overthink it, she threw on jeans, a striped blouse, and her Adidas Sambas, smudged a bit of concealer under her eyes, and dabbed on a bit of red lipstick, then she headed out the door. She kept her phone on in case Piper returned and wanted to know where she was, but she suspected that she'd be back before Piper knew she was gone. It was better that way, because how could she explain the magnetic pull of a dive bar she hadn't been to in twenty-seven years without telling her daughter how far she'd fallen from that former version of herself?

She was surprised to realize, as she walked, that her feet still knew the way, even all these years later. She made her way down the rue de la Huchette, which had changed little in the intervening years, and her stomach growled as she passed a storefront offering crepes and another one offering melted raclette and fondue. She would have one drink at The Red Telephone Box for old times' sake, and then she'd stop at one of these places on the way back to the hotel for a quick, greasy lunch, just like she remembered from the days when she'd lived here.

She turned right on the rue du Petit-Pont, left on the rue Saint-Séverin, and right again on the rue Galande, expecting to see the bar looming in front of her. But, to her surprise, in the spot where her bar—The Red Telephone Box—had once been, several anglophone flags flapped beneath a big sign that read LE MAISON GROG.

"Le Maison Grog?" she asked aloud as she stood frozen on the sidewalk. It looked the same as the bar she remembered, but she knew she hadn't gotten the name wrong. She pulled out her phone and googled *The Red Telephone Box bar, Paris*, and she felt her hope plummet when the only thing that came up was a Google Review noting that the bar had been bought by new owners from Australia fifteen years ago—and that they'd renamed it. She was indeed in the right place. But she'd missed her reunion with the past by a decade and a half.

She considered turning back to the hotel. But she had walked all this way, and she suddenly had a nostalgic desire for a pastis—a popular aperitif she'd discovered when she'd lived in France so long ago. She and Ellen had loved sitting on the terraces of cafés in the late afternoon, each of them slowly sipping an ice-cold pastis and believing that they looked very sophisticated and French while they watched the world go by. She hadn't had one in years.

She crossed the street, went down two steps to the entrance, and entered the bar, which was nearly deserted. From the sandwich board out front advertising a lunch special of fish and chips with a Foster's, she had assumed the place would be buzzing, but there were only three other customers there: a middle-aged couple in the corner wearing clunky sneakers and matching fanny packs, and a man about her age, maybe a few years older, sitting at the bar with his back to her.

She almost turned around and left. Though the place still looked surprisingly like The Red Telephone Box on the inside, the vibe was completely different. Then again, she'd never been here in daylight hours, had she? And it was barely three in the afternoon.

She made her way to the bar and sat two stools down from the man, who was wearing a baseball cap pulled low over his eyes. He nodded politely at her and then returned his attention to his beer as a bartender came over with a smile.

"G'day," the bartender said in the most exaggerated Australian accent she'd ever heard. "Welcome to Le Maison Grog. What can I get you to drink?"

"You don't have pastis, do you?"

"Sure we do," the bartender said. "Ricard or Pernod?"

"Ricard sounds great," she said. "Thank you."

"My pleasure." He gave her another smile and returned a moment later with a highball glass filled about an eighth of the way with translucent amber liquid, along with a small pitcher of cold water and a long spoon. "Need an ice cube, too?" he asked.

"No, thanks, this is perfect." She could feel the gaze of the man just down the bar as she picked up the pitcher and slowly poured water into the glass, instantly turning the translucent liquid milky. She filled the glass halfway, then put the pitcher back on the table and stirred the drink with the spoon. Finally, she closed her eyes and took a small sip, the anise and licorice flavors zinging her taste buds and taking her back to that summer so long ago when her whole life lay ahead of her. When she opened her eyes again, the man two seats away from her was still watching her. She gave him a small smile, and his face lit up in return.

"I'm sorry," he said quickly. "I don't mean to stare. It's just . . . what *is* that?" His accent was American, his voice deep and smooth. His eyes, she noticed without meaning to, were a beautiful shade of hazel that reminded her of warm honey.

"Well, this is basically my early twenties in a glass."

He laughed. "A fountain of youth?"

"More like a portal to a time that doesn't exist anymore. It's pastis, which comes from the south of France. You mix it with water, and it turns into something completely different."

"Like magic." The man smiled. "Alchemy, if you will."

"Exactly. I haven't actually had one in years. I lived here for a summer when I was twenty-two, and my friend and I used to think we were very fancy and grown-up when we drank them at outdoor cafés and flirted with French boys."

The man laughed, a sound that rose from low in his throat and sent a strange little shiver down her spine. "Well, you still look very fancy and grown-up, for what it's worth."

"That's what I was going for," she said, and he laughed again.

"And what brings a fancy grown-up like you in to day-drink magical, transportive beverages in a bar like this?" the man asked.

"The same thing that made me order my first pastis in twenty-seven years, I guess. Nostalgia. I used to come here that summer I lived here, back when it was called—"

"The Red Telephone Box," the man cut in, and her eyes widened.

"You remember it, too?"

"Yeah. I used to live a few blocks away, on the rue Xavier Privas. Summer of 1993."

"I was here the summer of '96."

"Well, now I wish I'd come back. I could have been one of the boys you flirted with. Or would I have been disqualified for being American?"

"No," she said, feeling uncharacteristically bold. "You would definitely not have been disqualified." He stared at her for long enough that her heart began to thud. "I'm, uh, Julia," she said, breaking eye contact and sticking out her hand.

He shook it and seemed to hesitate for a split second before saying, "Sam."

"Sam. Nice to meet you. What brings you to Paris?"

He hesitated again. "Work. You?"

Now it was her turn to pause. It wasn't as if she could tell him that she was here for one last hurrah before she kicked the bucket. That would instantly kill the electricity she could feel sizzling between them, and she wanted to enjoy it for a few seconds more. When was the last time a man had looked at her like she wasn't invisible? Like she had something to offer? She couldn't remember. "I'm on a trip with my twenty-three-year-old daughter. She's out wandering around a bit on her own."

"An adventurer, then," he said with a smile. "So what does that pastis taste like, anyhow?"

"Like licorice, believe it or not."

"Well, I like licorice." He gestured for the bartender. "Hey, Russ, can I try a pastis, too?"

"Sure, mate, coming right up," the bartender said and went to get a glass for Sam.

"You're on a first-name basis with the bartender," Julia noted, and Sam laughed.

"Only because I wandered in here yesterday when it was nearly as empty, and we struck up a conversation. Nice guy; he owns the place. He and his friend bought it from the owner of The Red Telephone Box fifteen years ago and they changed the name right away."

"It *was* a pretty silly name."

"That's what I said!" Sam exclaimed as Russ delivered his pastis. "Could you show me what to do?" he asked her, contemplating the glass, the pitcher, and the spoon in front of him.

"Sure."

"Mind if I scoot closer?" He gestured to the seat beside her.

"Please," she said with a smile.

He pushed his pastis and the pitcher of water down the bar and then stood and crossed to resettle beside her. Up close, he smelled like a tantalizingly masculine combination of vetiver and cedar. "Okay," he said. "Ready for my lesson."

She showed him how to slowly drizzle the water in, and he stared in disbelief as the liquid turned instantly cloudy. She handed him the spoon, and after he'd stirred, they clinked glasses and looked each other in the eye. "To Paris," she said.

"To meeting a beautiful girl in the old Red Telephone Box while discovering the strangest beverage I've ever seen," he said with a laugh, and she could feel her cheeks heating up as they each took a sip of their drinks.

Just then, his cell phone, which was sitting on the bar between them, buzzed and lit up with an incoming call from someone named Cash. Sam stared at it for a moment, and then, seeming to make a decision, he grabbed the phone and looked up at Julia. "I'm sorry, but I've got to take this. Don't leave, okay?"

"Okay," Julia agreed, and, looking relieved, Sam hopped off his barstool and headed outside to take the call. She stared after him as he walked away.

Surely this was too good to be true. Maybe he wouldn't come back. Maybe she'd be stuck with the bill for his pastis. It would almost be a relief, because the alternative was that she had just met the perfect guy while she was in the process of dying, and that really wouldn't be fair at all, would it?

CHAPTER TWELVE

Why on earth had he said his name was Sam?

It was the name he'd used to check into hotels in the '90s when he was on tour and needed a bit of anonymity—Sam Cleveland, a nod to his hometown—but he hadn't used it in thirty years, yet here it was, a lie between them that he couldn't take back without sounding like a lunatic.

As the call from his manager vibrated in his hand, Jackson stepped outside the bar and slapped himself dramatically on the forehead, earning a strange look from an old woman passing by. The thing was, Julia hadn't recognized him; he was sure of it. If he'd given her his real name, everything would have changed. And he didn't want that. He just wanted to have a conversation with a pretty girl without worrying that she already had an idea of him—or of his bank account—fixed in her head. He had the sudden unsettling sense that he'd been missing out on something fundamental for decades.

"Hey, Cash," he said, finally answering the phone.

"Jackson, you can't just go dark on me," his manager snapped.

"You've got interviews lined up later with *C à Vous* and TV5 and France 24, and we still have to talk about your set list for Friday. I've texted you twice in the past half hour, man."

"Well, you've got me now," Jackson said, rubbing his forehead as the beginnings of a headache began to set in. Cash tended to have that effect on him. "What's up?"

"I've got a guy here who wants to ask you a favor."

"Isn't that your department?" Jackson asked.

"He's a songwriter from your past, Jackson. Old dude named Henry McGee."

"McGee? The guy who wrote 'City of Light'?" Jackson said instantly.

"You know him?"

"Never met the guy. But I owe him my career, don't I?"

Cash made a growling sound. "You owe *me* your career, Jacks."

"Right." Jackson rolled his eyes. Cash had long believed he'd created Jackson from scratch, as if Jackson had been a lump of clay waiting for an artist to come along and sculpt him into something worthwhile. As if Jackson's years of singing on street corners and pounding pavement to hone his skills as a performer had nothing to do with it. "So what's the favor?"

"What?" Cash barked.

"The favor Henry McGee wants."

"Oh. Right. Something about a woman he loves," Cash said. There was a muffled male voice in the background and then Cash added, "He says he wants to talk to you. But I can get rid of him if you want."

"Cash, is he standing right there?" Jackson asked in disbelief.

"Yeah."

"Of course I'll talk to him."

"Fine," Cash said. "Then get your ass back here."

"Can't you just hand him the phone?"

"Says he wants to talk to you in person and that he's happy to come to you," Cash said. "But you're due back here for blocking, anyhow. I didn't fly you to Paris four days early so that you could wander around with your head in the clouds. This is where we launch your tour, Jackson. It's make or break for you, and you don't seem to get that. If the critics trash this show, man, you're dead in the water."

"Right, of course." If Jackson left the bar now, though, where did that leave him with Julia? But was that a ridiculous thought? Maybe he was making his conversation with her into more than it was. Besides, he'd started off with a lie, hadn't he? "I'll leave now. McGee doesn't mind waiting?"

"He says he's got all day. But I don't." Cash hung up before Jackson could say another word.

He shoved his phone back into his pocket and returned to the bar, where Julia still sat, sipping her pastis. The Aussie bartender, Russ, smiled at him as he settled back onto the stool beside Julia.

"Sorry about that," Jackson said with a smile.

"Nothing to be sorry about."

"Yeah, well, I'd prefer to spend the next hour sitting here with you, but unfortunately, that was work, and I have to go."

"Oh, you do?" Was it his imagination, or did Julia sound disappointed? "I mean, of course. Work has to come first."

He scratched his head. What was he going to do, explain that he had to get out to the arena to meet with the guy who'd penned his biggest hit song? No. Instead, before he could chicken out, he said, "Look, I hope I'm not being too forward, but I'd love to see you again."

Surprise flickered across her pretty features, followed by something else he couldn't quite place, something that looked almost like sadness. But it was gone so quickly that he was sure he must have imagined it. Or that's what he thought, anyhow, before he noticed a sheen in her eyes.

"Are you okay?" he asked, concerned.

"Oh, yeah, of course. Fine." She smiled at him. "It's just, I'm not sure if that's a good idea."

He felt instantly foolish. "Of course. I mean, that was way too forward of me."

"No, it isn't that," she said quickly. "It's that—" She stopped abruptly. "It's nothing. I just . . . I'm not a good person to get involved with right now."

He studied her. "Neither am I. But I think sometimes life doesn't hand us enough chances, you know? Like we think we'll have a million opportunities, and the older we get, the more our lives are already on a single track we chose a long time ago, and . . ." He trailed off, realizing he was not only rambling, but also probably sounding pathetic. "I'm sorry," he said. "It's just not that often I meet someone I get along with for the right reasons." He grabbed a napkin from the bar. "Do you have a pen? I'm going to give you my number, just in case you change your mind, okay?"

She nodded and handed him one from her purse.

He quickly jotted down his number and passed it to her. "No pressure. I just . . . Life's too short."

"Life's too short," she repeated, and then, after a pause, she grabbed the napkin and slipped it into the pocket of her jeans.

Feeling like he'd already lost her, Jackson signaled for Russ and handed him a fifty-euro note. "For my drinks and the lady's," he said.

"You don't have to buy my drink," Julia said.

"Please," he said with a smile. "You led me to the fountain of youth. It's the least I can do."

"Let me just get your change, mate," Russ said, but Jackson waved him away.

"Keep it, man," he said. His phone dinged with an incoming text, and he glanced at the screen. His driver had arrived and was waiting outside. He raked a hand through his hair. He would come back here tomorrow, because it already felt like a place where he could be himself, but he had the feeling he'd never see Julia again. He looked at her. "I have to go."

"Okay. It was nice to meet you. And . . . Thanks for the drink."

He smiled. "Call me if you change your mind, okay?" And then, before he stayed there forever, he forced his feet to carry him toward the door and out into the sunny afternoon, where his sleek, black luxury car idled at the curb, waiting to take him away from the only place in Paris he wanted to be.

After Piper had a quick coffee with Nicolas at a little café around the corner from Café Le Petit Pont, he walked her out to the side-walk, brushed the hair from her face, and stood there with his hand on her cheek, looking into her eyes for such a long time that she nearly stopped breathing.

"This has been nice," he said. "But I have to be back at work. And I know your mother is expecting you."

"Right, of course."

"You know," Nicolas said, "we haven't even exchanged numbers yet. But I'd love to be able to text you later to see how your dinner with your mother was."

Her heart raced, but she fought to sound nonchalant. "Cool."

With a smile, Nicolas pulled out his phone and swiped it open, then handed it to Piper. "Would you like to give me your number?"

With a nod, Piper quickly tapped the new contact button—*nouveau contact* on his phone—and added her name and number before handing it back to him.

"I'll text you from work," he said, sliding the phone into his pocket. "And I'll call you tonight. If that's okay."

"It's very okay," Piper said.

"Good," Nicolas said with a smile, his hand returning to her cheek, his eyes locked on hers. And then, as the world went by around them, he leaned in and kissed her softly, gently, and though it wasn't her first kiss, it felt like something new entirely. When he finally pulled away, her whole body was humming. "Have fun with your mother."

"Have a good night at work," Piper said, still dazed.

He held her gaze for another long second. "I'll talk to you tonight, okay?"

"Cool." Apparently, it was her new favorite word. "And, Nicolas? Thanks for today. I can't remember the last time someone listened to me the way you did. You're . . . well, you're amazing."

"You are, too, Piper."

And then, with one more quick kiss, he turned and walked away, leaving her staring after him, missing him already.

Jackson knew he had screwed up with Julia.

He wasn't accustomed to dating like a normal person. He hadn't done that in thirty years. In his heyday, there'd been movie stars and pop stars; just past his prime, there'd been a constant supply of fans thrilled to score some alone time with their favorite singer, though more than one had made off with his boxer briefs as a souvenir the next morning. There'd been two broken engagements—both to models—and even an attempt at dating a seemingly nice kindergarten teacher, only to discover after a month that she secretly had a shrine to him, candles and all, in her basement. There had been other women over the years but, normal or famous, they all saw him as a rock star. And while that was well and good for a fleeting affair, it couldn't exactly be the foundation of anything lasting.

But Julia had been different. She had looked him in the eye. She hadn't giggled like a schoolgirl. She'd liked that he'd remembered the bar when it was The Red Telephone Box, just as she had. She had even flirted with him—he was sure she had.

And then he had walked away. He had asked to see her and she'd said no, and he'd given her his number, anyhow, like a loser, and he'd left the bar before he could change her mind.

"Is everything all right, sir?" Manon asked from the driver's seat, giving him a look of concern in the rearview mirror.

"Yeah," he said, turning to stare out the window at the gold-domed Hôtel des Invalides on the left. But things weren't actually all right at all. Jackson felt like someone had just turned on the light after many years in the dark, illuminating all that was wrong with his life.

Forty-five minutes later, Manon dropped him at one of the arena's loading docks, where Cash waited in the shadows, checking his watch and looking like some kind of mobster.

"You're late," he said.

"Traffic," Jackson said. "Where's McGee?"

"In the greenroom," Cash said, giving Jackson a can-you-even-believe-it look. "I didn't know where else to put him. The guy's almost a hundred years old."

"A hundred? Come on." Obviously, Cash was exaggerating. But as they rounded the corner into the snug room backstage where Jackson would hole up before his set this weekend, his jaw nearly dropped when he saw the white-haired man sitting there, squinting at him through the thickest glasses Jackson had ever seen.

"Hello, Mr. Quick," said McGee, standing with effort and sticking out his hand. He looked nervous, and his palm was sweaty as Jackson grasped his hand and shook it.

"Please, Mr. McGee, call me Jackson."

"Only if you'll call me Henry." The old man smiled. "I do apologize for dragging you down here, Jackson. I could have explained myself on the phone."

"Yeah, but then I would have missed the opportunity to meet the man who wrote the biggest hit of my career." Jackson ignored Cash's soft snort of derision. "Really, Henry, I can never thank you enough."

"Well, it's I who should be thanking you," Henry said modestly. "If you hadn't made a hit out of it, I never would have won a Grammy *or* been able to afford to put my granddaughter through graduate school."

Jackson chuckled. "And I never would have had the chance to have the life I've had, sir. So what is it you wanted to see me about?"

"Ah." Henry looked uncomfortable. "Well, to be plain, I need your help."

Jackson felt a familiar bristling, his walls starting to go up. Anything Henry asked, he would do it if it was within his power—he'd meant it when he'd said he owed his career to the song Henry had written. But Jackson had forgotten, just for a few hours, that everyone in his life wanted something from him. The bubble of Le Maison Grog—with a bartender who didn't treat him like a celebrity and a woman who laughed at his lame lines because they were moderately funny, not because he was famous—had left him in a fog. "Right, of course," he said stiffly.

Henry seemed to quickly read his tone. "I'm sorry, I'm not explaining myself well. I don't need you to give me anything. Nothing like that, Jackson. It's more—it's a matter of the heart."

"Of the heart?"

Henry took a deep breath. "Eighty years ago, there was a girl . . ."

Jackson listened as the old man told his devastating story of being shot down over France during World War II and losing the girl who'd saved him.

"I spent my whole life thinking she'd died," Henry concluded, his voice breaking. "But she's alive, Jackson. She's still alive and she's in an assisted-living home in Paris, but her dementia is advanced, and the song I wrote—the one you made famous—is the only way I can think to reach her."

There was a lump in Jackson's throat. "You wrote 'City of Light' for her?"

"I modernized it over the years, but I used to sing the verses to her as we lay in bed together, staring up at the sliver of night sky we could see from her bedroom window."

"*The moon and the stars have nothing on you,*" Jackson sang softly, a line from the second verse. "*In this city of light, your light carries me through.*" He had never understood the words before, but now he could imagine a much younger Henry staring out from his hiding spot, knowing that he had to go, but at the same time, not wanting to leave the woman he'd fallen in love with.

"That's right," Henry said. "But I can't sing anymore. And she can hardly hear. And I just thought that maybe, if I could bring her to your concert, if we could sit near the stage, she could *feel* the song in her bones, the way she once did when I was lying beside her, holding her in my arms."

"My God, of course!" Jackson said without hesitation. "But, Henry, we have to do more."

Cash stepped quickly between the two of them. "Jackson, all the man's asking for is house seats. You're under no obligation to—"

"Come up onstage," Jackson interrupted, stepping around Cash to look a startled Henry in the eye. "Play the song with me. You can sit in on piano. That is, if you want."

Henry stared at him. "You'd do that for me?"

"Are you kidding? It's the best love story I've ever heard, Henry. It deserves to be told. And *you* deserve every chance to show her how you feel." Jackson again pushed thoughts of Julia from his head.

"Well." Henry didn't seem to know what to say.

"Cash will set it up. Do you have any family you'd like to bring? We'll get you as many tickets as you need." Jackson turned to Cash, who was staring at him in disbelief. "Cash'll get you backstage passes, too, okay? Come see me before the show."

"Thank you, Jackson," Henry said. "You might have just changed my life."

"Well, Henry," Jackson said with a smile, "you've already changed mine."

CHAPTER THIRTEEN

By the time Henry made it back to the Left Bank, it was past 6 p.m., and visiting hours at Celeste's assisted-living home had ended. It was probably just as well, because if he'd gotten back earlier, Henry would have tried to drop in on her again, which would have been yet another heartbreak.

Instead, he let his feet carry him from the metro back to Melanie's apartment, where he let himself in with the key she'd given him yesterday.

The floral smell assaulted him first. When he reached over to flip on the light switch to the right of the door, he gasped. The parlor was filled with at least two hundred red roses, probably more, some of them in vases, some of them in pitchers, some of them in mixing bowls.

"I ran out of places to put them." Melanie's voice wafted in from the kitchen. "Gilles sent two hundred forty roses, Grandpa Henry, but no vases."

Henry crossed the flower-filled room and entered the kitchen where, unbelievably, there were even *more* flowers. The sink itself was filled with water and held at least fifty of them, and there were several bouquets on the counter still wrapped in wax paper and plastic. Melanie was seated at the kitchen counter, her eyes bloodshot. "Two hundred *forty*?"

"A dozen for every year we've been married," she said flatly. "His attempt at being romantic, I think."

"Have you just been sitting here in the dark?" he asked her carefully.

"I guess so."

"And where is Gilles?"

"I told him to go stay in a hotel."

Henry looked around the room. "Before or after the flowers arrived?"

"Before," she said dully. "This morning. He told me he'd broken things off with Amandine."

"Well, that's good, isn't it?"

Melanie shrugged. "I suppose. But he only did it because he was caught, don't you think? Besides, does he think a few flowers are going to change things?"

"Well, it appears that's exactly his hope," Henry said, giving the room another sweeping look of disbelief. "What else did he say?"

Melanie shrugged. "That he loves me."

"And how do you feel?"

She looked defeated. "Honestly? I don't know anymore."

"I see." Henry fought the urge to tell her that perhaps that was the best thing that could have happened to her.

Melanie wiped her eyes and smiled at her grandfather. "Anyhow, how did it go with Celeste today?"

"Not well, I'm afraid. But I had an idea. What do you think about coming with me to the Jackson Quick concert this Friday?"

"Jackson Quick?" Of course Melanie knew that her grandfather had written Jackson Quick's biggest hit, but still she looked perplexed.

"'City of Light' is about Celeste," he explained. "I wrote the first version of it for her when we were together in Paris during the war. *Before* I met your grandmother," he added hastily. "I updated and modernized it over the years, so it's not quite the same as it was back then, but I thought perhaps if she hears the same words I sang to her, the same melody . . ."

"Oh, Grandpa Henry," Melanie said. "What if it doesn't make her remember?"

"I don't know, Melanie," Henry said. "But what if it does? I have to try, don't I?"

"I guess you do," she agreed. "It's amazing that you still love her so much, Grandpa Henry."

"I'd do anything for her," Henry said. As Melanie walked away to tend to the rest of the flowers, he found himself wishing fervently that whether it was with Gilles or with someone entirely different in the future, Melanie would know what it felt like to be loved that way, too.

Julia was propped up in bed, reading a book, when Piper came in just past seven, her cheeks flushed and her eyes shining. It didn't take a mind reader to ascertain the reason.

"How did it go with Nicolas?" Julia asked with a smile before Piper had even said hello.

"He's kind of amazing."

Julia closed her book. "I want to hear all about it at dinner."

"You're sure you're up to going out?"

"I wouldn't miss it for the world."

While Piper ducked into the bathroom with a change of clothes to freshen up, Julia stood, too, and slipped on the sleek black dress that she'd left hanging on the hook near the bathroom. It was just her and her daughter tonight, but this was still Paris, and she wanted to feel like someone attractive, not someone ill.

She touched up her mascara, swiped on some French-red lipstick, and nodded approvingly at her reflection in the mirror beside the door.

She sat back down on the bed, and as she waited for Piper, she pulled out the napkin with Sam's number and stared at it again. The truth was, she'd barely made it through ten pages of the book she'd been reading in the past two hours; every time she skimmed a few sentences, her mind wandered back to Sam and what on earth she'd been thinking when she'd turned him down.

Well of course she *knew* what she'd been thinking. She'd been thinking that she was dying and she didn't want to lead him on. It would be irresponsible to form another human connection now; she already felt guilty enough.

But isolating herself—cutting everyone off so that she left minimum wreckage in her wake—was lonelier than she'd anticipated.

Maybe she was overthinking this. Sam was a nice man who happened to be in Paris at the same time she was, but less than a week from now, they would both go back to where they came from. She didn't even know where he lived or what he did for a living. Maybe it didn't matter. Maybe she could learn to live in the present for once. Maybe she could allow herself to spend time with a man with a kind smile and a deep voice that made her shiver, and the most magnetic honey-colored eyes she'd ever seen. Maybe there was no harm in that as long as he wasn't expecting anything, either.

"Mom?" Piper had emerged from the bathroom at some point,

all dressed for dinner in dark jeans and a sheer black shirt over a lacy cami. "You okay?"

Julia realized she'd been standing in the middle of the room, clutching Sam's napkin and staring off into space. She shoved the napkin back into her purse and forced a blank look of innocence. "Sorry, yes. Just thinking about something funny."

Piper gave her a suspicious look but seemed to accept the explanation. "I love that dress, Mom. You look really pretty."

"Thanks, hon. So do you." The thought that Sam might like her in the dress, too, flickered through Julia's mind, and she pushed it away. She was acting like a teenager with a crush. "Should we go? I don't want to miss our reservation."

Thirty minutes later, Piper and Julia were being shown to terrace seats at Chez Francis on the Right Bank, overlooking the Eiffel Tower just across the Seine. "I can't believe how magical this is," Julia said as she and Piper ignored their menus and stared out at the monument, glowing against the darkening sky.

"It's unreal," Piper agreed. She reached across the table and squeezed Julia's hands. "I'm really glad we're here together, Mom."

Julia turned her attention from the tower to her daughter, who looked delicate and beautiful in the pale lighting of the terrace. "I'm so glad, too, honey. So how did you leave it with Nicolas?"

"He asked for my number and said he'd call me tonight after he finishes work."

"You should see him tomorrow," Julia said.

"I mean . . . maybe." But the smile Piper seemed to be trying to suppress belied the casual words. Julia had to turn away to hide a smile of her own. Her daughter was smitten, and she'd never seen her like that before. It was a beautiful thing to witness.

Their waiter arrived and they ordered glasses of champagne and bowls of French onion soup to start, and for dinner, Piper chose a filet au poivre while Julia ordered steak tartare, which came with matchstick fries. When they'd finished with their meals, they were both completely full, but the waiter talked them each into a second glass of champagne, along with an order of Camembert cheese with Isigny Sainte-Mère cream, served with grilled bread.

"They're going to have to roll me out of here," Piper said with a groan as the waiter cleared their empty plates and the Eiffel Tower's lights began to sparkle for the second time since they'd sat down, a dazzling five-minute show that began at the top of each hour.

"Me too," Julia agreed. "But it was worth every bite. And every pound that I probably added to my hips tonight."

Piper smiled a wobbly smile, but then suddenly, she was crying, and Julia didn't know what she'd said wrong.

"What is it, honey?" she asked, reaching across the table to wipe a tear from her daughter's cheek.

"It's that . . . you say things like that . . . and it reminds me how little time there is," Piper managed to say through sobs. "I mean, you don't have to think about adding pounds because . . ."

She trailed off, and Julia sucked in a sharp breath. "Honey . . ."

"I just forget sometimes, you know?" Piper said. "I didn't think of it once during dinner. But now . . ."

"I know. And I'm sorry."

"Yeah," Piper said, sniffling as she grabbed the napkin from her lap to dab at her damp eyes. "I am, too."

After they'd paid the bill, they strolled across the Pont de l'Alma, the Eiffel Tower illuminating the Left Bank like a magical nightlight just off to the right, piercing the blanket of sky. Halfway across the bridge, Piper looped her arm through Julia's and put her head on her mother's shoulder.

"I wish we could make this week last forever," she said.

"In a way, it will," Julia said after a moment, leaning her head into her daughter's as they strolled. "You can choose, Piper. You can decide that you'll never, ever forget these moments. I know that I won't."

"I won't, either," Piper said.

"But, honey?" Julia said a moment later as they turned right into a small park that would take them along the river's edge as they walked toward the tower. "That doesn't mean you should get stuck here in this memory, either."

Piper turned to look at her mother. "What are you saying?"

"That you're the best daughter in the world," Julia said. "But there's more to you than that. You're also a twenty-three-year-old woman in Paris for the first time. I was right around your age when I lived here for the summer, and it's the summer I became who I am. It's the summer I found myself. I want that for you, too."

"I already know who I am," Piper protested.

"Do you, though?" Julia said gently. "You've spent the past couple of years setting aside everything that makes you who you are in order to be there for me. And I can never thank you enough for that. But it's time you become *you* again—the you who laughs at *Friends* reruns and loves being with her friends and makes the world's best chocolate-chunk cookies and reads every novel she can get her hands on. Nothing would make me happier than seeing the woman you'll be when I'm gone and knowing in my heart that you'll be all right. Okay, honey? You can't stop living."

Piper opened her mouth like she was going to protest, but finally, she nodded. "Okay."

"Good."

They made their way across the quai Jacques Chirac until they were standing just beneath the tower itself, its warm light washing over them, illuminating their faces. Julia stared up at the tower for a moment, and then she looked over at her daughter, whose eyes were wide as she gazed up at the extraordinary iron lattice framework stretching a thousand feet into the sky.

"Piper?" she said after a moment, and she watched as her daughter's eyes moved from the glory of the tower down to her.

"Yes, Mom?"

"I love you so much," Julia said, her voice breaking. How many more chances would she get to say the words? Would Piper know, after Julia was gone, just how much she'd meant them with every fiber of her being?

"I love you, too, Mom," Piper said, and they put their arms around each other and returned to staring up at the Eiffel Tower, which had been there for more than a hundred and thirty years and would still be standing long after both of them were gone.

The Eiffel Tower was sparkling as Kayla crossed through the Esplanade David Ben Gourion. Usually, she kept her eyes fixed on the magical light show of the tower, but tonight, she was hoping to see Nadim. No one had ever looked at her as closely or as tenderly as he had last night, and though she figured it was simply an artist soaking in the details of his subject, she had liked how it had felt. His gaze had been warm and intimate, and every time he'd spoken, his melodic voice had done something to her.

As he'd sketched, he'd told her that by day, he was an accountant for a shipping company but that he found the work soulless and looked forward to stopping here by the river each evening with his pastels before the sun went down. He'd asked about her job, and she'd explained how rewarding it was to work with elderly dementia patients but that, sometimes, seeing their loved ones try in vain to reach them broke her heart.

Now, as she walked, she noticed Nadim in the same spot he'd occupied yesterday, the shadows falling over him as night approached, a single streetlamp illuminating his easel. He looked up and saw her, a grin lighting up his face.

"Kayla!" He called, waving to her, and she couldn't stop a smile from spreading across her face, too, as she hurried over.

"Hi." She felt instantly shy.

"I was hoping I would see you this evening," he said, beckoning to the open spot beside him on the bench. "I thought you might like to see one of your paintings."

"Really?" She smiled, but then she glanced down at her watch. "Shoot, I only have a few minutes before I have to go."

"A date?" he guessed.

She laughed. "No. Actually, I took your advice and invited my dad out for a drink tonight. I actually haven't been on a date since I moved here." She promptly pressed her lips together, embarrassed. Why would she admit something like that aloud?

But Nadim didn't look like he was judging her. "I would think a beautiful woman like you would be asked out on dates all the time."

She could feel herself blushing. Was he flirting with her? Or was she reading too much into it? "Well, you would be mistaken," she said. "I don't really meet people my age working in a nursing home, you know?" In a hurry to change the subject, she sat down beside him and looked at the pastel painting on his easel. The image he'd created there made her gasp and pull back. "Nadim," she breathed. "This is . . . beautiful."

"Because it's you," he said, his voice low.

Kayla stared at the painting, which was similar to the ones he'd shown her yesterday: a lone woman with the Seine behind her, her face aglow with the lights of the Eiffel Tower. But instead of the vague suggestion of her face from a distance, this one captured her more closely, from the trio of freckles just below her left earlobe to the single dimple in her right cheek. He had painted her with the vaguest reflection of the Eiffel Tower in her blue eyes, a small smile playing across her lips. She didn't even have the words for how impressed she was. "It's . . . incredible."

He grinned. "I'm glad you think so. This one is yours, if you'd like." He picked it up off the easel and handed it to her.

She blinked at him, startled, and then looked down at the painting in her hands. "Mine?"

"Of course. You are very kind to allow me to paint you. It's the least I can do to repay you."

"I don't know what to say."

"Say you'll return and talk with me again. I would like that very much."

"Um, yeah." She was flustered, overwhelmed by the reflection of herself in his painting. "Of course. I'll . . . I'll come see you again tomorrow on the way home."

"I hope you enjoy your drink with your father, Kayla. You are doing the right thing by talking with him. Doors open when we say what we mean, I think." He smiled at her once more and took the painting back from her, signing his name on the bottom right, followed by two *x*'s. Then he rolled the painting up, extracted a rubber band from his pocket to loop around it, and handed it to her, looking her in the eye in a way that made her heart beat a little faster.

CHAPTER FOURTEEN

Kayla made it to the Bistrot Le Champ de Mars two minutes before the time she'd agreed to meet her father, but already he was there, sipping a slender glass of beer on the patio. He raised a hand in greeting when she arrived, and she hurried over.

"You look like your mother when you are frazzled," he said in greeting as she fumbled with her work bag and the rolled-up painting before dropping into the seat beside him.

"I hope that's a compliment," Kayla said with a half smile. He'd made it clear since she'd gotten here that he had no regrets about cutting things off with her mother all those years before.

"*Mais oui*," he said as he beckoned to a waiter. "What would you like to drink, Kayla?"

She ordered a glass of rosé and settled back in her chair, trying to get ahold of herself. Between the conversation with Nadim in the park and the awkwardness she felt around her father, her nerves were jangling. "Thanks for meeting me," she said, because she couldn't think of any other way to open the conversation.

He took a sip of his beer as he studied her. "You are my daughter. Of course I would meet you if you asked."

"Well, that's kind of the thing," Kayla said, Nadim's words replaying themselves in her head. *Perhaps he feels he doesn't know how to be a father.* "I haven't seen much of you since I got here, and I just thought, well, maybe I should just come right out and tell you that the main reason I moved here was to get to know you."

"To know me?" He looked genuinely confused.

"Yeah, I mean, you're my dad," Kayla said. She could hear Nadim's voice in her head again: *Maybe he's even feeling guilt over his absence from your life, and he doesn't know how to face that.* "I just want you to know that you not being there during my childhood . . . It's okay. You know? I feel like this is a second chance for us. I hope it is, anyhow."

He leaned back in his chair and studied her. "Kayla, me not being there during your childhood . . . That was because of choices your mother made. She could have stayed in France, but she chose to raise you in the States."

Kayla bristled. "But . . . she said you didn't want to be with her. How could she have stayed? Her tourist visa would have run out."

He shrugged. "She could have found a way."

"But . . ." This wasn't going how she'd thought it would. "Even if that's true, I was only a phone call away for all those years. If you'd wanted to know me, you could have called. At least to, like, say happy birthday or something. Not that I'm blaming you," she added hastily, not wanting to push him away. "It's just, well, I don't really think that was about my mom's choices, exactly."

He shrugged again, his lips pursed, and something occurred to her.

"Wait, do you even know when my birthday is?"

His gaze slid away. "I'm terrible at recalling dates, Kayla."

"Right, but . . . I'm your child." She felt a swell of sadness. *He's lucky to have the chance to get to know you*, Nadim had said, and Kayla had come here buoyed by hope. But now, she was deflating by the second.

"Well, do you know *my* birthday?" He arched an eyebrow at her, a challenge.

"July tenth," she said without missing a beat, and he looked away from her again.

"All right, yes, fine, so your mother told you the date. I'm not sure what that proves, Kayla." Before she could reply, he gestured to the rolled-up canvas in her hand, changing the subject. "What do you have there?"

"Oh, just a painting," she said, flustered.

"A painting?" he repeated, sounding amused. "Did one of those street artists by the Seine con you into a print of the Eiffel Tower for your wall back home?"

She hated the way he made her feel as if she didn't belong here, as if she was just a silly visitor to a city that was only his. "Actually, it's a painting of me."

His eyebrows rose slowly. "Of *you*?"

She nodded, and his eyebrows went up even farther.

"And here I thought you were working in that home for old people. Instead, you've been wandering around Paris serving as an artist's muse?" He chuckled.

"No, of course not. This just kind of . . . happened."

The waiter arrived with her glass of wine, and when he whisked away again, Kayla looked up to find her father studying her pensively.

"What?" she asked.

"Nothing, it's just . . . Well, I suppose it isn't my business, but a naïve young girl like you . . . I am just concerned you are being taken advantage of."

She frowned. "He gave me this as a present. How would that be taking advantage of me?"

Her father reached for the rolled-up art. "Let me take a look."

She wanted to tell him no; his skepticism was souring the moment, and his outstretched palm felt like an invasion of her privacy. But she found herself reluctantly handing the painting over and watching as he unrolled it and studied it for a long moment, his lips pursed.

Finally, he looked up at her. "You are sleeping with this artist, yes?"

She was so startled by the accusation that she choked on the sip of rosé she'd just taken. "What?"

Her father looked back at the image. "Yes, the way he painted you, it is done with the eyes of a lover."

"No!" She wanted to snatch the painting back before he could ruin it for her further, but she was afraid of tearing it. "I've only known him since yesterday." She might even feel flattered that her father was trying to protect her honor, except for the fact that he seemed amused rather than upset.

"Anyhow, it isn't as if you'll stay here in Paris, will you?" he said with a shrug. "Which is perhaps part of the appeal. These street people target tourists, you see."

"He isn't a *street person*," she said through gritted teeth. "And I'm not a tourist. What do you mean that I won't stay?"

He stared at her for a moment. "I assume this little vacation will come to a close soon, yes? You were not raised here."

"Yes, I'm aware of where I was raised. But I've studied French since I was a kid. I'm trying to make a life here for now. This isn't a vacation."

He shook his head. "But you are American, not French."

"I'm both," she said. "I have dual citizenship through you, don't you remember?"

"Bah." He thrust the painting back toward her. She took it and rolled it carefully back up, already feeling like it had been sullied. "People should stay where they are. Fine, come for a visit. But staying? It's a burden to our social system. You don't want to be contributing to the immigration crisis, do you?"

"The *immigration crisis*?" she repeated, trying to keep her tone even, though it was getting harder by the second.

"These people flowing across our border from all sorts of places . . ." Her father leaned back and took a sip of his beer. "People should stay where they belong."

"And where exactly is it that you think I belong?" Kayla asked stiffly.

He shrugged. "I can see that you do not agree with me. But you Americans, you're part of the problem, aren't you? Coming and traipsing through Paris with your loud demands in English and your expectation that your culture should be accommodated."

"I'm not like that," Kayla protested. "Nor are the majority of Americans. And besides, isn't tourism a huge part of the economy here?"

"I'm not talking about tourists, not really," her father said, taking another casual sip of his beer. "But if we let the whole world in, we cease to be France. Our culture becomes diluted. You must see that."

"Or maybe opening up a society to more viewpoints makes it *better*," she snapped. "And maybe you'd be better off if you welcomed people like me—who care about your country and want to be a part of making it stronger and more beautiful. Instead, you're closing your mind to anyone who isn't just like you."

"Ah." Her father leaned back in his chair. "Now you sound *just* like your mother. She had a temper, too, if I recall."

She felt a stab of regret. "I *don't* have a temper," she said, trying not to sound as outraged and disappointed as she felt. "I'm just saying that I don't agree with the things you're saying."

"Kayla, calm down. You're embarrassing yourself."

"*I'm* the embarrassment?" She could feel herself getting angry again. "No, I think that distinction is yours. You have a daughter who has moved halfway across the world because she'd like to know you, and instead of taking that opportunity, you're telling me I don't belong here because it's not where I was born. But you know what? Maybe it's closed-minded people like you who don't belong. The world's changing. Catch up."

Without waiting for a reply, Kayla stood, threw down a handful of euro coins for her wine, and strode away from the table, out onto the sidewalk, resisting the urge to look back.

The devastation began to set in before she'd gone a block. What had just happened? She'd tried to tell her dad that she forgave him for his absence, and somehow, it had spiraled into a conversation about whether she had a right to be here? She felt furious and lost and deeply hurt.

Her head spinning, she passed by her own street, the rue du Général Camou, on the right, and a few minutes later crossed the quai Jacques Chirac into the riverside esplanade. She knew it was illogical to hope that Nadim was still there and could help untangle the conflicted way she was feeling, but she had nowhere else to go. She hadn't made any real friends in Paris yet.

A handful of couples strolled near the river, and another pair was making out on a bench. But there was no sign of Nadim, and as Kayla turned to trudge back to her shoebox of an apartment, her heart was heavy.

What if she was the biggest idiot in the world for coming here to try to establish a relationship with her dad? And what if, at the end of the day, her father turned out to be a man she didn't particularly like at all?

Shelby's friends were very, very drunk.

They had dined earlier in the evening at Le Refuge des Fondus, a hole-in-the-wall fondue restaurant on a side street in the Montmartre neighborhood that Vanessa had seen on Instagram. The place—a long, dimly lit, graffitied cave—was so narrow that there was room for just two very long tables, and to get to her seat against the wall, Corinne had to climb over the table with the assistance of a couple of cute waiters. Not that she'd seemed to mind.

The meal had started innocently enough—meats, cheeses, olives, and potatoes served in little glass bowls and a kir—white wine with black currant liqueur—for each of them. But then the fondue course—great steaming pots of melted cheese with giant baskets of bread cubes—had arrived, and along with it, red wine in baby bottles.

"Uh," Shelby said, holding up the bottle in confusion when the waiter plunked it down in front of her. Indeed, the English translation of the menu had promised a "baby bottle" of wine as part of the meal, but she had assumed that was a cute way of saying a *small* bottle. Instead, the wine was served in the exact same container that an infant would drink from, complete with a rubber nipple.

"It's, like, their signature thing!" Vanessa chirped. "All of their wine comes in these! Isn't it fun?"

And it *was* fun, Shelby had to admit, even if the baby bottles reminded her of what she didn't have. But the fondue was amazing; the place was loud and friendly; and they snapped dozens of photos toasting with their little baby bottles of red wine.

The problem was that the meal was *too* fun—and it was too easy to order a second round—and before they knew it, they were all stuffed full of cheese and bread, somewhat drunk, and posting food pics with abandon on Instagram.

"So you're holding out on us," Corinne said, leaning across the table and stabbing her fondue fork in Shelby's general direction. Beside Shelby, Vanessa burped demurely and took another swig of her red wine. "Did you sleep with that hot bartender last night or what?"

Shelby glanced from Corinne to Vanessa. Both of them were staring at her hopefully. "We just made out," she said with a small smile.

"Booooooooo!" Corinne said dramatically. "That's no fun! You're supposed to hook up in Paris to get Brandon out of your system."

"*Brandon*," Vanessa repeated bitterly, like it was a bad word. "Blech."

Shelby smiled; at least her friends had her back. "I know. Instead, I got drunk and cried."

"Oh, Shelb." Corinne's disappointment was palpable as she exchanged looks with Vanessa. "You cried?"

Shelby looked down, embarrassed. "I know. It's ridiculous. And Russ was, like, the nicest guy in the world. But somehow, all I could think about was Brandon. Totally pathetic. And Russ deserves better."

"*You* deserve better," Vanessa said sharply. "This is about you, Shelb, not about Brandon *or* some random bartender."

"He actually owns the bar," Shelby protested weakly, and Corinne rolled her eyes. "Really, he was a nice guy."

"You're not supposed to meet a *nice guy*," Corinne said. "You're supposed to meet a hot dude who takes you to bed and ravages you and makes you forget all about the fact that Brandon ever existed in the first place."

"I know," Shelby said in a small voice as the waiter arrived with three servings of chocolate mousse. The other two girls ordered a third round of drinks, but Shelby, whose stomach was already swimming, declined. "I'm supposed to go see him tonight, actually," Shelby added in a small voice, and both Vanessa and Corinne whooped and shrieked their approval, earning them annoyed looks from the groups on either side of them at the communal table.

"Good," Corinne said. "We'll go have some more drinks first, and then you can go meet up with him. This time, no crying. You're getting laid."

After they'd polished off their chocolate and paid the check, they stumbled down the cobblestone streets and stopped into a maroon-awninged bar called La Fourmi. They ordered two plates of french fries and a bottle of À Temps Perdu red wine and giggled as French guys flirted with them, and then they walked farther down the Boulevard de Clichy to gawk at the red neon windmill of the Moulin Rouge before wandering down another side street and into a lively bar called Le Valois, where Corinne ordered a round of Tequila Bang shots with salt and lemon. The girls were just ordering a second round when Shelby's phone buzzed.

Maybe it was Russ, calling because his shift was almost over. The girls weren't wrong; the best way to get over Brandon was to get under someone else, right? And why not Russ? Just because he seemed like a thoughtful guy didn't mean he couldn't be a fling, as long as she was honest.

But then she pulled out her phone and checked the caller ID and her heart skipped. It was Brandon. They hadn't spoken in more than a month.

"Hello?" she answered breathlessly, already moving toward the exit. She half hoped one of the other girls would snatch her phone away and save her from herself, but neither of them seemed to notice her leaving; they were flirting with a charming French bartender, who was offering to mix Vanessa and Corinne a specialty cocktail that he claimed he reserved for only the prettiest girls.

"Shelb?" Brandon's Southern twang should have sounded wrong to her in the midst of Paris, but instead, it made her stomach hurt, because it hit her like a bag of bricks how much she missed hearing it. "I can't hear you. Where *are* you?"

"Paris," she said, stepping outside onto the rue de Bruxelles, which was blissfully quiet once the door to the bar behind her closed.

"Paris . . . France?" Brandon sounded incredulous. "Who are you with?"

"Corinne and Vanessa," she answered automatically, without bothering to think about the fact that it was no longer his business.

He chuckled, low and deep. "And here I thought you were just reposting their pictures to make me jealous."

It took Shelby a few seconds to understand what he meant. "You're looking at my Instagram?" Then her brain caught up. "Wait, why would I be trying to make you jealous?"

"I don't know. I just mean, you're obviously trying to prove you've moved on."

She could feel the beginnings of a headache setting in. "I *have* moved on, Brandon. We're getting divorced, remember? And it seems like you've moved on, too. Alexis, is it?"

Brandon was silent for a few seconds. "You heard about that."

"Yeah, congratulations," Shelby said stiffly, hating that there were tears in her eyes, and grateful that he couldn't see them. "And I hear you're having a baby. Just what you always wanted."

He cleared his throat. "Actually, Alexis and I broke up." Shelby was stunned into silence, and when she didn't say anything, Brandon continued haltingly. "So the thing is, you're right. Alexis is having a baby. It's just . . . not mine."

"What? How do you know that?"

"Well, there's, uh, a problem with my sperm."

Shelby's whole body felt cold. "What?"

"I went in for a physical . . . Reduced motility and atypical morphology, the doctor said. Turns out Alexis was sleeping with some guy in her office. Can you believe that?"

"Wait, go back." Shelby's head was spinning. "*You* have fertility problems? So all that time we were trying to have a baby and thought I couldn't get pregnant because I had PCOS . . ." She trailed off, too stunned for words. Her fertility doctor had been Brandon's old fraternity brother, and Brandon had said it was too weird to have his sperm checked by someone who'd once held him up while he'd done keg stands, adding that there was no point, anyhow, if they already knew she had polycystic ovary syndrome. "It was your fault, too," she finished softly.

"'Fault' is a strong word," Brandon said.

"It sure is. And it's a word you used an awful lot on me."

She could hear him breathing. "I'm sorry, Shelb. I really am."

"Yeah," she whispered. "Me, too."

"Do you think . . ." He coughed and restarted. "Do you think we could try again?"

She was certain she'd misheard him. "I'm sorry, try what again?"

"Us. We were good together, weren't we?"

She was definitely in bizarro world now. "We were," she said evenly. "Until you decided that I was to blame for everything that wasn't perfect in our marriage."

"Yeah, well . . . I was wrong."

She closed her eyes. She never thought she'd hear him say the words. But they were too late. Weren't they? Suddenly, she was very confused. "Yes, Brandon, you were," she said. "I have to go." She hung up before he could say another word, and then, before she could second-guess herself, she set off toward the metro.

She didn't want to think about Brandon anymore tonight. She didn't want to face Vanessa and Corinne and their demands that she move on by sleeping with a new guy, either. She just wanted to be by herself.

But as she walked away, she found herself thinking of Russ. There was no future with him—she knew that—but still, he had shown her more care and respect last night than Brandon had in years. And now, as she felt the tug back into Brandon's orbit, she forced herself to think, instead, about what it had felt like to wake up in bed this morning with someone who didn't expect her to be anyone but who she was.

It was nearly closing time, and Russ's hopes were fading as the minutes ticked by.

Shelby had said she was going out with her girlfriends tonight but that she'd try to come by before the bar closed. Yet it was 1:45; he'd just shouted out that it was last call, and still, she hadn't appeared.

"If you're so desperate to get laid, there's a girl over there who's been eyeing you all night," Benji said as he squeezed by Russ with four pints of Foster's.

Russ glanced in the direction Benji indicated, where, indeed, a pretty brunette in her twenties was batting her eyes at him. "I'm old enough to be her father," he said dully as Benji returned.

"So what? If you're not going to hit on her, I will," Benji said brightly.

"Have at it."

"You sure?" Benji didn't wait for an answer before adding, "You're giving off sad-sack energy, anyhow."

"That's very nice, Benji, thanks."

"Just calling it like I see it." Benji grinned and then slithered like an eel over to the high-top where the brunette stood with some friends. In a second, she was giggling at something charming Benji had said, having already forgotten that she'd spent the past hour staring at Russ.

Fifteen minutes later the bar had emptied out, Benji had vanished with the brunette, and Rob had almost finished counting the cash in the till. Russ went out front to lock up, and he couldn't resist looking up and down the street, just in case Shelby was headed his way.

But the rue Galande was empty except for a few stragglers from Le Maison Grog.

No Shelby, then. Russ thought about calling her, but he didn't want to seem desperate. She knew where to find him.

He stepped back inside, pulled the doors closed, and vowed that one of these days, he'd have a hard conversation with himself about what he was doing with his life.

CHAPTER FIFTEEN

Nicolas hadn't called, and Piper couldn't believe it.

Why had he bothered listening to her pour her heart out as they'd walked around Paris if he'd intended to ghost her? Why had he asked for her number at all? Why had he gazed at her so tenderly and made her feel like she mattered?

"Did you talk to Nicolas last night?" her mom asked as they waited near Notre Dame for the hop-on, hop-off Big Bus. They'd just finished a quick breakfast in the hotel lobby—an almond croissant for Piper and a chocolate croissant for Julia, with plenty of coffee—and they were planning to spend the whole day riding around the city to visit several monuments and shops. Piper knew it would be exhausting, but that's why her mom planned to turn in early tonight instead of napping this afternoon. Besides, she'd have some time to rest on the bus between stops.

"Uh, yeah," Piper said, forcing a smile. She hated lying, but this trip was supposed to be perfect, and she knew her mom would fret about it if she thought Piper had been hurt. Fortunately, Piper had had plenty of practice pretending things were okay when they weren't.

"Oh, good," her mom said, putting an arm around her. "So you'll see him again tonight, after I go to sleep?"

"Mom, honestly, he's just some guy in a city I don't live in," Piper said, shrugging her mom's arm off. "I think you're making too big a deal of things. Let's not talk about Nicolas. Let's enjoy Paris, okay?"

Her mom gave her a suspicious look as the bus—double-decker and maroon with big yellow lettering—pulled up. "You're sure everything's okay?"

Piper bit her lip. Nothing had been okay in two years. "Of course," she said with a sunny smile. "Come on, let's grab seats."

A few minutes later, Piper watched from the bus's upper deck as they turned onto the street that ran along the river and drove directly past the Café Le Petit Pont on the left. Piper averted her eyes. Seriously, was the universe messing with her?

"You remind me of me when I was your age," Piper's mom said a few minutes later as the weeping willow at the edge of the Île de la Cité rolled by to their right, which felt like another dagger to Piper's heart. She looked quickly away, focusing on her mom.

"I do?" Piper asked, trying to shake off the feeling of rejection that had washed over her.

Her mom sighed. "I fell in love the summer I lived here, too. Or maybe it wasn't love, but it was something special. Something I hadn't felt before. It sounds crazy to say, but when I came back to the States, I came back knowing that I had value."

"Of course you did, Mom. You *do*."

"I know. But I don't think that's the kind of thing you necessarily know when you're young. And when you don't know you have value, you settle for less than you deserve." Her mom's voice was thick with emotion as she added, "Sometimes way less. That's what I was doing before that summer I spent in Paris. But being here, even for a small amount of time, changed me."

Piper didn't know what to say, so she reached for her mom's hand and squeezed.

"The thing is," her mom continued, "I didn't hang on to those lessons. And by the time I met your father, well, I think I had slid back into believing that I was lucky to have anyone pay attention to me."

They didn't talk much about Piper's father. When he and Piper's mom had divorced, he'd remarried in less than a year, and his new wife was pregnant within months. By the time Piper was a teenager, he had three preschoolers at home and hardly any time for her—but then again, he'd never had time for her when he'd still been married to her mom, either. Sure, he'd called dutifully every Sunday through her teen years, and she'd seen him once or twice a month for court-ordered visits, but she'd always felt like a guest in his new home rather than a daughter who belonged there. Once she'd gone off to college, her relationship with him had cooled; he was busy with her younger half siblings, and she no longer felt obligated to pretend she and her father were something they weren't. Since her mother's diagnosis, though, he had been calling more frequently, which she supposed was nice. He was trying.

"I'm sorry, Mom," Piper said after a minute. "I know things with Dad didn't work out the way you'd hoped."

Her mom shrugged. "We were both young and naïve and didn't know what we were doing. I only wish that he'd left more room in his life for you."

Piper swallowed the lump in her throat. "I think he's trying now."

"I think so, too, and I'm glad," her mom said. "And, look, I don't know what will happen between you and Nicolas. Maybe you'll stay in touch. Maybe you'll never see him again. But the way he looks at you is the way you should always be looked at by someone you care about, Piper. You deserve to be adored, and in the future, wherever your life goes and whoever you date, if you don't feel that way, give yourself permission to walk away. I'm glad I finally had the courage to do that with your dad, you know? But I did it years too late. I don't want you to make the same mistake."

Piper looked away from her mom as the bus came to a halt in front of the Musée d'Orsay. "You're not supposed to be telling me all these things now, Mom. You're supposed to say them along the way."

"I'm so sorry, honey," Piper's mom said. "I know." Piper sniffled and put her head on her mother's shoulder, and they stayed like that as the bus pulled away from the curb and chugged toward the next stop.

Melanie's bed felt empty without Gilles in it.

That was a pathetic thing to admit, and Melanie hated herself a little for feeling that way, for regretting, even for a second, that she'd banished him. The thing was, she *wanted* to be in love with him, just as she had been when she'd married him two decades earlier. Instead, she felt like she was waking up and realizing she no longer belonged in her own life.

She swung her legs out of bed and made her way to the kitchen, where, to her surprise, her grandfather was already up, clutching an oversized garbage bag.

"Morning, Grandpa Henry," she said with a yawn, moving past him to the Nespresso maker as she tried to pinpoint what felt different to her about the kitchen. She placed a cup under the spout, inserted a pod, and pressed the brew button.

"Morning, dear." He was already dressed for the day, and she knew without asking that it was because he was eager to visit his old girlfriend again.

"What are you doing?" she asked as he tied the garbage bag shut.

"I thought I'd do you the favor of getting rid of some of the flowers. A few roses are nice, but twenty dozen are clearly overkill." He looked uncertain. "But maybe I've overstepped. If you wanted to keep the flowers . . ."

Melanie slowly shook her head. That's why the kitchen had looked different; there were two dozen or so roses arranged tastefully in a vase on the counter, but the rest were squashed into the bag her grandfather was holding. It was a relief not to have the evidence of Gilles's betrayal on every conceivable surface. "No," she said. "This is perfect. Thank you for doing that."

Melanie turned her back to him and busied herself with pouring sugar into her coffee so that her grandfather wouldn't notice her eyes welling up. She felt his hand on her shoulder a moment later, and she turned, wiping away her tears.

"You deserve more, Melanie," he said, looking into her eyes. "You know that, right? Whether it's with Gilles or not. And perhaps it *is* with Gilles, dear. It's just that you shouldn't settle for anything less than love."

She sniffled and forced a smile. "Right. But there's still the matter of being married to him, you know? Now, can I get you a coffee?"

Five minutes later, they were seated in the kitchen, each with a fresh cup, as the flowers decayed in a trash bag by the front door.

"Can I forgive him for cheating?" Melanie asked as her grandfather took a sip of his coffee. "I want to, I think. But I'm not sure if I can."

He set his coffee down and reached for her hand. "I think you need to do whatever your heart tells you to do. But I also think that you need to protect that heart until you know whether you can trust your husband again."

She looked down at her coffee. "I can't imagine my life without him. But that's not a reason to stay, is it?"

"No, it isn't," her grandfather said. "And in this moment, my dear, the future is up to you. Do you move forward with him? Or do you choose a path alone?"

"I don't know," Melanie said miserably.

"Just remember to listen to your heart, not the parts of your head that want to keep things on an even keel because it's easier," Grandpa Henry said. "Stay with Gilles because you love him and feel you can trust him again, not because you want him to be something he's not."

Melanie blinked back tears. She and her grandfather had never talked like this; it was disconcerting now to realize that she'd missed out on fifty years of his advice. "Thanks, Grandpa Henry," she said.

Her grandfather reached across the counter and squeezed her hands. "I love you, kiddo."

She looked him in the eye, sadness sweeping over her. He was nearly one hundred. He wouldn't always be here. And if she left Gilles, who would she have when her grandfather was gone? She'd be all alone—but that was no reason to stay, either, was it? She forced a smile. "I love you, too, Grandpa Henry."

Thirty minutes later, Henry walked into the Café Le Petit Pont, a charming place whose patio faced Notre Dame. He had arranged to meet Celeste's grandson, Jean-Luc, here for a late breakfast, and he was as nervous as a much younger man meeting his girlfriend's parents for the first time. He tried to tell himself that in the end it didn't matter what Jean-Luc thought of him, but that wasn't true at all. Jean-Luc could eliminate Henry's access to Celeste with a single phone call. And he could throw up a roadblock when Henry asked to take Celeste to the Jackson Quick concert, which was the real reason Henry was here.

He asked for a table and was already halfway through his first coffee when a fiftysomething man with silver hair hurried through the door, explaining in French to the waiter who greeted him that he was here to meet a "very old American man." The waiter pointed, and Henry obediently stood and waved to let Jean-Luc know that he was there, though the description smarted a bit. Of course, he *was*, in fact, a very old American man, but it had galled him for the past twenty years that once a person crossed the threshold of his late seventies, his one defining quality in the eyes of others was his age. Younger people reduced their elders to walking stereotypes in their minds, not realizing that if they themselves were fortunate to live long enough, they'd soon have their own identities erased, too.

"*Bonjour, bonjour,*" Jean-Luc said, hurrying up to the table. "Or hello, hello. A good excuse to practice my English. You are Monsieur McGee?"

"Call me Henry," Henry said with a smile, extending his hand. "Thank you so much for meeting me."

Jean-Luc's handshake was firm, and he looked Henry in the eye with a genuine smile as they both sat down. "I still cannot believe you have traveled all this way to visit my grandmother."

"She has always been the love of my life," Henry said, cutting right to the chase.

The younger man exhaled slowly. "You understand that this is very strange for me. You see, I loved my grandfather very much. To think that there was someone else my grandmother loved before him . . ."

"I, too, was married for many years, and I think my granddaughter, Melanie, is having trouble knowing that there was a woman before her grandmother."

Jean-Luc leaned back in his chair. "It is clear from my grandmother's diaries that she believed you had died."

"I believed the same of her. I went to visit her uncle after the war. I still can't understand why he lied to me."

"I can't say for certain, sir, but he was captured by the Germans and spent two years in a prisoner of war camp under horrific conditions," Jean-Luc said. "He took my grandmother in after the war, did you know that? I think he bore a grudge against Americans for the rest of his life; he thought you should have entered the war sooner."

"We should have," Henry agreed.

"My guess? He didn't want his last living relative leaving him for someone he blamed for his circumstances."

Henry looked down in dismay. He understood what Jean-Luc was telling him, but it was almost inconceivable that his whole life had been shaped by a lie borne of one man's misplaced anger. "Had I known your grandmother had lived, Jean-Luc, I would have waited for her until the end of time. But that means I never would have had my son, and he wouldn't have had Melanie. And if your grandmother had married me all those years ago, you wouldn't be here, either."

Jean-Luc blinked. "I suppose that's true. And now that you have seen her, what do you think? Do you regret coming to Paris? There is not much of her there anymore."

Henry knew what the younger man meant, but he bristled at the implication that she was mostly gone. "Actually," he said as politely as possible, "I still see much of the Celeste I once knew."

"How so?" Jean-Luc looked unconvinced.

"Well, for one, she still speaks fluent English."

Jean-Luc squinted at Henry. "My grandmother speaks English?"

"Indeed she does. And her spirit. She's just as sassy as ever."

"Sassy?" Jean-Luc looked confused. "But when I visit, she has so little to say."

"How often do you see her?"

Jean-Luc looked across at Henry with a guilty expression. "Not as often as I should, I admit. It is very sad to me to realize that she has mostly disappeared."

"But what if she hasn't?"

They were interrupted then by a waiter asking if Jean-Luc would like a cup of coffee and if Henry would like a second cup. They both agreed, and each ordered grilled toast with butter and jam. There was nothing in the world like the bread in Paris. When the waiter had departed, Jean-Luc leaned forward. "Sorry. You were saying?"

"Your grandmother is still in there," Henry said. "Dementia is like a slow stripping away of the years, and the memories that go with them. But I also think that a person remains who she is at her very core for a long time, even after the memories are gone. And I think that in many cases, the older memories are still there, locked somewhere deep inside."

Jean-Luc drummed his fingers on the table. "You've thought a lot about this."

"I lost my wife to dementia," Henry replied. "Many years ago. And even as the memories slipped away, she was still herself in many ways until the very end. I just had to be patient and wait for her to come back to me now and then."

"Hmm." Jean-Luc looked unconvinced. Their coffees and breakfast arrived then, and for a moment, they busied themselves with their food.

It was Henry who broke the silence between them. "I'd like to take your grandmother to a concert this Friday."

Jean-Luc looked up from spreading jam. "Pardon?"

"A concert. I'm a songwriter, you see, and my biggest hit song—'City of Light'—was performed some thirty years ago by a fellow named Jackson Quick. I wrote it for your grandmother."

Jean-Luc's knife clattered to the table. "I'm sorry, you're telling me that 'City of Light' is about my *grand-mère*?"

"You know it?"

Jean-Luc choked out an astonished laugh. "The whole world knows that song, I think. But in Paris, we *are* the City of Light. That song was like an anthem to us in the 1990s. You really wrote it?"

"I did. And I am hoping that if your grandmother can hear it, too, it will remind her of who I am—and of who we were together."

"Hear it?" Jean-Luc looked unconvinced. "She has lost much of her hearing, I'm afraid."

"All the more reason to bring her to the concert, where she'll be able to feel the music in her bones. Jackson Quick himself is arranging tickets for us. You're welcome to come."

"To a Jackson Quick concert," Jean-Luc repeated dubiously. "With you and my grandmother."

"And my granddaughter, Melanie." Henry held his breath as Jean-Luc stared at him, clearly trying to make up his mind.

"Well," Jean-Luc said after a long pause, "I suppose there is no harm. But, Henry, I don't want you to get your hopes up. She isn't the same person she was then, you understand?"

Henry smiled. "I think, Jean-Luc, that life pushes us this way and that and bends us to its will. But we are who we are our whole lives through."

Jean-Luc frowned. "I'm not sure I believe that."

"You'll see," Henry said. "Your grandmother is still in there. We just have to find a way to remind her who she is."

CHAPTER SIXTEEN

Russ arrived at Le Maison Grog the next day at 10 a.m. to open, a job he and Benji took turns doing.

He was exhausted. It wasn't just that he'd slept poorly last night; it was that running the bar day in and day out, opening and closing, with only one day off per week, was enough to break anyone. And he'd been doing it for fifteen years.

He and Benji had tried hiring managers with whom to share the duties of running the place, but every single one had been a disaster. Lee skimmed money from the register for months before Russ figured it out. Johnny was a bigger flirt than Benji—which was saying something—and after he'd been their manager for about two months, he and Benji came to blows one night over the same girl. Then there'd been Chris, who had a serious drinking problem; Scotty, who kept forgetting to lock the front door when he left for the night; and Annie, who was the most promising manager they'd ever had until she moved to Majorca with her girlfriend and neglected to tell them.

After that, Benji and Russ had decided that they were done

handing over the keys to their livelihood to anyone. Unfortunately, that meant that between the two of them, they had to handle open-to-close seven days a week, with few exceptions. Sometimes, they both ducked out midday while Rob the bartender and Jagger the cook held down the fort, but it was always one of them arriving before 11 a.m. to open and departing after 2 a.m. to close.

And more often than not, lately, the responsibility fell to Russ.

As he wiped down sticky tables and restocked the bar, he called up Jackson Quick's debut album, *Skylight*, on Apple Music and blasted it through the speakers. He'd forgotten how many good tracks were on it; the only one to hit No. 1 had been "City of Light," but the album was deep with underrated songs that had been a few years before their time.

He still couldn't believe that the rock star had sat at his bar. Russ had played it cool, but now, listening to the songs that brought back memories of secondary school dances, he couldn't help but grin. What would he have thought if someone had told him, the year "City of Light" had come out, that one day he'd own a bar in Paris and Jackson Quick would come in? Life was strange, wasn't it?

That's what he was thinking about—the way that life surprised you in ways you couldn't see coming—when he was snapped out of it by a sharp knock at the front door of the bar.

He turned the music down, rolling his eyes. Who needed a drink so badly that he couldn't wait until the bar opened in forty-five minutes? Annoyed, he turned, ready to bark at whoever was there to come back at a decent hour. But to his surprise, it was Shelby, two cups of takeaway coffee in a carrier, her blond hair pulled back into a ponytail that showed off her sharp cheekbones.

Her smile was a question mark as Russ stared at her for a second. He crossed to unlock the front door and let her in. "Shelby," he said, looking down at her. He was glad to see her but couldn't help but wonder why she hadn't come last night.

"Coffee," she said, holding up the steaming cups. "And an apology."

"I'll take the coffee," he said, holding the door open for her, "but you don't owe me an apology."

"Sure I do. I said I'd come see you last night, and I bailed." She slipped under his outstretched arm and headed for the bar as he locked the door behind her. He joined her a moment later and accepted one of the coffees.

"God, I needed that," he said after a long sip.

"I'm not even human in the morning until I've had caffeine," Shelby said with a smile, taking a small sip of her own.

"So," he said, "good time with your friends last night?" He could hear Benji's voice in his ear telling him he sounded like a needy girl, so he added for good measure, "The bar was so busy, I hardly looked up at all last night."

"Oh, good." Shelby smiled at him again. "And yeah, we went to dinner in Montmartre and stopped at pretty much every bar between there and the Place de Clichy metro stop."

Russ laughed. "Ah. So you must be feeling really good this morning."

She laughed, too, and took another sip of her coffee. "I really did mean to come and see you."

"It's okay," he said quickly. It was bad enough that his feelings had been wounded; the last thing he needed was for her to know that he was being so pathetic. "Like I said, busy night. But do you have some time to hang out now? I could see if Benji could cover for me."

"My friends would kill me if I ditched them," she said with an apologetic shrug. "We're supposed to go shopping on the Champs-Élysées."

"Ah, retail therapy. Right, of course. But maybe you could come by tonight?" He hoped he sounded nonchalant.

"Yeah, sure." She looked relieved, but there was something else, too. Uncertainty? Sadness? He couldn't quite put a finger on whatever had just flickered across her face, and then it was gone, replaced by a bright smile. "I'll see how the day goes."

"Sure, right, yeah." He hesitated and then leaned in to kiss her, just a quick peck on the lips, before he could second-guess himself. "Sorry, I hope that was okay."

"Yeah, totally," she said, blinking back what looked like tears, but that couldn't be right. "Of course."

The passenger van of Vietnam vets pulled up outside of the Peninsula Hotel just before 11 a.m., disgorging its load of passengers outside of the palatial building near the Arc de Triomphe. George was the first one off after their tour guide, Pierre, because it was beginning to feel like the walls were closing in on him.

Today's outing was an early lunch at the famed hotel, where the treaty ending the Vietnam War had been signed in 1973. Pierre had arranged a private meal for them in Le Bar Kléber, which didn't open to the general public until noon. Pierre hustled the group across the lobby and through a pair of double doors. George felt a bit like royalty as they were ushered into the dark, oak-paneled bar lined with mirrors and silk tapestries. Quiet classical music played over the speakers, and a tuxedoed bartender told them in perfect English that the three tables in the corner had already been prepared for them.

"It is here that your secretary of state, Henry Kissinger, negotiated the Paris Peace Accords," Pierre said as George, Lou, and Cliff—who was once again wearing his beret—settled into three enormous chairs around a table, which sat beneath a huge vase and a stunning indigo tapestry with a white peacock in the foreground. The three couples sat at the table to one side of them, and the two nurses shared a smaller table on their other side. Cliff, of course, couldn't seem to stop himself from ogling them.

"Right here in this bar?" Cliff asked, looking around in awe.

"Indeed," Pierre confirmed. "It is why a visit here is the highlight of each Vietnam veterans' tour I run. I'll leave you to it, then."

He moved to sit at the far end of the bar, and the bartender whisked over to him immediately with a cup of coffee and a folded newspaper. A tuxedoed waiter hurried over with menus, and after a bit of consultation, they ordered a bottle of Sancerre for the table.

After the waiter had poured them each a glass of wine, the three men toasted the past and looked around the room for a moment in silence. Beside them, the three couples were chatting away, and the two nurses had pulled out a guidebook and were reading to each other.

"You can feel the weight of history here," Lou said reverently, glancing first at Cliff and then at George, whose gaze he held for a long moment. "The end of an era."

Being in Vietnam had altered George at his very core—he had come back unable to sleep for months, haunted by nightmares of men beside him being shot dead, tormented by the lives he'd taken in combat. He and Lou had grown especially close in the year after they'd come home, when they'd returned to a country that, to their surprise, reviled the soldiers who'd served. They'd been spit on numerous times, and Lou had once been kicked so hard in the torso by a protestor that George had had to take him to the hospital to rule out kidney damage. It had taken both men years to reconcile their guilt over their involvement in a war they hadn't fully understood and their pride in doing their duty to their country and serving with honor. George still wrestled with the conflicting feelings all these years later.

"The closing of the most formative period of our lives," George agreed, his heart heavy. He looked around at the stately room, which must have looked much the same fifty years earlier. Hard to imagine that Kissinger himself might have sat in this very spot as he helped put an end to the war that had taken so many lives and changed them all. Lou put a hand on his arm and nodded gravely, and George felt a thousand unspoken words pass between them. When you'd shared something like Vietnam, sometimes words weren't necessary.

Fearing that Cliff would feel left out, George finally looked away from Lou, forced a smile, and said, "Amazing, Cliff, isn't it?"

Cliff sighed. "It's just hard for me to appreciate anything here in my current state," he said in a low voice.

George and Lou exchanged looks. "Is something . . . the matter?" Lou asked.

Cliff heaved another dramatic sigh. "It's just that I'm in love with Diane over there, and she won't give me the time of day." He stared wistfully at the taller of the two nurses, who was utterly ignoring him.

"I'm sorry; you're in *love* with her?" George glanced at Lou again, confused. Lou merely shrugged.

"Well, aren't *you*?" Cliff asked with a despondent laugh. "How could anyone not fall instantly for her? She's only the most extraordinary creature to have ever lived. And look at those legs . . ."

"But . . ." George drew the word out. "You just met her. And you've hit on literally every woman we've come across since we arrived in Paris. Including Diane's friend. Sheila, is it?"

"That was just to make Diane jealous," Cliff said, blinking at George like he was a dolt. "Obviously."

Their waiter arrived then to take their orders—a club sandwich for Cliff, chicken pad thai for Lou, and a wild mushroom omelet with a green salad for George.

"Don't you think," Lou said after the waiter had departed, "that it might be easier just to talk to Diane? Instead of playing games?"

Cliff glanced at Diane, a look of horror crossing his face. "*Talk* to her?"

"Tell her how you feel, in other words," Lou said. "Instead of flirting with everyone around her in the hopes she'll notice you."

"That isn't how the game is played," Cliff said blankly.

"But what if it isn't a game? What if you could have something real with her?" Lou asked, glancing at George, whose mouth felt dry. "Tell her how you feel, Cliff. What's the worst that can happen?"

"Well, she could say no."

"Maybe," Lou said. "But then it wasn't meant to be. You can never regret honesty, though, can you?"

Cliff looked pensively at his own reflection in the large mirror on the opposite wall. Lou raised his eyebrows at George, and George knew that his friend was urging him to weigh in, but George's tongue felt heavy in his mouth, and he couldn't summon the right words. *You can never regret honesty*, Lou had said. But what could George say now that wouldn't make him a hypocrite?

"George?" Lou urged after a moment. "Don't *you* have any advice for Cliff?"

Cliff looked at George, his expression miserable and pleading. George felt compelled to say something.

"I do think," George said carefully, "that Lou is right. You will always regret not telling the truth if you choose not to do it."

Beside him, Lou nodded, and though George meant the words, he felt like a fraud.

"All right, then, you two convinced me," Cliff said. "I'll talk to Diane today."

George gave Cliff what he hoped was an encouraging smile, then shot a look at Lou, who was watching him. They'd just dispensed the right advice to Cliff; of that, he was sure. But when it came to taking his own advice? Seizing his own moment before it was too late? George wasn't sure he had the courage to do that.

Piper and her mother got off the Big Bus three times, first on the Champs-Élysées for a bit of shopping and an early lunch of croque monsieurs and rosé, then at the Trocadéro to snap some pictures with the Eiffel Tower in the background, and, finally, at the Opéra Garnier, where they admired the gilded exterior of the famous theater and then walked over to the Galeries Lafayette for more shopping and salads at the café on the ground floor.

It was nearly five by the time they walked through the doors to their hotel, and Piper's mom was rubbing her eyes and yawning.

"That was an awesome day," she said as she unlocked the door to their hotel room. "But I hope you won't mind if I turn in early."

"Of course not, Mom," Piper said, trying not to notice how frail her mother looked. The more exhausted she became throughout the day, the more her whole body seemed to deflate. "Are you sure you're okay?"

"Oh, I'm fine," her mother murmured, heading for the bathroom. "Nothing a little rest won't fix."

"Right, but—"

"No buts!" her mother called from the bathroom. "Go out with the boy! Your old mom needs her beauty sleep!"

Piper swallowed her hurt. She had checked her phone a hundred times, and Nicolas still hadn't called or texted. She felt foolish to have believed he could be something special. "Yeah, okay."

Piper's mom emerged a moment later, already wearing pajamas, her face scrubbed clean of makeup. "What?" she asked, and Piper looked away; she hadn't meant to stare at her mother.

"Nothing, Mom," she said, and when her mother continued to look at her, she added in a small voice, "It's just that you look . . . sick."

There. She'd said it. She'd acknowledged the elephant in the room, which was that Piper's mom wasn't just taking a quick rest before the next round of sightseeing; she was sleeping off the effects of an illness that was gaining on her.

"Well," her mom said, smiling a smile that Piper knew wasn't real, "I feel perfectly fine, and I'm sure I'll feel even better after I get some sleep."

"What about your dinner?"

"That salad was more than enough. And if I wake up later and I'm bored, I can wander around the neighborhood a bit on my own. I promise, sweetheart, I'm fine. Just text me if you'll be very late so that I know you're safe, okay?"

"Okay," Piper murmured. It used to drive her crazy that her mother wanted to keep tabs on her, but who would do so after her mom was gone? She had the terrible feeling that the things she had pushed away were the things she would miss the most. "Are you *sure* you're okay?"

"Positive." Piper's mom yawned again.

"Okay." Piper still wasn't certain that she was doing the right thing by leaving her mother, but already, her mom was crawling into bed, her lashes fluttering as she fought to keep her eyes open. Piper had to blink back tears as she crossed the room to kiss her mom on the cheek. "Get some rest."

"Have fun, honey."

"Sure." As she walked out of the hotel a few minutes later, she resolved not to go anywhere near the Café Le Petit Pont—and to stop thinking about Nicolas. As she strolled north across the Pont Saint-Michel toward Notre Dame, she tried to imagine her mother here nearly thirty years ago, when she was a young woman, before she was married, before Piper existed. Had she walked this same path? Seen these same sights? It was incredible to think that so many of the buildings that dominated Paris had been here for hundreds of years without change. It wasn't like that anywhere in the States, where cities were constantly reinventing themselves. Buildings were ripped down and rebuilt; restaurants and businesses came and went; nothing was permanent.

But Paris was like a time capsule. Sure, the vehicles and the storefronts, the electric streetlights and the mopeds, were all new in the past hundred years, but Piper could close her eyes and imagine that she was here almost thirty years ago, when her mom was young, or eighty years ago when World War II raged, or nearly two and a half centuries ago during the French Revolution. Notre Dame had been here for some eight hundred years. The Eiffel Tower, clearly visible in the distance in the opposite direction, was a much newer arrival, less than 140 years old, but it, too, had witnessed its share of history.

It made Piper feel small and insignificant in the grand scheme of things. People came and went, but these great monuments they built—much like the paintings they painted and the sculptures they sculpted—stood the test of time. Art lived on in a way people never could.

As Piper passed Notre Dame and headed for the bridge behind it that would take her to the Île Saint-Louis, the small residential island where she'd seen on TikTok that there was a great, decades-old ice cream shop called Berthillon, she felt a sort of peace settle over her. Maybe a piece of her mother would survive, just as the streets of Paris had survived, just as the artwork in the Musée d'Orsay had survived, as long as there was someone here to carry her memory forward. Maybe, as long as Piper was here, walking this earth, her mom would be, too.

Twenty minutes later, after ordering a salted butter caramel glacé from Berthillon, Piper strolled back toward Notre Dame, reveling in the taste of the sweet, creamy ice cream, hands down the best she'd ever had. She finished the last of the cone as she crossed through the public square in front of the church, and she was just about to reach the rue de la Cité when she saw a familiar figure hurrying across the bridge from the Left Bank, his head down. It couldn't be, could it? She ducked her head and averted her eyes, but not in time.

"Piper?" Nicolas's deep voice called out, and as he strode over, Piper wished she could disappear into the pavement.

But when she looked up, he was smiling, which threw her off for a moment. "Uh, hi, Nicolas."

"What are you doing here?" he asked.

"Ice cream," she managed, wondering why she seemed unable to string sentences together in his presence. "I mean, I'd read about Berthillon, and I thought I would try—"

"The caramel au beurre salé," he said, his smile widening as he correctly named the flavor she'd just polished off.

"How did you know that?"

"Because you still have some, just here," he said as he reached out and gently touched her chin, just below her lip.

Piper could feel her cheeks growing warm, though she wasn't sure whether the heat was from his touch or from the embarrassment of realizing she'd been wearing a glob of ice cream on her face. "Oh," she said, wiping her chin quickly. "Uh, thanks."

"Anytime." His eyes lingered on her lips for a moment before traveling up to meet her gaze. "I tried to call you, Piper."

Piper frowned. "No, you didn't, Nicolas."

"I think," he said, pulling his phone out of his pocket and typing something in, "that you gave me the wrong number." He held out his phone to show her.

"What?" She had hastily typed her own number in yesterday, still flustered from their kiss, and as she stared at the screen now, she realized, to her embarrassment, that she had entered 0211 as the last four digits instead of 0212. "Oh my God," she murmured.

"I reached a very confused man instead of you," Nicolas said, raising an eyebrow. "I thought at first it was a boyfriend you had not mentioned."

"I don't have a boyfriend," she said quickly.

He smiled at this. "And then I thought perhaps you'd given me the wrong number on purpose."

"I would never."

Nicolas shrugged. "Well, perhaps I'm not as charming as I hoped."

"No, you are *very* charming," she said quickly. "I am obviously just an idiot. Here, let me correct the number."

"Only if you're certain." Nicolas hesitated, holding the phone just out of her reach and waiting until she looked him in the eye.

"Believe me, I'm certain," she said, holding out her hand.

When he finally gave it to her, she changed the last digit and then, just to be sure, she texted herself a smiley face from his phone. Her phone dinged with the incoming message, and she held it up to show him. "See? Now you have my number, and I have yours. I'm so sorry."

He smiled at her as he took his phone back.

"I thought I'd scared you away," she added in a mumble.

He slid his phone into his pocket and took a step closer, reaching for her hand. "Why would you think that?"

"I'm an emotional basket case, Nicolas. I'm pretty sure you're not actually supposed to sob openly on the first day you meet a hot guy."

"A hot guy?" he asked with a grin.

She could feel the color returning to her cheeks. "I assume you own a mirror."

He laughed. "Where are you off to, now?"

"My mom is already asleep. I'm just wandering, I guess. Maybe trying to find the peace and joy you told me about."

He held out his arm with a grin. "In that case, what do you say we wander together for a while?"

She blinked at him. "You don't have somewhere to be?"

"I just finished work. I was on my way home. But I'm in no rush. And if you have a bit of time . . ."

Piper gave him a shy smile. "I do."

"Well then, *allons-y*," he said with a smile of his own. "Let's go."

CHAPTER SEVENTEEN

If Amandine was a betting woman, she would have wagered that Gilles would be back in less than twenty-four hours. As it was, it took nearly forty-eight, which was alarming because it meant that he was perhaps not as enamored with her as she would have liked.

She was doing this all wrong, and she knew it. The goal had been to have her apartment and living expenses paid for, and to be lavished with a bit of attention. It had been a game she had played continuously—without getting emotionally involved—for the past few years, switching middle-aged men every few months, dismissing them before they could dismiss her so that she always had the upper hand.

But to her dismay, she had developed *feelings* for Gilles, which was enormously inconvenient. She honestly couldn't even explain it; he was old and had a rather squishy body. Plus, when she was able to seduce someone so easily, she didn't normally think highly of that person's intellect. However, she had also discovered that Gilles was kind and genuinely cared about her; the other men she'd liaised with had all understood that a transaction was taking place, and they'd seemed okay with the terms. Gilles, however, looked at her like she mattered—and *not* just when she was naked.

That had thrown her for a loop, and it was why she'd made a mistake. She'd let her emotions get the best of her and she'd texted him while drinking a bottle of champagne by herself one evening—not discreetly, as they'd agreed to communicate, but in a way that would make it clear to his wife that he had a mistress, if he'd been foolish enough to leave his phone lying around.

And that, apparently, was just what had happened. Amandine realized now that there'd been a piece of her hoping to blow up his marriage. Perhaps then she could see whether what she felt for him was real or just an infatuation. Maybe it was time she stopped these games and tried to have something real with an older man who could support her long-term. But what she hadn't counted on was Gilles telling *her*, almost immediately, that he planned to slink back to his wife with his tail between his legs. It was almost unbelievable—as was the fact that it had hurt her.

Enough with the feelings. Love had never gotten her anywhere—and she was outraged with herself that she'd let her guard down. It was time to return to the playbook.

"What do you want?" she asked coldly when she opened the apartment door. He appeared thrown off by her tone, but really, it was a page from Mistressing 101. Make yourself seem just out of reach to the married man, for the thrill was in the chase. Forcing a man to pursue you triggered some caveman instinct that seemed to shut off all logic.

"You're angry with me," Gilles said, and Amandine crossed her arms over her chest, secretly delighted. He was responding exactly as he was supposed to. Good, she was back on familiar footing.

"Of course I'm angry with you," she said as righteously as she could. "You made love to me and then left me to go back to your wife!"

He swallowed hard, his Adam's apple bobbing up and down. "I'm so sorry, Amandine. I didn't mean to—"

"Didn't mean to what?" she interrupted savagely. "Didn't mean to use me? Didn't mean to make me feel worthless? Didn't mean to treat me like a whore?"

He flinched with each sentence she lobbed his way. "Forgive me. Please. I'm trying to be a better man."

She rolled her eyes dramatically and turned her back on him, swishing her hips seductively as she walked into the apartment. She knew he would follow, and a second later, when she heard the door close and his footsteps behind her, she smiled to herself. Her relief, however, was short-lived.

"I bought her flowers," he said miserably as he followed Amandine into the kitchen.

She froze, too stunned to respond for a second. "You bought *who* flowers?" she asked icily, turning to glare at him and jutting her bottom lip out in an exaggerated, sexy pout just in case he'd forgotten what she could do with that mouth.

"Melanie," he said, appearing not to notice her sulking lips or the hip she'd skillfully jutted in his direction. In fact, he wasn't even looking at her. What was wrong with him? "I bought her twenty dozen roses—one dozen for every year of our marriage—and she hasn't even called."

Amandine felt like her eyeballs were about to pop out of her head. "You bought your wife hundreds of flowers, and you're *telling* me about it?"

"Roses, yes," Gilles said, entirely missing the point.

"You've never bought me roses." It was the wrong thing to say. She knew it the moment the words were out of her mouth. Show any sort of neediness, and you've lost your edge.

Gilles looked confused. "Amandine, I *cheated* on my wife. With *you*. The roses were an apology. What have I ever needed to apologize to you for?"

Relieved to be back in more familiar territory, she fixed him with her best withering look. "What do you need to apologize for? For trying to leave me for your wife, that's what!"

His look of confusion deepened. "But you knew I was married."

She took a deep breath and switched from confrontational to wounded. She was taking acting classes through the Cours Candela, and she had learned to seamlessly switch gears like that just this week. She was quite good at it. "I thought," she said, "that you were going to leave your wife for me."

Gilles's mouth fell open. Of course he had promised her no such thing. But the guilt the words induced could not be underestimated. "Amandine, I . . . I'm sorry," he stammered. "I didn't mean to mislead you."

She wiped her eyes dramatically. "To think," she said, her lower lip quivering, "I put my life on hold for you."

"Amandine." Gilles looked stricken. "I never meant to hurt you. But I love Melanie. This was a mistake, all of it."

"Then why are you here now?" she asked. She jutted out her lower lip again, hoping that it reminded him of the last blow job she'd given him. This time, at least, he seemed to notice, his gaze snagging on her mouth for a long time. Some of the color drained from his face.

"B-because . . ." He trailed off. "Honestly, I don't know. She threw me out. I can't go home. And I thought . . ." He stopped abruptly, and to her astonishment, he began walking toward the door. "I'm sorry, Amandine. You're right. I shouldn't have come. I don't know what I'm doing."

What on earth was happening? She was losing him. "Gilles," she said seductively, already unbuttoning her blouse. She threw her shoulders back, her generous—and expensive—breasts straining against the lace of her bra. When Gilles turned, his eyes were on her nipples, not on her face, which was just what she wanted. She crossed to him and grabbed him by the tie. "Now that you're here," she murmured, "you won't leave me lonely, will you?"

"But . . . my wife," he said, his right hand already roaming to her left breast as if it had a mind of its own. He fondled her gently, and a shiver ran through her. What was it about this man that turned her on so much?

"Your wife is not here, is she?" she purred, reaching for the zipper of his pants. Unsurprisingly, he was entirely ready for her. He groaned as she touched him. "But I am."

"I can't," he said, his voice strained as she unbuckled his belt. "I shouldn't."

"Just admit that you want me, Gilles."

"I—" They were interrupted by the buzzing of his cell phone in his pocket. He fumbled for it, and Amandine felt a terrible, sinking feeling of dread.

"Don't answer it," she said, but he was already zipping his trousers, already fastening his belt, already backing away from her.

"It's Melanie," he said, his eyes shimmering. "I have to take this."

"You really love her," she said in awe, feeling a ripple of guilt, albeit a tiny one. Gilles had made his own choices. She was not responsible for them. The surprise, though, was that the guilt was followed by a swell of grief. He was really leaving. He was leaving *her.*

"I do," Gilles said. "And I'm afraid I won't be able to pay your rent anymore, Amandine. I'm sorry. That's what I came to say."

Before she could reply, he was already walking out into the hall, the phone to his ear, stammering something to his wife. He closed the door behind him and Amandine put her hands to her face, startled to feel it damp with tears, as she stared after him in disbelief.

Melanie held the phone to her ear, already doubting herself.

"Hello?" Gilles sounded breathless when he answered, and Melanie frowned. She wanted to ask him where he was, what he was doing, but she was the one who'd told him to get out, wasn't she? Maybe it wasn't her business where he was, as long as he wasn't with his mistress.

"I just wanted to say thank you," she said, sounding more formal than she'd intended to. "For the flowers. That was generous of you."

"I'm so glad you liked them." She could hear the distant ding of an elevator, the swooshing of doors.

"There were . . . a lot," she said, then immediately winced. Did she always sound this critical? This judgmental? He'd done a nice thing for her, and here she was telling him that he'd done *too much* of a nice thing. She closed her eyes and forced herself to add, "Not that I'm complaining. It was nice of you."

"Oh, good." He sounded relieved. "I'd worried that they would overwhelm you."

"No." She was doing a spectacularly bad job of having a mundane conversation with her husband. She heard another ding and imagined Gilles exiting an elevator somewhere. Again, she resisted the urge to ask him where he was.

"How are things with your grandfather and his long-lost girlfriend?" Gilles asked.

Melanie felt herself soften a bit. "You won't believe this, but he got some tickets to the Jackson Quick concert on Friday and is planning to take her."

"To a rock concert?" Gilles sounded perplexed. "At their age?"

"Apparently, Grandpa Henry wrote 'City of Light' for this Celeste woman eighty years ago."

"*Tu me fais taire!*" he said. "And now he's trying to win her back with the song again?"

"It's kind of incredible, isn't it?" Melanie felt a surge of connection to her husband, something she hadn't experienced in a long time. She was surprised how good it felt.

"When it comes to love, perhaps anything is possible." Gilles hesitated. "It would be nice to be there to support your grandfather, wouldn't it? And I want to prove to you that I'm committed to working for your forgiveness. Melanie, what if you and I go to the concert, too?"

Melanie shook her head in astonishment. "Like . . . a date?"

"Is that too much to ask? To see a concert with my wife?"

"No. I mean . . . I guess that sounds good." She felt uneasy, but she couldn't put a finger on why. Wasn't this what she wanted? To feel that he saw her? That she mattered to him?

"I will see about getting us some tickets, then," Gilles said, sounding relieved.

"My grandfather actually has a few extras. It's just . . ."

"What?"

"I can't remember the last time you asked me out. And it's . . . well, it's nice," she said. But when he didn't reply, she squirmed uncomfortably in the silence. "Gilles?" she ventured after a moment.

"I'm sorry, I'm sorry," he said quickly, the background of the call coming alive with the sounds of traffic and construction. She realized he had muted himself for a moment, and she resisted the urge to ask why. Suspicion tugged at the back of her mind, and she quickly shrugged it off. "I missed what you said, mon amour," he said.

It was the perfect opportunity to change her mind about the concert. But she wanted to forgive him. She did. And maybe this would be a first step.

"Melanie?" he prompted. "Are you still there? What's wrong?"

She chewed her lip. "Gilles? Are things really over with Amandine?"

"Of course." He sounded annoyed, but then his voice softened and he said, "It was never really anything to begin with. Just a stupid mistake. I am all yours."

She took a deep breath. They would never get back on track if she didn't try. "Okay. I'll leave a ticket for you at will call."

"And then perhaps you'll allow me to come home?"

She wanted to say yes, but she wasn't there yet. "Let's just take it step by step, okay?"

Gilles hesitated before saying, "Right, of course. I love you, you know?"

"Do you?" She needed to hear him say it again.

"Of course I do, Melanie. You're the love of my life."

She exhaled. She wanted to forgive him. She wanted to live in a world where her marriage was worth fighting for. "I love you, too," she said, but as they hung up, she couldn't help but think that in giving Gilles a second chance he hadn't really earned, maybe she was doing a disservice to herself.

Julia woke up to a pitch-black hotel room, her mouth dry.

"Piper?" she croaked, groping around for her cell phone. She had no idea what time it was. Was it morning yet? Her hand landed on the light switch beside the bed, and she turned it on, illuminating the room.

No Piper. For a second, Julia couldn't breathe. She snatched up her cell phone to see if Piper had texted her, and that's when she realized it was only 6:45 p.m. Less than ninety minutes had passed since Piper had gone.

Feeling both ridiculous and relieved, she grabbed her bottle of ibuprofen from the bedside table, palmed two pills, and swallowed them quickly with a few sips from a bottle of water. She really needed to be taking the tramadol her doctor had prescribed instead, but she hated how foggy it made her feel, and she wanted to remember every second of this trip. Her head throbbed and her belly ached—obviously the cancer performing its usual smug victory dance in her organs—but, by God, she was in Paris, and she was wide awake, and she couldn't stay in this hotel room by herself for a second more.

She contemplated texting Piper to tell her she was going out, but that would only disrupt her daughter's date, and knowing Piper, she'd be racked with guilt if she didn't immediately come back to spend time with her mother. With any luck, in fact, her daughter wasn't thinking of her at all.

Julia threw on jeans, a black silk tee, and her Sambas, ran a brush through her hair, and headed out the door, stopping at the front desk to grab the key to lock her room. She was tempted to try someplace new in the neighborhood, but she also wanted very badly to step back into a past where she was young and her whole life lay ahead of her, and the only place she knew how to do that was at the place that had once been The Red Telephone Box.

She thought fleetingly of Sam—what if he was there, too?—but she quickly reminded herself that this was Paris, and he had a trillion dining options, and besides, he'd said he was here for his job, so he was probably out with coworkers. She could call him—he'd given her his number—but that would be irresponsible. She couldn't act like just another American tourist in Paris, because she wasn't. She was a dying woman in Paris. And she knew she shouldn't spend any more time with a man she was that attracted to without imagining a future that could never, ever exist.

She wove through the bustling Latin Quarter, dodging crowds of tourists on the rue de la Huchette, passing by the crowded Café Le Petit Pont with a smile, before turning right and heading toward Le Maison Grog. How many times had her feet worn this exact same path when she had lived here? And how could it be that this might well be the last time she'd walk it?

As she hurried along the rue Galande, her head down, she heard someone calling her name.

"Julia?"

Snapped out of her self-pity, she looked up in surprise to see Sam ten feet away, coming toward Le Maison Grog from the opposite direction. He was wearing the same baseball cap she'd already seen on him, along with a faded Rolling Stones tee and a pair of jeans that hugged him just right. He looked *good*—even better than he had the day before.

"Sam," she squeaked, feeling instantly embarrassed that she hadn't called him. Certainly he'd taken it as a rejection rather than what it was: an attempt to spare him pain.

"Well, if it isn't my favorite fancy day-drinker," he said with a small smile as they reached the door at the same time. "You came back."

"My reminiscing got the best of me, I think," she admitted. "A million places to eat in Paris, and I wind up at the same hole-in-the-wall bar because it reminds me of the past."

"Turns out you can't turn back time. But you *can* eat fish and chips that remind you of who you were in the last millennium." He held open the door for her. "That's what I'm doing here, anyhow."

She laughed. "But it's a risk, isn't it? What if the old owner took the recipe with him when he sold it to the Australians?"

"It's a chance we'll have to take."

"Living on the edge," she replied and then resisted the urge to immediately smack herself in the forehead. To say she was rusty at flirtatious banter was a vast understatement.

From behind the bar, the bartender who'd waited on them yesterday waved in recognition, and Sam waved back before ducking his head.

"Um, at the risk of sounding like an idiot who doesn't know when to stop putting himself out there," Sam said, "would you care to join me for a bite?"

"I would love to." The words were out of her mouth before she could censor herself, because the fact was, she *would* love to. She wanted to enjoy a meal with this deep-voiced, charmingly hesitant, beautiful man. She wanted to forget for a little while what she was going through and remember instead what it felt like to be a woman. She wanted to be looked at the way he was looking at her now.

He exhaled dramatically. "Phew. I was afraid you were going to say no and I'd have to sit at my own table, awkwardly pretending I wouldn't rather be with you." He beckoned to the bartender, who grabbed two menus and began to make his way over to them.

"I'm really sorry I didn't call," she said.

"And I'll just pretend I wasn't checking my phone every few minutes like a middle schooler with a crush," he said, and then arched an eyebrow at her as the bartender showed them to a table in the corner. Julia was glad for the dim lighting, because she was certain she was blushing furiously.

"What can I get you two?" the bartender asked.

Julia ordered a kir royale, and Sam shrugged and asked for the same. As the bartender hurried off, Julia looked back at Sam. "I really am sorry. I'm in kind of a complicated situation."

"Ah." Sam leaned back. "I'm sorry. I know you mentioned a daughter, but are you also here in Paris with a boyfriend or a husband, or . . . ?"

"No," Julia said instantly. "I haven't had either one of those things in a very long time."

"Me neither," Sam said, then laughed and amended, "A girlfriend or wife, I mean."

Julia didn't know why that made her feel so much better. "My daughter's got this flirtation going with a cute French waiter, so . . ."

"She's twenty-three, you said?" Sam laughed. "God, it's so easy when you're young, isn't it? Not so much when you're fifty-five."

"Forty-nine," Julia said, raising her hand.

"Fortunately, we don't look a day over thirty," Sam said, and then they both burst out laughing.

"These days," Julia said as the bartender delivered their drinks and then slipped away, "I feel every one of those years. But I wouldn't change it for the world. The chance to have had all this time, you know?"

She felt instantly silly for being so sappy, but Sam was nodding vehemently. "I know exactly what you mean. When I was in my twenties, I thought getting older would be the worst thing that could happen to me. Turns out, though, that along with giving me all these laugh lines, it also made me into a different kind of person. I was not the most mature or self-aware twentysomething."

She laughed. "I don't think anyone is supposed to be mature or self-aware in their twenties." She took a sip of her wine. "And for the record, I like your laugh lines." She swallowed hard; had she gone too far?

But his face softened and his gaze held hers for a long moment. "And I like everything about you so far, Julia."

"You don't even know me yet."

"But I'd like to," Sam said. The bartender returned to take their food orders—fish and chips for both of them, and a bottle of wine to share—and as he walked away, Sam added, "I hope that's not too forward."

"No," Julia said, looking into his honey-gold eyes, and she was struck again with a sudden sense of familiarity that disappeared before she could put a finger on it. "So, Sam, what brings you to Paris? You mentioned work?"

He shifted in his seat and took a long sip of his kir royale. "Yeah. I, um, have a work thing this week a little bit northwest of Paris, but I'm staying in the city. How about you? What do you do?"

"I am—was—in advertising for a local paper back home."

"Was?" he asked, tilting his head to the side.

"I'm taking a hiatus." She was almost relieved that he'd been vague about his job, because it allowed her to do the same. "So where in the States are you from?"

"Born and raised in Cleveland," he said with a smile, "but I've been in Los Angeles the past thirty years or so. You?"

She shook her head in disbelief. "I'm from the Columbus area. Worthington."

He stared at her. "My mom was from twenty minutes away in Bexley."

"You're kidding me."

"What are the odds?"

The bartender hurried out then with two steaming baskets of fish and chips balanced on a tray with a bottle of white wine, two glasses, a bottle of ketchup, and a bottle of malt vinegar. In the moment it took him to get the food served and to open the wine for them, Julia couldn't stop staring at Sam, and it seemed that he, too, was just as powerless to look away.

"Hey," he said after they'd both thanked the bartender and he'd left them alone, "after we eat, is there any chance you might like to walk around with me for a bit? Maybe get a coffee or something?"

Julia hesitated, the *yes* she wanted to say caught in her throat.

"Please?" Sam added after she'd been quiet for too long, his forehead creasing beneath the brim of his cap. "There's no place in the world like Paris in the moonlight. It's been a really long time since I've had the chance to share that with someone."

"Okay," Julia said, her heart forcing the word out of her mouth before she could stop it.

Sam grinned at her. "Yeah?"

"Yeah." She smiled back, and for a moment, as she stared into the eyes of someone she wished she'd met decades ago, she could imagine that she was someone whose best days lay ahead of her rather than behind.

CHAPTER EIGHTEEN

Russ felt a bit like he was watching a reality show unfold. The woman who'd shown Jackson Quick how to mix pastis the other day seemed to have absolutely no idea that she was dining with a rock star.

He'd heard her call him "Sam" a few times, and after Russ had delivered their food, he'd heard the woman ask what brought Jackson to Paris. It would be almost funny if it wasn't sort of sad. Russ supposed that a man like Jackson probably couldn't be himself very often, for fear of people wanting to be around him for all the wrong reasons. But with this woman, who didn't seem to have any idea who Jackson was, he seemed loose and relaxed, and Russ had caught him gazing at the woman with stars in his eyes more than once.

It was all very sweet, except for the fact that eventually the woman would figure out the truth. And then, would she feel betrayed? Or would she understand why Jackson Quick might want someone to see him for the man he was rather than for the fame he'd achieved?

Anyhow, it wasn't Russ's business. If there was one thing he knew about owning a bar in this city, it was that you had to let people do their own thing and, at times, make their own mistakes. He'd sure made plenty of his own.

As the clock ticked past 8 p.m., the bar was filling up. Four American girls had come in a little while ago, and Benji—who still hadn't noticed that the man eating at the corner table was actually a rock star—was in his usual flirt-with-tourists mode, which meant that Russ and Rob were mostly on their own behind the bar. Aside from checking on Jackson Quick and his date now and then, Russ was in his own world, pouring beers and shaking martinis and trying not to think about the fact that Shelby had said she might come back after spending the day with her friends.

He couldn't figure out what it was about her that had him turned so inside out. She was beautiful, yes, though she didn't seem to realize it. And she had a vulnerability that made him want to wrap his arms around her and protect her from the world. But he'd met plenty of beautiful, vulnerable girls before—hell, he worked in a bar—and he hadn't felt that way about any of them.

But then, as he delivered the check to Jackson Quick's table around eight thirty, interrupting a moment when the rock star and the woman were gazing into each other's eyes, he had a realization.

Shelby had looked at him like that, too. She had from the very first moment she'd walked into the bar, and it wasn't because she was hoping for free drinks or that she wanted to sleep with an Australian bartender, which were the two reasons women usually looked at him that way. No, he had a feeling that she was seeing him beneath the surface, and he'd liked the version of himself he'd seen reflected in her eyes.

But what did that matter? Maybe she saw who he was, but she was also in the midst of a divorce, and on top of that, she was only in Paris for a few days. So why was he still thinking about her?

He ran Jackson Quick's credit card and delivered the card and receipt back to the table, and a few minutes later, he waved to Jackson as he and the woman headed for the door of the restaurant. Jackson nodded back and held the door open for the woman, but she paused to let someone else in before she exited, and when Russ looked up quickly, he almost dropped the glass he was drying. It was Shelby entering the bar by herself, her eyes scanning the room until they locked on his. She smiled slowly, and he couldn't stop himself from grinning back like a madman.

"You came," he said as she sidled up to the bar and leaned in. She was wearing a pale pink dress that fell to her calves and a pair of flat shoes, her hair long and loose.

"I told you I would try to."

He caught a whiff of her perfume—something with jasmine in it—as she closed the distance between them, propping herself on the bar momentarily to land a peck on his cheek.

"How was the Champs-Élysées?" he asked.

"Expensive," she said with a smile. "Plus, I found myself thinking the whole time that I wished I was here instead."

"Oh, yeah?" Russ raised an eyebrow in surprise.

"So I was wondering if there's any way you can go to dinner with me."

Russ glanced around, feeling a stab of regret. "I don't usually leave early."

"Right, of course, I didn't mean . . ." She hesitated and then added in a spill of words, "It's just, I don't know what this is. I don't know why I can't stop thinking about you. I'm not in a place to start anything new, and no one would mistake me for anything but a total mess right now. But . . . that didn't seem to scare you away."

"Maybe I like messy."

Shelby blinked, like the words had hit her hard. "That's good, because maybe that's who I am—not just now, but all the time. I'm not perfect. I never will be. But maybe that's okay, too. Maybe it's time to stop trying to become what everyone else wants me to be. Maybe I'm done with making the decisions everyone else wants me to make. Maybe it's time *I* choose."

Russ stared at her. He couldn't remember the last time someone had said something so starkly honest to him.

"Right," he said, setting down his towel and scanning the bar for Benji, who was now seated at the table of American blondes. "Would you hold on a second? I'll be right back."

"Sure."

Shelby watched him as he headed over to tap Benji on the shoulder. "Hey, mate," he said when Benji looked up at him in surprise. "The bar's all yours tonight. I have something I need to do."

"Now, wait a minute," Benji said, standing, and from the way he wobbled on his feet, it was clear that he'd not just been sitting with the girls but had also been drinking with them. His eyes were glassy and unfocused. "You didn't tell me you needed time off tonight."

"We're partners, Benji, remember? I cover for you most nights of the week."

"I never miss a night of work!" Benji snapped back.

"Doesn't mean you're here doing anything useful. You're always off drinking at a table with tourists, leaving me to run the place."

Benji glanced over his shoulder to see if the girls were listening, but they were absorbed in conversation. "Why are you trying to cock-block me?"

"I'm not." Russ was hit with a wave of exhaustion. "Look, mate, I'm going, whether you like it or not. Rob is fine behind the bar for now, but if things get busier, you should go help him pour drinks, all right?"

"Now you're talking to me like I'm a guest in my own bar?" Benji squared his shoulders and glared at Russ like he wanted to fight him. "Who do you think you are?"

Russ stared at him for a minute, at the anger and the alcohol burning in his expression, and he tried to remember the last time he'd actually felt like they were friends, rather than just two men who happened to own a bar together. There had once been a time when they'd laughed together, confided in each other, even lived together as ill-matched roommates as they'd embraced the adventure of moving to Paris to start a new life.

But those days had disappeared long ago, and Russ hadn't realized until that moment how sad he was to think that their friendship felt entirely behind them now, too. "I think I'm a man who wants more out of his life," he said. "And I think I'm a man who's done with picking up the slack for a friend who checked out a long time ago."

Benji seemed to take a few extra beats to process the words before his face darkened. "You don't want to run a bar with me anymore, mate, you just have to say the word."

Russ sighed. "I think maybe I don't, Benji. And I owe you a conversation about that. But let's save it for tomorrow when we're both sober and thinking with clear heads, okay?"

Benji scoffed. "You're too busy with some slag to talk to me now?"

"Careful, Benji." Russ swallowed down his anger. "All I'm saying is there's got to be a better way to live life than being trapped in the same useless cycle for fifteen years." And with that, as Benji gaped at him, Russ moved back to the bar, where he offered his arm to Shelby. "Can I take you to dinner?" he asked.

"You sure about this?" she replied. "I've just made possibly the worst romantic speech of all time. Plus, your friend doesn't look too happy."

Across the bar, Benji was glaring at him.

"Shelby," Russ said, "I've never been more sure of anything in my life."

Kayla walked through the Esplanade Ben Gourion quickly, cursing her lousy luck.

She'd only been on the schedule until four today, and it had been her plan to settle by the Seine as soon as her shift ended to wait for Nadim. The conversation with her father last night had made her long to speak with someone who hadn't seemed to judge her.

But her coworker had called in sick, and Kayla hadn't had a choice about staying until the next shift clocked in at eight thirty. By the time she hurried out of the train station, it was well past nine and the sun had fully set, which meant that Nadim had lost the light he probably needed to paint by. She was far more disappointed than she should have been, considering that she barely knew him.

She glanced up at the Eiffel Tower, which glowed with promise, and she felt a stab of despair. She shouldn't be here. How had the search for identity taken her across an ocean to the home of a father who had never cared about her—and who was apparently not such a great guy?

She was just about to head back to her tiny apartment for another lonely night when she heard a deep voice call out, "Kayla, wait." Startled, she turned.

"Nadim?" she said as he emerged from the shadows, holding his folded easel under one arm, a bag slung over his other shoulder. He was smiling at her, but his open expression turned to one of concern as he joined her in a pool of light cast by a streetlamp and saw her distress.

"Kayla? What is it? Are you all right?" He reached for her, touching her lightly on the arm, which sent a shiver through her.

"I . . ." She didn't know what to say. How could she tell him that she was feeling devastated because she thought she'd missed him?

"Kayla?" he prompted, moving closer, his brown eyes deep with concern.

"Yeah. I mean . . . yeah." She forced a smile. "I'm fine."

He studied her for a moment. "How did it go with your father last night?"

How had he read her so clearly? Her shoulders slumped. "He just said some things I didn't agree with," she mumbled.

"What did he say?"

"He's kind of a jerk, actually. He said . . ." She trailed off. "He said I should go back to where I came from, basically. That immigrants like me are destroying the fabric of France."

Nadim sighed. "Oh, Kayla. I'm very sorry. I'm afraid there are many here who feel that way about immigration. But to say such a thing to his own daughter . . ."

"It was just . . . he was so unkind and condescending about it," she said miserably. "You know what's bothering me most, though? The fact that I still feel this desperation to know him, despite everything. Like, what's wrong with me that I want a relationship with a father who very clearly doesn't want me here?" She felt foolish and vulnerable the moment the words were out of her mouth. Why was she telling him all of this?

But Nadim didn't seem to be judging her. In fact, he stepped even closer, close enough to kiss. "There's nothing wrong with you," he said. "It is only human to want to know one of the people who gave you life, I think."

"Even if that person isn't all that great?" She couldn't bring herself to look up and read the expression on his face.

"Even then," he said. "I think, though, that when people close their minds, it's often due to a lack of knowledge. Maybe in getting to know him better, you can introduce him to a different point of view." He touched her chin lightly, tilting her face up. His brown eyes, she noticed for the first time, were flecked with green. "Kayla?" Nadim said after a moment. "I'm afraid I have to head home now; my parents are expecting me."

"Oh, right," she said, trying not to sound as crushed as she felt.

"There's someplace I'd like to show you, though," he said. "Do you have time to meet me tomorrow?"

Her heart skipped; was he asking her out? "I have to work a double, but I'm off on Friday. Would that work?"

"Sure. Would you meet me at this address?" He pulled a pencil from his bag and scribbled down a place in the fifth arrondissement on the back of a receipt, handing the slip of paper over to her. "Say eleven a.m.? I'll take the afternoon off."

Kayla slid the piece of paper into her pocket, butterflies fluttering in her stomach. "Yeah, okay, I'll be there," she said, trying to sound more confident than she felt.

"Good." Nadim took a step closer. "I look forward to seeing you again. And, Kayla?"

"Yeah?"

"If your father can't see what a gift you are," Nadim said, holding her gaze, "that's his failing, not yours. Don't forget that."

Jackson knew, as he and Julia strolled toward the Seine, that he'd made a huge mistake in not telling her who he really was.

After all, if she was a fan, she would have recognized him already. So maybe it wouldn't matter. Maybe he could tell her that he was a musician named Jackson Quick, and she'd simply shrug. But the problem was that he'd lied to her; how could he explain that?

"I don't know why I didn't come back to Paris sooner," she said, interrupting his guilty thoughts as they strolled. He wanted to reach for her hand, but he didn't want to be too forward. He'd never felt this nervous with a woman before.

He tilted his head and looked at her, waiting for her to go on. She looked up at him with a sad smile.

"This was the place where I think I was the best version of myself," she said. "When I came back to the States, I told myself I'd be back all the time. I imagined an adulthood full of strolls along the Seine with my future husband and pushing boats in the fountains with my future child. And then, the years passed and life happened, and I never returned."

"It was the same for me. This was the last place I felt like myself before—" He cut himself off abruptly before he said too much.

"Before what?" Julia asked with a smile.

He swallowed hard. "Just before. Before I grew up. Before life got in the way."

She nodded. "I wish I'd come back earlier."

"But maybe we can make a promise to ourselves," he said. She looked up at him. "A promise that we'll come back again soon. That we won't waste the years we have left. That we'll try to find those versions of ourselves again."

Julia looked away, but before she did, he could have sworn he'd seen tears in her eyes. "What if there isn't time?"

"There's always time."

"Not always."

He was about to ask what she meant, but they had reached the river, and she grabbed his hand as she looked over at Notre Dame glowing across the water. "When I lived here, I used to walk by

Notre Dame every night and think about everything it had survived. I mean, it's been here for more than seven hundred years, and it's just as solid as it was in the thirteenth century."

Jackson looked down at her hand holding his and intertwined his fingers with hers. He waited for her to pull away, but to his relief, she instead looked him in the eye and then gently squeezed his hand. "When the fire happened in 2019, I was afraid it would collapse," he said. "And then, when the spire came down . . ."

Julia shuddered. "It would have been an unimaginable loss. There's something about knowing that it has borne witness to history—and that it still keeps watch over the city—that makes me feel like nothing is ever gone, not really." She went silent for a few seconds and then added, "If the places that have held us remain, then a piece of us is always here, too, isn't it?"

"I like that thought. That we leave a piece of ourselves wherever we go."

"Would you . . . walk with me to Notre Dame?" She sounded hesitant.

"Of course." They crossed the short pedestrian bridge just ahead of them and strolled to the front of the grand cathedral, still holding hands. Jackson felt as giddy and nervous as he had a lifetime ago when he'd gone on his very first date at the age of fifteen. How could it be that he was fifty-five now and had never felt that blend of butterflies and happiness again until now?

"I wish," Julia said, "that we could stay longer, too."

"We can stay as long as you want."

She smiled and looked up at him. "No, I mean, on this earth. How do we only get such a small number of years? Our lives are so insignificant in the grand scheme of things, aren't they?"

"Not if you leave something behind that matters."

"Like what?"

"I don't know. Like art that outlives you, maybe."

She squeezed his hand again. "What kind of art would you make?"

"Honestly? I've always wanted to write songs." He couldn't believe he'd admitted it aloud—not only because it skirted dangerously close to revealing who he really was, but because he'd never said that to a soul. Since he'd become famous, he'd always sung words and melodies written by other people, and the few times he'd tried to share things he'd worked on, Cash had dismissed him. But maybe Julia was right. Maybe it was time to leave a piece of himself behind in the world, even if no one listened, even if it didn't sell records.

"Songs?" Julia smiled. "Are you a musician?"

It was his chance to come clean, but he chickened out. "I, um, dabble."

"That's amazing. I've always wished I had musical talent, but I can't carry a tune."

"But you've raised a child, haven't you? Piper, you said? Your daughter is the future in a way that a song could never be."

Her eyes filled. "Do you have kids?"

"No, I don't." It was one of his many regrets; he thought he might have been a good father, but it was too late now to know. Sure, he could pull a Mick Jagger or a Billy Joel and get himself a younger girlfriend and become a father anytime. But he couldn't see that happening. Parenthood was a ship that had sailed long ago, when he wasn't looking because he was too busy worrying about his career. "I wish I did, though," he said honestly. "Tell me about Piper."

"She's incredible. She's getting her master's in English, and she's one of the smartest, kindest people you'll ever meet. I know parents are supposed to feel that way about their kids, but she really is something special."

"That's something to be proud of," he said. "Having raised a good person."

"Thanks." She looked up at the cathedral for a moment and then looked back at him. "So what would you write a song about?"

"I would write a song about you," he said before he could think it through, and then he immediately closed his eyes, mortified. "I'm sorry. That was too much."

"No." Julia was staring at him when he opened his eyes again. "That might be the nicest thing anyone has ever said to me. What would your song say?"

He hesitated, lyrics tumbling over themselves in his head. He sang to her softly before he could stop himself. "*I wish I could tell you what I'm starting to feel. That the way you inspire me is so new and so real. I wish you knew how perfect you look in this light. That as long as I breathe, I won't forget tonight.*"

He stopped, abruptly, because there were tears in her eyes. "That bad?" he asked.

"No. That was the most beautiful thing I've ever heard. You just wrote that? Just now?"

"It wasn't that good. The meter wasn't even right."

"It was incredible," she whispered.

His heart thudding, he reached down and touched her cheek and then her chin, aching to kiss her. Summoning his courage, he slowly lowered his lips to hers, and when she responded, moving so that her body was tucked against his, he let go of her hand and pulled her close to him, cradling her head gently.

When he finally pulled away, she looked as dazed as he felt. "I hope that was okay," he said.

"I've never been kissed like that, Sam."

Hearing the false name he had given her jolted him out of the moment. If he was going to bare his soul to this woman, he needed to go all in, didn't he? "Julia, there's something I need to tell you."

Something that looked like regret flitted across her face. "There's something I need to tell you, too." But just then, her phone rang, and as she fumbled in her purse for it, the moment was over. "My daughter," she explained before answering the call. He took a polite step back, not wanting to intrude. "I'm fine," she said into the phone. "No, I just went out to dinner. Why are you back so early?" She waited for a reply and then said, "Honey, you don't need to worry about me." Another pause and then she said, "I know. I know. I'll come back now, okay?"

Jackson's heart sank, and he waited as she said her goodbyes to her daughter. There was so much more that he wanted—no, *needed*—to say to her. "Everything okay?" he asked after she'd hung up.

"Yeah. I—I didn't realize how late it had gotten. I should get back."

He nodded. He wanted to beg her to stay, to walk around Paris with him until the sun came up, to let him kiss her again because it made him want to write a thousand more songs about her. But she was already moving away from him, back toward the bridge they'd crossed over to get here. "I'll walk you to your hotel," he said.

Hand in hand, they headed back over the Seine and turned right, strolling along the river. The lights of Paris glowed around them, magical and warm. "I'm sorry," she said after a moment. "It's just that this trip is supposed to be about Piper and me spending time together. And I could hear it in her voice; she was worried about me."

"I'm a bad influence, I guess," he joked. He took a deep breath and said, "Can I take you out tomorrow night?"

"I—I don't know if that's a good idea."

He glanced down at her, thrown. "I was just kidding about being a bad influence," he said, attempting levity. "I promise, my intentions are honorable."

"I know. I just—" She stopped abruptly, whatever she was about to say lost. "The thing is, what if this can never go further than this? What if this week was all we had? Would you still want to see me again?"

"Yes," he said, confused. "Unless you really do have some husband or boyfriend at home . . ."

"I don't," she said immediately. "It's just . . . this isn't real life."

"What do you mean?"

She bit her lip and looked away.

"How about Friday?" he asked after a moment, realizing a beat later that obviously he couldn't take her out on Friday; that was the night of his concert. He'd nearly forgotten that it was why he was in Paris.

She smiled. "Actually, my daughter is taking me to a concert on Friday."

He nearly tripped over his own two feet. "A . . . concert?"

"Yeah, Jackson Quick. Remember him from the nineties?"

He was so thrown, he didn't know what to say. "And are you . . . a Jackson Quick fan?" Had she known who he was all along? Was this some sort of a game?

"Piper *thinks* I was. She planned this whole trip around the concert, thinking that he'd been my big crush in high school."

"But . . . he wasn't?"

"Nope. I was a big Jon Bon Jovi fan. I don't know how Piper

mixed it up. But it's not like I can tell her now. She'd be so disappointed. I mean, I know 'City of Light,' of course. But beyond that, I couldn't tell you anything about the guy."

This was too strange. Now was the time to tell her, of course, to say, *Speaking of Jackson Quick, I have a funny story for you.* But again, he couldn't bring himself to do it. "Tomorrow, then," he said. "Whenever you can fit me in. I know you're here with your daughter, but even if it's a half hour for coffee at four in the morning . . ."

She smiled and then seemed to consider his request. "I have dinner plans with Piper. But what about a drink beforehand? At Le Maison Grog, five o'clock?"

"I'll be there," he said instantly.

"This is me," she said, stopping in front of a hotel with wooden, glass-paneled doors and light spilling out from inside. "Sam, I don't know how to thank you. Tonight was . . . magic."

"It was," he agreed. And then he leaned in and kissed her again, softly, tenderly, and they stayed that way for a long moment before she pulled away.

"I have to go." Were her eyes full of regret, or was that his imagination?

"I'll see you tomorrow," he said.

And with one last nod, she disappeared into the hotel, taking with her the evening's last opportunity for truth.

CHAPTER NINETEEN

When Russ awoke the next morning, Shelby was lying beside him, her hand on his bare chest, gazing up at him.

"Hey," she said with a smile, running her fingertips along his collarbone, which sent shivers coursing through him.

"Good morning." He smiled at her. "How long have you been awake?"

"Not long," she said. "Last night was amazing, Russ."

He grinned. "It was."

After she'd shown up at the bar, he'd taken her to dinner at Le Balzar, where they'd shared a Comté cheese soufflé and a bottle of Côtes du Rhône before having beef bourguignon and roasted chicken for dinner. They'd talked for hours, lingering over coffees and a shared tarte Tatin before finally strolling several blocks back to his place, where they'd talked for an hour more, in between increasingly deep kisses, and, finally, fallen into his bed together. He'd taken his time with her, gently undressing her and pausing several times along the way to make sure she was all right. Afterward, she'd fallen asleep in his arms, a smile across her face.

Now he watched her pull on the shirt he'd worn last night, which had been discarded on the floor. She smiled at him again and then padded into the bathroom, grabbing her purse and her dress and bra along the way. When she emerged five minutes later, she was dressed and had fixed her mussed hair and applied some lipstick. But there was something else different about her, too.

"I have to go," she said, her voice flat.

It was then that he noticed she was clutching her cell phone, her hand so tight around it that her knuckles were white. "Everything okay?" Maybe something had happened to one of her friends; when she'd called them last night to tell them she wouldn't be back to the hotel until morning, they had been out at a bar somewhere doing shots with guys they'd just met, and Russ had felt a ripple of concern. "Did your friends get back safely?"

"What?" She looked confused. "Oh, I mean, I don't know, but probably. I doubt they're awake yet."

Russ glanced at the clock. It was only eight in the morning. "Are you sure you have to go so soon?"

She nodded, glancing at her phone again. He tried not to notice how stiff her posture had become and how she was already inching toward the door. Maybe she was worrying that this hadn't meant anything to him.

He hurried to say, "Shelby, I'd love to take you to dinner again tonight if you're around."

Now she looked physically pained. "That's really sweet. I'll call you, okay?"

"Yeah, sure." Russ felt unsettled as she crossed the room and planted a quick kiss on his lips. He wasn't sure what else to say. "I'll see you later, then."

Shelby hesitated a second before smiling at him. "Right. See you later."

And then she was gone, the door to his apartment clicking closed behind her. After a moment, he pulled on his jeans and moved to the window. When she emerged from his building, hurrying away without a glance back, she was already on her phone, listening with a stricken look on her face, and Russ had the terrible, sinking feeling that whatever had happened between them last night was already lost.

After a moment, he turned away, ready to face the day—and his growing certainty that whatever happened with Shelby, he needed to make some changes in his life. It was time to get out of the rut. It was time to sell his share of the bar.

Jackson had been up half the night, his guitar in his hands, a notebook beside him, as he coaxed out melodies that matched the words that were suddenly pouring out of him. It was like someone had unlocked a vault, and every thought he'd had about love over the past several decades had all come tumbling out at once in a jumble of lyrics.

But none of them were *good*. At least they weren't good in the same way that Henry McGee's lyrics in "City of Light" were, and Jackson should know, considering how many times that song had come out of his mouth.

The notebook he'd filled overnight was, of course, about Julia. It didn't make sense how much he felt for someone he hardly knew yet, and many of the words he'd written were about that.

How can I feel what I'm feeling so far
When there hasn't been time to know who you are?
How can I feel what I'm feeling for you?
And is it too much to hope you feel it, too?

Everything he wrote filled him with dread, though. He was writing love songs—dozens of them, if the filled pages were any indication—for a woman who didn't even know his real name.

In the Hollywood version of this, she'd learn who he really was and they'd have a good laugh about it and live happily ever after. But he knew that the real-life version was more complicated. She didn't seem like a woman who'd be all that impressed by fame. Her daughter was clearly the center of her life, and who knew if there was room in it for a normal guy like Sam, never mind a one-time rock star like Jackson?

If I told you the truth, would you turn away?
Would you go or would you stay to hear what I might say?
Would you see all the reasons that drove one deception?
Would you listen to me and make an exception?

He sighed and pushed the notebook to the side, his head a jumbled mess of lyrics and lies. He wanted to sing to her. He wanted to explain everything. He wanted to use his words and his music to set everything right.

But the more he wrote, the more tangled it all became for him. Finally, just past nine in the morning, he made a decision. He picked up his phone and dialed a number he'd just added a few days earlier. Henry McGee answered on the third ring.

"It's Jackson Quick," he said. "Am I catching you at a bad time, Mr. McGee?"

"Please, it's Henry." The songwriter's warm voice came through the line. "And I have a few minutes. I'm just having coffee with my granddaughter, Melanie, before I go see Celeste."

"The woman you wrote 'City of Light' for."

"Yes. She hasn't remembered me yet, but there are glimmers. And where there are glimmers, there is hope."

His words, delivered so easily, sounded like song lyrics, and Jackson was momentarily filled with even more doubt. If Henry could effortlessly put such delicate thoughts into such beautiful phrasing, what was Jackson even doing? Maybe he should leave the songwriting to the professionals.

"Is there something you need, son?" Henry asked after a moment, and Jackson realized that he'd been so caught up in his own thoughts, he hadn't said a word.

"Oh, yes, sir," Jackson said. "I—I'm trying to write a song, and I was wondering whether you might have the time to sit down with me for a few minutes this afternoon. The thing is, I'm not sure how to make any of it sound the way I want it to, and, well, it's very important to me to get this right." He felt like a fool admitting it, but Henry's response was warm and immediate.

"A song? Why, that's wonderful. I always thought you should write your own music. Did your label discourage you from doing so?"

"I can't blame them. The songs I brought to them at the beginning weren't very good."

"But no one can write great songs until they've known great love," Henry said. "That's what I think, anyhow. Have you known great love, Jackson?"

"Not yet," Jackson admitted, feeling pathetic. All these years of living, and it was something he'd never found. "But there's a woman here, in Paris, who's different from anyone I've ever met before, and these words are pouring out of me, and I don't know if they're any good, or if they're terrible, or . . ." He trailed off, embarrassed.

Henry chuckled, but the sound was warm rather than unkind. "My favorite part of a love story. The beginning."

"I'm not sure it will turn out to be a love story."

"Ah, but Jackson, it already is. A love doesn't have to end in happily ever after in order to change your life forever. But let's hear what you have, shall we? I could meet with you in a few hours, after I've had a chance to visit with Celeste. Would that be all right?"

Jackson thanked him profusely, and after they'd spent a few minutes exchanging details and agreeing to meet at Henry's granddaughter's apartment at 1 p.m.—he hung up, put his guitar to the side, and got up to take a quick shower before the car arrived to take him to sound check at the arena.

Henry hung up with the rock star, shaking his head to himself. Something about Paris brought love to the surface, made people open their hearts in ways they never had before, made lovers out of strangers. That such a thing was happening for the first time for a musician in his fifties who'd probably had every romantic opportunity in the world? Well, that was no small feat.

"Did you just invite Jackson Quick to my apartment?" Melanie asked as she came back into the kitchen. She had drifted away while he'd chatted on the phone to give him some privacy, but it was clear she'd heard at least part of his conversation.

"I'm sorry, is that not all right?" Henry asked, worried. "I should have asked you first. I can call him back."

"No," Melanie said, looking flustered. Some color had risen to her cheeks. "It's just, well, I've never had a rock star in my apartment."

Henry gave her a look. "He's just a person, like you and me."

"Easy for you to say. You didn't have a crush on him in the nineties."

Henry laughed. "You never told me that. I would have tried to use my connections to introduce you—though, admittedly, my connections never amounted to much."

"I would have died of embarrassment, anyhow. In fact, I might just die of embarrassment today to have him here. If I lose the ability to string words together, just cover for me, okay?"

He laughed. "You're going to be fine. You're sure it's all right, though? I could arrange to meet him at a restaurant, if you'd prefer."

"No. My home is your home, Grandpa Henry. I mean that. Invite all the rock stars you want." She took a step forward to kiss him on the cheek. "Now, go see Celeste. I know you've been itching to get over there."

He hesitated. There was a heaviness to her, a strain in her voice. "Melanie? Are you all right?"

"Just fine. Now go."

"Thank you, sweetheart," he said, still uncertain about leaving her but desperate to get to Celeste. "I'll see you in a few hours."

Twenty minutes later, he was walking through the door of Celeste's assisted-living home. The receptionist buzzed him in with a smile, and he traced the now-familiar path to room 0-B. He knocked, and when she opened the door, her blue eyes blazing, he felt breathless for a moment, just like he always had all those years ago whenever he'd seen her.

"Do I know you?" Celeste asked in French, staring at him.

His heart broke for the hundredth time since he'd returned to Paris. "You did once," he replied in English. "And I'm determined that you will again. May I come in?"

Slowly, her eyes searching his face, she moved aside, and Henry stepped over the threshold.

Shelby sipped her latte, trying very hard to pretend to herself that she hadn't just had the best sex of her life the night before, because that complicated everything.

"So?" Corinne said, staring at her across their table at the café down the block from their hotel. "How did it go with the bartender?"

Vanessa was focused on her, too, and Shelby squirmed under the intensity of their gazes.

"Um, good," she said.

"'Um, good'?" Corinne repeated with a laugh. "Shelb, you've got to give us more than that. This is your divorce party! Did you get laid?"

It sounded so crass when she said it like that. "Yeah, I slept with Russ," she said, pushing away thoughts of his body pressed against her, his lips on her skin. But it was just a vacation fling, wasn't it? What did it matter that in the hours before he'd taken her to bed, he'd listened to her with such intensity and tenderness that she'd wanted to cry? That he hadn't judged her even when she'd told him about her infertility and her years of ups and downs with Brandon? That he'd kissed her like she was a treasure to be valued, not a conquest to be won? It had been perfect, but she'd be insane to think that there was any future with him.

"I *knew* it!" Corinne crowed, leaning in to fist-bump Shelby across the table. "Girl, you have to tell us *everything*."

Shelby glanced at Vanessa, then back to Corinne, who was staring at her with wide eyes. "It was amazing, actually. We talked for hours and then we . . ." She trailed off, feeling heat rise to her cheeks.

"So why do you look like you're about to cry?" Vanessa asked gently.

Corinne cut Vanessa a sharp glance. "She doesn't look like that," Corinne snapped. "Do you, Shelby? You're just tired. From a night of amazing sex."

"Right," Shelby agreed, glancing at Vanessa, whose brow was creased with concern.

"Shelby?" Vanessa prompted, and then, to Shelby's embarrassment, big fat teardrops were running down her face.

The waiter arrived with their breakfast order then: avocado toast for Vanessa; granola and yogurt for Corinne; and a croissant with jam for Shelby, who had just lost her appetite. The waiter politely pretended not to see her heaving sobs before hurrying away. Vanessa moved over to rub Shelby's back.

"What is it, Shelb?" Vanessa asked, peering at her with concern.

Shelby hesitated. They were going to kill her. "Brandon," she said in a near-whisper, because maybe if she said it quietly, it wouldn't land as hard.

"Brandon?" Vanessa was staring at her. "I'm sorry, I could have sworn you just spoke the name we agreed never to say again."

"Shelby, sweetie, we know he hurt you," Corinne said. "But we're here to forget about him, right?"

"And you just slept with the hottest Australian in Paris," Vanessa said. "Why are we talking about Brandon?"

"He called me," Shelby blurted out.

Vanessa and Corinne exchanged looks.

"What could that bastard possibly have to say to—" Vanessa said.

"He doesn't want to get divorced," Shelby interrupted. "He said he'd made a mistake. He said he's still in love with me."

The noise of traffic on the road beside the café seemed very loud in the stunned silence that followed.

"I'm sorry," Vanessa said, rubbing her temples. "Brandon is still in love with you?"

Shelby sniffled. "That's what he said."

"And when exactly did he say this?" Vanessa asked.

"The night before last. When we were at that bar near Montmartre."

"That's the call you took outside while we were doing shots," Corinne said, and Shelby nodded miserably. "Before you vanished on us."

"I didn't tell you because I didn't think he was serious." Shelby quickly recapped the conversation about Brandon's infertility and his breakup with his rebound while the other two women gaped at her. "He said he realized he was wrong and that he wants to try again with me."

"And you believed him?" Vanessa asked.

"Honestly? Not really. I mean, it's too little, too late, right? And besides, I figured he was just lonely after his breakup." Shelby's skin still crawled at the thought of him with someone else. "I—I think it's why I went to see Russ yesterday. I needed to prove to myself that I'd moved on." She closed her eyes and let a surge of guilt wash over her. She had dragged Russ into this mess with her, and that wasn't fair. "I figured I wouldn't hear from Brandon again, honestly, until I saw him at the divorce hearing next week. But . . . I woke up this morning to four voicemails from him."

The two other women exchanged glances again. "What did he say?" Corinne asked.

"The first three messages were all about how much he loved me and how he couldn't stand to lose me."

"And the fourth?" Corinne prompted.

"The fourth," Shelby said slowly, still not believing it, "was him telling me that he's on his way to Paris."

The other women stared at her. "He's coming to Paris?" Corinne repeated.

"I tried calling him back." Shelby snuck a look at their shocked expressions and then dropped her gaze again. "But his phone's off. It went right to voicemail. I—I think he's already on a flight."

"What are you going to do?" Vanessa asked.

"I don't know."

Corinne put a hand on Shelby's arm. "Do you still love him?"

"I . . ." Shelby exhaled and looked at her lap. "Yeah. I think maybe I do."

"But he hurt you," Vanessa reminded her.

"I know," Shelby said.

"But now that he's changed his mind, it's okay that he threw in the towel on your marriage?" Vanessa's tone was gentle but firm. "It's okay that he made you feel like the baby thing was all your fault? It's okay that he got himself a new girlfriend before you were even divorced?"

"No," Shelby said, swallowing the lump in her throat. "But he really sounded sorry. He even said he's started seeing a therapist."

Corinne snorted, and Vanessa gave her a warning look.

"All that matters is how *you* feel," Vanessa said quickly. "*Not* how Brandon feels or whether or not he's seeing a therapist for two seconds to impress you."

"Is he coming to our hotel when he gets here?" Corinne asked.

"I didn't tell him where we were staying."

"Um, I may have," Corinne said in a small voice.

Shelby blinked at her. "You what?"

Corinne hung her head. "When he couldn't reach you last night, he called me to make sure you were okay. I, um, told him where to find us. I thought he was going to send flowers or something, not get on a plane."

Shelby put her head in her hands as Vanessa hissed at Corinne that she should have stayed out of it.

"So, what are you going to do?" Corinne asked after a moment.

Shelby sighed. She could still smell Russ's cologne on her, could still feel his hands on her body. Was it the magic of being with someone new? Or was it the way things were supposed to feel when a man's motives were pure and true?

Things with Brandon were so tangled, and she'd been so hurt by him. But he was her husband, at least for the time being. If he was willing to try again, didn't he deserve another chance? Wasn't that the right thing to do? Her mother would certainly tell her it was. "I don't know," she said honestly, checking her watch. "I think I should hear him out. I owe him at least that."

"The only person you owe is yourself," Vanessa said.

"Maybe he really is sorry," Corinne said tentatively. "He must really love you, Shelby."

"Maybe." Shelby was silent for a moment as she thought about how frustrated Brandon had grown with her in the last year of their marriage because she wasn't exactly who he wanted her to be—and how Russ, in contrast, had seemed to accept the good, the bad, and the ugly about her without batting an eye. Still, was it fair to compare something new to a marriage that had spanned a decade and a half? Didn't all marriages go through ups and downs? "Maybe," she said again.

Corinne nodded, but Vanessa's expression remained impassive

as she looked up at the gray storm clouds rolling in overhead. "Looks like rain," she said.

"We should get our check," Corinne replied, looking around for the waiter as the first raindrop fell.

"What are you going to do about the cute bartender?" Vanessa asked.

"I—I should probably tell him that my life is too complicated right now," Shelby said. "That I shouldn't get involved."

"Is that what *you* want?" Vanessa asked.

"It's not like there was a future with him, anyhow," she said, trying to ignore the lump in her throat. And with that, the sky opened up, shedding teardrops from above, like the city itself was mourning Shelby's words.

CHAPTER TWENTY

George and Lou were strolling through the residential neighborhood just west of the Eiffel Tower when they felt the first drop of rain.

Lou groaned, looking skyward. "I forgot an umbrella."

"We can share mine," George said, pulling a miniature, collapsible umbrella from his pocket. Small enough to fit almost entirely in his palm while folded, it had been an impulse buy at the airport.

Lou looked at the umbrella in George's hand and laughed. "That thing looks barely large enough to shield a mouse from the rain."

George glanced at him and then looked hurriedly away. "We'll just have to squeeze in close."

It was just the two of them. The rest of the group had gone to Giverny to see the home of Claude Monet and the water lilies that had so inspired him, but Lou had admitted that he got carsick these days unless he was at the wheel and didn't think he could stomach four hours round trip in the passenger van, and George had happily agreed to stay in Paris with him. Ever since Cliff had taken their advice and declared his amorous feelings for Diane—which, to everyone's surprise, she had reciprocated—the two of them had been inseparable, holding hands and cooing at each other like they were all by themselves. Neither George nor Lou thought they could stand being in an enclosed space with them for the duration of the ride.

George felt terrible for Sheila, the other nurse Diane had taken the trip with, but Sheila didn't seem bothered. "Diane falls in love with someone new everywhere we go," she'd said with a shrug when George had expressed his concern. "She's been like that since we were in our twenties. Drives me crazy because it always fizzles out, and then she's devastated. But on the other hand, it's inspiring, really. Makes me think it's never too late for new beginnings, you know?"

George thought about her words as the Eiffel Tower came into view at the end of a side street. *It's never too late for new beginnings.* But what if it was?

He and Lou had been strolling around Paris for the past two hours, losing themselves in the crisscrossing streets and avenues of the city as they chatted easily, catching each other up on the latest goings-on in their lives and agreeing that they needed to make more of an effort to see each other back in Florida, despite the ninety-minute drive between their homes. Lou had just confessed that he'd been thinking recently of moving into a fifty-five-plus community like The Villages, just to have some company, and a surprised George had said he'd been considering the same thing. As they'd wound their way past The American Library in Paris on the rue du Général Camou, the Eiffel Tower looming ahead of them, Lou had just suggested that they might think about moving into the same community, because then they'd both start with a built-in friend.

The word *friend* had echoed in George's ear, because of course that's how Lou saw him. A friend. His oldest friend. A friend he'd met and relied on in Vietnam and had trusted with his life.

And that was all well and good, because George considered Lou his closest friend, too. But as the rain began to fall lightly, giving Paris a misty, ethereal feeling, and as he popped his tiny umbrella open and beckoned Lou to move in closer, he ached to say more. "Well, come on in, before you get soaked," George said instead, raising his arm and jerking his head to indicate that Lou should come into the fold.

Chuckling, Lou moved closer, and George's arm fell over his shoulders as the two men huddled against the rain, which was coming down harder now. "George Gallagher, you've been saving me for fifty years," Lou said as drops of water deflected from their umbrella in a soft pitter-patter. "What would I do without you?"

George knew how lucky he was to still be in touch with Lou all these decades after they'd first met, to share such a close friendship with a man who knew him better than anyone in the world, and who was as good and decent as anyone he'd ever known. "I don't know what I'd do without you, either."

Lou slipped his arm around George, too, so that the two of them took up as little space as possible beneath the umbrella. Matching each other stride for stride, they began to make their way toward the Eiffel Tower, the rain drumming down all around them. As they approached the monument, they were passed by dozens of people dashing in the opposite direction, some using maps or plastic bags as makeshift shields against the downpour.

"We're going against the tide," Lou pointed out as a fleeing tourist bumped into him, jostling him against George and shouting an apology over his shoulder.

"Haven't we always?"

Lou laughed. "I'll give you that."

They crossed into the tree-lined Champ de Mars, where the dirt paths were already dotted with puddles. "Watch yourself there," Lou said quickly, pulling George to the side to avoid splashing through water.

"Thanks," George said, leaning into Lou. They emerged from a cluster of trees and stopped to stare up at the Eiffel Tower, which loomed above the park just two hundred yards ahead. With the gray clouds as a backdrop and no sunshine to light it, the monument looked nearly black, a silhouette against the sky. The rain was slowing, but drops continued to drum against the umbrella as the air around them turned misty. "Beautiful, isn't it?" George said.

"Like something out of a classic movie," Lou agreed. He glanced at George. "If this were a film, this would be the moment the lovers would kiss, wouldn't it?"

George wasn't sure how to respond. "Well, too bad Cliff and Diane aren't here," he said after a moment. "They'd be kissing up a storm."

Lou chuckled, but he didn't say anything.

"Are you missing Lavonda?" George guessed after a few seconds of silence.

Lou seemed to consider this. "I miss her often. She was a wonderful companion. But in this moment, George? No, I wasn't thinking of Lavonda at all."

There was something in Lou's tone—a deepening of his voice, a tremor that felt like a little earthquake—that made George turn and look at him. Rain and mist drifted down around them, but in the shadow of the umbrella, it was just the two of them, nearly alone in the park. "You weren't?" George asked, hardly daring to hope.

"No."

"Who, then," George said slowly, "were you thinking of?"

Lou held his gaze. The rain fell. The clouds rolled. The Eiffel

Tower stood watch over the quiet morning, a witness to this and a million other moments. "You," he said, and George stared because Lou couldn't possibly mean what George thought he meant.

"Me?"

"George," Lou said, "I understand if you don't feel the same way. But for me, it has always been you."

Henry and Celeste sat by the window, staring out at the rain. They said little as they watched the drops fall, but when Henry had reached for Celeste's hand, she hadn't pulled away, and after a few seconds, she'd threaded her fingers through his, and they had been sitting like that, side by side, ever since.

Henry was afraid to move, for what if he broke this spell? It was enough, in this moment, to have Celeste's hand in his, to be gently stroking her palm with his thumb, to feel the warmth of her coursing through him.

"It's romantic, isn't it?" Celeste finally broke the silence. "Paris in the rain. Like . . . a promise of new beginnings."

Henry swallowed hard. It was the most lucid he'd heard Celeste sound since he'd returned to her. "I fell in love in the rain once," he dared to say.

She looked at him, and for a split second, he could have sworn that she saw him, *really* saw him. But then her eyes clouded over again, and when she smiled, it looked vacant. "How wonderful."

"It was," Henry said, the memories tumbling back in. Being walked through the waterlogged streets of Paris just before the curfew by a Resistance contact who introduced himself as Claude. Knowing that he was marginally safer than he otherwise would have been, because the Germans and the French police were huddled in cafés, staying dry. Seeing Celeste for the very first time, framed in the arched doorway of the building on the rue Dante, her hair damp, her dress clinging to every curve of her slender body. Knowing that, somehow, his path was meant to intertwine with hers, even though he didn't yet know that she was the next stop on the Allied escape line. The insistent patter of the rain on the zinc roof as she hid him in her top-floor apartment. The way he'd longed to kiss her for the first time as she'd perched by the window to look up at the drops falling from the sky. Their first kiss, just a week later, when the skies had blessed them with a second rainfall, turning the streets luminous.

"And did she fall in love with you, too?" Celeste asked, and when Henry looked at her, he again thought he could see a glimmer of recognition.

"She did," he said softly. "We promised that we would love each other forever. That we would find our way back to each other, no matter what."

"And did you? Find your way back?"

"We did." Henry's voice cracked. "But I'm afraid it might be too late."

Celeste absorbed this for a moment. "It's never too late, though, is it?"

Henry did his best to keep his voice from shaking. "That's my hope, Celeste, it really is."

"I was in love once," she said after a moment. "A very long time ago."

"Were you?" He was afraid that she was about to tell the story of her husband, and he knew he'd have to withstand hearing the details of the man she'd spent her life with instead of him, even if it broke his heart.

Instead, she sighed and said, "It was here, in Paris. He was an American. We were both very young."

Henry stared at her. "You remember?"

She looked at him blankly. "Remember what?"

"Falling in love with an American." He had the terrible feeling that he was already losing her.

She scrunched up her nose. "That isn't something I can talk about. It isn't safe. The Germans could be listening."

"The war is long since over, Celeste."

She narrowed her eyes at him. "So you say."

"I promise, it ended eighty years ago. We've been apart all that time, Celeste, but I've found you."

She peered at him. "But who *are* you?"

"I'm Henry." He blinked back tears. She'd been so close to a breakthrough, but as the rain slowed to a trickle outside, it seemed that the fog of confusion had already begun to descend again. "I'm the American you loved in Paris, a very long time ago. I loved you, too, very deeply. I still do."

She frowned and looked him up and down. "I don't know you."

"But you did, Celeste!" He could feel his desperation rising. "We used to lie in your bed and listen to the rain pounding on the roof. I used to sing to you. Do you remember?"

Her lips opened and closed, almost as if she was searching for lyrics she'd lost long ago. "There were love songs once."

"Yes. Yes, there were."

"I—I don't remember the words." Tears pooled in her eyes. "Why don't I remember the words anymore?"

As tears streamed down her face, Henry's eyes stung, too. "*Wherever you are, you make the world bright*," he said, his voice raspy. "*You light all the flames. You're my City of Light.*"

She stared at him for a long time. "But that isn't a song. You aren't singing."

"I had cysts on my vocal cords," he said, touching his throat.

"They tried surgery and voice therapy, but nothing has helped. My singing voice is lost."

She frowned. "It's terrible to lose things, isn't it? I think I have lost many of my memories. Don't tell anyone. They'll think I'm crazy."

"You're not crazy, Celeste. And though your memories may not all be here anymore," he said, tapping his head, "they are here." He put a hand over his heart. She stared at his hand for a moment.

"Because I feel them," she said softly, "even if I can't recall the details."

"Exactly."

They sat in silence for a few minutes more as the rain continued to fall. "I do not know you," Celeste said at last. "But I trust you."

"Hold on to that, then," Henry said. "And I promise, I will find a way to remind you of all the ways we live in each other's hearts."

George could not find the words to reply to Lou as the two men stared at each other in the shadow of the Eiffel Tower, raindrops landing like gentle drumbeats on George's umbrella.

"What do you mean, it's always been me?" George finally managed to say, his heart hammering.

Lou looked down at the ground for a long time as George's pulse raced. "I mean," Lou said slowly, without looking at George, "that I felt something different with you the very first time we met. It was easier, though, wasn't it, for me to love a woman? To know that whatever else happened, we would always be friends, as long as I didn't rock the boat?"

"And now?"

"Now," Lou said, finally looking up to meet George's gaze, "the boat is rocking. And if I wind up alone in the sea, so be it."

George could see anguish in his friend's eyes, and confusion. "What are you saying, Lou?"

"Well, George, I'm saying that I love you."

For a moment, George couldn't breathe, couldn't speak. He simply stared at Lou, a lump in his throat.

"Say something," Lou said, with a nervous laugh after a long beat of silence. "If I've misread the situation, if I've made you uncomfortable, perhaps we can just forget that I—"

"Lou," George said abruptly.

Lou stopped speaking and looked at him.

George inhaled, gathering his courage. And then he took the leap he had always assumed would never be his to take. "I love you, too, Lou," he said. "Always have, always will."

"Really?" Lou asked, his voice hoarse.

As the rain drifted down, they stood there under the umbrella looking into each other's eyes. And then, slowly, George leaned forward and touched his lips gently to Lou's, something he had dreamed of doing for so many years. There had been men in the time since Sally had died, but George's heart had always been right here, with Lou.

They stood like that for a long moment, their lips touching, the world going on all around them, not a single person giving them a second glance. Finally, George pulled away, and the two men stared at each other in disbelief. "Really," George whispered.

Lou's eyes filled with tears. "All this time . . ."

"All this time," George said, his voice breaking. "It has always been you, too."

CHAPTER TWENTY-ONE

Shelby stood on the sidewalk outside Le Maison Grog for a long time, holding an umbrella and trying to make a decision.

She was supposed to be touring Versailles with Corinne and Vanessa today, but she'd insisted that they go on without her. Brandon was going to be here in a few hours, and she needed to end whatever this was with Russ before then, or she wouldn't be able to live with herself.

But as she stood there in the rain, looking through the fogged-up windows into the bar, she found she had lost both her courage and her conviction. Was she making a mistake? But no, she could hear her mother's voice in her head, reminding her that her wedding vows were promises she'd made for life. What was she going to do, throw away a chance at reconciling with her husband because of one night of amazing sex with a bartender? That was ridiculous. And Russ would get over it; it was hard to imagine that a hot, Aussie bartender in the middle of tourist Paris wasn't getting hit on every night. He would be fine.

Right. Shelby took a deep breath and before she could stop herself, she opened the door to Le Maison Grog and went in.

Nineties pop music was playing over the sound system, and the bar was even more sparsely populated than it had been when she and the girls had arrived on their first day. In fact, except for a middle-aged couple at the far end of the bar, the place was entirely deserted.

She approached the bar slowly, scanning the room for Russ as she dragged her feet. She was doing the right thing, but a big part of her wanted to delay the inevitable.

The other bartender, the one Russ co-owned the bar with, emerged from the back, and spotting her, broke into a smile. "G'day," he said cheerfully as she approached. Then his forehead creased, and she could tell he was trying to place her.

"Hi," she said. "Benji, is it? I'm looking for Russ. Is he here?"

Recognition flickered across his features. "Ah. You're the girl." It wasn't said warmly.

"Um . . ."

"Russ isn't here." He began to wash glasses, which made eye contact impossible. "I thought he was with you, actually."

"He was. But I had to go meet my friends, and now, well, I need to talk with him. I'm Shelby, by the way." She extended her hand for a handshake, but Benji pursed his lips, raised his right arm up to show her that it was covered in soapy water, and then returned to his washing.

"Do you, um, know where I might be able to find him?" she asked after another minute had ticked by and Benji still hadn't said a word.

"I'm not his keeper."

"I know, of course." She had seen the two men argue last night, but Russ had told her Benji would forget all about it by the next day. "It's just that I really need to talk to him, and I'm not sure where—"

"Look, I don't know where he is, all right?" Benji finally turned off the water and slammed the glass in his hand down so hard that it chipped on the bottom. He cursed and threw the glass out, then grabbed a towel and dried his hands. When he looked up at Shelby again, he was glaring at her. "And I've got to say, you've got some nerve coming in here."

"What?" Shelby asked, completely thrown. "What do you mean?"

"I *mean* that everything was aces between me and Russ. Then he meets you and in two days flat, he's telling me he thinks he deserves a better life than this."

"He . . . what?"

"Besides, it's not like you'll stick around, Yoko." Benji sounded like a petulant teenager, but his words still cut her to the core. "You're a *tourist*." He said it like a bad word. "You'll have your fun and then you'll head home to wherever it is you came from."

"I—" She wanted to protest—after all, just a few hours earlier, he would have been wrong—but she had come here today to tell Russ she couldn't see him again, hadn't she? "That's not who I am."

"Honestly, I don't care."

As Benji glared at her, she felt even worse. "If you see Russ, would you tell him I came by, please?"

Benji snorted. "Now I look like his secretary?"

"Actually," she said, "you look a lot like someone Russ is better off without." She left before she could dig her hole any deeper—and before she had to admit to herself that the same words might apply to her, too.

Jackson hurried through sound check at La Défense, his mind still spinning with lyrics. It was good to hang with the musicians he'd spent four weeks rehearsing with back in Los Angeles, and he made plans to join them for dinner later in the evening after he'd seen Julia, but for now, he just wanted to get back to the Latin Quarter so that he could meet with Henry and commit his song to paper before he lost the thread of it.

Henry's granddaughter lived on a side street not far from where Jackson had stayed in his twenties, and she buzzed him in immediately when he rang.

"My grandfather just called and is on his way back," she said quickly when she answered the door, her cheeks flushed. She was about Jackson's age, maybe a little younger, with shoulder-length brown hair and a kind smile. "Melanie."

He shook her hand. "Jackson."

She laughed. "Yes, I know. Anyhow, my grandfather wanted me to apologize for keeping you waiting."

"Not at all," Jackson said as she ushered him into an apartment that was warm and homey, the tables piled high with magazines and art books, and the walls lined with bookshelves and framed black-and-white photos of Paris. "I'm sorry to impose."

"It's not an imposition at all. Can I get you a drink? A coffee, maybe?"

"That would be wonderful."

"Espresso? Americano? Latte?"

"Just a regular black coffee if you have it." Jackson smiled.

"Just like my grandpa. Coming right up."

He followed her into the kitchen and set his guitar at his feet. "So what brought you to France?" he asked as she scooped grinds into a French press and plugged in a kettle to boil water.

"I married a French man," she said, and there was a tightness in her voice when she said it.

"That sounds very romantic."

She looked away. "Yeah, well, I thought so, too. But now—" She stopped abruptly and busied herself with preparing the coffee before finally looking up at him. "Can I ask you a question?"

"Yeah, sure."

"Have you ever . . . cheated on anyone?"

He raised his eyebrows in surprise. "Wow, that's a big question."

She blushed. "I'm sorry. And you don't have to answer. It's just . . . my husband had an affair recently, and I think I'm just trying to wrap my head around it, you know? And I figure that since you're a rock star . . ."

"That I must have cheated on someone?"

Her blush deepened. "No offense. I'm sorry. I shouldn't have asked that."

"No, it's fine," Jackson said, feeling terrible for the poor woman, who looked completely flustered. "And no, I haven't. But I also haven't ever been that serious with anyone. So you and your husband—well, you're already a step ahead of me in terms of commitment."

"You've never been married?" She shook her head. "I mean, I should probably know that from your Wikipedia page or something."

He laughed. "Believe me, I'm glad you don't. No, I never married. But if I had, I'd like to think I wouldn't have cheated."

"The thing is, I'm not sure whether to forgive him," she said in a small voice. "Do I owe it to him to keep trying until we find our way back? I don't know what to do."

"Look, no one in the world would mistake me for the guy to

come to for relationship advice," Jackson said. "But if you want my opinion, I'd say it should be about what *you* want for your future—not what you owe him, you know? When you have an affair, don't you lose your say over what happens next? Just my two cents."

She exhaled heavily. "You sound an awful lot like my grandfather."

"I'll take that as a compliment," Jackson said with a smile.

The front door opened then, and they were momentarily distracted as Henry bustled into the kitchen, propping his walking cane against the doorframe and apologizing for his late arrival. Melanie busied herself with pouring them each a cup of coffee, and then she hurried out of the room, mumbling an excuse about having to check her email.

"She's going through a bit of a rough time," Henry said.

"She told me about her husband," Jackson said, and Henry raised an eyebrow.

"Did she?" Henry sighed. "Melanie has the biggest heart of anyone I know, and sometimes that complicates things; she's so busy trying to do the right thing that she forgets to ask herself what she wants. She's invited him to your concert, you know."

"Has she?" Jackson was surprised; he figured that with the way she'd spoken about her husband's affair, she wouldn't want him to be there. "Well, that's fine, of course. I just—I hope she doesn't get hurt."

"I hope so, too," Henry said. "But she'll be okay. She's stronger than she gives herself credit for. Now she just has to figure out how to move forward."

"She's lucky to have you, Henry."

"Ah, I'm lucky to have her, too. Now, what was it you wanted to see me about?"

"It's silly, really," Jackson said, embarrassed. "It's just . . . there's a woman. And, well, I can't seem to stop thinking in lyrics since I met her."

Henry smiled. "Sounds like love to me."

Jackson felt like an idiot. "I hardly know her."

Henry didn't reply for a moment. Instead, he beckoned for Jackson to follow him into a smaller room off the parlor, where Jackson was startled to see a full piano tucked against more bookcases.

"Is your granddaughter a musician, too?" Jackson asked.

"She plays a bit of piano. I like to think it's the one legacy I'll leave behind."

"All of those songs you've written are a pretty impressive legacy, too."

Henry shrugged. "The older I've gotten, the more I've realized that it's not the things you accomplish in life that matter, or even the art you create. It's how you love the people you're fortunate enough to share your time on earth with."

The words hit home. "See, you even speak in lyrics."

Henry smiled. "Well, what is a song but the truest expression of what lies in one's heart? I simply do my best to say what I mean."

"I'm not so good at that," Jackson admitted. "For a long time, I think I went into every relationship on the defensive, with all my walls up, assuming that women were interested in me for the wrong reasons."

"And you may not have been wrong," Henry said.

"But I may not have been right, either."

"I won't pretend to know what it's like to be a rock star, Jackson. But it seems to me that a certain amount of self-protection is not only wise but essential."

"The problem is that once those walls are up, it's hard to tear them down."

Henry sat down at the piano and beckoned for Jackson to

take the chair just to his left. "Go on, then. I'd love to hear what you've got."

Jackson felt nervous as he pulled his guitar out of its case. "It's not as good as what you write."

Henry fixed him with a look. "It's apples and oranges, son. You write with your life experiences, and I write with mine, and we both create art in our own way."

"Did it ever bother you? Not to have the chance to sing your own songs?" Jackson asked.

Henry chuckled. "I'm a writer, not a performer. Never did have much of a singing voice, even before I lost it. No, I think I'm exactly where I'm meant to be, Jackson. And you? Did it bother you not to write your own songs?"

"I was never good enough."

"I doubt very much that that was ever true," Henry said, "and if you had people in your circle who made you feel that way, perhaps they didn't have your best interests in mind."

"Maybe not." Feeling like he was about to leap without a safety net, Jackson began to strum his guitar and sing. "*I wish I could tell you what I'm starting to feel. That the way you inspire me is so new and so real.*"

For a moment, Henry just listened with his eyes closed, and Jackson was certain it was because the older man thought that his lyrics were terrible, that the melody was even worse. He was just about to stop singing when Henry's fingers began to move across the keys, softly at first and then with more conviction, accompanying Jackson flawlessly.

"*I wish you knew how perfect you look in this light.*" Jackson sang, with a bit more confidence. "*That as long as I breathe, I won't forget tonight.*"

For the next three and a half minutes, he sang from his soul, and Henry played along, his eyes still closed, his forehead creased in concentration. When Jackson finished singing, Henry opened his eyes and smiled at him.

"Well?" Jackson asked hesitantly.

"I think you might have your next hit song on your hands, son. I mean it. It's beautiful."

"You're not just saying that?"

"It's beautiful because it's real. When you let your heart bleed into the music, people can hear that. Heck, they can *feel* it." Henry paused and took his hands off the piano keys, turning to look Jackson right in the eye. "You asked me a few minutes ago how it could be love with this woman of yours when you hardly know her yet."

"Oh," Jackson said, startled by the change in subject. "Yeah."

"It might interest you to hear that I had only known Celeste—the love of my life—for two days when I began to write 'City of Light.'"

"Two *days*?"

"Sometimes you just know, Jackson. It's in our nature as human beings to search for logical explanations for everything, but sometimes, all we need to do is find space in the quiet to listen to what our hearts are telling us. I listened when mine spoke to me about Celeste—and I love her still, eighty years later, even though we were separated for most of our lives. I am hoping beyond hope, son, that when I bring her to your concert tomorrow, when she feels the rhythm of the song that I first sang to her all those years ago, that her heart will remember, too. And whatever happens with this new lady friend of yours—whether you're together many years from now or whether you have only a moment in time, as Celeste and I did—you can't regret it. You can only listen to your heart, for that is what makes you a better artist and, more importantly, a better man."

"Thank you, Henry," Jackson said over the lump in his throat.

"And for what it's worth, I'll be rooting with everything I have for your Celeste to remember."

Henry smiled. "And I'll be rooting for you, son, to know the kind of love that is possible only when we open our hearts without fear."

CHAPTER TWENTY-TWO

Piper and her mother strolled down the rue des Rosiers in the Marais neighborhood of the city, sharing an umbrella as the rain slowed to a drizzle, marveling at the way the wet cobblestones caught the light and the way that ivy and flowers tumbled from balconies and awnings, a vibrant burst of springtime in the city. The street was lined with boutiques and restaurants, and as they walked, peering into the windows of crowded falafel shops and stationery stores, Piper could almost imagine what it would feel like if this were her life, if she lived in Paris and strolled the market streets each day.

But alas, she was an American who would have to go home in just two days. Already, the city had stolen a piece of her heart, and admittedly, Nicolas had, too. Last night, they had walked all the way to the gleaming Basilique du Sacré-Coeur, which overlooked Paris from Montmartre, the hill on the northern side of the city. It had taken them an hour and a half to get there, and when they'd reached the top, they'd bought chicken, tomato, and mayonnaise sandwiches on fresh baguettes and had enjoyed an impromptu picnic on the basilica's steps, gazing out at the city, before walking back along a different route. By the end of the evening, her feet were aching, but her heart was full, and when he'd kissed her, deeply and tenderly, outside the front door of her hotel, she'd forgotten for a few minutes about the tragedy that was coming and the sadness that had cast a shadow over this whole trip. She was just a girl falling for a boy in the most beautiful city in the world.

But then she had floated upstairs to her hotel room, touching her tingling lips, and the wind had been knocked out of her when she'd realized her mother wasn't there. She had called her in a panic, worried that something had happened, but her mother had sounded weird and hadn't explained where she was—only that she would be back right away.

"So?" she prompted her mother, who'd been unusually quiet all morning. "Are you going to tell me about the man you were with last night? Or are we just going to pretend that didn't happen?"

Her mom looked sharply at her, guilt written across her face. "How do you know I was with a man?"

"I was watching out the window when you came home. Mom, he kissed you." Piper knew that the words sounded like an accusation, but what was her mother hiding? "I thought you were sleeping."

"I was," her mom said. "But I woke up and decided to go get something to eat."

"And picked up a random dude along the way?" Piper asked, incredulous.

"He wasn't exactly random," her mom said, looking away.

"What?"

"I just mean I met him the day before. He gave me his phone number, but I wasn't planning to call him. And then, there he was again."

Piper stopped walking, which forced her mother to stop, too. "So, what, you were out on, like, a date?"

Her mother shrugged. "No. Maybe. I don't know. I don't think you could call it that."

"Do you like this guy?" Piper pressed, then she lobbed another question before her mother could answer. "Who is he, anyway?"

Her mother started walking again, and after a beat, Piper hurried after her. "His name is Sam," her mother said. "He's American, and he seems . . . wonderful."

"Okay, so forgive me for not understanding this, but you and I are on a trip together to Paris, and you sneak out at night to go out with some guy when you're supposed to be sleeping?" Piper knew she sounded petulant, and she couldn't quite place why she was feeling so aggrieved that her mother had met someone.

"I didn't sneak out." Her mother sounded hurt. "I woke up and went to grab some food by myself, because I was hungry. I ran into someone I'd met the other day. And we went for a walk."

"A walk," Piper repeated. "And what exactly is the game plan with this guy? Like, is he going to call you in the States once we're home?" Her mom had so little time left, and it should all belong to Piper, shouldn't it? There wasn't room for some random man to share her mother's final months with her.

"I have no idea, Piper. Where is this coming from?"

"I don't know," Piper mumbled, because it was easier to say that than to admit she was jealous that someone else had stolen her mother's attention. "So he knows about your cancer?"

Her mom didn't say anything as they passed two more falafel shops with lines down the block. "No," she finally said, and Piper gave her a sharp look.

"You didn't tell him?"

Her mom glanced over at her, tears in her eyes. "You make it sound so simple, Piper. But when exactly do I bring that up in a light conversation? 'Where are you from, what do you do, and, oh, by the way, I'm dying'?"

"Mom." Piper felt a hitch in her throat. "No, I didn't mean—"

"It's just . . . I don't have a road map for this, honey." Her mom wiped a tear away. "I don't have a road map for any of it. But I want to live in the time I have left, you know?"

"That's what we're doing here." Piper gestured to the shopping street, which was filling up as the rain finally stopped. "We're living."

"I know. But . . ." Piper's mom looked like she wanted to say something, but she trailed off. "I can't even remember the last time someone looked at me the way Sam looked at me last night. Okay? And this will be the last time in my life someone looks at me like that. I know there's no future in it."

"Well . . . do you like him?" Piper asked. Since her parents had divorced thirteen years before, her mom hadn't dated, so this was completely new territory for both of them.

"I do, honey." Her mom's voice was sad. "I do, and that kind of breaks my heart."

"Why?"

"Because I have to tell him, don't I? I can't pretend to be anything other than what I am, which is a woman who didn't live enough in the years she had—and whose time is running out far too soon."

They stopped in front of a modern-looking patisserie as Piper grappled for words. "Mom . . ."

"It's fine, honey," her mom said, pasting a smile on her face though her eyes still shone with tears. "It's fine, and it will be fine, and I will do the right thing. I just . . . it was nice to have one night where I was just *me*. Not an ad executive for a failing newspaper or a divorcée or a cancer patient. I was just . . . Julia. I can't remember the last time I was just Julia. And I wasn't ready for that to end. The second I tell him, he'll only see me as The Woman Dying from Cancer."

"I'm sorry, Mom." Piper felt like her own heart had shattered into a million pieces. The truth was, she'd been treating her mother that way, too.

"I know." Piper's mom sniffled, wiped her tears away, and gestured to the door of the patisserie. "Now, what do you say we grab a tarte before lunch? In fact, we should eat dessert first more often, don't you think?"

Without waiting for an answer, she entered the shop, which smelled of yeast and sugar, and Piper had no choice but to follow.

"Your girlfriend came by," was the first thing Benji said when Russ walked into Le Maison Grog just past one o'clock. The place was completely empty, save for Benji cutting lemons. Russ was there earlier than he'd promised to be—today was Benji's day to open—but he had hoped to catch him during a lull in service to have a calm conversation about dissolving their business partnership. He had hoped that last night's animosity between them was fueled by alcohol, but today, Benji looked even more furious, and from the glazed look in his eyes, it was clear that he'd already been drinking for hours.

"Shelby?" Russ asked. He hadn't been able to find his phone that morning, and he'd run out of time looking for it. She must have come here after trying to call him.

"I don't know her name. The American. The one with the tits."

Russ clenched his fists, urging himself not to take the bait. "You're such an arse."

"Have I offended you, Russ?"

"Come on, Benji," Russ said, trying to keep his tone light. "Can we talk like adults?"

Benji sliced a few lemons with violent slashes before speaking. "Fine, you want to talk like adults? *This* adult thinks *that* adult is being a twat and throwing away everything we've worked for, all for some random bird."

"Benji, I'm not throwing away anything, and this has nothing to do with Shelby. I've been feeling like this for a while. I feel like I blinked and the past decade has just disappeared in a haze of whiskey and late nights, and . . . I think I'm just realizing I want more."

"Just because you've turned into a pensioner overnight doesn't mean I feel that way." Benji slammed his knife down and finally looked Russ in the eye. "Think about what you're doing here. You and I have a good thing going. A great thing. We make a profit every month—"

"A small one."

"*And* we have all the women we could possibly want. You get laid *one* time, and all of a sudden you're rethinking your whole life?"

Russ closed his eyes. "Benji. This isn't about women. It's just, this isn't the life I want, you know? I want stability and normal hours and a wife and maybe even kids."

"Do you hear yourself? A *wife*? Kids? Does the American with the big rack know you're planning her future like that? She's a tourist. She's on holiday. She'll go home with a story that she got laid by a hot Aussie bartender, and then she'll forget all about you."

"Screw you."

Benji managed to look both amused and pitying at the same time as he shook his head at Russ. "You're an idiot, mate. You've spent all this time pretending you walk on higher moral ground than I do, just because you don't take advantage of what's available to us every night. But in the end, you've done the exact same thing I do. Only, you don't have the brains to see it for what it is."

"I think we're done here," Russ said, thanking his lucky stars that he and Benji were separated by several paces. He wanted with every cell in his body to punch the smug look off Benji's face.

"Yeah, we're done, all right," Benji said, returning to cutting lemons. "You want out? I'll buy your share. But you're going to regret it. And when the American girl dumps you in a few days and you come to your senses, don't come crying to me."

"It's not about her."

"Sure." Benji snorted. "I can handle things here until we start getting busy at five. But don't think you're going to bail on your responsibilities, princess. You still own half the bar."

And then, he was gone, striding into the kitchen, the door banging closed behind him.

Shelby's stomach hurt as she waited outside her hotel, checking her watch.

Brandon would be here any moment now, and she still didn't know how she felt about that. She was afraid that when she saw him, she would revert back to the role of needy wife, the one she had played to perfection for nearly fifteen years. But that's not who she wanted to be anymore.

Could she open a new chapter with Brandon? Was she capable of being who she wanted to be in that relationship, if she returned to it? Or would she turn over a new leaf, only to return to the bad habit of putting her own needs on a shelf to accommodate Brandon? Could the rules of their relationship—the ones she'd largely created herself to try to be the wife Brandon wanted—even be rewritten?

But Shelby didn't want those rules anymore. No, she wanted to finally be her authentic self. She wanted to have bad hair days and to not worry if she had five extra pounds around her waist. She wanted to say what she thought and be listened to, because how she felt mattered.

In short, she wanted to be who she'd been with Russ for the past few days. But being with Russ himself wasn't the answer, was it? What was the expression? People come into your life for a reason, a season, or a lifetime. Maybe her path had crossed with Russ's for a purpose—to show her that there was a different way forward. After all, there was no realistic future here in Paris with him. She could just imagine calling her parents—who were already so disappointed that she'd thrown away the life they'd always dreamed of for her—to tell them that she wasn't coming home because she'd met a guy in a bar. It was laughable, really.

And maybe she had played a purpose in Russ's life, too. Benji had said that Russ was rethinking their business partnership. But what if getting out of the bar was the best thing for Russ, too? When he'd talked about the long hours, his sense of doing something meaningless, and his desire for something more, he had sounded so unhappy. Maybe something about meeting her had given him the push he needed—and therefore, maybe she had somehow changed his life for the better, too.

That's what she told herself, anyhow, as she called him for a third time. Her calls were rolling directly into his voicemail, which made her uneasy. Had she done something to offend him? She hadn't left a message at first because she didn't know what to say.

But now Brandon was coming. And she owed it to Russ to do the right thing before he arrived.

"Russ? It's Shelby," she said once his voicemail had beeped. "I came by the bar earlier because I wanted to catch you to say . . ." She trailed off and dove in again before she could second-guess herself, adding in a rushed tumble of words, "I had so much fun with you. I really did. And if things were different in my life—if we lived on the same continent, even—I think maybe there'd be a chance for us. But I think I'm being unfair to you, because, let's be honest, there isn't a future in this. I have to go home at the end of this week, and I know you have things to work out here, and . . ." She cut herself off because she was babbling. "Anyways, maybe I'm overthinking it, right? We had fun together, and maybe that's all this is. The thing is, I wanted to say thank you, because you reminded me of who I want to be as a human being, and that's worth everything. I—I wish I'd met you sooner, before so much of my life was already written. But I'm so glad to have had the opportunity to get to know you and, well, I wish you the best. And I'm . . . I'm sorry."

She hung up quickly before she could sound even more pathetic. Would he roll his eyes at her rambling message? Maybe she was ascribing meaning to something that had none. Maybe he hooked up with tourists every week. Maybe she was imagining that he'd looked at her like she was something special. Maybe he'd play her lame message for Benji, and they'd laugh their heads off.

Regardless, it didn't matter. She could fix everything that was broken in her life just by saying yes to Brandon, and she wanted that. She wanted what she'd had before he'd blown it all up. But this time, it couldn't be all on Brandon's terms.

"Shelby?" Brandon's deep voice came from behind her, and she spun around in time to see the man she'd married approaching from a half block away, a duffel bag slung over one shoulder. He looked like a Ken doll—blond hair, broad shoulders, narrow waist. Her stomach did the same little flip-flop it always had when she'd spotted him across campus in college, when their relationship had been new and magical. Could it be that way again?

"Brandon," she said as he reached her, her voice breaking, and then she was in his arms, and he was dipping her for a dramatic kiss, and she was laughing, and he was laughing, and for a moment, it felt like no time had passed at all and that he hadn't filed for divorce and she hadn't realized how happy she could feel with someone who wasn't him.

"I screwed up, babe," he said, finally letting her go and giving her a dazzling smile. "I love you, and I'll do whatever it takes to win you back."

Her heart fluttered again as he slung his arm around her. It was everything she'd wanted to hear, but somehow, it didn't fill her up the way she'd imagined it would. Still, he was her past and her future. "I love you, too," she said, and she meant it.

But as they turned to walk into the hotel, she realized she was crying, and she honestly didn't know whether they were tears of joy at the possibility of a new beginning or tears of sadness at the end of something that could have been a new kind of happily ever after.

CHAPTER TWENTY-THREE

Piper and her mom had wandered around the Marais until their feet hurt, and then they'd parted ways with a promise to meet back in their hotel room at seven for dinner at La Nouvelle Seine, a restaurant inside a barge permanently docked opposite Notre Dame.

Piper's mom wanted to meet the guy she had kissed to come clean with him about her diagnosis, so Piper had texted Nicolas to ask if he had a bit of time before dinner to meet up. He responded instantly that he'd see her in her hotel lobby at five and would take care of everything.

Piper let herself out of the room and headed downstairs, her heart heavy with worry for her mom. She was so lost in thought about how exhausted her mother looked that it took her a few seconds to register that Nicolas was already there waiting for her.

"Bonjour," he said, standing as he spotted her. "I was off a little early, so I walked over. I hope that's okay."

"Yeah, it's perfect," she said, but when she tried to smile at him, she could feel her eyes filling with tears.

"Piper, what is it?" Nicolas crossed to her quickly and pulled her into his arms. "Is your mother all right?"

"No," Piper said. "And there's nothing I can do about it."

"That isn't true. You are here, in Paris, helping to make a magical experience that she—and you—will always remember."

"But it won't save her life," Piper said, pulling away just far enough to look into Nicolas's eyes. "How is any of this enough?"

"It isn't," he said. "But it's never enough, is it? When we're children, we think the moments will be endless. But in the end, they slip through our fingers before we know how much they mean."

She stared at him. "How come you always know just the right thing to say?"

He looked at her for a moment. "'For every atom belonging to me as good belongs to you,'" he said slowly.

"What?"

He smiled. "It's a quote from 'Song of Myself,' and, Piper, I think it means that we're all connected to one another."

"I can't believe I'm in Paris with a French guy quoting Whitman to me," she said with a small smile. "My professors would be so proud."

"Happy to help." He grinned. "But would you prefer to stay with your mother right now, Piper?"

"Believe it or not, she has a date."

"A date? Oh la la. This really is the city of romance."

Piper laughed and then sobered. "I actually think she's going to get hurt, and I'm afraid it's my fault."

"Your fault?" Nicolas prompted gently.

"She met some guy, and I got upset and told her she needed to be honest with him. I think I made her feel like she needed to do that before she was ready."

"But she owes him the truth, doesn't she?"

Piper shrugged. "Does she, though? Maybe she deserved to just make a memory and to do it in her own way. And now she's going to get her heart broken."

"But then you will be there to help."

"I guess." But the weight still felt heavy on her shoulders. She knew she'd pushed too hard. "Anyhow, I'm sorry. What should we do for the next two hours?"

"Are you hungry?" Nicolas asked. He reached down and grabbed a large canvas bag she hadn't noticed earlier, which had a long baguette protruding from it. "I know you don't have much time today, but I've packed a little picnic for an early *apéro*."

"Apéro?"

"It is a tradition here—drinks and a bit of food before dinner to whet the appetite. I just thought we might enjoy being outside now that the rain has let up."

Thirty minutes and one RER train ride later, they were in the Champ de Mars, the huge rectangular green park that stretched from the Eiffel Tower down to the imposing École Militaire. The morning rain had given way to a crisp late afternoon with an impossibly blue sky and light the color of lemons.

Reaching into one of the canvas bags, Nicolas pulled out a waterproof picnic blanket, which he unfolded, laying it out on the still-damp grass. He gestured for Piper to sit, and then, as she watched in astonishment, he unpacked a small array of cheeses along with the baguette, a bottle of champagne, and two plastic cups.

"When did you even have time to pack a picnic?" she asked. No one had ever done anything like that for her before.

"I went on my break today to the rue Mouffetard," he said with a smile. "The market street near the café. I hope that's all right. Everyone who comes to Paris should experience apéro, and where better to enjoy a glass of wine?"

She was speechless as he popped the cork on the champagne and poured them each a plastic cup.

"*Santé*," he said, touching his cup to hers and taking a sip of his wine. "To you and to your mother."

"Why are you being so nice, Nicolas?" she asked before she could stop herself. "I'm only here for a couple more days."

But he didn't look like he was judging her. "The world is small, Piper. Who knows what the future will bring, and in the meantime, you can call me whenever you need someone." He began to unwrap cheeses, naming them as he went. "A Bleu d'Auvergne, a Camembert from Normandy, and a Tomme de Savoie from the French Alps." He handed her a cheese knife with a smile and gestured to the baguette. "I went a bit overboard—usually apéro is smaller—but these were all things I wanted you to try, in case you hadn't had them yet in France."

Piper felt like she was in a trance as she wedged off a bit of runny Camembert, spread it on a torn piece of baguette, and took a small bite. "Oh my God, how is it this good?" she moaned, closing her eyes. When she opened them again, Nicolas was smiling at her.

"I see you like the cheese. Now you must try the rillettes."

"Rillettes?"

He pulled from the tote bag a red container that looked like a tub of margarine. But when he opened it and began to spread it on a piece of baguette for her, she could see that it was some sort of pâté. He handed it to her and reached into the bag once more for a jar of small pickles. "Try it with a cornichon," he said, opening the jar and holding it out to her.

Tentatively, she took one of the pickles, placed it atop the meat spread, and took a bite.

"Well?" he prompted as she chewed, her eyes wide.

"That might actually be the best thing I've ever tasted," she said.

"Ah, then you will definitely need to return to France," he said with a laugh. "There are so many more things to try. Go on, taste the other two cheeses."

As she sampled the blue cheese and the tomme, moaning again with each heavenly bite, he unpacked some sliced saucisson, too, as well as a small bag of potato chips.

"I can't believe this," she said when the entire spread lay before her. They were in the shadow of the Eiffel Tower, eating the most beautiful cheeses she could imagine, and drinking champagne. She never wanted to leave this moment; it was like something out of a dream.

"Is there really not a man back in America waiting for you to come home?" Nicolas asked after they'd eaten in comfortable quiet for a moment.

Piper shook her head. "There's no guy back home. There . . . there never really has been." She couldn't believe she'd admitted something so embarrassing aloud. She was nearly twenty-four years old, and she'd never had a serious boyfriend. "I mean, I've gone on dates," she clarified quickly. "But nothing has . . . stuck." She snuck a look at him, expecting to see judgment on his face. Instead, he was nodding thoughtfully.

"Because you needed to care for your mother?" he asked.

She hung her head. "Maybe I can blame a bit of it on that. But before that . . . I don't know. I just never really met anyone who felt right to me. I feel like I watched my friends pair off one by one. It felt like some kind of race to a finish line I couldn't see, you know? They were always dragging me on double dates with their boyfriends' friends, and some of them were nice enough, but every time I thought about making a commitment like that, it felt like my world was getting so small, I could hardly breathe." She stopped abruptly. "I know, I sound like a lunatic."

"No," he said gently. "You sound like a woman who knows what she wants."

"But that's just the thing. I have no *idea* what I want. How am I supposed to choose someone else when I don't even know who I am yet?"

Nicolas took another sip of wine and seemed to be choosing his words carefully. "But I think you do know who you are. You're a woman who isn't done becoming herself. And I think you're exactly where you're meant to be."

"Sitting in a park in Paris eating cheese?"

He laughed. "Actually, yes. I think you are meant to be here. With me. With the whole world in front of you." He swept his hand out wide, encompassing the Eiffel Tower, the park before them, and all of Paris spreading out beyond. "Right now, your life is about your mother, as it should be. But when the time comes, the world will be yours. And you'll get to choose."

"Choose what?" she asked in a small voice.

"Everything. You were right to think that your world might have become small if you had chosen one of those boys in university. All of the paths you could have walked would have narrowed to one—which would have been fine for the right person, but not if you'd settled for a wrong one."

"What if the right one lives thousands of miles away from me?"

Nicolas held her gaze. "When something is right, it has a way of working itself out."

She turned to look at the Eiffel Tower for a moment, soaking it all in, before looking back at Nicolas, who was watching her. "It's all so beautiful," she whispered.

"Yes," he said, taking her hand. "It is." He didn't look at the tower at all as he leaned in and kissed her, his lips soft on hers as he handed her the possibility of a future she couldn't see yet but knew she wanted just the same.

Le Maison Grog was mostly empty, and Julia sat at the bar, sipping a glass of champagne and trying to steel her nerves for what she knew was inevitable. She had to tell Sam the truth. It was time to let the chips fall where they may.

She turned, pulse racing, when the door banged open a few minutes before five, sending a man into the room in a burst of afternoon sunshine. *Sam*, she thought, but as the door closed, she realized that the man striding toward her was the bartender who'd been so pleasant to them. She forced a smile at him, and he returned the smile with an expression that looked false and strained. She was just about to ask him if he was all right, but then the door opened again, and in the next flood of sunlight, Sam appeared like a vision, and her heart went from hammering to fluttering.

He spotted her at the bar and broke into a grin, crossing the room toward her and then awkwardly pausing before hurriedly kissing her on the cheek, as if he couldn't decide where to aim his lips and had settled for the safer option.

"Hey," he said, his deep voice making the hair on her arms stand on end.

"Hey," she replied, gazing into his honey-colored eyes and wishing she could stop time, could make this moment last forever. It was her last few seconds of the *Before*. Before he learned about her cancer. Before he knew that she was dying. Before he changed his mind about her.

She didn't realize that tears had sprung to her eyes until he reached up and wiped a teardrop away, his smile melting into an expression of concern. "Hey now," he said in that deep, rumbly voice. "What is it? Are you all right?"

This was the moment that she should have said, *No, as a matter of fact, I'm not.* But she opened and closed her mouth and when nothing emerged, she chickened out. "Um, want to grab a table?" she said, mentally kicking herself as she backed away from the perfect opening.

"Sure." Sam put a hand on her arm to steady her as she hopped down from the barstool and grabbed her champagne.

A moment later, they were settled in a corner booth, and the pleasant bartender had delivered a beer for Sam and a second glass of champagne for Julia, who was banking on liquid courage.

"I wrote a song today," Sam said abruptly after they'd toasted, and Julia was momentarily thrown. "Verses and chorus and everything."

"Sam," she began, but she couldn't seem to force words out, and after a second, he smiled.

"It's not very good. But you, ah, you inspired me." He looked down. "Sorry, that was corny. It's just—I've tried writing before. And I can never find the words. But now that I've met you . . ." His voice trailed off and he looked back up at her. "Sorry, am I making this weird?"

She shook her head, so moved that she temporarily forgot what she'd come here to tell him. "I inspired you?"

"I wasn't even going to tell you. I was going to surprise you when—" He abruptly cut himself off. "I just wanted you to know, Julia. And I wanted to say thank you."

"I'd love to hear the song sometime."

"I'll play it for you," he said, reaching for her hand. "But first, there's something I need to tell you."

All at once, she was yanked back down to earth. She pulled her hand away. "There's something I need to tell you, too, Sam."

Something undecipherable flickered across his face. "Oh. Okay."

She looked down and then forced herself to look him in the eye. "The thing is, I'm sick."

"Oh, man." A shadow of concern crossed his face. "Do you think it's food poisoning, or are you coming down with something?"

She could feel heat rising in her cheeks. She really, really didn't want to do this, but she had to.

"No, not that kind of sick." She took a deep breath, bracing herself. "Sam, I have cancer."

His mouth fell open, and though the pause only lasted a few seconds, it felt like an eternity. "Julia," he said, his voice hoarse. "Have you known for long? How are your doctors treating it? Are you on chemo, or . . ."

"I was." She let the words sink in, hoping he would understand without her having to spell it out, but she could tell from the tender, concerned way he was gazing at her that he hadn't gotten it yet. "I stopped."

"Okay," he said slowly, as if he was trying hard to process what she was saying.

"The chemo wasn't working anymore. I'm dying."

There. The words sat between them, cold and stark and impossible to take back. She'd said it. She'd done the right thing. And now, Sam looked like a deer in the headlights as he stared at her, and the seeds of doubt that had been planted in her mind began to sprout and blossom. He wasn't telling her it was okay, that it didn't change anything, that he still wanted to write songs for her. Instead, he was looking at her like she had the plague.

"Julia, I—" His voice cracked as he cut himself off. "My God, I don't know what to say."

She forced a wobbly smile. What had she expected him to say, that he was still interested in her? That he would come home to the States with her and be by her side as she wasted away? That he'd hold back her hair when she threw up and take her to the bathroom when she couldn't do it herself? God, she was delusional. This was a guy she'd met at a dive bar in Paris, for goodness' sake. "No, I'm sorry," she said. "You actually don't have to say anything. I just wanted you to know, you know?" She could feel tears in her eyes, and she wiped them quickly away. "I understand if this is too much. I—I should have told you sooner."

"I—" His voice cracked again. "Julia, I'm so sorry. What kind of cancer is it?"

"Pancreatic."

"My God . . ." He blinked a few times. "Are you in pain?" The look of concern and sadness in his eyes almost broke her.

"Sometimes. It comes and goes. Mostly . . . Mostly I'm just devastated to be leaving my daughter behind. It will shape at least a portion of her life, and it's my fault."

She watched his Adam's apple bob up and down as he looked at the table. When he looked up again, his eyes were glistening. "It's not your fault, Julia. Are you sure there's nothing more the doctors can do? A study you can get into, maybe? Or what about immunotherapy?"

She shook her head. "It's too late for all of that. Believe me, I asked my doctor all these same questions. I've been fighting this for more than two years and now, well, the road has run out. To be honest, I got way more time than the doctors told me I'd have when I was diagnosed."

He swallowed hard. "How long do you have left?"

She smiled sadly. "Best guess? Two or three months. It's why we're here, Piper and me. We wanted to take one last trip while I still felt like myself."

Sam put a hand over his mouth and sat back in his chair. "Julia," he said, his voice hoarse.

"It's a lot, I know. And it's not fair that I didn't tell you. I'm sorry. I didn't expect . . . I didn't expect to feel for you what I feel for you. But then you kissed me, and I . . ." She coughed. "I had to tell you."

He blinked rapidly and wiped at his eyes. "Would you . . . I'm so sorry . . . Would you excuse me for a moment?" And then, before she could answer, he stood from the table so abruptly that he almost knocked it over. His beer sloshed out of the glass, and he mumbled an apology as he hurried away, toward the stairs to the restroom in the back of the bar. She watched as he disappeared quickly down the stairs.

"Right," she said aloud, finally allowing the tears to come. "Right. I did the right thing."

She grabbed a tissue from her purse and quickly wiped her eyes. What was she getting so emotional about, anyhow? She'd long since digested the reality that she was dying; how could she let one guy's reaction thrust her back into heartbreak again when she'd worked so hard to focus on the positive?

And it wasn't exactly that Sam had reacted badly. The compassion in his eyes had been real. But then he'd hurried off like he couldn't get away from her quickly enough. And as the minutes ticked by and she drank the rest of her champagne, she began to wonder if he was coming back at all.

Five minutes later, with a sad wave to the friendly bartender, who was glancing over at her with concern, she slipped a twenty-euro note under her empty glass and, with one more look at the staircase leading down to the bathrooms, she headed for the door.

Sam would resurface eventually, but it was clear he was avoiding the ticking time bomb she'd dropped on his lap. And who could blame him?

Still, as she walked away, she had the strange sense of leaving something important behind, of closing a door on something she hadn't fully realized she wanted until she'd lost it.

CHAPTER TWENTY-FOUR

Jackson stared at his reflection in the bathroom mirror, willing himself to get a grip.

"Come on, man," he said, glaring at himself. "Just get it together and go back up there."

The problem was, he was crying like a baby.

He hadn't cried—at all—since the funeral of his mother ten years earlier. Before that, the last time he'd cried was when he was sixteen and his father had died after a short, terrible battle with lung cancer.

He knew, on some level, that what he was feeling now was wrapped up in that loss, at least a little bit. It felt like reliving the worst moments of his life. And of course knowing that a woman he'd just met was dying wasn't remotely the same as suddenly losing his father at such a young age. But he already cared for her, deeply. He hadn't even realized just how much he felt until she'd delivered her news, and it had seemed as if the bottom had dropped out from beneath him. He hated himself a little for the way he'd just abruptly stood from the table and hurried off, but he didn't want her to see him cry.

And it wasn't because he was embarrassed, at least not entirely. The issue was more that he knew he didn't have the right to that depth of pain when it came to her. And what kind of a support system could he possibly provide if she delivered news of a diagnosis dry-eyed and he burst into tears?

But she hadn't seen him cry—and she wouldn't. He'd be sure of that. He wiped his eyes, took a deep breath, and then turned on the faucet to splash a bit of water on his face. He dried off with a paper towel and then, giving himself one last look of warning in the mirror, he headed for the door.

He climbed the stairs back to the bar slowly, giving himself a pep talk on the way. *Right now, she needs your support. You've got to put your own issues to the side.* The thing he'd actually come here to do—telling her the truth about who he really was—was now the furthest thing from his mind.

Besides, even though she seemed convinced that it was the end of the road for her, what if it wasn't? What if there were strings he could pull that could help her?

He emerged into the bar, forcing himself to smile bravely. He could do this. He could be strong for her.

But then he realized that the table they'd shared just moments ago was empty. He scanned the bar quickly, dread rising in his chest, but she was nowhere to be seen. He locked eyes with the bartender, who shook his head and walked over.

"She left a minute ago," the bartender said, and without missing a beat, Jackson ran for the door and looked up and down the street. But there was no sign of Julia, and he knew she was gone and that he'd screwed it all up, perhaps irrevocably.

Deflated, he turned around and headed back into the bar.

"You okay, mate?" the bartender asked.

"I'm an idiot," Jackson said. "Did she . . . Did she look very upset?"

The bartender hesitated. "She didn't look happy."

Jackson cursed to himself. "Okay. Okay." He pulled out his phone and realized instantly that while he had given her his number, she had never given him hers.

He cursed again and then looked back at the bartender, who was watching him with concern. "The thing is, I think I'm falling in love with her," he said, and the bartender raised his eyebrows. "But I might have just lost her."

"Go after her, then, mate."

"Yeah," Jackson said, already heading for the door once again. "I will. Thanks, man."

Jackson started off walking toward Julia's hotel, but after a half block, he broke into a jog, earning stares from several passersby. There was something liberating about being gawked at for doing something strange as opposed to being recognized, though, and as he ran, he basked in the anonymity of being simply an American without manners in a city that prided itself on decorum.

He scanned the streets as he went, but no Julia. He was panting by the time he yanked open the door to her hotel five minutes later and hurled himself at the front desk. The man at reception stared at him as he caught his breath.

"I'm looking for Julia Glover," he managed to say. He really needed to start getting back to the gym for cardio.

"She is a guest here?" the man asked in perfect English.

"Yes. I don't know her room number, though."

The man consulted his computer. "Let me ring her." He dialed the phone and waited for several beats before shaking his head. "I'm afraid she isn't answering, sir."

"Did you see her come back? Beautiful woman, short, dark hair, the most dazzling smile you've ever seen?"

The man smiled slightly. "She sounds lovely, sir, but I haven't seen her."

Jackson slumped. "Yeah, okay. Thanks."

"Forgive me for asking, but are you Jackson Quick?"

Jackson blinked a few times, thrown by being recognized. He had forgotten, for a few minutes at least, that he was anything but a man on a mission to win back the woman he was falling in love with. "Oh. Yes. I am."

The man's smile broadened. "I'm a big fan, sir. Big fan. I'm coming to your show tomorrow."

"Oh, um, thank you."

"Shall I tell Madame Glover that you stopped by?"

"No. Please don't." The last thing he needed was the hotel clerk sharing his identity before Jackson had a chance to do so himself.

"All right, sir. Mum's the word."

"Thanks." And with that, Jackson headed back out the door, already moving toward the river.

He broke into a jog again, heading first to the bookstands along the Seine and then to the pedestrian bridge they'd lingered on the day before, but she was in neither place. He checked Notre Dame and then swung by the café across the river from the church—Café Le Petit Pont—because he remembered her mentioning that her daughter was interested in a waiter who worked there. But there was no sign of Julia—or, for that matter, of a twentysomething woman who might be her daughter.

He racked his brain; had she told him where she was going to dinner? She hadn't, and as he stood on the street corner outside the café, he looked helplessly around. In his direct sightline were at least six dining establishments; there were thousands more throughout the city. Trying to find her tonight would be like searching for a needle in a haystack.

Finally, he trudged back to her hotel. She and her daughter would return here eventually; they'd have to. Smiling halfheartedly at the front desk manager who'd recognized him earlier, he pulled his baseball cap from his back pocket, hoping for some degree of anonymity, and settled onto the small sofa in the lobby to wait.

Russ finally found his phone just past three in the morning, after he'd come home from a lousy night at Le Maison Grog and had turned his apartment upside down looking for it. It was dead and had slipped between two cushions of the couch; his best guess was that it had fallen out the night before when he was making out with Shelby, before they'd moved to the bed.

He plugged it in, tapping his foot impatiently as he waited for it to power on. Finally, his backdrop—a picture of him with his mum and dad, taken three years ago when he was last home in Oz—loaded, followed by a dozen notifications of new messages, emails, and voicemails. He swiped over to his voicemail inbox, realized he had a message from Shelby, and pushed play immediately, the smile fading from his face as she began to speak.

He replayed the message twice, just in case he'd misunderstood. But he hadn't. Her words were clear. She was thanking him for showing her a good time and telling him that there was no future for them.

His head throbbed. There was a part of him that wanted to call her back and fight for her. But it was the middle of the night, and if she was trying to break things off with him, she probably wouldn't appreciate being woken up. So what then? A grand gesture? Should he show up to her hotel and tell her how he felt? But he didn't even know where she was staying.

Confused and hurt, he finally settled for a text message, reasoning that she'd probably turned her notifications off before bed.

Shelby, I just got your message. I'm really sorry—I'd left my phone at home. I know it doesn't make any sense. I know we live on two continents. I know you're in the middle of something complicated. But I thought there was something between us, anyhow. Can we talk?

His finger hovered over the send button for a second as he considered, but then, before he could second-guess himself, he pressed it, sending the text zinging across Paris. When no answer came, he lay down in bed, hoping that tomorrow there would be a return message from Shelby.

Four hours later, as dawn began filtering in, Russ was still awake, staring at the ceiling. And there'd been no answer to his text.

CHAPTER TWENTY-FIVE

Shelby was woken up just past eight in the morning by Brandon's aggressive snores.

She'd forgotten just how loudly he snored. Sleeping beside him had always been like sharing a bed with a dying water buffalo. But it was one of those things she'd overlooked, which was what you were supposed to do when you loved someone.

So why, then, was she feeling so irritable this morning? Was it just the snoring? Or was it the fact that he'd insisted on putting off the conversation about the state of their relationship so that he could take her to go see the Eiffel Tower on his first night in Paris, despite the fact that she'd already been there with Vanessa and Corinne earlier in the week? Was it because she'd wanted the two of them to meet up with her friends, but instead, they'd wound up alone at the hotel bar, sharing a bottle of wine? Was it because they'd managed to talk about Alabama's upcoming football season, a new restaurant that had opened in Tuscaloosa, the renewal of their country club membership, and Brandon's decision to switch gyms, while avoiding anything that resembled a real conversation about their future?

Or was it because, deep down, she was beginning to wonder if she was making a terrible mistake?

As he snored on, she rolled over and grabbed her phone from the nightstand. There were no missed calls from Russ, but there was a text, and as she opened it up and read it, she felt even worse. He wanted to talk, but Brandon was back, and there was really nothing else to say.

So why was it taking every ounce of her self-control not to text him back?

Beside her, Brandon snorted loudly and stirred, cracking an eye open. "Babe?" he croaked.

Instantly, Shelby softened, pushing away thoughts of Russ. "Morning, babe," she said. How many nights had she prayed that she'd be waking up beside Brandon again? That he would come to his senses and remember how much he loved her? And now here they were, and she was worrying about some other guy? She needed to get it together.

"Water," he rasped, and she hopped out of bed to fill a glass for him from the tap in the bathroom. By the time she returned to bed and handed him his drink, he was sitting up, holding his head. He cracked open one eye and peered at her suspiciously. "What time is it?"

"Just past eight," she said brightly. "It takes a few days to adjust to the time difference."

He muttered several expletives and then took a giant sip of the water she handed him, draining the glass. "More, please," he grunted, and she immediately hopped up to refill his water, wondering halfway to the sink why she instantly leapt up to do his bidding whenever he snapped his fingers, even after everything that had happened.

She refilled the glass, but instead of bringing it back to him, she set it beside the sink and turned. A thousand questions—the ones she'd wanted to ask last night—were running through her head, but she started with the most important one. "Brandon? What are you doing here, really?"

He squinted at her. "What do you mean, babe?"

"I mean, why are things so different all of a sudden that you felt like you had to cross an ocean?"

His eyes narrowed further, like he was having trouble processing her question. "Wait, are you mad? I was trying to make a grand gesture."

"Right, and that's really nice. But, like, why now? You filed for divorce six months ago. I know things just ended with Alexis—"

"This has nothing to do with her."

"But it kind of does, doesn't it?"

"Look, babe, I'm man enough to say I messed up. Can't you just take me at my word? I want you back, Shelb."

"But . . . why?" She couldn't resist. Talking to him was like picking a scab.

"Because we're a perfect team, aren't we? Me and you? I love you."

"Did you love me when you left?"

"Babe, I told you, I was wrong." He swung his legs out of bed. He was wearing only boxer briefs, and for a moment, she was distracted. Why did he still have to look so good? "What's on the agenda for today?"

She looked away. "I told the girls we'd meet them for breakfast at nine. They have a tour of the Louvre booked today." She refrained from saying that she was supposed to be along on that tour, that as an art major, it was, in fact, the part of this Paris vacation that she'd been looking forward to the most.

"Why don't you just go meet them without me? I want to get some more sleep."

"Neither of them are going to believe your intentions are good unless you show up," she said bluntly.

He groaned and pulled a pillow over his head. "I don't have to prove anything to them, Shelb," he said, his voice muffled by the pillow. "I love you, you love me, end of story."

"But is it?" she couldn't resist saying.

He removed the pillow from his face and peered at her suspiciously. "What are you talking about, babe?"

"Is it the end of the story? I mean, I thought the story ended when you filed for divorce, and now you're here telling me it's not over after all. But you can't expect to just waltz back into my life without me and my friends asking some questions."

He looked away. "This has nothing to do with your friends."

"Actually, it has everything to do with them, because they're the ones who picked up the pieces when you broke me."

He half laughed. "Broke you? Wow, that's dramatic."

Anger rose in her chest. Did he really not know how deeply he'd hurt her? That there had been weeks where she could hardly get out of bed? That she had wondered—after learning about his new girlfriend and her pregnancy—whether there was even any point to living? It sounded pathetic and ridiculous now, but that was the kind of hold he had over her and, truth be told, she hated it. She hated that she had handed over control of her feelings and her sense of security to someone who didn't treat those things with care.

"Get dressed, Brandon," she said, not recognizing the steel in her own voice. "At the very least, you owe me breakfast with my friends, and if you can't do that, then you can go to hell."

She slammed the bathroom door, but not before she saw the look of shock on his face. Two seconds later, she could hear him scrambling to gather his clothes and shoes from the floor, and she knew without opening the door that he was doing as she asked. Maybe it was time to turn over a new leaf. To actually ask for what she needed. To remember that he was living in her world just as much as she was living in his. And to realize that if they were going to be together, things would have to be different this time around.

Russ had respected her. He had listened to her, considered her feelings, truly cared about what she had to say. Why shouldn't she expect the same from Brandon? Maybe the reason Russ had come into her life was to remind her that she mattered, and that if Brandon was going to be with her, he needed to prove that he knew that, too.

Julia woke up with her head pounding and her eyes raw from crying.

It was her last full day in Paris with Piper, the day they'd be attending the Jackson Quick concert together, and already, she felt a sense of grief over the end of the vacation, which had been all too short.

She sat up in bed and glanced over at Piper, still asleep in the bed beside hers. Her daughter was beautiful, her long hair splayed out on the pillow, her cheeks pink, her skin smooth and flawless. Piper would age one day, but Julia wouldn't be here to see it, and that broke her heart as much as anything else. She would miss every future version of who her daughter turned out to be; she would only know Piper as she was today.

She wiped her eyes and got out of bed, padding quietly into the bathroom. She shut the door, flicked on the light, and regarded herself in the mirror with dismay.

She looked awful. Her mascara had melted off overnight and

settled into her lines. Her eyes were bloodshot, and her hair looked like a rat's nest. She'd faked her way through dinner with Piper, pretending that everything was fine and smiling so hard that her face had ached, but her insides were twisted with hurt. She was dying, and Sam was a random man she'd met in Paris. That was all. What had she expected from him? Still, she had hoped that he would have had the decency to at least look her in the eye and tell her that it was all too much for him. Instead, he had slunk off to the bathroom and never returned. He clearly wasn't the man she'd thought he was.

She shook her head at herself and turned on the tap. No use shedding another tear over Sam. She would never see him again. This trip was about her and Piper.

She splashed water on her face and dried off, then she faced herself in the mirror again. "Enough," she told her reflection. "Enough."

She had no time to think about Sam today. Piper would be up soon, and it would be up to her to turn today into a day of memories. Piper would need a day like today to hang on to when Julia was gone, and she couldn't let anyone—least of all a virtual stranger—take that from them.

"Enough," she said one last time, and then she headed into the shower, vowing to herself that when she emerged, she would put Sam out of her mind once and for all.

Kayla took the RER C from Pont de l'Alma to the Gare d'Austerlitz station in eastern Paris, thinking of how at ease she felt with Nadim, whom she'd only known for a few days. She wondered if today was meant to be a date or if she was reading into things. Surely she hadn't imagined the spark between them, though.

When she got off the train, she followed the walking directions Google Maps gave her, heading away from the river, the elevated Jardin des Plantes on her right. She'd been meaning to go to the sprawling botanical garden and wondered whether Nadim's plan for today included a visit. She stopped short, though, when she turned right at the end of the long block and realized exactly what she was approaching.

She checked her phone just to make sure. Yes, she had nearly reached the address Nadim had given her the night before. But he hadn't mentioned that he was asking her to meet him at the Grande Mosquée de Paris, a broad white building with a leaf-green roof, Moorish detailing, and a soaring minaret with stonework so detailed that it looked like lace. It was beautiful.

She hadn't been here before, though she'd seen pictures, and as she started walking again, her stomach swam uneasily. She wasn't sure she belonged here. And obviously his intentions weren't romantic if he was taking her to some sort of religious gathering.

"Kayla!" She spun around, relieved but now a bit nervous to see Nadim jogging toward her from the direction of the train station. "I'm sorry I ran a bit late," he said as he reached her, pausing to kiss her on both cheeks.

She smiled at him and then gestured to the mosque across the street. "Is this, um, where you worship?"

"No. I grew up in Belleville, actually. You know it? A suburb just to the northeast of Paris? My family is not especially religious, but I try to attend at least a few times during Ramadan. Our mosque is there."

"How come you wanted me to meet you here, then?" She

glanced up once more at the building, feeling small and insignificant next to the physical embodiment of a culture she knew nothing about.

"Because I want to tell you a story." Nadim smiled at her. "And I think that this story is best served with tea."

She tilted her head, perplexed, and his smile widened.

"Trust me," he said, offering his arm, and as she looped her arm through his and followed him across the street, she realized that she did.

"It's okay that I'm not Muslim?" she asked. "I don't even have a scarf for my hair."

"Everyone is welcome here," he said. "You'll see what I mean."

They entered the mosque's grounds through a large archway shaped like a keyhole. Inside was a small, sun-dappled courtyard filled with café chairs and small blue-and-white-tiled tables shaded by leafy trees. Waiters in black pants and crisp white shirts hurried around with trays.

"Please," Nadim said, smiling at Kayla and gesturing to a chair at an empty table.

Tentatively, she sat, astonished that there was a little café inside the mosque's walls. Pigeons poked around for crumbs on the ground, and the place bustled with people.

"I hope you're hungry," Nadim said, joining her at the table as a waiter carrying a large tray heaped high with an assortment of pastries approached. Her eyes widened. What was this place? "Would it be all right if I chose a few of my favorites for us to share?"

She nodded, and as she stared in awe at the selection, Nadim greeted the waiter and then rattled off an order in a language Kayla didn't know, pointing to pastries one by one. The waiter plucked them from the tray with tongs and placed them on a paper plate before handing them to Nadim in exchange for a ten-euro note.

When the waiter walked away, Nadim turned to Kayla with a smile. "Would mint tea be all right?" he asked. "It's their specialty here."

"It sounds wonderful," Kayla said, overwhelmed.

Nadim beckoned to another waiter, who was walking around with a dozen small glasses balanced on a tray. "Two, please," he said in French, and he handed the waiter two coins. The waiter nodded and placed the drinks on the table before hurrying off.

"I ordered a few things you may not have tried before," Nadim said after Kayla had taken a tentative sip of her tea, which was hot and sweet. Kayla's mouth watered as he quickly explained the pastries between them. "*Loukoum*, which I think is called Turkish Delight in America," he said, gesturing to a wobbly, sugar-dusted cube. "*Basboussa*, which is an Egyptian semolina cake with syrup; a *corne de gazelle*, which is a Moroccan crescent cookie with sweet almond flavoring; *makrout*, which is filled with date paste and soaked in honey; and a *montecao*, a Moroccan cinnamon cookie that melts in your mouth. *Bon appétit*."

Kayla picked up the montecao first and looked up at Nadim in astonishment. "My grandmother used to make a cookie that looked just like this." She took a small bite, the taste taking her back two decades to the kitchen of her mother's mother when Kayla was just a little girl. "These taste exactly like her cookies, too."

"The world is always smaller than we think, isn't it?" He grinned and picked up the makrout. "Now let's eat our pastries, and then I'll explain why I brought you here."

"Okay." For the next few minutes, they said little as they filled their mouths with sugar and honey. With the exception of the montecao, the pastries were all unfamiliar to Kayla, but somehow, they all tasted like home, too.

"To the kinds of conversations that go best with sugar," Nadim said with a smile, raising his narrow glass of mint tea and clinking it against Kayla's.

"I'll toast to that." Kayla took a sip. "Now, what was this story you wanted to tell me?"

Nadim leaned back in his chair. "Once upon a time, during the Second World War, a Resistance network ran through this mosque," he said. "My great-grandfather was a part of it."

Kayla leaned forward, intrigued. "A Resistance network? What do you mean?"

"During the war, the Nazis mostly left Paris's Muslim community alone, for fear of upsetting the balance in northern Africa, which gave the mosque the ability to operate under the radar, so to speak. The mosque's rector came up with a plan to hide some Jewish refugees here, and others were smuggled out through the tunnels beneath the city, starting right here in this mosque. Still more were given false papers, identifying them as Muslims, which protected them from deportation."

Kayla stared at him. "The Muslim community in Paris saved Jewish citizens during World War II?"

"By some accounts, the mosque was responsible for saving more than a thousand Jewish lives," Nadim said with a smile. "My grandfather's father was a forger recruited by the rector to create false papers. He did that for a year before agreeing to take in Jewish refugees. In my family home, on the outskirts of Paris, more than a dozen Jewish citizens passed through on their way to safety."

Kayla could feel tears in her eyes. "Nadim, that's beautiful."

He leaned across the table and took her hand. "So you see, I wanted to explain how deeply immigrants are woven into the fabric here. It isn't that those from the outside damage a society. In fact, they strengthen it. My great-grandparents immigrated to France from Algeria just before the Second World War. But they risked their lives to save refugees—including some whose families had been here for centuries. It didn't matter to them where people had come from, or even how they worshipped. What mattered was that they were all human beings. Just like you, Kayla. Just like me. If your father closes his mind to you, to us, to *this*, he's missing all of this beauty."

Kayla nodded slowly and Nadim squeezed her hand.

"It's difficult to hear words of rejection from someone whose approval we want," he said. "But I wanted to make sure you heard a story of love, too, because that's what this world's really about, I think: the idea that our shared humanity comes before anything that separates us."

Kayla sat back in her chair, the wind knocked out of her by the deep thoughtfulness of his gesture. "Thank you," she said softly.

"We may trace our roots back to different places," Nadim said. "But in the end, we're all worthy of one another's respect, no matter where we've come from, as long as we're good people. And, Kayla, you're thoughtful and kind and you care deeply about others. Maybe I saw all those things in you even before we met, written across your face every time you hurried across the esplanade. It's why painting you intrigued me so much. You're a very special person, I think."

Nobody had felt that way about her before; she wasn't even sure that she felt that way about herself. But she wanted Nadim to be right about her. "I think you're someone very special, too," she said softly.

"Thank you, Kayla." He held her gaze for a long moment, and

she found herself wishing again that he'd kiss her but wondering if she was misreading the situation.

"Shall we go for a walk in the botanical garden?" he asked with a smile.

"I would love that," she said.

He grasped her hand, and together they stood, heading out of the mosque and into the sunshine, where the world somehow looked very different to her than it ever had before. But maybe it wasn't the world that was different; maybe it was her heart, which had been cracked open in a new and unexpected way, leaving room for the light to pour in.

CHAPTER TWENTY-SIX

Shelby and Brandon were fifteen minutes late when they sat down across from Vanessa and Corinne at Café Le Petit Pont.

Brandon had dragged his feet, muttering about how he hadn't flown all the way to Paris just to eat breakfast with people he could see back home. It had taken him an inordinately long time to throw on a polo shirt, pressed khakis, and his usual day-off boat shoes. He could not have looked more American if he'd Sharpied TOURIST across his forehead.

Corinne hopped up immediately when Shelby and Brandon walked in to give him a big hug, but Vanessa stayed seated, her arms crossed over her chest, evaluating him as Corinne gushed about how she was *so* glad he'd come to his senses and how it was *so* romantic that he'd flown all the way to Paris to win Shelby back.

"Be nice," Shelby muttered to Vanessa, who was watching the exchange with narrowed eyes.

"I'm always nice," Vanessa replied under her breath, giving her a sideways glance before returning her glare to Brandon.

"I mean be polite to him. This is my choice, Vanessa. I choose him."

Vanessa looked at her. "No offense, Shelb, but that's just dumb."

Shelby blinked at her a few times. "Are you serious right now?"

Vanessa took a sip of her coffee. "This is the guy who tossed you aside when it suited him. And now he's here to win you back because it suits him. Where do *you* figure into all of this?"

"Things are going to be different," Shelby said softly. "They really are."

"Yeah? What's changed?"

Brandon interrupted then, squeezing between them to lean down and give Vanessa a hug, which she politely accepted without really hugging back. As Brandon backed away awkwardly, his gaze darted between the two of them. "Everything okay, Vanessa?" he asked.

"Why wouldn't it be?" she asked with a broad, fake smile.

Brandon exhaled. "Phew. I thought you were pissed at me."

Vanessa's artificial smile widened, and she shrugged, but she didn't deny it. Concern flickered across Brandon's face, but before things could get more awkward, Corinne pulled him aside to regale him with a story about the crazy fondue bar in Montmartre.

Vanessa turned back to Shelby. "What about the hot bartender?"

Brandon glanced sharply at Shelby, his brow furrowing, and Shelby could feel heat rising to her cheeks.

"Shh," she said to Vanessa, lowering her voice and turning her back to Brandon. "Obviously I don't want Brandon to know."

"To know what?" Vanessa said, but at least she was whispering, and when Shelby looked over her shoulder at Brandon, she was relieved to find him fully tuned in to whatever Corinne was saying. "That you had real feelings for him?"

"It was just a fun fling," Shelby whispered, feeling a surge of guilt for minimizing how she'd felt with Russ.

"Yeah? Well, the way you talked about him the other day wasn't the way someone talks about a fling," Vanessa said in a low voice. "And the way he looked at you was not very flingy, either."

"Flingy's not a word." Shelby was stalling, and from Vanessa's eye roll, it was clear that she knew it. "What, like I'm going to move to Paris for some guy I hardly know?" Shelby added, feeling heat rise to her cheeks. "Besides, what I have with Brandon *is* real. He wants to try again. He's all-in, Vanessa."

"Is he?" Vanessa asked, her tone sad. "You're sure about that?"

Shelby followed Vanessa's gaze to Brandon, who had paused in his conversation with Corinne to stare out the window at a girl with long legs and a very short skirt smoking a cigarette just outside the café. Shelby's stomach flipped, and she felt woozy, disoriented. "Of course I'm sure," she said, anyhow, but she could hear the doubt in her own voice.

There would always be a girl with a short skirt, and Brandon was always going to look, wasn't he? He would never look at Shelby the way Russ had, like she'd hung the moon and the stars. There would always be something better he was striving for. She'd never feel like *enough* if she stayed in this marriage, and the truth of that settled on her shoulders, dark, heavy, and inescapable.

"He's not going to change, Shelby," Vanessa said softly.

"I know," she said, turning away from Vanessa, her throat beginning to close.

"Everything okay, babe?" Brandon turned and gave her an innocent smile, like he hadn't just been ogling someone right in front of the wife he was trying to win back. "What's good on the menu here?" he asked, settling into the seat beside her and grabbing her hand. In an instant, her palm was clammy and she felt like throwing up.

"Excuse me," Shelby said, abruptly pushing her chair back from the table.

"Babe?" Brandon asked, sounding concerned now.

But she ignored him. She couldn't be here anymore, pretending that everything was okay. She hurried to the back of the restaurant and down the spiral stairs to the bathroom in the basement.

In the ladies' room, she stared at herself in the mirror. "What are you doing?" she whispered. The answer should have been easy. She was reconnecting the dots of her life. She was getting back to normal. She was doing the thing her mother wanted her to do, that most of her friends wanted her to do.

But what about what *she* wanted? *Where do you figure into all of this?* Vanessa had asked. The truth was, Shelby didn't really know the answer. There were so many reasons to get back together with Brandon. But what about the one big reason that made everything else null and void?

"I don't actually want to be married to him," she said to her reflection in the mirror, stunned at the sudden clarity of the thought, almost breathless at the way that as soon as she'd said the words, it felt like a huge weight had been lifted from her shoulders. "*I don't want to be married to him*," she said more firmly, really listening to herself say the words this time. Once they were out of her mouth, she could feel the truth of them in the very marrow of her bones, and a powerful wave of relief swept over her.

She exhaled slowly, then she turned away from the mirror and went back upstairs, settling into her seat between Vanessa and Brandon.

"You okay?" Vanessa asked softly.

"Not yet," Shelby replied. "But I think I will be."

She turned to Brandon, who was studying his menu with a frown. "Why do you love me?" she asked abruptly.

He looked at her and blinked a few times, processing the question. "Because you're hot as hell, babe," he said after a few beats, giving her a charming, broad smile.

Did it say something about her that he expected this would be the right answer? "No, really," she said.

He darted a glance at Corinne. Vanessa crossed her arms over her chest again, waiting. Brandon cleared his throat. "You're my wife," he said. "We promised each other forever, didn't we?"

"I'm pretty sure that the divorce papers your attorney presented to my attorney promised the opposite of that," Shelby said.

"I told you. That was a mistake."

"No," Shelby said. "I think maybe *this* is the mistake."

He looked blankly at her, again shooting a nervous glance at the others. It was clear in that moment that what they thought of him mattered just as much as the conversation at hand. "What are you saying?"

"*This* is the mistake," Shelby said, the wobble in her voice disappearing as she went on. "This, Brandon. You broke my heart. And I thought that the only way to pick up the pieces was to hand them back to you and ask you to reassemble me. But that's not true. I can fix the broken parts myself, and even if my life doesn't look like I thought it would, it'll still be *my* life I'm living, not yours."

Brandon's nostrils flared, a sure sign that he was getting angry. He'd never raised a hand to her, but he had flown into a rage more than once, smashing glasses in their kitchen, slamming doors so hard they came loose from their hinges. She had managed to erase that from her collection of idealized mental pictures of their marriage, but now, looking at the fire smoldering dangerously in his eyes, she had a sudden memory of him punching a hole through their bedroom wall after demanding to know why she couldn't just get pregnant without so much drama, like all his friends' wives had.

That, she realized, was the image she needed to deliberately go back to every time she wavered. Brandon as he looked now, his face turning purple, his eyes bulging as he tried to control his anger. That was the real Brandon, not the smooth, polished version he presented to everyone else.

"I can't believe I'm hearing this," he said finally, some of the color fading from his face as he got ahold of himself. There were, after all, other people present. "You go to Paris for a week and suddenly you don't want to be married to me anymore?"

"*You* were the one who didn't want to be married to *me*, Brandon," she shot back.

"I told you, that was a mistake! I thought you wanted me back. And now, for some reason, our marriage isn't worth fighting for? What the hell changed, Shelby?"

"You did," she said quietly. "And I did, too. Or maybe we just both became who we really were, the way people do when they grow up. The thing is, Brandon, I want to be with someone who works to understand me, who doesn't blame me for everything that goes wrong, and who would never walk out when life got hard." Was it strange that it was Russ's face that flashed across her mind for an instant? She barely knew him, but she knew she could trust him to care for her feelings with a respect Brandon had never shown her. How had she convinced herself that Russ was the one she needed to walk away from?

Brandon's eyes darted to Vanessa and Corinne again. Vanessa was glaring at him, and the warmth had even gone out of Corinne's expressions. "Nobody will give you the life I'm able to give you, Shelby," he said after a long pause.

"But maybe I don't need *anyone* to give that kind of life to me. I think I have to figure out for myself the kind of life I want." She took a deep breath. "I'm sorry, Brandon. I'm sorry I didn't realize—

before you came all this way—that I've spent my whole life chasing after the wrong things, thinking they'd make me happy. I'm sorry I spent our whole marriage trying to mold myself into what I thought you wanted instead of just being me. It's my fault, too."

Vanessa piped in quickly, saying to Brandon, "But mostly, it's yours," which made his eyes narrow even further.

"Vanessa, this is between me and Shelby," he said tightly.

"No, Brandon," Shelby said. "It stopped being just about us when you walked out the door. I'm lucky I have a friend like Vanessa, who has spent the last six months telling me—even if I didn't listen—that your decision to leave was your failing, not mine."

"Now you're letting your friends make your choices for you?" he asked, incredulous. "That's not the Shelby I know."

She looked across the table at Vanessa and Corinne. Their advice wasn't always perfect, and maybe a divorce party in Paris was the dumbest idea in the world, but she knew they had her back in a way he never would. "Then maybe you never bothered to know me at all, Brandon," she said at last, standing up again. "But for now, I have somewhere to be."

"But . . . where am I supposed to stay?" he demanded. "I flew all the way to Paris for you!"

"You know what, Brandon?" Shelby said, a great sense of peace settling over her. "That's not really my problem anymore." She walked out without another word, ignoring his sputtering protests behind her.

Melanie had come to Café Le Petit Pont alone this morning to get a cup of coffee and to get her thoughts in order before seeing Gilles at the concert. She couldn't think clearly in the apartment she shared with him, surrounded by reminders of how deeply enmeshed they were in each other's lives. Plus, even though most of the flowers were gone now, thanks to Grandpa Henry, the place still had the cloying smell of decaying roses.

She had thought that being at the café, popular with tourists, would be a perfect break from her real world, but now, she felt like she couldn't breathe as she watched the pretty blond American at the next table over storm out of the restaurant, her head held high, as a glossy-looking man in preppy clothes stared after her, his face red with anger.

There were two other young women at the table with him, and after the blonde had gone, the brunette stood and glared down at the man. "Go back to Alabama, Brandon," she said. "And leave Shelby alone."

The redheaded girl stood up, too. "Also, don't you think it's maybe time to stop dressing like a frat boy? You look like a jackass."

He gaped at them as they dropped a few bills on the table and hurried off, and then, perhaps feeling Melanie staring at him, he turned and narrowed his eyes at her.

"What are *you* looking at?" he snapped, and she was taken aback by the intensity of the fury that was now directed at her.

She almost mumbled an apology and averted her gaze. But seeing the way the blonde had stood up to him had done something to her. *Your decision to leave was your failing, not mine*, the woman had said, and Melanie realized with a jolt of certainty that the same could be said for Gilles's affair. It was his failing, not hers. And so as the absurdly preppy man glared at her, she resisted the urge to look away. Instead, she replied, "I think maybe I'm looking at what my future could be, too, if I have the courage to choose happiness."

"What the hell are you talking about, lady?"

But Melanie was already standing, a confusing jumble of emotions coursing through her. She didn't know the blonde's story, nor did she know what this angry man had done. She knew only that seeing the girl choose herself had made Melanie wonder if that's the one thing she'd been forgetting to do.

"The redhead was right, by the way," Melanie said to the glaring man as she put a few euros on the table and turned to leave. "You really do look ridiculous."

She ignored his sputtering protests behind her as she walked from the café into the sunshine and the promise of a different kind of life, if only she had the courage to choose it for herself.

Before she could chicken out, she pulled her phone from her pocket and dialed her husband's number.

Piper and her mother planned to take it easy on their final full day in Paris, because her mom would need to conserve her energy for the concert that evening.

So when her mom suggested a walk over to Café Le Petit Pont for a late breakfast, Piper protested at first, though she really did want to see Nicolas, who was working that day. "I don't want to wear you out before the concert, Mom," she said.

"Didn't you say Nicolas had a surprise for you?" her mom prompted. "I don't know about you, but I want to know what it is."

Piper smiled. Actually, Nicolas had told her the night before that the surprise was for her mom, too, and that he hoped they'd both be able to come by. "Are you sure?"

"Positive. And we should wander around after that, too. Maybe the Louvre today?"

Piper hesitated. "Won't all that walking make you tired?"

Her mom reached for her hand and squeezed. "Honey, I don't

want to miss another moment with you. I'll take a nap before the show tonight. But for now, let's make the most of the time we have."

Piper nodded and pasted on a smile so that her mother wouldn't notice her misty eyes.

As they left through the lobby of their hotel, Piper glanced at the sofa against the far wall. When she'd come home from dinner with her mom the night before, there'd been a man deep in conversation on the phone, his head in his hands, saying something about not having time to talk to every blogger who came calling. He hadn't looked up at her when she'd walked past, but Piper could have sworn the man looked just like Jackson Quick. That didn't make any sense, though, did it? Rock stars probably stayed in the swankiest hotels wherever they went, and the hotel Piper and her mom were staying in was not exactly luxurious. It was fine, but it didn't really seem like the place you'd spot a celebrity.

"There was a guy in the lobby last night," Piper said, anyhow, as they headed out onto the street, "who looked just like Jackson Quick."

Her mom laughed. "How would *you* know what Jackson Quick looks like?"

Piper rolled her eyes. "Duh, Mom, the internet? I looked the guy up before I bought our tickets."

"And does he still have Billy Idol hair?"

Piper looked at her mom in confusion. "Does he have who what?"

Her mom smiled. "Never mind."

"Anyways, you're the big Jackson Quick fan, not me," Piper pointed out.

"Right," her mom said, her eyes sliding away. "I definitely am."

"Anyways, the guy last night obviously wasn't him, right? Like, what would a rock star be doing in the lobby of *our* hotel?"

Her mom laughed again. "Can you imagine, though? Hey, we could hitch a ride to the concert with him."

They reached Café Le Petit Pont a few minutes later, and Piper felt a current of electricity sizzle through her body when she noticed Nicolas across the room. He looked at her at the exact moment her eyes found him, and they held each other's gazes for a long, charged moment. When she finally exhaled and looked away, her mom was watching her with an arched eyebrow. "What?" Piper asked, embarrassed.

"Are you sure you want to go to a concert with me tonight when you could be spending your last night in Paris with Nicolas?"

Piper's eyes widened. "How can you even ask that? Of course I want to go with you."

"Okay." Her mom held up her hands. "Just wanted to give you an out if you wanted one."

Piper started to protest, but she was interrupted by the arrival of Nicolas, who offered her his arm and ushered her and her mom to a table just outside, overlooking the quai and Notre Dame across the narrow sliver of river.

"I'll be out with cappuccinos for you both in a moment, but first, I have a bit of a surprise," he said with a smile after kissing each of them on both cheeks and handing them their menus. He glanced at Piper, and then his smile widened as he turned to Piper's mom. "I have a friend who owns a limousine company. He has offered to drive you two to the concert tonight, on the condition that I come along to keep him company. So, ladies, if you'd like, you'll be going to the Jackson Quick show in style."

Piper squealed. "No way!" She turned to her mom, who raised

her eyebrows with a smile. She turned back to Nicolas. "This is seriously amazing!"

"Nicolas, are you sure?" Piper's mother asked. "You don't have to do this. We're totally okay just taking the metro."

"Please," he said with a smile. "I want to help make it the most memorable evening possible for both of you."

Piper's mother shook her head. "I don't know what to say."

Nicolas glanced at Piper again. "You don't have to say anything. But if you want, maybe you can say I have your blessing to spend time with your daughter in the future."

Piper could feel her cheeks heating up. "But, Nicolas, we live an ocean apart." She wasn't going to say it aloud, but she had begun to wonder if this was just a weeklong flirtation. What future could there possibly be in it?

"I've always wanted to visit the States," he said. "And I hope you'll come back to Paris one day, too."

"I will." Piper swallowed the lump in her throat as she glanced at her mom.

"Good, then," her mother said. She turned to Nicolas. "You don't need my blessing, Nicolas, but of course you have it. Piper will need all the support she can get in the next few months."

Piper blinked back tears. Nicolas put a hand on her shoulder and gave her mom a solemn nod.

"I promise you, Madame Glover—"

"Julia," her mom corrected with a small smile.

"I promise you, Julia," he said gravely. "I will do all I can to make sure that Piper is all right."

Piper's mom held his gaze, and Piper had the strangest sense that, in that moment, something passed between them, an understanding of sorts, a sacred vow. Finally, her mom nodded, and Nicolas turned back to Piper.

"Shall Bastien and I pick you up at six at your hotel?" Nicolas asked.

"If you're sure," Piper managed to say. Nicolas smiled and hurried away to get their coffees, and Piper turned back to her mom, drinking in the sight of her, unable to imagine a world in the not-so-distant future where she simply didn't exist anymore.

CHAPTER TWENTY-SEVEN

Russ had come to work early that morning, because he couldn't sleep. He kept checking and rechecking his phone, hoping that Shelby had called back, and hating himself a little for how much he cared.

Clearly he'd done something to push her away, and until he figured out what that was, he didn't know how to go about winning her back.

He was distracted, too, with worrying about what came next, after he sold his share of the bar. He knew in his gut that doing so was the only choice. Shelby had been like a wake-up call, reminding him that he had to make better decisions if he was going to be happy. But would he stay here in Paris? Move home to Australia? Find a new place to put down roots? And was there something wrong with him that, for a fleeting moment the other night, he had wondered what his life might look like on American soil?

He was just wiping down the bar when the front door opened, spilling light and noise into the quiet darkness of Le Maison Grog. "Not open yet, mate!" he said before he'd looked up, annoyed at himself that he'd forgotten to lock the front door after he'd entered.

But then he looked up and froze, because in the doorway stood Shelby, her eyes red-rimmed and bloodshot. His surprise immediately melted to concern.

"Shelby?" he said, hurrying around the bar toward her. "Are you all right? What's happened?"

"What's happened?" She barked out a laugh. "What's happened is that I was a complete idiot, and I didn't see what was right in front of my face."

He didn't know what to say because he wasn't sure what she was talking about. "Okay," he said, now just inches from her. He longed to close the remaining distance, to pull her into his arms, but maybe she wasn't there for that. Maybe she was here to deliver in person the message she'd left on his phone.

"My husband showed up yesterday," she said flatly, and his heart sank. *Her husband.* He'd known her divorce wasn't quite final yet, but he'd thought it was just a matter of paperwork. Hearing the words from her lips now made him realize that there was more to it than that.

"Oh," he said, taking a step back. "I see. What did he say?"

"He told me he wanted to try again." She took a step toward Russ, again closing the distance between them. "He told me he wants me to come home."

Russ tried not to let his hurt play out on his face. "Well. If that's what you want, I'm happy for you."

"It's not what I want, though."

"It isn't?"

"No." She reached up and touched the side of his face, sending a shot of electricity sizzling through him. "I want someone who only wants me to be me, not some idealized version of who

I could be. I want happiness without the weight of someone else's expectations. I want someone I can share the joys with, but also the failures, someone who wants to carry the sadness with me, not just the happiness. I want a future that I shape myself, not one that has already been drawn for me. I want to stop playing the role I think everyone wants me to play and to figure out who I am."

"Who you are," Russ said softly, "is wonderful. And I wouldn't change a thing."

She stared into his eyes like she was trying to ascertain the veracity of his words. He stared right back, because he meant them with all his heart.

"The thing is, Russ, I think I need to be alone for a little while," she said softly.

"Oh." Disappointment coursed through him. "Yeah, of course. I understand."

"But," she went on, "I also want you."

He peered down at her, not sure he'd heard her right.

"I have no right to ask you to wait for me, Russ," she continued. "And no reason to expect that you'll still be here when I get my head on straight. But I feel something for you that isn't like anything I've felt before. And I hope . . ." She trailed off, seeming to search for the words. "I hope that once I figure out who I am, you might like to get to know that person, too."

Russ swallowed hard. And then, because it was the best response he knew, he gently took her face in his hands and touched his lips to hers, tenderly, slowly. When he pulled away, she opened her eyes and they stared at each other for a moment. "I would like that very much," he said.

"Okay," she said softly. And then, she turned and walked away, leaving him alone in Le Maison Grog, wondering whether he'd ever see her again.

It was four o'clock and they were two hours away from the doors opening for the seven-thirty show. Jackson wouldn't go on until nearly nine, after an opener named Stephen Kellogg, a singer-songwriter he'd always liked and respected.

They'd caught up an hour ago when Stephen had arrived at the arena for sound check, but he'd stopped himself before he'd spilled his guts about Julia to the poor guy. It wasn't up to his opening act to fix his mistakes. Jackson was old enough now to know that he had to solve his own problems. It was just that he had no idea how to solve this one. He had hurt Julia, and he hoped that it wasn't too late to make things right with her. But how would he navigate the next chapter, the one in which he fell in love with her as she died? Was he brave enough to take that journey? Would she even want him to? Maybe she'd never want to talk to him again, especially once she realized he'd been dishonest with her from the start.

There was a knock on the greenroom door, and when Jackson got up to answer it, it was Henry McGee standing there with his granddaughter, Melanie.

The old man was dressed in a suit and tie, and he looked as nervous as a teenager going on his first date. "I can't thank you enough for the tickets, Jackson," Henry said, still hovering in the doorway like he wasn't sure whether it was appropriate to enter. "Celeste is on her way with her grandson."

"Come in," Jackson said, pulling Henry into a spontaneous hug and then giving Melanie a quick hug, too. "I'm glad you two are here; I wanted to talk to you about how we're going to do your song for Celeste."

"And *your* song for Julia," Henry said with a smile.

Jackson's heart raced. He had called Henry last night to ask whether he'd be up for accompanying him on piano as Jackson sang the song he'd been writing for the past few days. It was his grand gesture, his apology—and he knew he'd have to perform the song at the start of the show, because the moment the lights went up and Julia saw him onstage, she'd realize he'd lied. Hell, she'd probably know it the moment she walked into the arena, because it was his face plastered on the concert posters and T-shirts. He wanted to make sure she knew that was the only thing he'd been less than forthcoming about. From now on, he planned to be an open book for the rest of the time they had together. "Thanks again for doing that, Henry."

Henry smiled. "Anything for love. And thank *you* for allowing me to stay onstage with you for 'City of Light.'"

"Anything for love," Jackson echoed, patting Henry on the back. He was as nervous about that part of the evening as Henry was. What if Celeste didn't recognize the song? What if her response wasn't what Henry hoped? It would break the old man's heart. "Is your husband coming?" he asked, turning to Melanie. "Your grandfather mentioned the other day that you'd invited him."

"Actually, I tried calling him earlier to tell him not to come after all, but he didn't pick up and his voicemail was full." Melanie's reply sounded strangely hollow. "So I guess he'll be here."

Jackson and Henry exchanged concerned glances. "And is that okay with you?" Henry asked.

"Honestly? I don't know." Melanie sighed. "But you know what? This is your night, Grandpa Henry. We shouldn't be talking about Gilles right now." She glanced at Jackson, and her face reddened. "Also, maybe we could not talk about my disintegrating marriage in front of my favorite rock star from the nineties." Melanie turned to Jackson with an embarrassed smile. "And on that note, I'm going to go get a drink."

Jackson smiled and waved to the catering table, which was full of liquor bottles. "Help yourself to anything here."

"Actually, that was just my excuse for getting out of here before I humiliate myself even further." She leaned over and kissed Henry on the cheek. "I'll see you after the show, Grandpa Henry. Good luck, both of you."

She strode out of the greenroom, and Henry turned to Jackson with a sigh. "I never understood what she saw in that man. She loves him, I think, but sometimes love isn't enough to fix things when you're simply not right for each other."

Jackson shook his head, trying to push away the doubt that was nibbling at the edges of his mind. Was it enough to care about Julia if there was no room in her life for him? If all her thoughts were tangled up in the future she wouldn't have? He swallowed hard. "Relationships are complicated, aren't they?"

"I suppose that's why we write the songs we do," Henry said with a smile. "And why people listen to them. None of us have figured this out yet."

"But you have, haven't you?" Jackson asked. "You've loved Celeste from the day you met her."

"But look at all the mistakes I made along the way," Henry said. "Knowing you love someone isn't the same as having it all figured out."

"Do you regret it? Spending your life loving someone who wasn't there?"

"Not for a second. To love fully and truly is everything, Jackson, no matter how it turns out."

Jackson swallowed the lump in his throat. "Well, then, I hope that tonight Celeste remembers that."

"And I hope," Henry said, patting Jackson on the shoulder, "that your Julia does, too."

Traffic was snarled on the N13, so by the time Julia and Piper reached the arena on the outskirts of Paris, the lights inside were already down, and the opening act was already on stage, crooning about seeing the love of his life in blue jeans the day they met. As Piper led them quickly to their seats—on the second level—Julia had a fleeting burst of sadness. Sam had written lyrics for her, too, but that was before he'd run away to live forever in the bathroom of Le Maison Grog.

But the ache in her chest wasn't really about song lyrics; it was about the thought that her last chance for love had gone up in smoke this week. That was another ridiculous thought, though. Even in perfect health, could she really believe that an attraction sparked during a vacation in Paris would turn into anything? She and Sam would almost certainly have gone their separate ways at the end of the week, anyhow.

Somehow, still, she genuinely couldn't shake him—so much so that when they'd entered the arena, she'd had the weirdest thought that the posters of Jackson Quick—all stylized and shadowy and shot from the side—looked a little like Sam. But of course that was ridiculous; in the photos, you couldn't even see Jackson Quick's face except in profile.

She shook herself out of her cloud of self-pity and nudged Piper. "I'm sorry we had to leave Nicolas outside."

Piper smiled. "He and his buddy are going to try to scalp some tickets in the parking lot. He'll text me if they get in. Besides, Mom, this is *our* night."

Aside from the traffic, it had been a dream traveling to the concert in the back of a limo. Nicolas had even provided a bottle of champagne on ice, and he'd insisted on sitting up front with his friend to give Piper and Julia some time together. They had popped the cork, poured some bubbly, and spent a wonderful hour toasting to the week they'd had in Paris and the magical memories they'd made. "It was really nice of him to do that for us," Julia said. "He's a good guy."

"He really is." Piper got a dreamy look on her face as the opener started singing again, a song about high highs and low lows, and for a second, it felt to Julia as if the song was speaking directly to her. It was amazing how music could do that sometimes, how a universal message could feel so specific in the moment you needed it most. This week had been full of the highest highs and the lowest lows, and Julia supposed that she was lucky to have felt so much—even the heartbreak.

When the song ended and the singer began talking again, Piper turned to Julia. "Do you actually think Nicolas and I will stay in touch?"

"Of course," Julia said without hesitation. The way Nicolas looked at her daughter wasn't the way one looked at a fling, and when he'd promised Julia at the café that he'd look out for Piper, she had felt the weight of his words. "And I think you should plan to come back to visit him soon, or have him visit you."

"Mom," Piper said softly, tears shimmering in her eyes.

"But also," Julia said, putting an arm around Piper, "stay open to all the possibilities, okay? Nicolas may be an incredible man, but who knows yet if he's the right one for you? Sometimes people come into our lives to show us the way to the next step instead of staying around forever." Sam flickered across her mind once more, and she pushed the thought away. "And maybe Nicolas will be here forever. Maybe he won't be. But however it turns out, it'll all be okay in the end."

"How will it ever be okay if you're not here?" Piper said softly.

Julia blinked away tears. "Because life goes on, honey. And you're going to have a beautiful, brilliant one."

Up onstage, the opener pulled a piece of paper from his pocket. "Before I dive into the next song, which'll be my last, I've been asked to do a favor." The singer squinted at the paper. "Okay, I'm supposed to ask Julia and Piper Glover to go to guest services behind section 103. Ladies, looks like you're getting some upgraded seats."

Julia turned to Piper, who was looking at her with wide eyes. "Did he just say *our* names?" she asked in astonishment.

Piper's cheeks had gone pink. "Oh my gosh, Nicolas must have arranged something!"

Julia put her arm around her daughter again. "This really is the perfect evening. I can't believe he did so much."

Piper grinned. "Come on. Let's go see where our seats are. Can you imagine if we get to sit right by the stage?"

Linking arms and laughing in disbelief, they set off to find section 103.

The opening act had just ended and Melanie had reached her seat—front row, to the right of center stage—when a handsome man about her age arrived, guiding a very old woman with long white hair shuffling toward them with the assistance of a walker. As they made their way toward her, she realized with a start that this must be Celeste.

"*Bon soir*," said the man as they reached the seats beside hers. "You are the granddaughter of Henry McGee?"

Melanie smiled. There was an openness to the man's face and

a charming gap between his front teeth. "And you must be the grandson of Celeste."

His smile widened. "I am. Jean-Luc Manard. And this is my grandmother, Celeste Didier."

"Melanie Chaulet." She smiled first at Jean-Luc and then at Celeste. The old woman nodded politely, but her eyes were darting around, and she looked nervous. "Here, why don't you have a seat, madame?" she said to Celeste, helping her into one of the chairs facing the stage. "That's it. Jackson Quick will be on soon."

"I don't know him," Celeste said, her gaze alighting on Melanie for a second before flitting away. "I don't know why I'm here."

Jean-Luc and Melanie exchanged glances. "We're here because your friend Henry has invited us," Jean-Luc said with a gentleness that moved Melanie. "He has a surprise for you."

"Who is this Henry?" Celeste asked, and again, Melanie met Jean-Luc's eyes. This boded poorly, the way the old woman already looked so overwhelmed. Melanie hoped Grandpa Henry knew what he was doing.

"Henry is someone who loves you very much," Melanie said. "He is also my grandfather."

Celeste studied her for a moment and seemed to relax a bit. "You don't say."

"Yes, madame. A long time ago, he wrote a song, and he wanted you to hear it tonight."

Celeste looked concerned. She leaned forward and said in a whisper, "But you see, I can't hear very well."

"It's why he wanted to bring you here," Melanie said with a smile. "You'll be able to feel the song as well as hear it. He hopes it will bring back memories."

Celeste looked at Jean-Luc. "Did you know about this?"

Jean-Luc glanced once more at Melanie. "Yes, Grand-mère. Henry has written you one of the most famous songs of the past thirty years."

Celeste put a hand over her mouth. "For me? How romantic."

Jean-Luc glanced at Melanie again and smiled. "It is indeed."

Just then, out of the corner of her eye, Melanie saw Gilles approaching. Her heart began to hammer. She still wasn't sure what to do, but seeing the scene between the American couple play out this morning at Café Le Petit Pont had reminded her that she needed to ask herself what she really wanted, not just what she owed her husband.

Still, as Gilles came closer, she realized she'd missed him, despite herself. And she was relieved that he hadn't let her down this time; he had shown up just as he'd said he would. He was clearly trying, and that had to count for something.

"Mon amour," Gilles said, kissing her on both cheeks as he arrived beside her. "You look wonderful."

"Thanks. You do, too." But as he pressed up against her, she was startled to feel a sudden and visceral need to pull away.

"I'm very sorry about everything," he whispered, oblivious to her discomfort, his breath tickling her ear. "I've been such a fool, Melanie. I'll do whatever it takes to make things right."

"I—I don't know if that's enough, Gilles. But this isn't the time," she replied softly. She glanced at Jean-Luc, who was watching them. "Gilles, this is Jean-Luc Manard, and his grandmother, Celeste Didier. They are my grandfather's guests tonight."

"*Enchanté*," Gilles said briefly, effectively ending the conversation by turning his back to them. Jean-Luc caught her eye, raising his eyebrows as if to ask if she was all right. She gave him a small nod.

"If you could just give me a second chance, Melanie—" Gilles began again.

"Please, Gilles. Let's just enjoy the concert, okay? This means so much to my grandfather." As the lights in the arena dimmed, and as the crowd began to scream, she leaned pointedly around Gilles and smiled at Celeste and Jean-Luc. "Show's about to begin!" she said. Jean-Luc smiled at her, but Celeste just looked worried.

"Why are people yelling?" she asked, looking back and forth from Melanie to Jean-Luc.

"Everything's going to be okay," Jean-Luc said, putting his arm around his grandmother and then catching Melanie's eye, and for a second, Melanie wondered if his words were meant for her, too.

Julia couldn't believe their luck; when she and Piper got to the customer service kiosk behind section 103, they were presented with four front-row tickets, four VIP passes, and no explanation. "How on earth did Nicolas manage to do this?" she asked Piper, who beamed at her.

"I have no idea. Maybe he has a friend who works here," Piper said. "I'll call him now and tell him and Bastien to come sit with us."

"Right," Julia said as Piper stepped away, her phone to her ear. But it didn't make sense. If Nicolas was outside the arena, why hadn't he kept two of the tickets so that he and his friend could get in? Besides, seats that good had to be worth thousands, and who knew how much the VIP passes were? How could he have afforded them? But if not from him, where did they come from?

Piper returned a moment later, looking puzzled. "He swears they're not from him," she said. "But he and Bastien managed to buy some nosebleed seats, so they just got inside. I told them to join us."

"Okay," Julia said, completely confused. A few moments later, Nicolas and Bastien hurried up, and after a quick series of hugs, they all headed for the seats; the opening act had ended, and Jackson Quick was due to take the stage at any moment.

Sure enough, an usher showed them to the front row, where they settled into the four empty seats beside a white-haired woman who looked far too old to be a Jackson Quick fan. Maybe she was the singer's grandmother.

"These seats are *amazing*," Piper gushed, her eyes bright with excitement. "I've never sat so close to a stage before. We're going to be able to see right up Jackson Quick's nose."

Nicolas laughed and put an arm around her, and Julia settled back in her seat, perplexed.

The lights dimmed, and the screams of the crowd drowned out any opportunity Julia had to lean over and ask Piper where on earth she thought the tickets had come from.

The stage was still dark when a piano began to play, a beautiful, piercing melody. Then, a single spotlight came on, illuminating a baby grand, and behind it sat an elderly man in thick glasses, wearing a suit. The old woman beside Julia sat up straighter, staring at the pianist.

At that moment, Jackson Quick's voice dropped in, and though he still hadn't emerged onto the stage, the crowd went wild. "Today, ladies and gentlemen, I'm going to start with a new song, one that I wrote in just the past few days," said the rock star, and then he emerged from the wings of the stage in a beam of light, and the screaming escalated, but suddenly Julia couldn't breathe, because what she was seeing made no sense. The man standing in the spotlight looked just like Sam. "This one," the singer continued, looking down at the front row and locking eyes with Julia, "is for Julia, who I hope can forgive me."

Her mouth fell open. What on earth was happening? Sam was *Jackson Quick*?

Beside her, as she gaped, Piper grabbed her arm. "Mom?" Piper shouted over the din of the crowd. "Is Jackson Quick talking about *you*? How do *you* know Jackson Quick?"

"I have no idea," Julia said weakly, completely confused and flustered now. She hadn't recognized him, of course, because she'd never been a Jackson Quick fan in the first place. But why had he told her his name was Sam? None of this made sense.

Still looking right at her, Jackson began to sing along, the old man's fingers still flying across the piano keys in a beautiful melody. "*I'm sorry*," the singer sang, looking right at Julia, "*that I wasn't better. That I wasn't what you needed when you shared with me your heart. I'm sorry I couldn't find the words to say. The truth is, I failed you from the start.*"

Julia felt like she was having an out-of-body experience. How was this happening?

"*I'm not a perfect man, which I'm sure you know by now. What you don't know is that I want a chance to love you, anyhow.*"

The crowd roared and the rocker stepped closer to the edge of the stage, gazing down at Julia, who could do nothing but stare back, dumbstruck. *I'm sorry*, he mouthed to Julia, and she could see in his eyes how much he meant it, but she was still completely frozen. Her brain didn't seem to be catching up; she was still in disbelief that this was really happening.

But then Sam—Jackson Quick?—turned to Piper and mouthed, *You must be Piper*, before grinning and waving *hi* to Julia's suddenly starstruck daughter, and something in Julia cracked open. As Jackson—it was still so weird to think of him that way—backed away, heading to the middle of the stage for the next verse, she had the weirdest urge to call after him, to beg him to come back, because he was already too far away from her.

"Mom!" Piper shrieked over the screams. "Jackson Quick knows my name? How does he know my name?"

"He's the guy I met this week. I just—I didn't know he was Jackson Quick."

Piper's eyes shimmered. "But aren't you a huge Jackson Quick fan? How did you not recognize him?"

"The real truth?" Julia hesitated, giving her daughter a guilty smile. "The thing is, I'm not exactly a Jackson Quick fan."

"What?" Piper looked stunned.

"You were so excited to surprise me with tickets, honey. And I didn't *not* like him."

Piper stared at her. "Oh my God. Who did you like, then?"

"Jon Bon Jovi. Several years before Jackson Quick ever recorded a song." Julia grinned just as, up onstage, Jackson dove into the next lines. "*You trusted me with your story; you gave me the gift of your time. You shared your truth, your heart, your life, and I didn't know how to share mine.*

"*You make me want to be a better man! A better man. You make me want to be a better version of myself. And I sure as hell hope I can.*" It was the chorus to the song, apparently, and as Jackson repeated the lines once more, the crowd joined in, singing "Better man" right back to him.

The song went on for two more verses, and two more repetitions of the chorus, ending with Jackson singing the chorus a capella, looking straight at Julia, as the crowd clapped along. "*You make me want to be a better man! A better man. You make me want to be a better version of myself. And I sure as hell hope I can.*"

He finished the song, holding Julia's gaze for one more second, before waving an arm at the piano player and saying, "Ladies and gentlemen, Henry McGee on the piano!" The crowd cheered, and beside Julia, the old woman went still. "You all may be interested to know that it was Henry who wrote 'City of Light.' And Henry's going to join me and my band now in playing it for a very special woman in the audience. Henry?"

The old man leaned into the mic atop his piano and said, "This is for you, Celeste. They've all been for you."

And then, Jackson plunged into his biggest hit and Julia stood, shell-shocked, as the rest of the fans in the arena rose to their feet and sang along with every word of the first verse of "City of Light."

She was in love with Jackson Quick. And, it seemed, he was in love with her. And maybe, just maybe, even in the face of the overwhelming sadness she knew was coming, Julia would get her happily ever after, after all.

CHAPTER TWENTY-EIGHT

Celeste stared up at the man playing the piano. She *knew* this song. She was certain she did. She had never seen the young man onstage before, the one the crowd seemed to be cheering for, the one with the kind eyes and the charming smile. But the man at the piano. Him, she knew. But how? And from where?

"Who is that man?" she leaned over and asked the young man to her left, who was someone she was nearly certain she should recognize. Was he her son? Her grandson? Why couldn't she remember?

"That's Henry McGee," the young man—almost certainly her son—said loudly, though she had to read his lips to understand him over the din of the crowd. "He loves you, Grand-mère. He's been in love with you since you were teenagers."

Celeste's eyes widened. In love with her? Since they were teenagers? He looked far too old to have been a teenager at the same time as Celeste, in any case. "In love with *me*?" she repeated, just in case she'd misunderstood.

"In love with you," the young man confirmed. "He wrote this song for you many years ago."

This was flattering, but also perplexing. "Why is the other man singing it, then?"

"He was the one who made the song famous. And Henry can't sing anymore, anyhow," the young man reported. "But he hoped you would hear this song and remember."

Celeste looked back at the old man at the piano. His eyes were closed, and he looked lost in the music, and she had the strangest sense of having seen his face before, seeing his eyes closed, just like that, of sleeping beside him, of kissing his cheeks in the morning when his skin was far less wrinkled than it was now.

But had those things really happened? Or was she imagining them? She felt so lost within the maze of her own mind these days, so confused about what had really happened and what hadn't, and why people seemed to know her when she didn't know them at all.

But then the man opened his eyes and, even though he was still playing the song, he was looking directly at her. There was something about getting lost in his gaze for a moment, with the song swirling all around them, that unlocked something for her, and before she knew what she was doing, she was singing along, her lips moving to words that she didn't know, but somehow also knew, and when she sang them, she could feel them in the very depths of her soul. "*Wherever you are, you make the world bright. You light all the flames. You're my City of Light.*" And when the man at the piano looked at her, tears rolling down his face, she knew that the words were for her, and that some time ago, in a different place, he had sung these very words to her, whispering them while they lay side by side in her bed, dreaming about forever.

"Henry," she whispered, and beside her, the young man gasped.

"You remember, Grand-mère?" he asked, and suddenly, she knew exactly who he was, too.

"Jean-Luc," she murmured, and his eyes went wide with surprise. "Jean-Luc, I once loved that man."

"Yes, you did," Jean-Luc said, his eyes damp.

"And he loved me, too."

"Yes," Jean-Luc agreed. "He still does, I believe. He has been coming to see you every day."

"He has?" Celeste asked, panic beginning to rise within her. "Why don't I remember?" She wanted to hear the rest of the song. She wanted to stay in this moment, to remember the man named Henry who was playing the piano so beautifully, but already, the fear was like a fog rolling in from nowhere, covering everything that had been so clear just seconds before.

"Grand-mère, try to listen to the words," the young man beside her said. She couldn't hear him at all—she could hardly hear anything—but she could read his lips clear as day. "They are for you."

Celeste swallowed the fear that was rising in her throat. "But who *are* you?" she demanded. "Where *am* I? I—I don't want to be here!"

She looked once more at the stage, where there was an old man at the piano who was staring at her oddly, and she suddenly felt confined and uncomfortable. "Why is he looking at me?" she demanded of the man next to her. "What's happening?"

"Grand-mère," his lips said, and it was strange, because she was certainly not his grandmother. She could not remember the names of her grandchildren, but they couldn't be older than school-aged, and this man next to her was a full-grown adult.

"I think," she said, trying not to sound as frightened as she felt, "that you have confused me with someone else. I would like to go home now."

"But—" the man began.

Celeste would not take no for an answer. She was already rising, already shuffling unsteadily away with her walker when the young man caught up with her.

"I'll take you back to Paris," he said sadly.

"*Back* to Paris?" she asked, her panic rising. "Where on earth are we? Where have you taken me?"

Up onstage, the old man watched her go, and she could feel—even after she'd turned away and was no longer looking at him—the sadness in his gaze. She could hear the tears in the notes of the music he was playing.

And there was a part of her, a part she couldn't explain, that wanted to stay, that wanted to hear the rest of the song, that wanted to walk right up to that old man and say, "I know you, don't I?" But she didn't know him. And she didn't know the song. And all of a sudden, she was very, very tired.

"It'll all be all right," the young man said as they exited the arena.

"I just want to go home," she said, but as the man gave her a sad smile, she had the sense that she'd just done the wrong thing, had missed something important that was right in front of her.

But as quickly as she'd had the thought, it was gone again, and so a few minutes later, as she allowed the young man to help her into his car, she had already forgotten why they were here, and who he was, and there was peace in the darkness that descended, because when the lights went out in her mind, she could no longer see her fear.

Melanie's heart broke for her grandfather as Celeste lurched out of her seat, grabbed her walker, and made a beeline for the exit. She could see devastation on her grandfather's face, replacing the elation that had been there just a minute before, when Celeste had begun to sing the lyrics before saying her grandfather's name and stopping abruptly.

Celeste had been there for a second. She had remembered. And then, just as quickly, she was gone again.

I'm sorry, Jean-Luc had mouthed to Melanie as he had quickly jumped up to escort his grandmother out. *Please tell your grandfather I'm sorry.*

Melanie had nodded in sympathy, because she didn't know what to say. She looked back to Grandpa Henry, still playing the piano along with Jackson's band, as the singer belted out the chorus that still had everyone in the arena on their feet.

"*You . . . and me . . . Underneath the stars. I want . . . to be . . . wherever you are. You . . . and me, it all feels so right. Wherever you are, you make the world bright. You light all the flames. You're my City of Light.*"

She looked over at Gilles, who was bobbing his head, mouthing the lyrics along with the rest of the audience. He looked over at her, throwing her a quick, tentative smile before returning his attention to the stage, and suddenly, she felt sick to her stomach. *You and me*, the lyrics said. *It all feels so right*. Had she ever felt that way about her husband? Or had she, with the best of intentions, simply thrown herself headlong into a marriage that had never really been a fit?

"*The world shatters around us. But, still, we are here*," Jackson Quick sang, words her grandfather had written for a woman he'd known for only a few weeks but still loved all these years later. "*Beside you always, the world so bright, together forever, you're my City of Light.*" Jackson Quick sang, and Melanie tried to remember the last time she'd felt that kind of deep love and hope with Gilles. She thought once again of the blonde in the café, who'd had the courage to take her future into her own hands.

Gilles must have felt Melanie's gaze lingering on him, because he turned, his brows knitting together, and asked, "What is it?"

Melanie took a deep breath and spoke the truest words she'd uttered since she'd learned of her husband's affair. "I think this is over, Gilles," she said tentatively, trying on the words, but the moment they were out of her mouth, she felt lighter than she'd felt in years. Yes, she was scared about what came next. Yes, she was worried that she didn't know how to be alone. But now there wasn't a single ounce of doubt in her mind that she was doing the right thing.

Gilles looked confused. "Pardon?" he shouted over the din of the applause and cheers that greeted the end of "City of Light." On the stage, her grandfather was joining Jackson in the spotlight, taking a bow as the crowd roared.

"Our marriage! It's over!" Melanie shouted, just as the crowd quieted down, which meant that her voice carried. Onstage, Jackson's eyebrows went up, and he gave her a small smile of encouragement, and beside him, her grandfather beamed. *Good for you, kiddo*, he mouthed, and Melanie felt tears of relief in her eyes.

"Is this a joke?" Gilles asked, staring at her blankly as her grandfather exited stage left and Jackson launched into another one of his hits.

"No," Melanie said. "I'm sorry, Gilles."

"This is just because I cheated on you?" he asked in disbelief. "People have affairs all the time, Melanie. We will work through this."

"The thing is," Melanie said, "I don't want to. We've grown apart, haven't we? The things that connected us at the beginning, they're not there anymore, and now you've cut through the last piece of thread holding us together—the thread of our trust. Your affair was the wake-up call I needed, and even though you hurt me deeply, there's a little part of me that's grateful to you, too, because I never would have had the courage to leave otherwise."

"Please, Melanie," he said, reaching for her hand. "Think of what you're doing."

"Actually, for the first time in twenty years, I know *exactly* what I'm doing." Slowly, she pulled away from him. "Goodbye, Gilles."

And with that, she turned and walked away, leaving him in his front row seat, staring after her, as up onstage, Jackson sang about a love story coming to an end.

Backstage, Henry sat in the greenroom with his head in his hands, trying to get ahold of himself. Celeste had recognized him, he was sure of it. She had known the lyrics to "City of Light," if only for a moment. That meant she was still in there, just as he'd known she was. And he was also fairly certain that it meant she still loved him, just as he loved her. But then he'd watched as she'd disappeared again, the light in her eyes going out.

He had tried calling Jean-Luc as soon as he'd walked offstage, his concern growing as the call went straight to voicemail. *She's okay*, Jean-Luc had texted him a moment later. *I'm taking her home. I'm sorry.*

Melanie appeared in the doorway then, looking at him with concern. "You okay, Grandpa Henry?" she asked softly.

He nodded, beckoning her closer. When she sat beside him, he put his arm around her and pulled her into a hug. "You're leaving Gilles," he said—a statement, not a question.

"I'm leaving Gilles," she repeated, sounding almost as if she didn't believe it herself as she pulled away from him, shaking her head in astonishment. "*I'm leaving Gilles*."

"I'm so proud of you, Melanie," he said softly. "You finally asked yourself what was right for *you*."

"I think maybe that's what I should have been doing all along," she said. She put a hand on his arm. "She remembered you, you know. Celeste."

"I know." Her grandfather smiled sadly. "I think she just became overwhelmed."

"But you reached her. For a moment."

"I did. And that means there's still a piece of her that knows me."

"So what will you do now?"

"I'll stay. As long as Celeste is here, I will be, too."

"Well, as it turns out, I have a brand-new opening for a roommate, if you're interested."

Henry smiled. "Are you certain, Melanie? I don't want to impose."

"Grandpa Henry, nothing would make me happier. Can I ask you something?"

"Anything."

"Can you tell me about falling in love with Celeste? I want to hear all your stories, because I need to believe that kind of love is possible. I need to believe that it might be out there for me, too."

"It is, my dear," Henry said. "And it would be my pleasure to tell you my stories. If we don't believe in great love, we'll never find it."

"I want to believe," she said.

"And you shall, my sweet Melanie," he said, pulling her back into a hug. "You shall."

Six miles away, in the shadow of the Eiffel Tower, George and Lou strolled through the Champ de Mars, holding hands, and no one—not a single person—looked askance at them.

They were in their seventies. One was Black and one was white. They'd been soldiers together in Vietnam. All of these might have been reasons that this love could never have been.

But they were here, in Paris, the most romantic city in the world, and it was possible to believe in magic and possibility and the idea that they could finally spend the rest of their lives simply being themselves.

Cliff and Diane hadn't even batted an eye when they'd met up for dinner the previous evening. In fact, the two lovebirds had been so caught up in their own flirtation that they'd hardly listened as Lou had explained, haltingly, how he'd loved George for fifty years but hadn't known how to say it, and George had said he'd felt a connection the moment they'd met, in basic training, all those years before.

"Well, then, it's about time you admitted it to each other," Cliff had said with a shrug. "Don't you think?"

"Yeah," George had said, glancing at Lou. "I do."

Now, as he looked at Lou, he had a terrible thought. Could this have been their lives all along if they'd been honest with themselves sooner? If they'd lived in a world where falling in love with another man—and a man of another race, at that—wouldn't have made them outliers? If they hadn't found wives to marry so that they could mold themselves into the sort of men they'd thought the world expected them to be?

"It was different for us," Lou said, reading George's mind, as he had done so many times over the years. "We came from a different generation. It wasn't just us that had to get here. It was society, too."

George nodded. Lou was right. Still, he wished he'd had more courage. More self-awareness. More of a sense that love came in more colors and shades and forms than he could have imagined. "The world is changing," he said.

Lou reached over and gave him a peck on his cheek. "And love is love," he said.

"Love is love," George repeated, and he knew, in the depths of his soul, that it wasn't that he and Lou had finally found it. Their love had been there all along. It was just a matter of opening their hearts wide enough that they could finally see what was inside.

Kayla held tight to Nadim's hand as they made their way through the illuminated darkness of the Champ de Mars. They passed a couple of older men holding hands as they walked in the other direction, and Kayla felt a surge of hope. If men of that generation had found a way to go against the tide, maybe there was a way forward for her and Nadim. She didn't even know if he was attracted to her or if he was just being kind. She loved the way he looked at her and the way he listened to her, and if he was open to being more than friends with her one day, she'd feel like the luckiest woman in the world.

"My parents loved you," Nadim said, smiling down at her as they strolled.

Her heart zinged. She had expected, when he spontaneously invited her home to dinner after their stroll through the Jardin des Plantes, that his family might tolerate her politely, but that she wouldn't really be welcome. But they had surprised her, asking her all sorts of questions about life in the States and how long she thought she'd stay in France, and how she liked her job at the assisted-living facility. She'd even told them the story of Celeste

Didier and Henry McGee, and they'd seemed as invested as she was in finding out what had happened at the Jackson Quick concert on the other side of town tonight.

"I loved them all, too," she replied, feeling emotional. Her own father had questioned her very right to be here, but these people who were strangers to her—who worshipped differently, whose lives were very different from hers—had accepted her without question.

After dinner, buoyed by her newfound sense of belonging, she had stepped outside for a few minutes to call her father. He hadn't picked up, but she'd left a voicemail. "Like I said earlier this week, I'm here because I want to know you," she said quickly before she could lose her courage. "I hope you feel the same. I'm your daughter, and I want you to be someone I care about, and if that isn't enough for you, then maybe I've made a mistake in thinking we could have a relationship. At the end of the day, we're all human beings, and we have to accept one another for who we are. I do hope you can accept me—and accept that I'm staying. But if you can't, well, I honestly think that's your loss. I'm proud to be an American living in Paris."

She'd felt lighter after that—and then, because it was the right thing to do, she had followed up with a call to her mom. "You were right about my father," she said. "But I'm still glad I came, Mom. I'm planning to stay for a while."

"I just want you to be happy, honey," her mom had said in reply, and Kayla had nodded, glancing through the window into the Haddad family kitchen, where Nadim was laughing at something his mother had said.

"I am, Mom," Kayla said. "I really am."

But later, as she and Nadim walked toward the Eiffel Tower, she felt a surge of uncertainty. "Can I ask you a question?" she said.

"Anything."

"I guess . . . I'm just wondering what this is between us. You and me. Am I just a girl who needed rescuing? Or am I something else to you?" It was too much to ask, but her emotions were raw, and she didn't have anything to lose by being honest. "Because I like you, Nadim. I like you a lot."

Nadim looked amused. "I like you, too, Kayla."

"But I mean . . . I *like* like you," she said, possibly digging her hole deeper.

He laughed. "I like like you, too."

"You do?"

"You're the first girl I've ever taken to the mosque," he said quietly. "And you didn't think I made a habit of picking girls up along the river and bringing them home to my family, did you?"

Kayla blushed. "I didn't know what to think. I thought maybe you just liked me as a friend."

"I think all relationships should start with friendship, don't you agree?" Nadim asked. "But to be clear, Kayla, if you were just a friend, I don't think I'd want to kiss you as badly as I do right now."

Her heart skipped. "You want to kiss me?"

He stopped and looked down at her, brushing her hair over her shoulders and putting a hand on her face. "Very much so. If that's all right with you."

"It is." She smiled up at him. Here in Paris, the world was her oyster, and the pearl was this man she'd never expected. Maybe this would be a romance that would run its course, like the one that had burned out between her mother and father. Or maybe it would be a flame that would glow for nearly a century, like the love between Henry and Celeste. Either way, she knew in the depth of her soul that it would change her life.

"What are you thinking?" Nadim asked, staring into her eyes as his thumb brushed gently against her lower lip.

"I'm thinking," she said, "that I'd really like you to hurry up with that kiss."

"I thought you'd never ask," he said. This time, when he tilted her chin up and lowered his mouth to hers, there were no more words that needed to be said. They were just a girl and a boy in the shadow of the Eiffel Tower. And finally, an ocean away from where she'd been raised, it felt to Kayla like she was exactly where she'd always belonged.

Jackson came offstage at the end of the show after two exhilarating encores, the cheers of the crowd still echoing through La Défense.

He had done it. He had held the crowd in the palm of his hand, just as he had been able to do thirty years before. He was back, and his feeling of relief was vast.

But none of that mattered. Not really. What mattered was whether Julia would be waiting for him in the greenroom, or whether she had left when the show had ended. He had tried not to watch her throughout the show, to focus on the rest of the audience, too, but he'd caught her eye several times, and each time, she'd been smiling. He hoped that was a good sign.

He jogged toward the greenroom now, desperate to know if she was there. As he hurried through the door, he stopped short, relief coursing through him, along with hope.

There she was, standing in the middle of the room. Her daughter was there, too, along with two young guys he didn't know, but he assumed one was the waiter Piper was seeing. It was why he'd left four tickets and backstage passes, on the off chance that they'd brought Piper's waiter or anyone else along. And in a moment, he would turn the rock-star charm back on and greet all of them and be the perfect greenroom host.

But for now, all that mattered was Julia.

"I'm sorry," was the first thing he said, and she nodded slowly.

"Why did you tell me your name was Sam?" she asked.

He shook his head, feeling like an idiot. "Honestly? I don't know. It's the name I used to use to check into hotels when I was on tour, and it was just what came out of my mouth. Once I said it, and I realized you didn't know who I was, I felt like I could be myself. I—I hadn't felt like that in a really long time, and then, afterward, I wanted to tell you, but I didn't know how."

"You could have been yourself with me no matter what your name was," Julia said softly.

"And I know that now." He took her hands, and he was encouraged when she didn't pull away. "I also need you to know that I wasn't running from what you told me the other day. I left so abruptly because I didn't want you to see me cry."

"You cried?"

"I cried," he confirmed. "I lost my dad to cancer, and I needed to untangle that in my own head before I could show up for you. I tried to pull myself together in the bathroom, but when I came back up . . ."

"I was gone," she filled in. "I didn't give you a chance."

"I don't think I earned my chance," he said. "But I hope I have now. I hope, at least, that you'll listen to what I have to say."

She swallowed hard. "You wrote a song for me."

"I told you that you inspired me," he said with a smile. "But that's not what I want to say now."

"It isn't?"

"No. What I want to say now is that I want to be here. With you. For all of it."

Her eyes filled with tears. "Are you saying what I think you're saying?"

"Yes. Julia, I think I'm falling in love with you, and it's not fair that we won't get years together. But if you'll have me, I'll take whatever time is left. I'll do everything I can to make your life better—and to make sure your daughter is okay. And I'll never, ever, walk away again."

"Jackson, I'm dying," she whispered. "These next few months will be hard."

"I know."

"The end might be terrible."

"I know."

"You're sure about this?"

"I've never been more sure of anything in my entire life."

Her tears spilled over, rolling down each cheek, and he wiped them gently away with his thumbs. "So what now?" she asked softly.

"Now," he said, cupping her face in his hands and thinking how very lucky he was to have even a moment with this woman. "Now is the part where I kiss you."

And he did. And she kissed him back. And for the first time in his life, he understood why people wrote love songs, because it was impossible not to want to put into words the magic and the possibility of a moment like this, a moment that he knew would stay with him forever.

EPILOGUE

TWO MONTHS LATER

Jackson's tour was over for now. He had talked to Cash and made clear that whatever plans his manager had for relaunching his career would have to wait. Energized by the success they'd had in Paris and at his five other shows in London, Dublin, Madrid, Munich, and Copenhagen, Cash had wanted him to head out on the road again as soon as possible, but Jackson had been firm.

His moments now all belonged to Julia. He would go on tour next year. After.

He couldn't bear to think of the after, but it was coming. He knew that. Julia was getting weaker and more jaundiced by the day, and there was talk of bringing hospice in to ease the final weeks for her. But first, she'd wanted to go to Paris one more time, and so they'd come.

It was where they'd met, and it was where Piper had met the earnest, poetry-reciting Nicolas, too. Jackson knew how much it meant to Julia to see her daughter so happy, and to know now not only that Jackson would always be a part of Piper's life, but that Nicolas might well be, too.

What Julia didn't know was that Jackson had brought along a ring today. Nor did she know, as they were about to duck into Le Maison Grog, that the owner, Russ—who was finalizing the sale of his share of the bar at the end of the week—had champagne chilling on ice for them, or that Piper and Nicolas were already there waiting.

"You doing okay?" Jackson asked as they got out of the hired car that had taken them from the airport to the Latin Quarter. "You sure you don't want to stop at the hotel first?"

"No," Julia said, her voice weaker now than it had been even a day or two before. She was fading before his eyes. "I missed this place."

She smiled faintly, and he kissed her. And then, he held open the door, and together, they walked through.

Inside, Piper and Nicolas sat at a table, smiling at them. Russ stood behind the bar, four champagne glasses at the ready.

"What is all this?" Julia asked, turning to Jackson in astonishment.

"This," he said, getting down on one knee and holding up the ring he'd bought for her, an oval-cut diamond solitaire flanked by pavé diamonds on a platinum band, which Piper had approved before he'd bought it, "is me proposing to you."

"Proposing?" she asked, staring at him and then at the ring.

"I know we haven't gotten as much time together as we would have liked," he said, looking into her eyes. "But I want to marry you, Julia, if you'll have me. I wasn't really living until I met you. And now, well, I want to be married to you for the rest of the time we have. This is the life I've been singing about all these years, the life I never really believed existed. But it's real, and I want to spend as much of it as I can with you."

Julia stared at him, and he looked up at her from on bended knee, hoping that he hadn't gotten this all wrong.

"I—I don't know what to say," she whispered.

"Say yes, Mom!" Piper called out, which brought a smile to Julia's face.

She looked Jackson in the eyes. "Yes," she said, and his heart did a somersault. "Yes, Jackson. Yes." And then he was on his feet, and she was in his arms, and he was kissing the woman he knew he'd marry, in the place where it had all begun, and even though he knew he wouldn't have her forever, they had this moment and all those that came after. And he was here for all of them.

Shelby paused outside the door to Le Maison Grog. She had arrived just hours before on the overnight from Atlanta, her first time back in Paris since her ill-fated divorce party. Was she doing the right thing? She didn't know, but for once, she was following her heart.

She had gone through with her divorce from Brandon, and though there were parts of the dissolving of their marriage that still devastated her, she had no doubt that she'd done the right thing.

She hadn't talked to Russ in two months, though, because she didn't want to leave one relationship only to dive headfirst into another. Doing that would have meant that she'd simply traded Brandon's expectations for Russ's, even if she knew Russ would never try to force her into a mold. The thing was, though, it wasn't just Brandon who had tried to make Shelby into something she wasn't. Shelby had done it to herself, because she'd spent her whole life believing that people loved you only when you became exactly what they wanted you to be.

She'd needed the time it took to find her way back to simply being herself. And she'd told herself that once she knew who *she* was, she would come back.

She knew there was a good possibility that Russ had moved on, that he had a girlfriend by now or that he simply wanted nothing to do with her after the way she'd left. And if that was the case, it would be okay. Shelby would still be Shelby at the end of the day, and she'd return home to the States ready for her next chapter.

But what if her next chapter was here? She would never know unless she opened that door. And so, steeling her nerves, she did.

Inside, Le Maison Grog was nearly empty, save for two couples sharing a bottle of champagne at a table. One of the couples was young, perhaps early twenties, and the other looked a generation older. From the way the man—who looked a bit like the old rock star Jackson Quick—was looking at the woman, it was crystal clear that they were in love. For a moment, Shelby hesitated, staring, caught up in wishing that someone would look at her like that one day.

And then, the door to the kitchen opened and Russ emerged, and he stopped abruptly, staring at her like he'd seen a ghost. "Shelby," he said.

"Is this a bad time?" she asked, glancing at the two couples.

Slowly, Russ shook his head, his eyes never leaving hers.

"Good," she said. "Because I've come to ask if maybe, if you have the time, you might like to go out on a date with me."

He held her gaze. Her heart pounded. She was walking into her next chapter, whether it included him or not, and there was something incredibly gratifying about realizing that, about knowing that she had turned the page and that she had done it by herself. Still, she held her breath, hoping.

"I would like that, Shelby," he said at last. "I would like that very much."

The monitors beeped a steady rhythm as Celeste's chest rose up and down. Henry paused in the doorway of her hospital room, tears in his eyes, collecting himself before he entered.

He had been in Paris for two months, living with Melanie in her apartment, which was a lot more cheerful now that Gilles had moved out. He had never seen his granddaughter happier, and he was so glad that she had discovered, before it was too late, that it was better to be alone than to be with the wrong person. She was finding her way, and he was honored to have been with her in small part on that path.

He had gone to see Celeste every day, talking to her, telling her stories of the past, waiting for her to come back to him. Sometimes, he could see the light flicker on in her eyes for just a moment. Sometimes, she tilted her head just so, and he knew that, for a few seconds, a part of her had remembered. But since the night of the concert, there had been only glimpses of her, and he could feel her drifting further and further away.

"Are you sure you want to stay in Paris?" her grandson, Jean-Luc, had asked Henry just last week, peering at him with concern. "I'm sorry to say, Henry, that I don't think she knows anyone at all anymore. You must have a life of your own to get back to."

"Celeste is my life," Henry replied. "And I will be here as long as she is."

She'd had her heart attack the very next day, just before Henry had arrived for his morning visit. When he had turned the corner to the rue Royer-Collard, he had been startled to see an ambulance out front, two paramedics pushing a gurney out the front door. He'd hurried over as quickly as he could using his cane, knowing somehow, before he got there, that the patient was Celeste. He had caught just a quick glimpse of her before the ambulance doors slammed closed.

He had been at the hospital ever since, spending the days in her room, the evenings sleeping in the waiting area. Melanie had tried to convince him to come home, but she didn't understand that his home was wherever Celeste was.

The doctors had solemnly told Henry and Jean-Luc that it was the end. For a week now, Celeste had drifted in and out of consciousness, waking for only a few moments at a time, hardly aware of her surroundings. When Henry sat by her bedside and squeezed her hand, sometimes she squeezed back, but mostly she lay motionless, her body slowly disappearing, cell by cell, before him. She seemed to grow smaller with every passing day.

Now, wiping the tears from his eyes, Henry entered Celeste's room, thinking, as he always did when he looked at her, that she was the most beautiful woman in the world. Even now, with her white hair unwashed, her face pallid, and her body wasting away, she was still a radiant angel.

He sat beside her, as had become his daily habit, and reached for her hand. Her breathing was slow, and he could hear a rattle in her chest as the air moved in and out of her lungs. "Good morning, my love," he said, squeezing her hand. "I've missed you."

Her eyes opened, and slowly, she looked around the room, her gaze finally settling on Henry. She stared at him for a long time, and he had the strangest sense that she looked different today, her eyes bluer, brighter. "I've . . . missed you," she said with difficulty, her voice barely more than a whisper.

He gave her a sad smile. It was, of course, a parroted response. He had gotten used to this over the past two months with her; he would say something, and she would repeat it back, her expression blank, the words devoid of meaning.

But then something different happened. She was still looking into his eyes when she said, "Henry?"

His heart skipped. Surely he'd imagined it. "Celeste?" he said. "Did you just say—"

"Henry," she repeated. She blinked at him a few times, as if trying to bring him into focus. "It *is* you. . . . isn't it? You . . . came back."

His breath caught in his throat. "I'm so sorry that it took me so long, Celeste. I came as soon as I could."

She closed her eyes, and when she opened them a few seconds later, he could see that she was already beginning to fade. "I dreamed . . . that you . . . would. I waited . . . so long."

"I have loved you from the moment I first laid eyes on you, Celeste," he said. "You were with me all the days of my life."

"Henry," she murmured, "I never stopped . . . loving you."

"I love you, too," he said, his eyes filling with tears, because he knew that this was the end, that it was the last time he would be able to say those words to the woman who had both saved and shaped his life. "Always have. Always will."

She held his gaze, and in her eyes, he saw the past and the present and all the moments in between, the moments that had brought them together and driven them apart and reunited them once more. "*The world shatters around us*," she rasped, words he'd first sung to her so very long ago. "*But, still . . . we are here*."

And then, her eyes closed once more, and her breathing stilled, and he could feel the very second that her soul left her body. The monitors began to beep, but Henry stayed there, holding her hand, long enough to finish the verse.

"*Beside you always, the world so bright*," he whispered, the last words of a song that would forever honor the love of his life. "*Together forever, you're my City of Light*."

AUTHOR'S NOTE

Over the past decade and a half, I've been known mostly as a writer of historical fiction, with novels such as *The Book of Lost Names*, *The Winemaker's Wife*, and *The Paris Daughter*. But my career actually began twenty years ago with the 2006 publication of a rom-com called *How to Sleep with a Movie Star* (not a real how-to guide, I promise!), and I wrote four books in that vein (along with two contemporary YA novels) before making the switch to writing about the past with 2012's *The Sweetness of Forgetting*. Since then, only one of my books—2014's *The Life Intended*—was set in the present day.

Until now.

I've been wanting for a while to write something in the style of *Love Actually*, one of my favorite movies, but it wasn't until recently that the idea fully materialized for me. What if I sent a handful of Americans from different walks of life to my beloved Paris at the same time? What if their lives overlapped and intertwined—just as the characters' lives do in *Love Actually*—as they found their way to who they were supposed to be?

What if some stories ended in sadness, while others ended in hope? What if the bitter mixed with the sweet, just as it does so often in real life? And what if I could write something that sent readers on a vacation to Paris within the pages of a book?

The result is, of course, *Meet Me in Paris*, a novel that features seven intertwining love stories, set in the most romantic city on earth. At its core—just like my historical novels over the past fifteen years—it is a story about losing and finding love, figuring out who we are, laying down our burdens, seeing one another for who we really are, finding a way to be a light in the darkness, and maybe—just maybe—finding our way to that elusive happily ever after.

If you've finished the book, you know that it features two big nods to the Second World War, my favorite time period to write about. Henry and Celeste's love story dates back to 1943 Paris, and Nadim shares pieces of his own family history, which involves the incredible story of Muslims saving Jews in the center of Paris during World War II. You might even remember that history from *The Sweetness of Forgetting*, in which the Grande Mosquée de Paris (where Nadim brings Kayla in this book) plays a role. If those storylines captured your imagination, there's plenty more where they came from with previous World War II–set books of mine, from *The Book of Lost Names* to *The Room on Rue Amélie*.

But why do I keep returning to Paris on the page again and again? It's because it's the city that changed my life.

I moved there on a whim in the summer of 2002, just after I'd turned twenty-three, and I spent several months there soaking up the city. I was working as a magazine reporter at the time, routinely putting in sixty- and seventy-hour weeks. That summer in Paris taught me to slow down and to ask myself what I really wanted out of life. And, it turned out, what I wanted was to be a novelist.

I started my first novel right there, sometimes stretched out on a picnic blanket in the Champ de Mars, sometimes with my legs dangling over the wall near the Saule Pleureur de la Pointe, both of which make appearances in this book.

That was the summer I became *me*.

I recently found my diary from that summer, and I want to share the last entry with you: *I'll have to stick to (writing) my book*, I wrote. *I think I have a decent thing going, and I'd like to stay with it. Wouldn't it be amazing to publish a novel?? Could I do it with this one??*

I also wrote in that same entry: *I want to stick with my book, my new attitudes, my freedom to travel, and the independence inherent in writing books. I really want this summer to be a springboard for changes in my life. I can't believe my time in Europe is over. But I think that it was the most amazing, wonderful, and influential few months of my life. I will take it with me forever.*

I'd like to think that the twenty-three-year-old version of me would be proud of the way Paris is still so deeply woven into my heart and soul.

Now, to share a bit of information about the locations in the novel:

When I lived in Paris, I had an apartment on the rue du Général Camou, overlooking the nearby Eiffel Tower. (In fact, it's where Kayla lives in this book, and where a teenaged Rose lived in *The Sweetness of Forgetting*). But my roommate, Lauren, and I spent much of our time in the Latin Quarter, near Notre Dame, which was and is a bustling social scene for twentysomethings, thanks to the number of universities nearby. On my very first night in Paris, we wound up at an anglophone bar in the Latin Quarter called The Long Hop—which serves as a very loose inspiration for Le Maison Grog in the book. We spent a lot of evenings at The Long Hop—and a lot of dinners at Café Le Petit Pont (where

Nicolas works in the book!). We got to know very well one of the waiters—a wonderful guy named Jean-Michel—and, in fact, he makes an anonymous guest appearance in this novel; in real life, he now owns Le Valois, the bar near Montmartre and Moulin Rouge that Shelby and her friends visit after dining at the fondue restaurant. (He's the one pouring them Tequila Bang shots with salt and lemon.) Go see him (20 rue de Bruxelles), and tell him I sent you!

Julia and Piper stay at a hotel based on the Relais Hôtel du Vieux on the rue Gît-le-Coeur, where I had the pleasure of staying on my last trip to Paris. It's a fascinating place; prior to its renovation into a four-star establishment, it was a run-down place known as the Beat Hotel, home to many Beat Generation poets, writers, and artists in the late 1950s and early '60s, including Allen Ginsberg, William Burroughs, Gregory Corso, Brion Gysin, Peter Orlovsky, and Harold Norse. If you're interested in learning more, the nonfiction book *The Beat Hotel* by Barry Miles is an excellent resource.

There are a number of other places in the novel that mean something to me, too. I passed the Esplanade Ben Gourion, the riverside space where Nadim paints, on the way back to my apartment from the train station most days. I've enjoyed meals on the terrace of Chez Francis, overlooking the Eiffel Tower, and countless picnics in the Champ de Mars. I've stood on the stones marking Point Zéro in front of Notre Dame and thought about all the directions my feet could take me. I've loved strolling the streets of the Marais, admiring art in museums such as the Louvre and the Musée d'Orsay, browsing in Shakespeare and Company, eating fondue at Le Refuge des Fondus, and eating ice cream at Berthillon. And I've loved visiting the Salon de Thé de la Grande Mosquée de Paris, where I've enjoyed incredible pastries and mint tea in the sunshine while surrounded by the beauty of a place that contributed to saving many lives during World War II. (It's worth a stop if you're in Paris; enter at the corner of the rue Geoffroy-Saint-Hilaire and the rue Daubenton.)

In other words, so much of my own love of Paris is woven through these pages. I hope you can feel that here—and that if you find yourself in the City of Light someday, you might discover some of these places for yourself, too.

I also want to note that while Jackson Quick and Henry McGee are fictional, Jackson's opening act—Stephen Kellogg—is real. He's a friend of mine, and he's not only an incredible musician and road warrior (and a great dad to four young women), but he's an author, too! When I thought about opening acts for Jackson's show, he was the first person I thought of, because he's one of my favorite people to see perform live. If you ever see him on the schedule of a venue near you, buy a ticket immediately!

A final note about Julia: The decision to have her dying from cancer was a difficult one for me, because I myself was diagnosed with breast cancer in 2022 and went through surgery, chemotherapy, and radiation therapy. I'm in remission now—knock on wood—and have every reason to believe I'll have a long, full life. But as I went through that, I thought a lot about how awful it would be to be diagnosed with a cancer that wasn't able to be cured—and especially how awful it would be to leave a child behind. In a lot of ways, I think the character of Julia is the embodiment of many of my own fears from that time period. But she's also a reminder of the importance of continuing to support cancer research. A beloved family member of mine is currently battling pancreatic cancer and is part of a clinical trial for a new miracle drug that seems to be making a difference. There are incredible things on the horizon, and as long as we keep funding research, I think there's real hope for the future. I'd like to think that if Julia was diagnosed even a few years from now, she'd have a real chance to survive.

My next book will be a return to the historical fiction I'm known for, and I'm excited to dive back into researching the past. But in the meantime, I'm so glad to have journeyed to present-day Paris on the page. If there's one thing I hope you take away from this book—aside from hopefully feeling like you've taken a little vacation to the City of Light—it's this: Wherever you are in the world, and wherever you are in your life, you have the right to choose happiness—and to pursue your own happily ever after with your whole heart.

Thanks for meeting me in Paris!

xo, Kristin

ACKNOWLEDGMENTS

A huge thank-you to my wonderful publishing team at Gallery Books, including Hannah Braaten, Jennifer Bergstrom, Jessica Roth, Sarah Schlick, Heather Waters, Cassidy Graham, Ali Chesnick, Jen Long, Eliza Hanson, Aimée Bell, Mackenzie Hickey, and Sally Marvin. And, of course, a huge thanks to my dear friend Abby Zidle, who was my editor for fifteen years before departing Gallery Books to start A to Z Editorial Services—and who did an excellent first round of edits for *Meet Me in Paris*.

I absolutely love my talented literary agent, Holly Root, and the entire Root Literary team, including Holly's assistant, Kat Miller, and Stacy Jenson, who expertly fields every accounting question I lob her way. Thanks, too, to my incredible foreign rights agent, Heather Shapiro, of Baror International, and to the amazing publishing teams I work with around the world, especially my friends at Simon & Schuster Canada, Headline Publishing Group/Hachette UK (plus the Australia/New Zealand team), and The Armchair Publishing House (in Israel).

Big hugs, also, to my phenomenal publicist, Kristin Dwyer of Leo PR, and to the whole team at Authors Unbound, including Christie Hinrichs, Jenn Hoffman, and Allie Arkema.

On the film side, I'm tremendously fortunate to be represented by fellow hockey fan Dana Spector at Creative Artists Agency, as well as Lauren Bishow and Andrew Hurwitz at Frankfurt Kurnit Klein & Selz PC, all of whom I adore. The film side of my career has been shaped enormously by my dear friend and manager, Jonathan Baruch, of Rain Management, who is one of my favorite people in the world. Special shout-outs to Luca Sosa at Rain, Kiana Lee at FKKS, and Hadley Jevon at CAA.

To my rock star oncological breast surgeon Dr. Anu Saigal, my oncologist Dr. Sonalee Shroff, my radiation oncologist Dr. Afshin Forouzannia, radiologist Dr. Clark Rogers, primary care physician Dr. Neha Doshi, physician assistant Rochelle Drayton, and chemotherapy nurse Tara Thomas: Thanks for helping to save my life.

To my Friends & Fiction family, including Mary Kay Andrews, Kristy Woodson Harvey, Patti Callahan Henry, Meg Walker, Shaun Hettinger, Ron Block, Lisa Harrison, and Brenda Gardner: I don't know what I would do without you. For readers who aren't yet familiar with Friends & Fiction, I hope you'll check us out on Facebook, YouTube, or FriendsandFiction.com. We're a huge reading community (run by four bestselling novelists), and we interview other authors on a web show and podcast each week. Joining us is absolutely free, and I guarantee that if you do, your TBR list will grow by a mile!

A huge thanks to the rest of the amazing people I work with, including Chelsea McGuckin, Lisa Litwack, Nancy Tonik, Susan Bishansky, Wendy Sheanin, Caroline Pallotta, the Book Club Favorites team, Molly Mitchell, Jeni Shirley, Amy Loomis, the library and sales teams at S&S, and at Simon & Schuster Audio: Gaby Audet, Sarah Lieberman, and Medina Cekovic.

And, of course, a big thank-you to the very talented actress and audiobook narrator Madeleine Maby, whose voice you'll hear on many of my audiobooks.

I'm also so grateful to the incredible Bob Greenblatt, Jon Wu, Stephanie Germain, Howard Braunstein, Jonathan Elkin, and Toby Ascher for helping me to grow and develop as a screenwriter—and for believing in me and my stories! It's such a pleasure working with you all. A huge thanks, too, to my dear friend Stephen Tolkin, with whom I have written and worked for a few years now, and who has become a real mentor to me in the film world. And to Aria Mia Loberti, Molly Stevens, and Heather Hach: I can't wait to see what we can create!

To the booksellers and librarians I work with—and sometimes get to visit on tour—thank you times one million for all that you do to get books into the hands of readers. I'm so lucky to be part of this literary community!

Thanks to my mom, Carol; my siblings, Karen and David; my dad, Rick; my stepmother, Janine; my in-laws, Mark and Wanda; my grandparents-in-law, Grandma and Grandpa Trouba; and to my whole family, including Barry, James, William, Emma, Johanna, Sophia, Donna, Jarryd, Brittany, Chloe, Steve, Janet, Anne, Fred, Courtney, Jeff, Anne, Bob, JoAnn, and the Trouba and Rivers families. I love you all.

To my dear friends Kristen Bost, Marcie Golgoski, Melixa Carbonell, Lisa Wilkes, Amber Draus, Megan Perretta, Wendy Jo Moyer, Albany Borregales, Aldo Pacheco, Melody Foxworthy, Dane Foxworthy, Jouti, Dema, Alla, Olga, Mark Given x 2, Weez

Given, Christina, Rob Given, Christina Sivrich, Lisa Proto, Jason Cabrera, Nathalie Sainpaulin, Shari Resnick, Amy Tan, Nancy Alvarez, Colton Bost, Eddie Bost, Robbi Lucas, and Lauren Elkin (my dear Paris roommate): I love you all!

And to my dear author friends Wendy Toliver, Allison van Diepen, Linda Gerber, Emily Wing Smith, Alyson Noel, Jay Asher, Kristina McMoris, Kate Quinn, Fiona Davis, Marie Benedict, Pam Jenoff, Lisa Scottoline, Alison Hammer, Stephen Kellogg (who makes a guest appearance in this book!), Jamie Brenner, Sadeqa Johnson, Madeline Martin, Eliza Knight, Leslie Lehr, Heather Webb, Sarah Penner, Mary Alice Monroe, Brad Meltzer, Elin Hilderbrand, Christina Hobbs, Lauren Billings, Lisa Unger, Laura Zigman, Colleen Oakley, James Ponti, Allison Pataki, Sarah McCoy, and more (there are too many to name!): Thank you all, from the bottom of my heart, for the inspiration you've given me with your words. And thanks to Ken Block and Sister Hazel for the inspiration you've given me with your music—and for running the incredible nonprofit Lyrics for Life, which funds pediatric cancer research. (Check them out at lyricsforlife.org.)

The biggest thanks of all goes to my husband, Jason, and my son, Noah, without whom none of this would be possible. You guys tolerate my early mornings, my late nights, my head-in-the-clouds moments, and all my travel—and you keep showing up for me again and again. I love you both so very much, and I know I'm the luckiest wife and mom in the world.

And, finally, to you, the reader: Thanks for coming with me on this journey. I know that *Meet Me in Paris* is a bit different than my typical fare, but for those of you who normally read my historical fiction, thanks so much for taking a chance on something new from me. For those of you finding me for the first time with this book: If you enjoyed *Meet Me in Paris*, I hope you'll pick up my historical fiction, too, if you're so inclined; I guarantee you'll find the same heart in all my historical novels!

Please visit me at KristinHarmel.com for more information on tour dates, breast cancer resources, and links to my social media. I hope to see you all over at Friends & Fiction. Thanks for reading!